The Rain King

A Murder of Crows

Book One

Selena

The Rain King

Unabridged First Edition

Published in the United States by Selena and Speak Now.

ISBN-13: 978-1-955913-61-4

For Michelle.

prologue

Content Warning:
If reading about fictional men who are toxic, manipulative, and abusive upsets you, please return this book for a refund. There is nothing comfortable or safe about this read.
If you are 18+ and have no triggers… Welcome to Faulkner, where the city limit is the only limit.

#1 on the Billboard Chart:
"If You Had My Love"—Jennifer Lopez

"Time to collect."

I glower at the plain brick townhouse as we cruise by. A light is on in an upstairs window, and her shadow moves inside the room. Low light filters through the blinds over the living room windows. A mixture of fury and finality simmers inside me as Reggie pulls to a stop.

"Sure you don't need backup?" he asks, leaning forward to pull his gun from the back of his jeans.

"I got it," I say, throwing open the car door. "This shit's personal."

"Just because he's a pussy, that doesn't mean he's not dangerous," Reggie calls as I climb out. I circle the car, and he cranks the window down and reaches out.

"He's still my brother," I say, clasping his hand and pulling us in close.

"Nah," Reggie says. "The Crows are your brothers."

"The Crows don't exist anymore," I remind him.

We all know it's bullshit. We will always belong to something greater, something deeper, a brotherhood that transcends blood.

"You got too much faith in the *malparido*," Daniel says from the back seat. "Mess with a guy's bitch, and he doesn't think straight."

"Learned that the hard way," I say, cracking a grin and leaning down to speak through the open window. If you can't joke about that shit, it'll drive you insane.

"We'll be here," Reggie says. "Give us a signal if you need us."

"I'm going around back to have a smoke," Billy says, pushing the empty passenger seat forward and climbing out. "In case he's still a little bitch, and he tries to run."

"He won't run," I say, the urge to defend my brother coming automatically.

There's no use with these guys, though. They are my boys, and he's not. He's not one of us anymore. He made that choice, and in their eyes, he deserves no respect. He's a rival.

But I know he made it for her. And hell, maybe I'd have done the same if she'd chosen me.

The thought makes the old rage rise inside me, a phoenix of fury that turns to ashes when I don't think about it but is ready to burst into incinerating flames the moment I do.

Reggie sets his gun on his lap and grabs his cigarettes off the dash. "No reason to live with unfinished business," he says. "Go take care of it."

"Gracias, parce," I say to him, then nod to the rest of my crew who rode with me tonight. Straightening, I tuck my gun in at the small of my back before heading for the door.

I haven't seen the inside of my twin's place since he moved here. He cut ties with more than the Crows when he dipped.

I've driven by, though. Imagined cruising by and scaring them, making them wonder if we're coming for them. If we're biding our time before payback. I've imagined sliding down the window, hanging my arm out, shooting him in the back while he carries in groceries for her.

It's a pussy move, but then, he knows all about those.

I've thought about putting a bullet in her head when she's in the yard, maybe a few years down the road, when they have kids and he'll be stuck with them.

Mostly though, I think about seeing them fucking. If the windows are open one day, the white curtains fluttering, and framed between them, I'll see his hands on her bare back as she rides him, her head thrown back and her long, dark hair tumbling down as she moves, so lost in her own bliss she doesn't remember I exist.

Or maybe he'll have her bent over the bed, pounding into her from behind like a man possessed, the way he used to fuck the initiates, so lost in his own lust he doesn't remember *she* exists.

After the crew girls, it's hard to fuck a girl normally, but I guess they worked it out. Rae wouldn't stick around if she wasn't into his game. She's a runner, after all.

Which will only make it that much sweeter to catch her tonight. To let her cry and beg, and make her think I'll have mercy, only to take what I'm owed in the end.

I don't have to worry about treating her right or having her stick around.

I'm not the one marrying her tomorrow.

I'm just here to take what I was promised last year, when things were simple and she was just a piece of ass. When I still had a brother.

Tonight, he'll pay for what he did.

And she'll pay for making him do it.

one for sorrow

one

Two Years Before

#1 on the Billboard Chart:
"Hypnotize"—The Notorious B.I.G.

Rae West

I look up from my book at the sound of a hard, insistent tap on the window startling out of my fictional world. I'm on the second floor, so there's no way a person could be tapping, but before my rational brain can supply that information, my heart lurches into my throat and I almost fall out of the window seat. My eyes don't meet that of a person or a tommyknocker from a nursery rhyme, though. They meet the solid black eyes of a crow.

"Poe," I say through a startled laugh. "You scared me."

I rise carefully, and the bird hops back a few steps and caws demandingly. After only a few weeks, she's barely afraid of me.

"Yeah, yeah, I'm hungry too," I mutter, crossing my room to grab the sandwich waiting on my plate for when she—or he—came back. I'm not really sure how to tell a male from a female crow. In fact, I named her after Edgar Allen Poe thinking she was a raven. By the time she cawed at me in her bossy, impatient way, it was too late. I figure Poe's a good name whether male or female, but I've decided she's a female looking for a place to make a nest.

I set the plate down and heave the window up with both hands. It was painted shut and doesn't have a screen, so I know it's not meant to be opened. But what my parents don't know won't hurt them. The porch roof extends under the window, so it's not like I can fall. Which *might* not be their number one concern if they knew that my only friend in Faulkner is a bird that eats carrion as well as my bread crusts.

Holding the window with one hand so the impossibly heavy thing won't fall shut and behead me like a guillotine, I quickly stack up a dozen fat paperbacks to hold it. Poe hops closer, giving me an impatient caw and cocking her head like she's trying to figure out my methods. She's a smart bird. I bet if she had hands, she'd show me an easier way to keep the window open. At this very moment, she's probably thinking how ridiculous I am.

Picking up my sandwich, I lean down and slowly push the plate out so as not to startle her. She hops onto the edge and caws angrily at me before I've even released the plate.

"Hungry little thing, aren't you?" I ask softly, tearing off a crust and dropping it onto the plate. She snatches it up with her beak right away. The poor bird always acts like she's starving.

The first few days, she stood on the porch roof and stared at me while I ate my sandwich in my reading nook. I felt bad eating when she had nothing, so I started to throw out the crusts and close the window before she arrived. But within a week, she knew she could trust me to put food out while she was at the far edge of the roof. Now, after only two weeks in the big new house, I've gained her trust enough that she'll eat off my plate while I'm so close I could touch her.

I'm working up to that, but I don't want to scare her off. For now, we share our lunch in companionable silence. I tear off each bread crust and toss it out when she finishes the last one. I hear other crows in the neighborhood, but she's the only one who visits.

Maybe she's new and without a flock, alone like me.

"Honey?" Mom calls, her voice a soft plea as she taps on my door. "Can you come downstairs? Your father wants to talk to you."

I quickly toss out the last crusts of bread and pull the plate in, close the window, and brush the crumbs off my cushion. Then I pick up the book I left open, keeping a finger in the yellowing pages of the battered paperback. Until I get a library card, I'm rereading the handful of books I snuck here in the bottom of my box of clothes before the move. My parents think books are not a necessity and should be left behind.

I hug *The Tommyknockers* to my chest like it might hear those ugly words echoing in my memory. "What does he want?" I call back.

"You need to get outside," Mom says. "You haven't left the house since we got here."

"Gee, I wonder why," I mutter to myself. I know it'll just piss off my stepfather if I don't obey, though. I quickly tear off the corner of a page in my composition notebook and slide it between the pages of my novel to mark my spot. I leave it in my window seat—the best thing about the new house—and join Mom in the hall. She smiles nervously and tugs my shirt straight, picking at me like a nervous little bird, nothing like Poe's assertive demands. If Mom was a bird, she'd be one who was scared of shadows. Her thin face is tense, her mouth drawn into a thin line and her eyes drooping with exhaustion.

I return her smile with an equally tight one of my own. She's not an ally, but she's also not the enemy. I try not to shoot the messenger more often than I can help it. I just have to survive one more year until I turn eighteen, until I graduate and move the fuck out of here.

"'*Late last night and the night before*,'" I sing under my breath as I follow her down the stairs, pressing my fingernails into my palms to steady myself before facing Lee.

I step into the living room where my stepdad sits smoking and squinting at the little boxy TV that looks too small for the room. I don't know how my parents could afford this place, though in all honesty, it's a dump. Or "fixer upper" as my mom said when she told me we were moving here. It's not a mansion, though it might as well be after our last place. It's at least twice as big as our house in Ridgedale, probably more like three times. It's also probably a hundred years old.

"You know we got a pool out back, or you been too busy holing up in your room with your nose in a book?" Lee asks.

"I didn't figure you'd want me bringing pies to the neighbors," I say with my sweetest smile.

"You getting smart with me, girl?" he asks, glowering at me from under grey brows on his protruding forehead. The asshole looks like a caveman elder, but I'm saving that little insult for when I walk out the door for good, flipping him the bird as I go.

"No," I say. "Just stating facts."

"Get your ass outside and start cleaning it," he snaps.

"I don't know how to clean a pool," I point out. "Do I just skim it or…?"

Lee grinds his cigarette out in the ashtray sitting on the arm of his worn chair, his eyes boring into me with such intensity I'm pretty sure he's imagining putting it out on my face. "I don't pay the bills around here for you to sit on your ass like some pampered princess, reading whatever nonsense is in those books of yours," he seethes. "You don't know how to do something? Fucking figure it out, Rae, or I swear to God…"

An involuntary quake goes through me despite my efforts to be brave, and I shake my head, my bravado gone. "I'll figure it out. Just sit tight while I get my shoes on."

I race back upstairs and shove my feet into my tennis shoes, my heart pounding. The minute my shoes are on, hugging my feet like a pair of familiar, comforting arms, the craving to run almost overtakes me. I glance up and see the roof empty outside my reading nook. A pang of loneliness goes through me.

If I were a bird, I'd fly away too.

Not really. People who say they want that for a superpower are crazy. Flying sounds terrifying to me—being buffeted by the wind, careening out of control, maybe caught up in storm if you weren't careful. I prefer my feet on the ground.

Lee is right, anyway. He does pay for everything, since Mom doesn't have a job and won't file for disability because then she'd have to explain all the mysterious injuries she never went to the doctor about. I haven't rushed to get a job, either, looking the way I have for the past few weeks. Not that Lee would have let me. He has to keep up appearances. But maybe I'll put in some applications now that I can leave the house without people staring.

Mom meets me at the back door, lowering her voice to a whisper. "Make yourself useful for an hour, just to get your father off your back," she says, giving me an apologetic smile.

"It's fine, Mom," I say, pushing her hands away when she starts picking at me again. "I could use the fresh air, like you said. I might even go for a run before I come back."

"What are you two hens squawking about?" Lee demands.

Mom cowers. "Don't be out too late," she whispers to me, darting a glance back to the living room. "Remember, Faulkner has a city curfew."

"I'll be in way before ten," I say, pulling open the door and then pushing the screen door beyond. It creaks on its hinges, the wood old and wobbly, probably rotted through.

I step out onto the porch and take a deep breath of the sweltering May heat, letting the steamy air fill my lungs as I take in my surroundings. Though the grass isn't uniform like it might be in a fancy neighborhood, the backyard has been mowed in neat stripes. Of course Lee had to take care of his lawn first thing. The man's obsessed.

Apparently the next door neighbor is, too. I can hear their mower running, though it's a damn sauna out here even at six in the evening. I catch a glimpse of a tall man through a hole in the privacy fence where three or four of the grey boards have been broken out to let neighborhood kids in. I can tell by the graffiti along the fence, mostly penises, swear words, and gang signs. There's also a giant bird painted across one whole side of the wooden fence, each feather detailed in black paint. Its impressive wingspan stretches wide, as if to encircle the yard in a hug. I know instantly that someone else has gotten a visit from Poe. Did the person who lived here before us paint this? It's not like the other graffiti.

I trot down the four steps, noting that the boards on the second step are loose, the nail heads sticking up half an inch. There's a shed at the far end of the pool that looks like it might collapse in the next gust of wind, and a big old oak at the far end of the yard. But the swimming pool is front and center, unshaded by trees or the shed. That's the main attraction. I cross the grimy white tiles to the pool.

And groan.

I pictured a scene from *90210* when Lee said we had a pool. Skim a few leaves and some tree pollen, and it would be a sparkling blue rectangle where I'd lay out and work on my tan while reading, like a rich girl.

This is… Not that.

The urge to run pops back up, wheedling for attention. It's not like Lee cares if I work or run first. Okay, maybe he'll care, but he won't know. He's off duty, and he's planted himself for the evening. He won't budge until dinner. As long as I stay out of the house, he won't complain.

Probably.

I weigh the risks, then turn and cross the yard to climb through the hole in the fence, only then realizing I'm in the neighbor's yard. He's gone around the back of his house with the mower, so I hurry along the fence until it ends and step into our front yard before he sees me. Then I stop to gather my thick, dark waves into a high pony. I stretch for a minute, taking in the other houses in the neighborhood. I've seen these from my window, unlike the back yard.

Our house sits on the northwest corner of our block, where Mill ends. The other houses on the street are basic, drab rectangles. Ours sticks out like a sore thumb, the only two-story house within eyesight down any of the streets I can see from the windows. It's big and white and shabby, with grungy white paint peeling away in places. The wraparound porch surrounds the entire lower level, and latticework hangs from the roof over it. It's completely out of place among the ranch-style brick boxes in the surrounding area.

I finish stretching and take off, turning off Mill and jogging the first block to warm up. Humidity lays over the town like a damp blanket, along with an occasional whiff of the paper mill that blows in on the hot breeze, but late afternoon sun slants through the trees, turning the leaf edges golden. I like this time of day, even the heat.

I let it wash over me, absorb me, and I let go. Sometimes I run to work out my fury, sometimes to escape, sometimes to think. Today, though, I run to move my body again after stagnating in the eggshell of my room for two weeks, to be free and shake off the lethargy, and leave behind the broken pieces of my home.

This is the kind of flying I do.

My shoes hit the pavement with satisfying impact, the ground solid and reassuring under my feet. It's nice to know it's always there for me, not shifting or disappearing on a whim. The earth is predictable and stable, there no matter what town I move to or what mood my stepdad is in. Needless to say, it's something I can totally appreciate.

I lose myself in the rhythm, letting my feet take me where they will. I'm not worried about getting lost. I have a pretty good sense of direction, and since I'm in a new place, I take note of each street name when I pass. I see a girl in overalls skateboarding with a Walkman in her pocket, headphones over her ears, and I make a note to grab my music next time I run.

Before I know it, the sun has sunk behind the houses, and the cars speeding by have their lights on. Well, shit. I lost track of time. I turn and retrace my steps as fast as I can, fear increasing my pace but making me reckless. Just as I turn back onto Mill Street, I run smack into a guy. The impact sends me flying backward, literally bouncing off the wall of tight muscle. I slam down on the cracked sidewalk, the breath knocked out of me so thoroughly I can't even cry out or cuss at the pain.

The guy towers over me as I lie on the sidewalk like an overturned turtle. From my vantage point, he looks like a giant, easily over six feet of solid muscle, wearing a pair of knee-length basketball shorts and running shoes. He's shirtless, which means I have a full view of all that muscle straining under his smooth light brown skin, like it barely fits. Tattoos ring his arms, spread over his chest and shoulders, peek out from the top of his low-slung athletic shorts, and wrap around the front of his neck like a threatening hand.

He studies me with emotionless eyes, dark and fathomless. The asshole doesn't even offer an apology or a hand to help me up.

I suck in a hideously ugly breath and scramble to my feet, brushing off my ass. "Watch where you're going, jerk face," I snap.

The barest spark of life flits through his eyes, which up close are a dark, deep, mossy green. The corners of his full, masculine lips twitch. Then he's back to stony indifference, a muscle in his square jaw ticking.

"Watch how you speak to people in *la olla*, little girl," he says, his voice a startlingly deep, annoyingly sexy growl with just a hint of an accent. His black hair is shorn on the sides but long enough on top to be a bit mussed by sweat and the wind. From the collision with his bare chest, I can tell he's been running a while too.

Now that I'm standing, he's not quite such a behemoth, though he still looms at least a foot taller than my five-foot-four frame. My instinct for self-preservation slightly outweighs my temper, and one look at this tattooed tower tells me I don't want to mess with him. I give him a two-finger salute. "Noted," I say. "Thanks for the heads up."

He looks down at me like I'm a roach he'd like to stomp. The feeling is entirely mutual.

"Anytime, little girl," he says, his voice dropping into a slow drawl as his gaze melts over me, taking me in from my messy ponytail to the loose strands sticking to the damp skin of my neck, my sweaty ringer tee, high-waisted shorts, and bare legs. Suddenly I do feel like a little girl, or at least an idiot who runs in jean shorts.

"Later, jerk face," I say, turning and starting up the walkway to our house. I'm on the porch before I remember I was supposed to clean the pool. Shit. I wanted to slam the door in that guy's face, but not as much as I want to avoid Lee's wrath. I veer around the side of the house, following the wrap-around porch. When I spare a glance over my shoulder, the guy is still standing there, watching me with a frown. Double shit. I thought he'd be gone, continuing on with his run. Now he saw me look back at him, like I wanted to know if he was watching me walk away.

I dart around the house and take a minute to gather my wits and examine my elbows, which are scraped to hell from biting the dust so hard. At least I didn't crack my skull open.

I sigh and head down the back steps to survey the job ahead. As I stand there listening to the drone of a weed eater next door, excitement starts to replace the dread at such a huge undertaking. So, it'll take more than a quick skim with a net before I'm enjoying a California-blue teenage dream. So what? It's not like I've never gotten my hands dirty or done hard work before. This time, I have something better than money waiting at the end. My stepdad just takes all my money anyway. He can't take this. Hell, he probably won't even use it much.

But I'll use it.

I can barely contain myself as I close my eyes and imagine it, something I've never even hoped for, it was so far out of the realm of possibility. A *pool.* Only rich kids have pools in Ridgedale. My friends and I listened with envy while the popular girls talked about pool parties and laying out working on their tans. I never dreamed *I'd* have something so posh.

"Hey," calls a warm, masculine voice behind me.

I spin around, my eyes sweeping the yard before landing on a guy standing with his hands braced on either side of the gap in the fence, his head ducked under the crossbeam at the top.

Everything about him is sweet as honey. Eyes like warm, melted gold peer out at me from behind a pair of wire-rimmed glasses set on a prominent nose above wide, full lips that are smiling at me in a way that makes funny things happen in my lower belly. His jaw is strong and square, his cheekbones sharp as saw blades, his skin beaded with little droplets of sweat that gleam in the twilight like he's running with honey. A shock of messy, damp black hair completes the image of the guy who is too gorgeous for words.

My throat sticks as I try to swallow. Yep, words have deserted me. The guy is… Breathtaking.

The weed eater is no longer running, so he must have shut it off while I was lost in thought. The silence in the neighborhood seems to throb in the stifling evening air.

"You okay?" he asks, his smile widening at one corner only, so it goes all crooked.

My stomach careens sideways too.

"Hey," I say, trying not to sound as nervous and jumpy as I feel suddenly. I don't like being taken by surprise, especially not by guys who look like they belong in movies instead of a rundown neighborhood in Faulkner, Arkansas.

"Mind if I join you?" he asks, gesturing to the gap in the fence. "I figure introducing myself is the neighborly thing to do, but I like to ask before I come in a girl's hole."

If I wasn't already sweating from the heat, I am now.

I'm also wondering what kind of jerk talks like that to a stranger.

"There's already a lot of dicks in here," I say, gesturing to the graffiti on the fence. "I'm sure I won't even notice one more."

He laughs and steps through the gap, his long legs taking him across the grass to join me in moments. I try not to ogle the way he moves; the way his jeans sit low on his hips; the wallet chain that swings casually against his thigh with each step or the earrings glinting in each ear; the way his sweat-soaked white t-shirt clings to the lean muscle underneath.

Try being the operative word.

"Looks like a good day for a swim," he says, planting his hands on his hips and gazing down into the pool.

I jerk my attention back to the task at hand. Just because he's hot—volcanically so—doesn't mean he's interested, or that I'm interested in him. Besides, the guy looks at least twenty. I've had my share of catcalls from gross old guys, but I'm not used to them making me flustered. It's just thrown me for a loop because he's *so* not gross.

"You first," I say, trying to shake off the star-struck moment.

"What, you chicken?" he taunts.

"Um, yes," I say. "That's a festering vat of disease."

He laughs again, the sound rich and rolling through the dense heat like it's part of it, like he's part of the air itself, the town, the rustle of the oak tree swaying lazily in the summer evening.

He makes his voice dramatic, like he's reading Shakespeare, and sweeps his arm wide. "Who knows what rusty needles and used condoms lurk in ye murky depths?"

A snort starts to escape me before I realize how ugly that sounds and try to change it to a giggle, which I'm pretty sure is a sound I've never made in my life. The hybrid snort-giggle is less attractive than if I'd just gone all in for the snort.

The guy laughs again, the warm sound making me want to disappear into the ground after my failed attempt at sounding cute.

At least someone's finding humor in the situation. I turn my attention back to the half-foot of sludge at the bottom of the blue rectangle. A mixture of rainwater, rotten leaves, acorns, dead mosquitos and their larvae, and other sticks and bugs forms a thick stew of nastiness in the pool that should be full of clear, sparkling, Beverly Hills water.

The guy sobers but smiles sideways at me, a dimple sinking into his cheek. God, it's not even fair how fine he is. "Well, I just saw you over here and figured I'd come by and introduce myself, since it seems we're neighbors," he says. "I'm Lennox."

"Like Annie?" I ask, smiling up at him.

"Sure," he says, tipping his chin toward me. "What about you?"

"Rae."

"Like Billy Ray Cyrus?" he asks. "Ray Charles? Ray of Sunshine?"

"With an E," I correct.

"You look like a ray of sunshine to me," he says, and I'm startled to see him checking me out from the corner of his eye.

"It's actually Rae West, like Mae West. My mom's a big fan of old movies, and we have the same last name, but she wanted to add a little Southern flare so…" I realize I'm rambling, thrown off by having a guy who looks like him looking at me like he is.

"Wait, your last name is West?"

"Yeah," I say. "So?"

"No way," he says with an easy laugh.

"What?" I insist, halfway embarrassed and halfway irritated that I'm not in on the joke.

"Lennox North," he says, pointing to his chest. "Just think, if we got married, we could be the North-Wests."

I laugh, flustered by a guy I just met talking about us marrying, when he's clearly older than me and a million times too hot.

"The neighborhood could use some fresh blood," he says, his manner turning more serious. "Fresh faces. A pool…"

I roll my eyes. "So that's why you're really here? To ask if you can use our pool?"

"Not just me," he says, his eyes lighting up as he paints a scenario in his mind. "A lot of kids around here… They don't have stuff like pools. It might be cool if they could come swim here. You could be the neighborhood hot spot, where we all hang out." He gives me such a winning smile my knees nearly melt, and I want to give him everything he's asking just because he said he'd come hang out with me.

God, I'm such a ditz.

"If you're up for it, of course," he says when I'm too busy drooling to answer.

"*I* wouldn't mind," I say, reality punching back into me like a familiar fist. "It's just, my dad—my stepdad... He's not, like, super friendly. In fact, you should probably go. He wouldn't want me talking to strangers, even if you are the neighbor."

That's putting it so nicely I almost laugh. If the neighborhood kids started frequenting our pool, Lee would sit on the back porch with his Glock and use them for target practice. My family keeps things behind closed doors. We don't go meet the neighbors—hence it being two weeks since we moved in before any of us met him. We sure as hell don't invite the neighbors over for a pool party. The only reason Lee wants this back in working order is so he can have something no one else has, something worth coveting, and maybe invite a few officers over to show it off.

Our job is to make sure everyone knows he's the best. To shine a light on his goodness and hide the badness in shadow. Telling the neighbor, a virtual stranger, the truth would lead to dire consequences. I may only be seventeen, but that lesson comes from experience, not age. We don't tell strangers our problems. We tell them they're unwelcome when they ask to use our pool, and we pretend we don't see their face fall, and we stop ourselves from backtracking and offering a compromise.

This is family business. We don't air our dirty laundry in public. No one else needs to know what goes on behind those doors. Letting someone in, letting them come over on the regular, lounge beside the pool and draw me in with dirty jokes and criminal smiles, would be too risky.

I'm afraid to look at Lennox, afraid he'll see something I don't want seen. So I stare into the mess at the bottom of the pool while he says goodbye, and I tell myself it's better this way. Tempting as it is to flirt with the hot neighbor, it's the last kind of trouble I need to bring into my life. I'll be gone in a year anyway. I just have to make it to graduation—no distractions, no connections that will tie me here.

So, with my stupid heart screaming at me that I'm the one being stupid, I let him walk across the lawn and disappear back onto his own side of the fence.

He'll probably never talk to me again.

two

Lennox North

"I met the neighbor," I say, kicking the door closed behind me and tossing my work gloves on the side table. I drop my sweaty ass onto the couch beside my twin.

"Yeah?" he asks, not looking up from Mortal Kombat.

"She's fine as hell," I say, watching him like he might ejaculate at the mention of hot pussy. With my brother, it's a very real possibility.

"I didn't think you were into old women, but okay," he says, manhandling the controller. "Maybe you and Billy can double date before the cop splatters your brains. If you have any."

"Not the mom," I say, grabbing the other controller. "The daughter."

"Didn't think you were into little kids, either," he says. "Guess it explains why you never get any action outside the crew. I'll let Mom know to keep the kids away from Uncle Lennox next Christmas."

"Fuck off, *cabrón*," I say. "I didn't even know they had a kid. They moved in two weeks ago, haven't seen her once."

"Yeah? Maybe her mommy doesn't let her play with strangers."

Remembering she said something similar about her dad, I throw my leg over his, slumping down next to him. "You seen her?"

"*Sí,* I seen her," he says. "What about it?"

"You think she's fine?"

"I think it doesn't matter. You don't fuck with a cop's daughter, *parce.*"

"Maybe he lets her date."

Maddox laughs. "Since when do we *date* bitches?"

I shrug. "I could date a bitch."

"Stay away from that one unless you want to spend eight to ten years in prison."

I just laugh. "She's not that young."

"Bullshit."

"Well, she's fine as hell anyway."

"You'll never get a girl like that. She's all wholesome and shit," he says. "Besides, you're only into crew girls."

"Maybe it's time for a change," I say, though his words eat at me. "If you're not into her, I've got a chance."

I hate that he might be right, hate that my words are even truer than his. Most of all, I hate that I have to feel him out about every girl before I make a move, because every fucking time they end up falling for him and leaving me to eat shit.

"You have *no* chance," he says, shoving my leg off him. "Get your *pecueca* off me and go take a shower, or even the crew girls won't lick your smelly ass."

I laugh and toss down my controller like it doesn't matter. "So you *are* into her," I say. "You're just trying to trick me into not being interested, so you can mack on her."

"I don't have to *mack* on anyone," he says, focusing on the game. "If I wanted her, I could get her to bounce on my dick without lifting a finger. Meanwhile, you wouldn't know what to do with a chick that cute if you had her, you fucking freak. *Necesitas un cucha para calmar tu arrechera.*"

I don't let myself wince at his words. I am a freak. He knows it, but it's funny to him.

It's not funny to me.

"Knew it," I say, swinging up from the couch with a smug grin that makes him glare like he wants to bust out my front teeth. Better that than having him guess the truth of how deeply it bothers me. I laugh and slug his shoulder. "You think she's hot, too."

"Fuck off," he says, shoving me with his foot. "Or I'll nut in her ass just to piss you off."

"If she's too wholesome for me, she's sure as hell too wholesome for your sick mind," I shoot back, heading down the hall to shower. And maybe picture her pouty pink lips begging for mercy and her eyes streaming with tears when I jerk off and imagine giving her none.

three

#1 on the Billboard Chart:
"MMMBop"—Hanson

Rae West

Half asleep, I stumble out from the dim interior of our house into the blinding sun, step into my rubber boots, grab the bucket and shovel I found in the decrepit old shed, and head for the pool. It's close to a hundred degrees out, but I'd rather work in the heat than in the evening under Lee's critical eye. He's not impressed with my progress, and to be honest, I can't blame him. After two weeks of work, I've only managed to lower the level of sludge by a couple inches.

I come to an abrupt halt when I reach the edge of the pool and see four men below. Still groggy after staying up until 4 A.M. finishing *Christine* and then sleeping until noon, I didn't register the sounds coming from my own backyard. I've gotten used to the neighborhood noises—old men smoking on porches, their wives gossiping over fences, TVs blaring, babies crying. Everything happens in slow-mo under the molasses of summer heat.

Everything except the four men shoveling sludge into a dozen buckets, their pants and boots slick with mud, brown droplets splattering their arms and sunburned shoulders.

One of them looks up, and I'm startled to see the guy I've affectionately deemed Jerk Face. I haven't had any more close encounters, but I've seen him from my window.

Not that I was watching for him or anything. Total coincidence.

He just happens to run by at around seven every evening, and I happen to sit in my window seat around that time, and it's hard not to be distracted by all that tan skin, muscle, and ink. He's shirtless again today—all four of them are—and sweat tracks down his taut abs, glistening in the blistering sun. Our eyes meet, and he glares like I've assigned him this odious task.

"Gonna get down here and help, little girl?" he asks. "Or are you afraid to get your hands dirty?"

"What are you doing?" I demand.

"Bailing your ass out," he says, glowering. "Unless you don't need help."

I'm tempted to mouth off and tell him I don't need anything from an asshole like him, that I'm dead set on getting this done and I can do it myself. But the truth is, they've already done as much in one morning as I've done in two weeks working alone. It's not like they're swooping in on the last day and taking all the credit when I did all the work.

"But why?" I ask, climbing down the rusty ladder to join them.

"I told you, Sunshine," says my neighbor, who's also hard at work. "It'll be good to have a pool on the block."

"Did you talk to my stepdad?" I ask, scooping a shovelful of rotting leaves and muck into my bucket.

"Nah," he says. "But we waited for him to go to work before invading."

He flashes me a smile and swipes a forearm over his forehead, leaving behind a smudge of brown mud above his glasses. It's somehow endearing, which is a good thing, because I'm in danger of fainting from the heat waves coming off him. If he was gorgeous with a shirt on, he's heart stopping without one. He's built more like a runner than the other guy, muscular but lean, with long limbs. He's also tattooed, a black crow stretching its wings across his entire chest, a skull superimposed over its body, and its tail spread over the top of his abs. A raised, brown scar runs over his hipbone and down into the top of his jeans, where a wallet chain hangs. But the dimpled smile and warm gaze soften what would otherwise be a scary sight.

"Well… Thanks," I say, continuing to work. I feel sweat trickling down my chest between my breasts, and I'm glad I pulled on a loose t-shirt this morning, too sleep-fogged to think ahead. The last few days, I've worked in a sports bra. Might as well work on my tan one way or another. Not exactly the California dream situation, but I can work with what I'm given.

Suddenly I wonder if my neighbor saw me struggling to make progress on the pool, and I'm glad the heat's already flushed my face so no one can see my blush under my ballcap.

Lennox must have seen me out here working or he wouldn't have come over to help.

And brought a whole crew.

I decide that whatever he's seen of me, it's totally worth it if that's what prompted him to pitch in.

When the buckets are full, Lennox and the runner climb out of the pool. The other two guys start handing up the buckets, and to my surprise, my neighbor grabs two buckets and dumps them over our fence, into his yard. Figuring out what to do with the stuff has been a problem, so I've just been dumping it into our trash can. For two weeks, with just one person climbing up and down the ladder every time my bucket got full, it's been slow going. These guys have a whole system worked out, and I can see how they got so much done this morning.

One of the guys, a tanned, tattooed guy with a blond mullet peaking out under a ballcap and a pair of sunglasses over his eyes, grabs my bucket. "I'm Billy," he says, hooking a thumb back over his shoulder at the last one, a beefy guy who sports paler skin singed red by the sun, frosted tips, and a pair of mirrored shades. "That's Tommy."

"Y'all live in the neighborhood?" I ask, accepting an empty bucket from Tommy. It's smeared with brown, and some of the murky water drips off the bottom and runs down my leg, but I don't complain. I'm grateful as hell they're here.

"Nah, I play ball with Maddox," he says, nodding toward the runner. "Go Wampus Cats."

"Same," Billy says. "I live over in the trailer park on the east side of town."

"Couldn't resist a pool job, could you?" Tommy says, elbowing Billy.

"Fuck off," Billy says, shoving him in the shoulder. His hands are clad in work gloves, and I can tell they've seen their fair share of use already. He looks like the kind of guy who worked for his muscles, like a farm boy who isn't afraid to get his hands dirty. He'd fit in better in Ridgedale than what I've seen of Faulkner.

"He's just waiting for your mama to come out and offer us some lemonade," Tommy says to me. "He's been eyeing your house all morning, trying to catch a glimpse."

"I said, fuck off," Billy growls, bending to scoop a handful of slime and tossing it at Tommy. It splatters over his pale belly and onto his sunburned chest.

Tommy throws a bucket aside and leaps at Billy, collaring him with a muscular arm. They wrestle around, trying not to lose their footing in the slippery ooze, before Maddox hops down and casually strolls over, grabbing the back of both their necks and yanking them apart.

"*Ustedes pueden calmar!*" he snaps.

Billy shoves him off before stalking to the far end of the pool and digging back in, angrily flinging sludge into an empty bucket.

Lennox climbs back in too, looking as unbothered by the fight as if they were playing, though Billy was obviously pissed. I cast a curious glance at Maddox, but he just scowls, his gaze catching on the muddy water dribbling down my leg before he attacks the job as angrily as Billy.

I work my way over to Lennox, who seems to be the only one who hasn't become irritable in the heat.

"How do you know these guys?" I ask. "They said they played ball with Maddox."

Maddox knows where I live, but there's no way the jerk face recruited people to come help me.

Lennox gestures around. "Meet *mi parceros.* Mad's my brother—my twin. Billy runs with our crew, and Tommy was just bored and promised free beer. A couple more are on the way."

"Free beer?" I barely manage to speak past the racing of my heart. If we raid Lee's beer stash, I'm dead meat.

"It'll be here any second," Lennox says, giving me a quick wink.

"Oh," I say, covering my nervousness with a laugh.

I catch Maddox watching us from across the pool, a frown on his face. Before I can ask what his problem is, Lennox speaks.

"You a square?"

"What?"

"You looked so freaked when I brought up beer, and you don't look like the kind of girl who's already on the wagon. You ever even had beer?"

"Of course I've had beer," I say, reaching up to readjust my cap and pull my long hair through the hole in the back. "And I'm not a square."

"Sure," he says, smirking at me. "How old are you anyway? My brother says you're jail bait."

I gulp and cast a guilty glance at Maddox. I think about telling them I'm eighteen, but there's no way they'll buy that. Besides, seventeen is legal here, so if they wanted to date me…

I push the thought away and go for the truth. "Seventeen."

Lennox raises a brow like he doesn't believe it, but he doesn't challenge me.

"So, what's this crew you have?" I ask. "Like a work crew?"

"Sure," Lennox says, smiling as he scoops.

"What?" I ask, getting that same feeling I got when he asked about my last name, like I'm missing something.

"We do work together," Lennox says. "But it's our street crew. All of Mill and the next few blocks. *Nosotros nos cuidamos el uno al otro.*"

I shake my head and give him an apologetic look. "I don't speak Spanish. Sorry."

"We just make sure everyone's taken care of, *sí?*"

He flashes me a grin that almost distracts me from the sinking feeling in my belly. Almost.

"Yeah," I say awkwardly. "*Sí.*"

Before I can ask more, he finishes his bucket and climbs out of the pool for dumping duty again. I can't even imagine what his yard looks like right now, with a hundred gallons of sludge flooding it. When he comes back, though, I force myself not to chicken out.

"Does your crew have a name?" I ask carefully.

"Sure," he says. "But we don't need to get into that with you, Sunshine."

"Maybe the Skull and Crossbones?" I venture, narrowing my eyes.

He frowns. "*Vení,* we just make sure everything in our neighborhoods runs smoothly and everyone's safe. Like a Neighborhood Watch."

"That's why you wanted to fix up my pool?" I ask incredulously. "So you could invite your *gang* over?"

Lennox rolls his eyes and finishes yet another bucket, filling four to every one of mine. "The Skulls are not a gang," he says. "It's an organization. Gangs sell drugs and shit. We clean things up, take care of the people in our neighborhood."

I narrow my eyes, but now it's my turn to not challenge his word. Besides, I'm one girl, and though I'm not afraid to get my hands dirty, there are four big gang members in my pool right now. Not exactly the odds I want in a fight.

And they're *gang members*. They probably have weapons hidden in their muddy jeans and work boots. I find myself watching them from the corner of my eye. Maybe he says it's not a gang, but the news is always featuring stories about the gangs in Little Rock, and they don't call them organizations. I wonder if Lennox really believes that, or if they're supposed to tell outsiders that. The news never distinguishes between the Skull & Crossbones and Lucifer's Disciples or the big, nationwide *organizations*. They're all lumped into the "crime problem."

The silence between us has just started to get awkward when Billy calls, "Hey girl, you wanna get dirty?"

I start to turn, and just then, a handful of soft, silty mud splatters my side. I yelp in surprise as the clump of muck slides down me, warm water trickling down my skin. Billy laughs and bends to scoop up another handful.

"You pig," I yell, grabbing for some of the mud that's left at the very bottom. I have only a second to remember Lennox's warning about needles and condoms before another missile of mud and leaves flies at me. I duck aside and hurl some back at Billy. He ducks, laughing, but the mud hits the wall of the pool behind him and splatters his back.

"Oh, you're in for it now," he says, grabbing a double-handed scoop.

I shriek and turn to run, only to find Lennox with mud in his hands right behind me. He tosses it against my chest, and it covers the front of my "Soylent Green is People" shirt. I give a cry of anger and throw some back at him. Another load hits my back, and I spin and try to defend myself from the attack by throwing mud at both Tommy and Billy, who are laughing and slipping in the muck as they come closer.

Within minutes, I'm drenched in warm, muddy water and coated with brown gunk and slime. I shriek again and duck, holding onto my hat to protect the top of my head as they close in, all three of them laughing as they gang up on me. I feel a hand slide down my bare leg, painting me with mud, and I look over to see Lennox grinning big enough to make his dimple sink in, a mischievous look in his eye as he smears me in filth.

My heart does a flip when his hand slowly glides up my thigh.

Suddenly, I can't breathe, and the others don't exist.

And then cold water drenches my back, and I scream and cover my head again. I spin around and get a face-full of water straight from the hose. Maddox stands over us, smirking from beside the pool. I was so busy defending myself from the other three in the mud fight I didn't even see him climb out.

Spluttering and spitting, I scramble backwards, only for my foot to slip. I go down, planting on my ass for the second time in front of him. He smiles wider, dousing me with water until I'm thoroughly soaked, my shirt clean again and plastered to my skin. Lennox holds out a hand, pulling me to my feet, and turns me around so Maddox can rinse my back.

All four of them are staring at me with expressions ranging from resentful—Maddox—to wolfish hunger—Tommy. I cross my arms, aware that they're all staring, that my nipples are pebbled from the cold water and my clothes are painted to my skin, leaving little to the imagination.

"Damn," says an unfamiliar voice behind me. "Looks like we missed all the fun."

Lennox pulls me into his arms, as if sensing my discomfort, and the cold water stops. I turn my head and see two more men standing beside Maddox, holding a heavy cooler between them. One of them is a stocky guy with hair that's short on the sides and squared off on top, and the other is an Asian guy with a grey bandana around his head.

"Beer time," Tommy whoops, pumping his fist. He starts out of the pool, Billy following.

"Let's grab a beer and then finish this up, Sunshine," Lennox says, his hands circling my waist before he hoists me up.

Maddox grabs my hands and pulls me out of the pool, setting me on my feet.

"You good?" he asks.

I nod. I'm only inches from his chest, from the bulging muscles of his pecs, the smooth skin, the ink. I gulp, my eyes slowly rising, taking in the delicate dagger on his sternum, nestled between his powerful, bulging pecs, to the crow with outstretched wings on his neck.

My heart does a little flip. As soon as I see it, everything clicks into place. It's a gang tattoo. There are words in another language circling his neck below the tattoo, but aside from that, it's the same design that's on Lennox's chest and on Billy's back—a crow like an avenging angel with its wings spread over his shoulder blades.

"Go get changed," Maddox says, frowning down at me.

His eyes are heated when they meet mine.

"You're wet, too," I point out, feeling brave.

"I don't look like… that," he says flatly, his eyes raking down me again.

I swallow hard.

He's wrong.

His lips pull into a smirk. "Unless you want six guys jerking off thinking about wrecking your tight little ass later," he says. "Maybe you're into that kind of thing. In which case, you can strip for us and hang out in your panties. We can see everything, anyway."

"Jerk," I manage. I can't meet his eyes, so I turn around and flee into the house to catch my breath. Mom is on the couch watching one of her soaps and smoking a cigarette. She doesn't even look up when I grab a crust of bread from the end of the loaf before sneaking up the stairs, dripping wet. She must have heard us in the back, as we got pretty loud during the mud fight, but she doesn't say a word.

I'm disappointed to see the porch roof empty beyond my window. I missed Poe's visit. I slip the piece of bread out, though, hoping she'll come back for it, even if she's not here to calm my nerves. I've taken to talking to her like the crazy person I am.

I hurry to the bathroom after closing the window. There, I try to steady my breathing and let my heartbeat return to normal as I peel off my wet clothes and hang them over the edge of the clawfoot tub. Of course those guys are going to talk rough. They're gangsters, for fuck's sake, and a lot older than me.

I stand in front of the full-length mirror and examine my bare body, running my hands over my slight curves. I'm built more like an athlete than a stripper, with small boobs and hips, a boyish figure that I've never really thought was sexy.

Do they really think I'm sexy?

I quickly towel dry my hair and pull on a pair of cut-offs, the shortest pair I have, that show off my muscular runner's legs. Then I slip into a black baby tee that says, "Strangers Have the Best Candy," on the front. I think about a pair of chunky sandals, but that feels like trying too hard, so I twist my hair up into a bun, secure it with a handful of butterfly clips, and head back out. I still smell like a swamp, but I'm afraid I'll miss something if I take the time to shower. Besides, they're all filthy and stinky.

I hurry back downstairs and along the back hall, ducking out onto the porch. Maddox is still at the end of the pool, rinsing mud from the bottom with the hose.

The buckets are stacked along the edge of the pool, now emptied. There's barely anything left at the bottom. The Asian guy is standing at the far end, where it's deepest, scooping up anything that clogs the drain and tossing it into the lone bucket that remains, the yellow one I brought.

Feeling both guilty and so grateful I could cry—they did all this in one day—I start toward the ladder, about to go help.

Billy holds out a can of beer toward me before I can climb down.

"*Vení,* take a load off," Lennox says, patting the spot beside him. They're all sitting along the edge of the pool, their feet dangling in.

"I should help," I say, nodding toward the two still working. "It's my pool…"

"It's *our* pool," he says, flashing me that smile that makes my knees nearly buckle.

"I told you, my stepdad…"

"Once it's full, you'll see. There's room for everybody."

I start to sit, but he pulls me down onto his knee instead of the ground. Wrapping an arm around my middle, he pulls me back against him and rubs his chin against the back of my neck. “I promise,” he says softly, his hot breath against my skin making my eyes roll back in my head.

His promise and his arm around me feel so reassuring, I almost believe it. It’s not like I can tell them the truth, go into detail about Lee’s temperament and how much trouble I’d be in. They’ll think I’m a baby, that I still care what my parents think even though I’m basically a senior already. That’s my own shit to sort, so I laugh it off and pretend everything is okay.

I’ve never sat on a guy’s lap before, and I’m painfully aware of my body against his, my weight on his leg, the sweat on his bare chest soaking into my clean t-shirt. I should be disgusted, but I melt instead.

I see Maddox watching us with an even fiercer scowl, and I grab the beer and open it, trying to collect myself and act like an adult instead of a freak who’s so afraid to get close to anyone that she's never even kissed a boy.

I take a slug of beer, forcing myself not to make a face at the nasty taste. I've drank before—my friends and I snuck some from our parents on occasion—but I don't really like beer. Everyone around the pool is drinking it like it's water though, and I don't want to look like a prude, so I drink up too.

"Why does your brother hate me?" I ask when I've had a beer and my defenses start to lower. I know that's dangerous, so I sip at the next one instead of drinking it fast to quench my thirst and quell the heat. Beads of condensation dot the can, and I run my thumb over them, wiping them from the red and blue emblem.

"He doesn't hate you," Lennox assures me, squeezing me back against him. My heart swells with warmth, but Billy laughs.

"What'd you do to him?" he asks.

"Nothing," I protest. "He seems to be holding a grudge because I got in his way while he was running. Although I'm the one who paid the price."

I rub my elbow, still whitish pink from where the scabs just cleared.

"Don't take it personal," says Michael, the guy who brought the beer. He leans over to bump his can against mine. "Mad's got a hit list a mile long. Dude never forgets a grudge."

"Give it time," Lennox says. "Some people take longer to warm up."

"Yeah," Billy says. "I'm sure you didn't really piss him off. If you had, you'd be buried in his backyard, and he'd be dumping that shit on your grave."

Lennox chuckles. "*Verdad que sí.* You don't want to get on his bad side. His wrath is like no other. But don't worry, Sunshine. He'll learn to love you in time."

When I catch Maddox glaring at us like he wants to murder me for sitting on his brother's lap, I'm not so sure. I don't think time will cure whatever's wrong with him.

four

Maddox North

"It's done," I say, kicking off my boots next to the front door. "Leak's patched and holding. Pool's in business."

"Fuck yeah," Lennox says, hopping up and throwing an arm around my neck. "We did it!"

"I still think it's a shit idea," I mutter, shoving him off.

"*Quíubo?*" Mom asks, sticking her head out of the kitchen. "What's this idea?"

"Nothing," I say.

"We fixed up the pool next door," Lennox says. "Now that it's up and running, we're going to have a block party, so everyone knows it's open. Can you imagine what it'll do for the kids in the neighborhood, to have a pool to hang out at all summer?"

"It's not a fucking community center," I point out. "It's our neighbor's, and he's a cop. How's that for a stupid fucking idea?"

Mom plants a hand on her hip. "Why wouldn't he want you there? You're not doing anything illegal."

"Not everyone's a fucking saint like Lennox," I say.

It's fucking annoying how selfless he is, how he's always looking for ways to help the neighborhood while I'm the dickhead who mostly just wants to help himself.

Mom clicks her tongue at me and stands on tiptoes to give Lennox a hug around the neck with one arm, and I'm reminded that he's not always a saint. Joining the Skull & Crossbones was his idea. He got his bones and became a full member first. I didn't kill a man for a full year after he did, and it still haunts me, though I'd never let on.

Still, I've done my share of dirty work since then, while he's kept his hands clean.

Sometimes I wonder if I made a mistake, if we should have just dealt with our problem on our own. After we avenged our mother, Lennox had no interest in defending the Skull's turf. Even after we formed the Murder of Crows, he's not keen on riding along when someone's stupid enough to disrespect our crew. He's more interested in building our local community and organizing the Skulls than tearing anything or anyone down. Sometimes even I forget how well our crew name fits his dark side.

Sometimes I forget he has one.

five

#1 on the Billboard Chart:
"I'll Be Missing You"—Puff Daddy & Faith Evans

Rae West

"*Hola, chica,*" calls Lexi, a girl who came over to help scrub the pool clean a few weeks ago. "You excited about the party?"

She sits smoking on a woven plastic lounge chair in the neighbor's front yard, wearing a baggy T-shirt and jeans despite the sweltering heat. Her shiny dark blonde hair hangs in two loops on the sides of her head, and a half-smoked cigarette dangles casually from her fingers.

Even though I want to pretend I didn't hear, I slowly make my way over. I've just returned from a run, and the last thing I want to think about is the horrible thing she just said. But she helped clean the pool for no reason other than Billy is her cousin and she apparently had nothing better to do that day, so I don't want to be a bitch.

"What party?" I ask, careful to keep my voice even.

Sweat clings to me like a sodden blanket, and I want to go take a cold shower and talk to my crow, not deal with what is clearly a total emergency. Even in running shorts and a baby tee, I feel grimy with the heat that doesn't seem to bother Lexi in the slightest.

"The party at your house," she says, like I'm missing something obvious. "Tomorrow night?"

I grit my teeth and glare at the house next door, but my heart is hammering wildly.

I close my eyes and squeeze my hands into fists, fighting to keep my composure. "There's no party."

"Try telling Lenny that," she says, puffing on her cigarette. "He told the whole neighborhood and all his friends."

He didn't.

He couldn't have. Surely…

My nails bite into my palm as my mind races over the conversations I've had with Lennox over the past few weeks as we got the pool ready. The crew finished filling it the other day, and it's now as close to the Beverly Hills version as an old pool in a rundown neighborhood can get. There are still cracked tiles around it, the grout between them stained brown, but we scrubbed down the entire inside of the pool and the area around it. We don't have chairs or umbrellas or anything fancy, but it still makes me feel like the richest girl in the world when I step out my back door and see a sparkling blue pool.

I'd be more than happy to share the pool with all the people who came to help, thanks to the North brothers next door. It's the least I could do to thank them. But I know Lee wouldn't see it that way. He'd say no one asked them to do that or promised them any payment, and if they made the stupid decision to work for free, that's their bad.

But I'm the one who will pay.

"And who exactly is coming to this party?" I ask.

"Oh, you know," she says. "All the Crows, a few of their friends…"

"The who?"

"The Crows," she says, like that's something I should know. "You know. Mill Street's crew—the Murder of Crows. The guys are all in it, plus some of the girls in their area…"

"Their gang," I clarify.

"The Skull and Crossbones is a gang," she says. "They're just a little street crew."

"That's part of the bigger gang."

She shrugs. "Yeah, I guess you could say that."

"And they thought it would be a good idea to have a pool party at a policeman's house?" I ask, not quite believing they could be that ballsy.

"It's not like they're going to hotwire his cruiser and do a drive-by in it," she says, rolling her eyes. "They're basically normal guys. They're just… Closer than other guys."

"I'm going to go over and talk to Lennox," I say, too mad to wait it out. Now that I've gotten used to Lennox's heart stopping good looks, I can actually talk to the guy without wanting to faint.

Sometimes.

I march up to their front door and bang on it. A minute later, a pretty Latina woman with black curly hair and the same warm, golden eyes as Lennox opens the door. "Can I help you?" she asks, glancing behind me.

"I'm looking for Lennox," I say, my words coming out uncertain, almost a question. "Is he around?"

"Come in," she says with a knowing smile. "You must be Rae, the pretty neighbor girl I keep hearing about."

"I guess," I say, glad the dim hallway hides how flustered I am when we step inside. "I mean, yes, I'm Rae. From next door."

Despite being neighbors and spending a lot of working hours together, none of us have crossed the threshold of entering the others' house. It feels like taking a next step, one I'm not sure I'm ready for. I'm awkward enough without the added pressure of knowing one of the boys called me pretty.

"My sons told me about you," she says, turning to me after closing the door. "I'm Valeria Cardenes, their mother and your neighbor, I hear. Sorry I haven't come by to say hello since you moved in. I work odd hours, and I seem to keep missing your parents."

"It's fine," I assure her quickly. "They're not really the meet-the-neighbors kind of people."

"Oh, okay," she says with a little laugh. "Now I don't feel so bad."

I shift awkwardly from one foot to the other. "I didn't realize they still lived with their mom."

I've seen a few girls coming and going, hanging around, or obviously trying to impress the brothers when they came over to help with the pool, but I've never seen this woman before. It strikes me how very little I know them. Despite Lennox's constant flirting, he hasn't divulged much about himself, and Maddox just glowers and hardly says anything to me. I learned more about them and their crew in the five minutes I just talked to Lexi than I have from them in the month I've lived next door to them.

"Of course they still live with me," Valeria says, gesturing toward the hall. "They might be big boys, but they're still kids. They'll be in Faulkner High with you, unless you're going to the fancy private school across town."

I shake my head.

"Go on back," she says. "I think they're in their room."

"Their room," I say, a little flutter of nerves shooting through me. I nod, psyching myself up, and then start down when their mom looks at me like she's wondering what I'm waiting for. I'm not sure myself. Maybe for her to tell me to leave the door cracked six inches or something. Though I've been in the rooms of a couple guy friends I had at Ridgedale, this feels worlds away from that. This isn't hanging out watching horror movies on beanbags on the floor with a handful of fellow nerds, both male and female.

This is being alone with a hot guy in his *bedroom.* Suddenly it seems like a foreign, fascinating concept, a place where mysterious boy things happen. Now that I know they're in high school like me, something shifts, like I'm closer to equal footing with them. Suddenly, there's potential. Lennox is not an adult who own this house. He's a prospective boyfriend—at least in my wildest dreams, he could be.

By the time I reach his door, I'm not sure I want to go in. Music thumps inside the room, a Ghostface Killah song turned up loud enough that he probably can't hear me if I knock. I'm about to turn the knob when I hear my name and freeze.

Are they talking about me?

I strain to hear over the music, but I can't hear anything more, not even voices. Then the song ends, and in the gap before the next one starts, I hear a guttural grunt that makes me shrink inside. It's a sound like I used to hear Lee make at night, when my room was next door to Mom's at our old place. I jerk my hand back from the knob like I've been burned.

Suddenly, a door opens at the end of the hall, and Lennox comes out, zipping his fly.

My face bursts into flames of heat.

"Hey," he says. "What are you doing here?"

"Uh, nothing," I say, stepping back from the bedroom door like I've been caught spying, so flustered I forgot why I came for a second. The music goes off, and Lennox glances at the door and then back to me.

"Well, come on, we can hang out," he says, passing me and grabbing the doorknob.

I almost protest, but he's already swinging the door open. I don't want to see what's inside, but when he walks in, Maddox is standing next to a dark wooden dresser, his back to us. He grabs something off the surface and tosses it into the trash, casting a furious glare over his shoulder.

"You couldn't wait two minutes?" he snaps. He turns back forwards without seeing me behind his brother, and I catch the distinctive movement of his shoulders and arms as he zips his jeans. Then he turns around, and his eyes fall on me.

My face gets even hotter, but instead of snapping at me, a smug little smile tugs at the corners of his lips. *"¿Qué hace esta chica aquí?"*

"She just came to hang out," Lennox says, flopping down on a narrow, twin bed under a life-sized painting of a man walking down a road. His side of the room is spotlessly clean—the bed tightly made, shoes lined up in neat pairs under the edge, a rolltop desk with a mug of pens on top, along with a globe and a lava lamp, each of them equidistant from the others. The only messy part is an easel set up with jars of paint, paint-stained cups, and a half dozen brushes dumped on a ledge at the bottom.

Lennox smiles at me and pats the bed beside him.

I want to marvel at his talent and the intricate detail of his painting, but then I remember why I'm there. I plant my hands on my hips. "You told everyone there's a party at my house?"

"*Si*, the kick-off party," he says, sitting up. "That way everyone knows where it is, and kids can use it before school starts. When they go back to school, they can talk about the pool just like the rich kids."

I glare at him. "My stepdad will never allow it."

"He won't even know," he says. "You said he plays poker on Thursdays."

I just gape, too furious to even speak. He used something I told him in casual conversation to manipulate the situation to get what he wants, and he's not even pretending to be sorry for it. He grabs my hand and pulls me down on his lap.

"Just think about it," he says, rubbing his chin against my neck, sending shivers racing down my body. "We'll introduce you to all our friends before school starts, let them know you're off limits…"

I almost let my eyes close with bliss at how good it feels, but then I see Maddox standing there watching us, and I remember what I just heard. Surely I heard wrong, but it still makes my body tense and embarrassment flood through me. Especially when I see, on his messy side of the room that has shoes kicked haphazardly in a pile, CDs scattered around a boom box on the desk, and clothes tossed over the back of his chair, a magazine with a girl in a see-through lace bikini sliding off a stack under his bed.

The distraction lets me grab onto my anger once more. I struggle against Lennox's hold, but he pulls me back, pressing his hips against my ass just hard enough for me to feel him stiffening.

"Let me go," I say, furious and embarrassed about how easily these boys can get under my skin. It was one thing when I thought they were older—grown men. Now that I know they're still in high school, they shouldn't have this power over me.

Lennox releases me, laughing. "Don't be such a buzzkill," he says. "It's just a party. Your dad will never even know we were there."

"No," I say fiercely, my heart hammering as I think of what Lee will say. There's no way he won't find out, even if he's gone all night for poker. "I told you, you can't have a party there."

"Relax and come here," Lennox says with a careless smile that makes me want to scream and throw something. He pats the bed and grins. "I'll make you feel better, little mama."

I want to cry with the desperate fury crawling up inside me. But there's no way I'm going to cry in front of these guys and look like a big baby. I already feel like I'm in way over my head when I'm with them, even if they are basically my age, and this only confirms it. They do whatever they want, regardless of what I tell them. I'm powerless against them, even when it's my pool they're using.

Something flutters in my lower belly as I stare at Lennox's big, paint-stained hand stroking the bed. I wonder what it would feel like on my skin, what his mouth would feel like on mine. He's kissed my neck and shoulders, but it's always been playful. But if he's not older, if he doesn't think of me as a kid… Does he like me? Will this gorgeous, older guy be my boyfriend at the new school where I don't know a soul?

I gulp, my gaze darting to Maddox, who's leaning on the dresser and watching us as per usual. Instead of his usual frown, though, he looks amused this time.

"What about him?" I ask, my throat tight.

Maddox breaks into a grin, but it's not one that makes me melt like his brother's. Instead, it's cold and sly, like a predator sneaking up on its prey. "If you think you can take us both at once…"

My heart starts galloping as I realize I'm alone in their bedroom, helpless against these two older, bigger boys if they wanted to hurt me instead of kiss me and be my boyfriend. I feel stupid and naïve just for having had the thought.

"What?" I whisper, barely able to speak as I step back toward the door.

"Don't worry, we've got practice," he says, prowling forward until he's looming over me. "We sex in all the crew girls with a gangbang."

I feel the color drain from my face, and I turn my gaze to Lennox, who's just watching without saying a word to fend off his brother.

Maddox looks positively feral at my shocked expression. "What's the matter, little girl?" he purrs, reaching out to play with a silky strand of my hair that came loose while I was running. "Cat got your tongue? Don't worry. I'll give your cat plenty of tongue if you hang around long enough."

A flutter bites into the flesh between my thighs, like a vicious butterfly. I back toward the door again, and Maddox chuckles.

"Look, Len, I scared her away. Don't go, little girl. I can just watch this time, if that's what gets you off."

I turn and flee, halfway expecting one of them to grab me as I yank open the door and race down the hall, my heart galloping faster than my feet. But the only thing that follows me is their laughter.

six

Maddox North

"You didn't have to be such a dick," Lennox says, watching me as he lounges back on the bed.

I open my drawer, pull out my gun, and check the chamber. "She shouldn't even be coming around here. She's a normal girl."

"Exactly why you shouldn't be such a dick to her."

"Just warning her what we're like," I say with a shrug. "She should know we're not the kind of guys she needs to fuck around with."

"You wouldn't fuck her?" Lennox asks skeptically.

"No," I say. "She doesn't belong in our world, and you know it."

"Maybe she could," he says, sitting up and swinging his legs off the side of the bed. "Not every girl wants the kind of guy who holds hands and watches the sunset with her."

I snort. "*Por supuesto*, but she does. I'll bet you fucking money that she's sitting there writing your names together in a little heart in her notebook. She wants a boyfriend. Not… Us."

"I could be her boyfriend," Lennox says.

That gets a full laugh out of me. "Yeah. Sure."

"I could," Lennox insists.

"What happens when you have to fuck a crew girl in?"

He shrugs. "I'll let her know up front I have those obligations. She's not like those girls, anyway."

"Exactly what I'm saying," I point out, pushing the drawer closed with my hip. "There are crew girls, and there are girls like her. I'm not saying there's anything wrong with her, but you don't fuck around with that type. Crew girls know what's up. That girl doesn't know shit."

"I'm gonna ask her out."

I shake my head. "She's not going to go out with you."

"You don't think I could get her?"

"I think you'd break her in a week."

He shrugs again. "What do you care?"

"I don't," I snap. "But she's too smart to fall for your bullshit."

Lennox's eyes turn ferocious. "Wanna bet?"

"Nah," I say, tucking my gun into the back of my jeans. "Go for it, *parce*. I don't have time to mess with little girls. I got real shit to take care of. The crew's driving by the Serpents' Nest tonight."

Lennox gets up and clasps my hand, pulling me in. "Be careful, brother."

"You should be there," I say. "We all ride together."

"You know I'm better behind the scenes," he says, squeezing the back of my neck.

He's wrong about that. He's more vicious than I am, though I'm working hard to remedy that. Time on the ground is what I need. He doesn't have to come to these things to prove himself because he's already where he needs to be. I need to toughen up.

"*Sin duda*," I say, pulling his head into my neck and crushing him against me. "One of us should be here to take care of Mom, anyway. In case."

For a moment, we just hold each other, and then we clap each other on the back before I leave, stepping out into the still, heavy darkness and letting it conceal the side of me I'm trying to erase.

seven

Rae West

I'm too embarrassed to turn away the first few guests who show up, both of them moms with kids hanging all over them and food to offer the party, looking harried and overwhelmed. Before I can muster up the heart to explain that this is all a misunderstanding, there are eight kids plunging into my pool with shrieks of pure joy. The mothers are both thanking me profusely and looking so grateful I wonder if Lennox told them I was babysitting all evening.

Probably guessing I'll try to break up the party before it starts, Lennox hurries over the moment he hears kids in the pool, bringing Reggie, our neighbor from across the street with him. I try to hiss at Lennox, but he's too busy charming the moms. He leads them to his house, and I panic that he really is leaving me to babysit eight kids whose names I don't even know. But he comes back with the moms a minute later, carrying plastic folding tables through the hole in the fence.

I really need to fix that.

I spend the next couple hours freaking out as more and more people show up. I should run away now, so I can get a head start, because I'm dead when Lee gets home. I pray he drinks too much or meets some woman and stays overnight, because if he gets home and all these people are here…

I'm surprised at the turnout. Apparently Lennox passed the word around that there's a block party, and everyone shows up, not just high schoolers. The neighborhood is always lively in the evenings. Kids run through sprinklers, ride bikes, yell up and down the street. Teenagers hang out, listen to loud music in their carports, and walk to each other's houses. Adults cook out on grills, chat with each other, and call out the doors for the kids to come home when it gets dark. Tonight, all those groups have converged on my house.

Someone brought a couple grills, and the men barbecue hotdogs, burgers, and elote while the women pile the portable tables with potato salad, tamales, coleslaw, greens cooked with bacon, watermelon, cherry fluff, churros, Jell-O molds, and cookies. A whole table is covered in pitchers of sweet tea, lemonade, Kool-Aid, and horchata; big bottles of soda; gallons of orange drink. Each table is flanked by coolers full of ice and beer.

My head spins with the number of people, each one adding to the mess. Mom has come out, since everyone wanted to meet her and pressured me until I went to get her. She wanders around the party looking like a lost owl chicklet, smiling vaguely into the distance and fussing with the stuff on the tables. I know she's as dazed and overwhelmed as I am—and as terrified.

Finally around ten, parents start rounding up their tired kids, most of them fussing at having to leave or crying from the crash after their sugar rush is over. Within minutes, the yard is cleaned up, the paper plates, cups, and napkins disappearing into trash bags tied neatly and set next to our trash can at the corner of the house. I start to relax, thinking maybe it will be okay. I assure Mom I'll stay up until everyone is gone and the back yard is clean, and she goes inside to bed.

"Here, have *unas polas* and chill the fuck out," Maddox says, roughly shoving a beer into my hand. "You've been running around acting *loco* all night. Did you even eat?"

I'm surprised he noticed. I didn't think he ever saw me except when I'm with his brother, and I'm too mad to have even spoken to Lennox tonight. Mostly I spent the evening pressing my nails into my palms until a dozen bloody crescent moons mark each one, and then biting my nails until they're raw to stop myself from doing more of the former. Y'know, totally normal stuff.

Maddox stands there smirking at me like a challenge until I take a drink. I stare back at him, refusing to let him intimidate me. It's time to put my foot down. "The party's over," I say. "All y'all need to leave. Now."

He laughs, and I realize it's the first time I've heard him laugh. It's deep and rolls through me with a vibration like thunder, his dark forest eyes crinkling at the corners as they fix on me in a way that makes me feel like I'm suddenly the most fantastic creature to ever grace the planet.

"The party's just getting started, *chica.* Buckle up. It's about to get wild."

"No," I say firmly. "That can't happen. You need to go home."

He pops the tab on his own beer, taking a long drink and letting the foam run down the side of the can before grinning at me. "There's nothing you can do about it, so you might as well enjoy it. Stop being so uptight for a minute and just go with the flow, little mama."

He winks at me and walks away, leaving me to stand there fuming. Looking around, I see that all the adults and little kids are gone. The people our age show no signs of going anywhere. I march over to Lennox, who currently has a tall girl in a bikini draped around his neck. "It's time to go," I say. "I told you, my stepdad will be home, and he's going to be pissed."

"Oh, relax," he says, letting his hand slide down the girl's bare back to her ass. He gives it a squeeze, his eyes on me. "Everything went great, didn't it? You have to admit, everyone had fun and the place looks great."

"Yeah, but—"

"Go sit down and finish your beer," he says. "Don't talk to me again until you're three beers in. Cool?"

I glare at him. "No, it's not fucking cool. You have no idea…"

I can't finish that sentence without explaining Lee, and that's not something I'm going to tell him, even if we didn't have an audience. No one needs to know about my fucked up family.

"Ooh, she swears," Lennox taunts, smiling down at the girl on his arm. "I bet it was her first time."

She giggles and gives me a smug look, nestling her head against his bare, tattooed chest. "Yeah, chill out," she says. "Don't be such a drag. We're just having a little fun. Aren't we, *papi?*" Smiling up at Lennox, she slides her hand down the front of his trunks.

"Get those three beers down, and I'll give you your first time for something else," Lennox says to me. "I'm too big for a virgin unless she's got a few in her to relax and help numb the pain."

I gulp down my rage and jealousy and take a swig of my beer like I don't even notice the girl jerking him off in front of me. Stupid me thought that he might like me, but it was all an act to get what he wanted. I glare at him, and he stares back at me coolly, his eyes hooded as the girl continues stroking him, looking up at him with such eager eyes it almost hurts. I can't hate her. I'm just like her—gullible and desperate for his approval.

Yeah, fuck that. Now that I know what he's about, and I'm not going to waste another minute falling for his sweet words and flirty smiles. He's nothing but a honey trap who was using me to get what he wanted all along, knowing I was too naïve to see through the manipulation.

I can't do shit about it now, and he's clearly not going to get anyone to leave, which means I have to. Gathering my courage, I tip back my head and down the entire beer, then go and start telling people it's time to go.

No one gives me the slightest indication they're going to obey my orders. Instead, they look to the North brothers, who are clearly here for the long haul. At last, I give up, grab a beer, and flop down on a chair, trying not to cry. Maybe I should give in to the night, like Maddox suggested. I can't do anything to stop it, so I might as well enjoy it. There are only two dozen people left here, but they're all drinking and having fun, with no intention of leaving until the guys who invited them tell them the party's over.

I'll just have to take Lee's wrath as it comes. Won't be the first time, won't be the last.

A shriek draws our attention, and I turn to see a handful of pink fluff from the marshmallow dessert flying through the air. It splatters onto Lexi, who's nothing like what I expected from our first few meetings. She's normally the wide-leg jeans and flannel kind of girl, but in a bikini, she's fucking gorgeous. She can't be more than five feet tall, but she's got curves where it counts, and her creamy skin beckons like an unopened invitation.

Four tall, dark-haired guys seem to have decided to answer the invite. They're surrounding her, wolf-whistling and taunting her while she curses savagely at them.

Maddox has parked himself on a plastic chaise, a beer in one hand while three girls sit on the edges of his chair, swinging their hair around and giggling and generally fawning over him. Lennox is watching the guys mess with Lexi, ignoring the girl hanging around his neck. Another flare of jealousy goes through me. Does he like Lexi?

One of the guys smears the pink goop down her hip and thigh, almost taking her bikini bottom with it. She tries to push him away, but he keeps groping her while she shrieks and struggles. I wonder if she's scared, surrounded like that.

A second guy picks her up and hurls her into the pool, and she comes up spluttering and cursing.

"Let's go in and steal her suit," says one of the guys, his voice deep and thick with a New York accent.

She starts swimming away as fast as she can, and they all laugh. One of them jumps in and swims after her, easily catching up. The others dive in and follow, surrounding her in the water. She screams and spins around when they untie her bikini top, clamping her arm to her chest to keep it covering her.

I hop up and go to the edge of the pool. "Cut it out," I yell.

Again, no one pays any attention.

When they start untying Lexi's bottoms, she has to let go of her top, shoving them and fighting as they all laugh and hoot and push her under the water. Pretty soon, they have her top and bottom, leaving her naked for all the party to see.

One of the guys swims away, holding her suit over his head like a trophy and whooping with joy.

"Give it back," she yells, swimming after him. She sounds furious and is clearly not playing the way they are.

The other three guys swim after her, grabbing her legs, groping at her bare skin. She screams as their hands move over her body, distorted and discolored through the water like some kind of nightmare.

I look around frantically, waiting for someone to stop them, but they're all just laughing. Even though I swore I'd never talk to Lennox again, this is an emergency, so I run over. "Help her," I cry, gesturing toward the pool.

"Nah, Lexi's not our girl," he says. "Besides, she's just playing hard to get. We've all fucked her already."

I spin around, searching for Maddox, and see him over beside the shed, his hand braced against the wall and his other behind a girl's head as she kneels in front of him, bobbing up and down. Too desperate to be shocked, I spin back around, finding a tight group of guys over near the fence. I race over, shoving past Reggie to find the familiar blond mullet I want.

"Billy," I say, grabbing his arm. "They're messing with your cousin."

Without a word, he shoves his beer bottle into my hand and flies past me, nearly knocking me to the ground as he charges across the yard with the speed of a football star and plunges into the pool. He streaks through the water, comes up next to them, and punches a guy in the face.

A shriek lodges in my throat as blood flies. All the guys jump on Billy, and I spin around, gesturing for someone to help before they drown him. The guys he was talking to move toward the pool to watch the fight, but no one jumps in. Lexi jumps onto someone's back, and when I see no one else is going in to help, I bend and smash the end of the bottle Billy thrust into my hand. Then I jump in and race through the water. I grab onto a handful of dark hair and wrap my legs around his hips for grip, reaching around to press the jagged edge of the bottle to his throat.

"Leave her the fuck alone," I scream.

The guy throws himself backwards, and we're plunged under water. I see blood floating up, and I know I must have cut him, but he's stronger than me and yanks my hand away from his neck, thrashes free, and swims back up. I surface a second later, horrified as I see how much blood is laced through the churning water as more people join the fight.

Strong arms grab me from behind, pulling me backwards. I turn, the bottle raised, but Maddox grabs my wrist to stop me from cutting him.

"You're a crazy bitch, you know that?" he says, ripping the bottle from my hand and throwing it. It hits the tile beside the pool and shatters, sending glass into the pool and along the edge.

"Let me go," I howl, twisting to free myself.

"You don't need to be in a fight with a bunch of grown men, little girl," he says, backpedaling through the water without letting me go.

"They were hurting Lexi," I say, a sob catching in my throat, much to my horror. My lip trembles, and Maddox's eyes soften for just a second.

He pulls me against him in the water, coming to a stop at the far edge of the pool. Wrapping his arms around me, he presses his nose to the top of my wet head. "She'll be okay," he says. "That's not your fight."

"It's my pool," I manage. "I tried to get Lennox to help, but he just—" I break off, hurt twisting in my chest at the memory of his callous response.

"Lennox gets off on that shit," Maddox says. "Don't ever underestimate anyone in our crew, little girl. We're all dangerous. Some of us are just better at hiding it."

I nod against his chest, grateful that he's holding me so close he can't see the tear slip through my lids.

"Come on," he says after a second. "Fight's over. I'll get you a beer."

I glance over and see that he's right. The dozen guys who fought and pulled apart the fight are climbing out of the water, and Billy's shielding Lexi's body from view while she wraps a towel around herself. The pieces of her swimsuit float near the edge of the pool, which is tinged pink on that end from the blood.

I gulp, feeling a little queasy. I don't need a beer, but Maddox is being so nice I can't say no. I don't want to go back to Maddox the Jerk Face, so I follow him out of the pool. He snags us both a beer and sits down on one of the plastic chaise lounges, pulling me down on his knee.

"Thanks," I say, leaning toward him, wanting to return to the comfort of his arms.

"Don't mistake this for something it's not," he says shortly, holding up a hand to block me from cuddling up to him. "I'm not your friend. I just didn't want an outsider winding up dead at a crew party. Cops don't give a shit if it's one of us, but if it's some innocent little white girl who's not affiliated…"

"Or his stepdaughter?" I ask. "In his own backyard?"

"Yeah, that," he says with a little smirk.

"Can I ask you something?" I say, settling in on his knee and not pressing for more intimacy.

"As long as you know this doesn't change anything."

"Got it," I say, rolling my eyes. "It's not like I think you're my boyfriend because you pulled me off a fight."

Maddox takes a swig of his beer. "Then shoot, little girl."

"How'd you get involved with the gang?"

"Don't let Lennox hear you call the Crows a gang," he says. "We're a murder."

"What's that?"

"A Murder of Crows," he says. "Like a flock. *Our* flock."

"But it's a street crew."

"It's more than that."

"Okay," I say slowly. "So how'd you join this *flock?*"

"Murder," he corrects.

Or maybe he's telling me how he joined. A shiver goes through me, but I don't ask. I don't want to know if I'm sitting on the lap of someone capable of the ultimate crime.

"You're not going to answer me, are you?" I ask instead.

He shrugs and takes another drink. "Someone had to look out for the family."

"It's just you and Lennox?"

"And our mom."

I nod. "Your mom's Mexican?"

"Colombian," he corrects. "Our dad was—is—a gringo."

"He's not around?"

"He's around," he says. "He just pretends he doesn't know us when we run into him."

"That blows," I say. "I'm sorry."

He just shrugs and takes another drink.

"My dad's not around, either," I say. "But I don't really remember him."

"At least you've got your stepdad," he offers.

A quiet scoff escapes me before I can stop it. "Yeah," I mutter. "At least."

Maddox watches me with unwavering intensity while he takes a swig, but he doesn't ask. He finishes his beer, wipes his mouth with the back of his hand, and sets the bottle down, his body tensing like he's about to stand.

Before he can, I put a hand on his arm to stop him. "One more question."

He sighs. *"¿Qué más?"*

"When I came over the other day…" I gulp and look away. "What were you doing?"

He chuckles, the sound low and delicious in his mouth. His hands slide around my bare hips, warm and so big they circle half my body. His touch sends an unexpected rush of shivery anticipation through me. He's usually so mean I don't even notice how gorgeous he is, and even sitting on his knee didn't have the same effect. But something about the way his hands settle on my hips, the gesture obviously comfortable and familiar for him but brand new for me, makes heat creep up my neck.

"I was jerking off," he says. "What'd it look like?"

Even though I was pretty sure I knew, hearing him say it so bluntly, so nonchalantly, shocks me into stillness. I gulp, unable to come up with a flippant answer to ease the tension. I'm sure as hell not going to tell him I heard him say my name right before he finished. Maybe I was only imagining things, anyway. The guy hates my guts.

His eyes seize on my mortified expression, and the cruel smirk I'm used to seeing on his lips returns. His eyes light up with malice, and he leans forward, until I can feel his warm breath feathering over my cheek.

"What about you, little girl?" he whispers, his lip just grazing the hairs on my cheek that are so fine they're invisible, but somehow full of so much sensation I nearly topple off his lap as it rushes through me in a tidal wave. "Do you touch yourself?"

"No," I mumble, too embarrassed to even meet his eye.

He leans his big body over mine, so his warm, bare chest presses into my shoulder. "I think you do," he murmurs, his voice a velvet purr in my ear. "Do you think about me when you finger this sweet little cunt?"

His hand slides from my hip around the front, dipping between my legs and cupping me, holding me tightly against him.

My heart is pounding so hard I can't breathe, and my body is frozen with indecision, a mixture of fear and arousal clashing inside me, harsh alarm bells clamoring in my head while my body chimes with the sweetest note. I wonder if he can feel how hot I am through my bathing suit, if he knows the wetness isn't just from the pool. Somehow, that's the most embarrassing part of all—not his words, but my own shameful reaction, something that should be hidden at all costs, so he won't know, so he won't have even more power than he does.

"Get off me," I say, shoving at his arm.

"I'd rather get you off, but okay." He gives a little squeeze, and I gasp audibly as his warm fingers pulse once against my soft flesh before slowly retreating. The most infuriating smile I've ever seen graces his lips. "You sure you're seventeen?" he asks. "Because I don't remember the girls in our grade last year being so sweet."

"Just because only sluts want you, that doesn't mean every girl is one."

"Well, you're too fucking innocent for us, that's for damn sure," he says, nudging me to get off his knee. "Why don't you go talk to the girls? Maybe you'll learn a little something you can use. Oh, and if you want to ride a gangster dick, ask them for tricks on taking one this big."

I jump up from his knee like it burned me and stomp away. I'm not even going to dignify his comment with a response, and since I don't have one, it works out. How can any family produce two sons that infuriating? Valeria was perfectly nice and even helped clean up after the party tonight. But her children are total jerks, and not just Maddox the Jerk Face. What was I thinking, sitting on his lap? I just saw him getting a blow job not an hour ago, for gods sakes. Her spit is probably still on his dick.

The thought sends me spiraling into fury, but instead of letting him know how much he got under my skin, I grab another beer and march over to a group of girls who are chattering about the fight.

"What's up, yo?" I ask awkwardly, stepping in to join them.

"Oh my god, this is her," Lexi says, standing on tiptoes and throwing an arm around my neck. She's now dressed in a long-sleeve T that swallows her tiny frame and hangs nearly to her knees. "This is the girl I was talking about—the one who rescued me."

"I don't know if I rescued you," I say, though a swell of warmth rises inside me at being praised.

"You totally jumped in there and tried to tackle Tony," says the girl who had her hand in Lennox's pants earlier. Apparently she's forgotten our beef, because now she bumps her beer against mine. "That was sick."

I laugh, the tension easing from me. "Thanks."

"This is Rae, everybody," Lexi says. "She owns the place. Rae, these are my homegirls—Mariana, Becky, Ines, Keisha, Lola, and my number one whore-bitch and homegirl, Marilyn."

Marilyn gives her a sullen look, her goth makeup ringing her eyes from the damp heat.

"This party's the bomb," says Mariana, the girl who was impressed that I fought. "I wish I had a pool."

"Well, now we do," Lexi says. "Lenny said we can come over any time."

I start to protest, but it's too late to shut this down for tonight, so I decide to just go with the flow and let the party play out. It'll be easier to explain things to them when they're sober and not in a pack. So I sink into the party and the severe buzz I've gotten off the beer. I talk and laugh with the girls, and no one would ever know that in the back of my mind, a dark cloud is creeping closer and closer.

Finally, around dawn, it slams back into me. If I don't get these people out of here, I'm totally dead. I start grabbing empty beer bottles and tossing them, urging everyone to leave. I see Keisha passed out on a lounge and try to rouse her to no avail.

"What's the big deal, Sunshine?" asks Lennox, pulling me into his lap. He kisses my ear, his breath smelling of beer and a hint of smoke. "Let them sleep it off."

"No," I shout, struggling to get up. "You have to leave! Now."

Everyone turns to look at me, like I'm a kid throwing a tantrum. Whatever. I'd rather them think that than know the truth, know how hard and erratically my heart is racing, or that I'm close to tears.

Lennox looks at me a long moment, then shrugs and stands from his chair. "You heard the girl," he says. "Let's bounce. *Abrasé!*"

Maddox picks up Keisha and throws her over his shoulder. "Later, little mama," he says to me with a cool tip of his chin. Then he turns and walks away, leading the procession of a dozen people who stayed all night. I'm so relieved I want to sink down and cry when the last of them disappears through the hole in the fence. But I can't afford to wallow in despair right now.

There are dozens of bottles and cans all around the pool, a few pieces of trash, and splatters of pink marshmallow on the tile. Cigarette butts float in the pool, and pieces of broken glass are scattered on the bottom. The blood has dissipated, and I'm not sure if we'll have to drain the entire pool, but I can't think about that right now, either. I race around, grabbing up bottles. When they're gone, I jump into the pool and swim around gathering cigarette butts. I nearly gag as I toss the stinky, soggy handful into the overflowing trash can. Then I drag the can and one of the bags out to the curb.

The sky is light now, but there's no sign of Lee's car yet. I race into the backyard and grab the last two trash bags, hauling them to the curb too. Then it's back to the scene of the crime. Someone left one of the tables, which is now laden with the melted pink dessert, a few mostly empty bags of chips and bottles of soda, and platter with nothing but cookie crumbs. I see a beer can against the leg of the table and bend to grab it, thankful I saw the evidence. Just then, I hear tires grinding on the front drive, and my heart stops.

I shove the can inside a chip bag, crumple it up, and look at the table with a sinking heart. There's no way I can hide this before Lee sees it and knows there was a party. Unless… Maybe he won't look out the back.

I grab everything up in my arms and scurry toward the corner of the house. Just as I reach it, the back door flies open. Lee's eyes fix on me with deadly fury.

"What the hell is going on in my house when I'm not here?" he demands.

I stand frozen, the blood draining from my limbs, leaving them heavy and numb.

"Well?" Lee thunders. "Why are there enough trash bags on the curb to last a month?"

I swallow, dread sticking my tongue to the roof of my mouth. I can't believe I did that. I've never had a party before, and I made the most rookie mistake imaginable. I almost deserve what's coming.

"Answer me, girl," Lee grinds out. "What do you have to say for yourself?"

He can see what happened. My arms are full of trash, there are chairs that don't belong to us all around the pool, and the lawn's seen enough feet tonight to leave a mark.

"We had a party," I say, swallowing the concrete block of terror in my throat. "To meet the neighbors."

I don't know what happens the next moment. There's a blank spot between saying the words, and when Lee reaches me.

His hand flashes through the air and sends me flying.

Before I can get my wits back, his fingers sink into the hair at the crown of my head. He drags me twisting and flailing up the back stairs. My head, shoulders, back, and hips hit each step with bruising force. I struggle in silence, biting down on my lip so I don't scream.

The only thing worse than the beating that's coming is for anyone to witness the shame of it. So I bite into the side of my cheek until I taste blood, so I won't taste it when Lee backhands me again. He tosses me on the floor in the back hallway, and I curl into a ball and protect my head with my hands while he kicks me until his fury is gone.

I'm still lying there trying to catch my breath when I hear him start in on Mom upstairs. I cover my ears and try to block out the screaming. I can still hear it, and I wince at every shriek, wondering with a shame that burns into the very marrow of my bones if the neighbors can hear her. In that moment, I hate her as much as him. Why can't she learn to shut her fucking mouth?

eight

#1 on the Billboard Chart:
"Mo Money Mo Problems"—The Notorious B.I.G.

Lennox North

"You can't be here."

"Well, well, well, look who's decided to show her face again," I say, pulling down my shades to look up at Rae, who's standing over me as I lay on the chaise lounge beside her pool. "I was starting to think you were avoiding us. *Qué onda?*"

"Seriously," she says, her voice harder than I've heard it before. "You can't use our pool."

Mariana giggles nervously and glances between Maddox and me, waiting for a cue on how we're going to play this.

"You mean *our* pool," I say. "We all pitched in to get it working. If it weren't for us, you wouldn't have a pool."

"True that," Billy says, holding up a beer. "Why don't you join us and take a load off, Rae Rae?"

"My mom said y'all have to leave," Rae says. "All of y'all."

"Oh, your mom said?" Tommy taunts, snickering.

I wait for her to threaten us with her dad the cop, like Tommy would, but she doesn't say anything. I don't like Tommy hanging around, but he plays ball with Maddox, and after he found out Rae's dad is on the police force with him, he thinks he has free reign of her pool any time and can talk to her any way he likes. It pisses me off, the way he's trying to upstage me to look good in front of my brother, even though he's a soft little bitch.

"Chill," Keisha drawls, taking a swig of her beer and moving her ass around on Maddox's lap. "We're just having fun." She's straddling my brother, facing the pool, while he lays back on his lounge chair. Of course the head cheerleader wants to ride his dick.

Pretending I don't notice, I laugh and open the cooler, digging out a beer. "Relax, Sunshine," I say to Rae, holding it out as a peace offering.

We've been using her pool for a couple weeks now, ever since the party. We leave our shit all over, and every day when we arrive, all the empties are gone, and it's fresh and clean for us to start over. There hasn't been a single sighting of Rae, though. I was starting to think her dad sent her to a boarding school for having a party or some shit.

Now I almost feel bad that she's been cleaning up after us this whole time. She starts picking up our empties, holding them to her chest, clad in a filmy black t-shirt that says "Atomic Love" on the front.

"Come have some *polas* and chill out by the pool," I say, waving the cold beer at her. "What's the point of having it if you don't enjoy it?"

"I enjoy it," she says through clenched teeth. "When you're not around."

"What happened to you?" Maddox asks, pushing up on his elbows and looking at her past Keisha and Mariana, who's on Billy's dick. I ignore the fact that no one's sitting on me, and I check out what Maddox is looking at.

He's watching Rae with a frown, and I move so she's not silhouetted against the blazing August sun. Her eyes are hidden by shades, but the bridge of her nose and cheeks are yellowed with an old bruising.

She shrugs and snatches up the last of the bottles, and I see that her legs are bruised below her little high-waisted shorts. "I fell down the stairs when I was tipsy after the party," she says. "I've never lived in a house with stairs before, and I'm still getting used to them."

"Chin." Mariana giggles and hides it behind her beer can.

Maddox raises his brows and turns to me. We share a look, and then he shrugs and lays back on the chaise. "We're not hurting anything," he says to her. "No one's stopping you from using the pool. In fact, we use it when no one's here. It's just sitting here going to waste."

"Yeah," Becky pipes up. "Don't be such a buzz kill."

Rae doesn't answer. She goes over and dumps the bottles into the trash can at the corner of the house, then walks back, kicks off her sandals, and strips out of her clothes. She's wearing a swimsuit underneath, but all five of the guys and probably a few of the girls sit there gaping, transfixed. There's something about a chick undressing... The way her body stretches when she reaches up to pull the shirt over her head, the way she bends to drop her shorts. My cock twitches in my trunks, and I wonder what it would take to get her to sit on my dick the way Keisha's sitting on Maddox's.

Still ignoring us, she dives into the pool. She swims up and down, not acknowledging us as she does laps for about twenty minutes. Then she climbs out of the pool, water streaming off her freckled shoulders. She twists her hair up into a wet bun, secures it with a scrunchy, and picks up her towel, pretending five dudes aren't getting a semi watching her.

"Come 'ere, *mi cariña*," I say. "I want to talk to you. No hard feelings?"

Showing no sign she heard me, she wraps her towel around her body and disappears into her house without a backwards glance.

nine

#1 on the Billboard Chart:
"Honey"—Mariah Carey

Rae West

Starting a new school where you don't know anyone sucks a big one. Especially when I've somehow become known for being the buzzkill who broke up the North's party. The first time someone says it, I roll my eyes.

Like, what the hell? It wasn't their party.

Okay, maybe it was their party, but it was at my house. I had every right to send them home at dawn. Not that it did much good. If I'd known my little tantrum that morning, when I kicked them all out before Lee got home, would become what I was known for at Faulkner High, I would have just let him find them all there. It's not like getting rid of them and cleaning up helped matters with my stepdad.

But thinking about him yelling at them, or worse, arresting them, makes me want to keel over and die of embarrassment. I'd rather be known as the crybaby who ruined their good time than the daughter of the pig who threw them in jail for swimming in his pool.

Luckily, Faulkner High is bigger than Ridgedale, and it's fairly easy to avoid my neighbors themselves. They spent the rest of summer coming to my pool on the regular, but after the day when I tried to get them to leave, I didn't bother going out when they were there. I tried getting Mom on board, since she took a beating for the party too, but she just looked at me and asked, "Did you tell them to leave?"

When I told her I had, she said, "What am I supposed to do about it? If they won't leave when you tell them to, they won't when I do."

She wouldn't even try, so I went back to reading in my room during the middle of the day and venting my frustrations to Poe when she visited. I'd rather be alone than be friends with assholes like my neighbors. I wasn't alone, though. I had my bird friend, and together, we made our own murder of crows. Fuck the Norths.

After that day, at least the guys cleaned up after themselves, and I no longer had to go pick up their empties every day. It wasn't a big deal. I hardly knew they were there, aside from the occasional splashing when they played pool games and shrieking when they were teasing the girls. I barely felt the pit of emptiness inside me, the loneliness and fury that I wasn't included in the fun going on in my own backyard.

But a girl's got her pride.

And who needs a tan anyway? It's not like anyone's going to see it.

Now that school's started, they come over less often. Apparently, social status is forgotten over the summer. Everyone from our block hung out, plus a few of their friends who had vehicles and could come over. Since I was new, I didn't realize that the summer group wouldn't be the same once school started. I just knew I didn't belong.

Once school starts, I'm startled to see everyone splinter off into different groups. Maddox and all the guys from the football team are top-tier popular, including Tommy, Billy, Michael, and Daniel. I didn't even realize one of the most popular girls in school was hanging out at my pool all summer, but Keisha's head cheerleader and pretty much the queen bee of FHS.

I'm just as surprised by those who aren't popular. Reggie, Jeff, and Lennox are more feared than adored, since they don't play football and are widely known for their gang affiliation. Lexi has a reputation as a slut, as do her two closest friends, and people make disgusting comments to her every day in our shared classes. I feel bad, but I'm too busy trying to keep my own head above water to defend her.

I never thought I'd be on the popular group's radar, but Keisha and the cheerleaders scoff and give me dirty looks, and the football players oink at me and call me a pig, like I called the cops, or a rat, like I ratted them out. Really, I didn't do anything, but they must have heard from the North brothers that I was in the house but refusing to come out and join the fun. Most of the people who give me shit weren't even at the party.

I ignore it, ignore the whispers, the comments. There's not much I can do about them. Responding will only give them more ammunition. And if Lee's fists don't break me, a few words sure as hell won't. I'm on my own, and I'm fine with that. They might need a crew, their flock of crow brothers, but I'm a murder of one. I focus on my grades and pick up some babysitting work on the side, since a few neighborhood moms remember me from the party.

A month into school, a coach gets fired for sleeping with a student, and it's all anyone can talk about. I'm just relieved that the focus has shifted away from me. I'm not magically forgiven, and my best friend is still a bird, but hey, at least people don't actively go out of their way to mess with me anymore. They seem to have forgotten I exist, and when they remember, they just call me a name and move on. They no longer give me shit, knock my books from my arms, or write nasty things on my desk.

A few weeks later, the North brothers find me at my locker one afternoon. I turn away when they walk up, studiously focusing on which books I need for the rest of my classes.

"You're hard to find, you know that, little girl?" Maddox asks, leaning against the locker next to mine like a towering wall of lickable muscle. Damn, he's a waste of all those good looks.

"Maybe it's a sign that you should stop trying," I say with a shrug.

"We haven't been looking," he says, crossing his arms and frowning down at me, like he's pissed that I called him out for being the one to seek me out. "Trust me, we'd have found you if we had been."

"Whatever," I say, closing my locker and turning away. He's probably used to girls falling all over themselves, chasing him to the ends of the earth. Fuck if I'm going to be one of them.

"*Vení*, don't be like that," Lennox says, giving me a smile that should be illegal, as it's clearly a weapon of mass destruction.

"What do you want?" I ask with a sigh, pretending I'm not affected. Sure, his smile is as lethal to me as any other girl, but I know what hides under it. "Now that people aren't relentlessly tormenting me, are you here to dig up some more ammunition to make everyone hate me again?"

"This one's got some bite to her," Maddox says, tilting his chin back and looking down at me with a smirk, totally unaffected by my fury. "Good thing we didn't fuck her. She'd probably bite our dicks off."

I turn away and start down the hall. Lennox falls into step beside me, giving me a smile that makes me nearly buckle, damn him. Maddox is on my other side, though, so I resist and try to be as unaffected as him.

"You can't still be mad at us," Lennox says, touching my elbow to recapture my attention.

"You mean because you ignore everything I say and refuse to stop trespassing in my backyard, so I can't even use my own pool in peace?" I ask. "Or because you told everyone I was a pig and a rat who broke up your party? Nah, I'm not mad. It's fine. Totally copacetic."

Maddox just chuckles, the sound twisting down into my lower belly in a way that infuriates me even more.

I get to my class, but Lennox grabs my arm firmly and pulls me aside before I can go in. "I just wanted to let you know we're planning an end-of-season party," he says. "It's getting colder, so this is probably the last chance to use the pool this year. We'll help you drain it and cover it up for winter afterwards."

"Are you crazy?" I demand. "You can't have a party there."

"Actually, we can," he says. "We'll help you clean up this time. Promise." He pressed a hand to his heart, smiling so his dimples show, waves of dark hair tumbling over his forehead. God, it really is criminal to look that good.

Maddox clears his throat and gives me a cool look. "And if you fall down any more stairs after this one, we'll take care of those, too."

My heart stops. I look up at him, squeezing my hands into fists so he won't see them shaking. They always come over when Lee's at work, so he doesn't even know they're using the pool. I've gotten backhanded a few times since then, but nothing like the post-party ass kicking. The guys didn't even see me those days, so there's no way they could know.

Right?

"You're going to fix the loose boards on the back steps?" I ask carefully, using the pain in my palm from my nails biting in to anchor me and keep me on an even keel.

"Sure, little girl," Maddox says quietly, his gaze so intense it makes me squirm. "If that's what we're still going with."

I swallow past the trembling mass of fear in my throat and stare at the wall behind him. "Thanks."

"So, we'll invite the block again," Lennox says. "When will your dad be gone?"

I want to cry, but I won't. I won't even argue. There's no use. He'll do what he wants, like he always does. "He's going hunting this weekend," I admit.

Lennox grins so big I almost smile back despite myself. Before I can, he grabs me up and spins me around, planting a hard kiss right on my mouth. I'm so stunned I don't even move as he sets me back on my feet.

He smiles when he sees my flustered expression, the dimple sinking into his cheek that makes me more lightheaded than the kiss. "I've missed you and your silly shirts," he says, tugging at the bottom of my old Coed Naked Volleyball shirt.

I don't say anything, because I'm too busy trying to comprehend that I just had my first kiss, in plain sight of all the people walking past and staring at the social pariah standing with what must be the two hottest guys on the planet.

Scarlet, a pretty blonde cheerleader who I've seen flirting with Maddox, gives me a look of pure loathing as she passes. The other girls give me dirty looks and whisper behind my back, but she does nasty stuff like spitting in my hair and drawing obscene sketches on my desks. Despite looking like she belongs in a J.C. Penny's catalog instead of on the arm of a tattooed gangster, she's been the worst of all the girls this year.

Ignoring her, Lennox steps closer to me, slowly stroking a strand of hair back that came loose when he spun me around. His fingers brush my cheek, and my head gets ten kinds of stupid. "Did you miss me?" he coaxes, that dimple sinking into his cheek like he's trying to make me expire on the spot.

"How can you miss something you never had?" I ask.

"Damn," Maddox says, his eyes lighting up with laughter. "She's cold, *parce*."

Lennox shoots him an annoyed glance. "Somehow I manage, Sunshine," he says to me. "We'll see you this weekend for the *rumba*. You won't regret it."

They turn and walk away before I can tell him that I most definitely will regret it. I sit in class, my heart pounding erratically, my thoughts swinging from what's going to happen if Lee finds out we had another party to the fact that Lennox North just *kissed* me.

Not that it means anything. Sure, he did it in the middle of the hall, for all the school to see. But that just proves how little it means to him. He probably kisses lots of girls in the hallway and everywhere else. Hell, I've peaked out the window and seen both the twins with a different girl draped over them every time they lounge at the pool, and Mariana jerked him off right in front of me at the first party. Granted, I've never seen Lennox with his dick down a girl's throat, which I've seen at least twice now with Maddox, but still. He wouldn't kiss me just because he was happy if it meant something to him.

And if it meant nothing to him, it'll just have to mean nothing to me.

By the end of the week, people are talking about the party. Every time it comes up, dread knots in my belly. I'm on my way to PE on Friday when a group of Maddox's football buddies corner me, a few of their girls trailing behind.

"We invited to your party?" asks Tommy.

"I'm not having a party," I say, which is true. The less people who show up, the better.

"Dude, everyone's talking about it," he says. "The North's have a party, everyone knows. Why you holding out on us?"

"I'm not," I protest, trying to continue past them to class.

"The pig doesn't want us at her party," says another guy, elbowing Tommy.

"It's not that," I say quickly.

"I think we're scaring her," says Tommy, stepping in front of me and backing me against the cinderblock wall in the hallway that leads to the gym.

"Let's crash the pig party," yells Randy, and a handful of them start oinking while the girls giggle and give me pitying looks. The bell rings, the loud jangling interrupting us, but no one moves to get to the gym.

"Look at her. She's shaking," Tommy says, grabbing me when I try to dart sideways. "Aww, is the little piggie afraid of the big bad wolves?"

He looks positively gleeful at the realization. Scarlet and her evil minions exchange glances and smirk at me with their cherry gloss lips.

"Leave me alone," I growl, jerking my arm free of Tommy's grip.

"I don't think we will," he says. "See, you offended me and my boys by not inviting us."

"I didn't invite anyone," I snap. "Take it up with the Norths. It's their party."

"I'd rather take it up with you, West," he says, crowding me against the wall again. "You're cuter."

The other guys crowd around, and my heart starts racing. The secluded hallway is empty other than us, and no one will be coming this way except maybe someone running late for class. Tommy takes the opportunity to reach down and goose me.

"Get away from me," I yell, dropping my books to shove him in the chest. He hardly moves. The books slap the linoleum tiles with loud cracks as they scatter around us. Good. If I can't fight them off, I'm sure as hell going to be loud enough to draw some attention.

Tommy takes the opportunity to grab my boobs now that they're not behind my books. He shoves me against the wall again, and suddenly my mind flashes to an image of Lexi being stripped in the pool, and how nobody helped. Adrenaline shoots through me, and I look for an opening, wondering if I can get my knee in his crotch for a good kick in the nuts.

"Maybe we can have our own party," Tommy says. "You and the football team. The senior girls are all sluts this year. Aren't you in the Slut Club with Lexi and Marilyn and—"

Before he can finish, someone shoves through the crowd and grabs him around the neck from behind. I get one glance of Maddox, and then Tommy hits the floor. Maddox is on top of him, his fists flying as he bashes Tommy in the face four or five times within seconds. The guys jump in and drag him off, and Tommy rolls over, coughing out a spray of blood and bits of tooth onto the smooth, pale floor.

Maddox shakes off the guys, his face red with exertion, and turns to me. I shrink back at the stormy, furious look on his face, but he grabs me by the back of the neck and pulls me forward. "This bitch is *ours*," he growls at the football players, shaking me like a rag doll in front of him. "In case that wasn't clear to you fucking *malparidos*. She's from *la olla* and she's hosting our party, which means she's the Crows' girl. She's off limits to every fucking person in this school who didn't ask our permission. Anyone else touches her, or even *looks* at her, you pay the price. *¿Comprende?*"

A few of the others nod and glance at each other.

"She's a Crow?" Randy asks.

"Why don't you fuck around with her and find out," Maddox snaps, glowering at him.

The guy shakes his head and steps back, as if he wants to disappear into the crowd.

"My dad's a cop," Tommy whines. "You're going to fucking pay for this, North."

"I don't give a fuck who your daddy is," Maddox says. "Let him come for me. You'll see what happens."

Tommy groans and spits more blood, pushing himself to a sitting position.

"Now pick up her books," Maddox says, his voice so cold it makes my blood freeze. He kicks Tommy lightly in the thigh.

Tommy groans and drags himself onto all fours, pawing my books into a pile before lumbering to his feet.

Blood is streaming from his nose and mouth, drown his chin, and onto the front of his Big Johnson t-shirt. He shoves the books into my hands and starts to turn, but Maddox grabs his shoulder.

"Apologize."

Tommy glares, his eyes full of belligerent hatred, and I can't help thinking that Maddox just made things even worse for me. Our dads work together, so there's usually a wary distance between us.

"Sorry," Tommy mutters.

"It's fine," I say quickly.

"Now get the fuck out of here," Maddox says, shoving him away. "All of you."

I start to go, but he pulls me back, securing me against his chest. We watch the others walk away. Scarlet glances over her shoulder with a look that says she despises me even more now that I have Maddox's blessing. Then she turns to follow her friends.

I can feel Maddox's heart pounding against my back, his ragged breath heaving in and out, the trembling in his arm as it holds me firmly against him. I can't help but wonder if it's just the adrenaline from the fight, or if he needs me in some way and kept me here for his sake, not mine.

"You good?" he asks quietly after everyone is gone and we haven't moved for a whole minute longer.

"Yeah," I say, leaning back into his solid chest and trying not to swoon at how good it feels against me. I close my eyes and inhale the scent of him, like rain falling on hay that's freshly dried in the sun. Then I jerk my eyes open and focus on the blood on the floor to bring myself back to reality. I do not need to be thinking about how good this boy smells, how right he feels against me, or how much I want to stay here.

"You?" I ask faintly.

"De nada," he says, releasing me. "Just a scuffle."

"Since when am I yours?" I ask, stepping away and turning to face him. "I thought you hated me."

I expect him to make a cutting remark, but he just looks down at me with hooded eyes and flexes his bloody fist. "You're growing on me, little girl."

"I can't say the feeling is mutual," I mutter, staring at the crow tattoo on his neck, the wings wrapping around it like a hand. "But thanks. For what you did just now."

He tips his chin in a quick nod of acknowledgement. "You live on our turf," he says. "That comes with certain… Benefits."

"Benefits?" I ask, my voice a little squeaky.

"Protection," he said, his voice a slow, accented drawl as his face settles into its usual maddening smirk. "As my mother would say, *no des papaya.* Always use protection."

"You do know that I have no clue what you're saying when you speak Spanish, right?"

He just levels me with that infuriating gaze and chucks me under the chin like I'm five years old. "Better study hard in your class, little girl."

With that, he turns and walks away.

ten

#1 on the Billboard Chart:
"4 Seasons of Loneliness"—Boyz II Men

Maddox North

The party is just like the one last summer—the block shows up with food and gratitude. Our little mama makes all the difference. Instead of rushing around like a chick having a panic attack, she flits around like a little bee, talking to everyone and encouraging them to take what will probably be the last swim of the season. I watch her with annoyance and awe. I can't figure her out, and it pisses me off. It would be easy to say she's being fake this time, but if she is, she's one hell of an actress.

I settle on the theory that it's her parents. Her mom doesn't come out this time, and her dad is gone all weekend, so there's no chance he'll come home and bust up the party.

I remember those bruises on her legs, her arms, her face. Our dad never laid a finger on us—Mom would have put him in the ground if he tried that shit. But I've been a Crow since I was fourteen, and I know what a beating looks like.

The thought makes a slow burn rage simmer inside me as I watch Rae swing her wavy, chocolate hair over her shoulder while she talks to Lexi, who's wearing a flannel shirt and daisy dukes instead of a bikini today. Playing with fire gets everybody burned eventually. The Dolce brothers might have scholarships to the fancy private school on the other side of the tracks, but they belong on this side of town. After the last party, Lexi won't forget it.

At around ten, the parents pack up their kids and leave us to do our thing again.

About an hour later, the sound of cars pulling up and slamming doors draws everyone's attention. Our host freezes, her big hazel eyes going wide and her face whitening. Before I can wonder who she thinks it is, Reggie jumps up and pulls his piece. I share a look with Lennox and Jeff, on alert for the appearance of the Skull Serpents. The rougher crew's been encroaching on our turf and is known for their quick and ruthless execution style. While we prefer the clean kill of a bullet, their preferred method is a brutal curb stomp.

But when the gate opens, a dozen or so guys from the team pour through, led by Tommy Hertz and followed by their cheer squad bitches.

"What are they doing here?" I growl.

"Relax," Lennox says, sinking back on the lounge chair beside mine. "It's just your teammates."

I glare at Tommy, remembering the way he was holding Rae before I sent him to the floor. "We brought drinks!" he yells, holding aloft two bottles of shitty vodka in his meaty fists.

Some of the others have rum and tequila clutched in their hands, though, and some of the guys are friends of mine. I sit back and watch, keeping an eye on things.

Our host looks uncomfortable, but she doesn't tell them to leave like last time, when she kept trying to break up the party. She should know we'll take care of things before we go, like we have at the pool ever since we saw what her dad thought of having people over.

After a while, I'm distracted when Scarlet comes gliding over, wearing a bikini top and a sarong wrapped around her hips. She parks her ass on the edge of my chair and bats her lashes at me. She's high on her status upgrade, since last year she was just a majorette, but thanks to her whoring herself out to Randy, she's now a cheerleader and part of the in-crowd.

"Hey, Maddox," she says, leaning on her arm in a way that makes her tits push up in her top. "I was hoping you'd be here."

Lennox snorts beside me. He doesn't play the game like I do. He only fucks crew girls, though he entertains others up to a point.

"Hey, Scar," I say. "Did you run out of guys with money to fuck, or are you just wondering if gangster dick is everything you've heard it is?"

"Maddox! You're so bad!" She giggles and plays with her blonde hair. I can tell she's already gagging for my dick, but I don't make things too easy for chicks like her. Eventually I'll fuck her to put her out of her misery, but she's a rich bitch, and I'm not about to be another pony or car or whatever she sets her eyes on and gets. She's going to have to work for this one.

"If you wanted a good guy, you wouldn't be drooling on my dick right now."

She widens her eyes and glances around like she's scared someone will overhear me talking to her like that—and see that she fucking loves it. Girls like her eat that shit up. They pretend they're all prissy and uptight, but they want to be treated like the dirtiest whores. I have to be careful of them, though. Their daddies don't like it when they fuck around with gangsters, especially ones who look like me. More than that, the chicks themselves get clingy and weird when you try to move on. It took me a year to shake the last rich bitch I played around with.

Only Lennox is watching us, and he gets off on that shit as much as she does, so I'm not about to take her somewhere private and spare her dignity. She doesn't want that much respect, anyway. If I told this bitch to bend over, she'd let me rail her in front of the whole party, and she'd cum harder than she's ever cum in her life.

It's tempting, so I mull over the idea for a minute. I spot Rae over by the shed, holding her hair up while Marilyn ties her bikini top, and my cock twitches.

"Go get me a beer," I say to Scarlet.

She huffs and looks indignant that I'm ordering her around.

"Actually, bring over a bottle of tequila," I say, shifting my position and pushing my hips up. "You can take a shot and lick my dick off for the salt."

Her eyes drop to my crotch, and she gulps. Then she scurries off to obey.

Predictable.

"You're savage with these chicks, *parce*," Lennox says, shaking his head.

"They love it," I assure him, crossing my arms and watching Scarlet convince Michael to hand over the tequila. Lennox frowns, like he disapproves, and I give him a cocky grin.

I may be gloating a little, but my brother could get chicks if he wanted. I don't know what his hang-up is, except that he likes initiating crew girls too much. It's like he saves up all his *arrechera* for them, so he can really give it to them when we get a new member.

Ten minutes later, I'm nursing a bottle of tequila and Scarlet's nursing on my cock. That's when our little girl decides to come over. She studiously ignores me and sinks down beside Lennox, angling her body to face away from me as much as she can.

I try not to look at the swell of her ass in her bikini bottom, curve of her back that makes it scream for attention. I picture sliding my hands around her hips, under her bikini bottom, and palming her ass while she rides me. My cock throbs precum into Scarlet's throat, and the whore moans around my dick like she fucking loves it. I shove her head down further just to hear her choke.

"So, a couple guys from your *crew* are asking me questions," Rae says to Lennox, ignoring the noises Scarlet's making.

"Oh yeah?" he asks. "What kind of questions, Sunshine?"

"Like, if I'm a member, and if I'm being initiated," she says.

Lennox's brows shoot up, and he casts his eyes toward me. "You have anything to do with this?"

"I told the team not to mess with her," I admit, wiping my mouth after taking another swig. "That she's Crows' property."

He nods, looking her up and down thoughtfully. She may be legal, unlike a lot of our members, but she's not like the girls in the crew. She might as well be a decade younger for how innocent she is.

"*Vení*, I've got to deal with this," I say, grabbing Scarlet's hair and pulling her head up. Her mouth makes a wet popping sound as it slides off my dick. "You can finish me off later, yeah?"

Her face flushes with fury, and she smooths her hair over her shoulder and gives Rae a murderous look before stomping away without a word.

"I didn't mean to interrupt," Rae says with a sweet smile as I tuck my dick back into my swim trunks.

"Sure you didn't, little girl," I say, snagging the bottle that I set down to square myself away. "Now what's this about you joining the crew?"

"I didn't know if that's what you meant when you said it at school," she admits.

Lennox pulls her back to lie on his arm, so they're squeezed into the chair together. It pisses me off. She's too innocent for both of us, not just me, but he can't seem to keep his hands off her.

I glare at her. "You can't join."

"Why?" she asks, a challenge in her voice. "You said I was a Crow girl."

"I said you belong to the Crows," I correct.

"So?" she asks. "What's the difference? What if I want to join?"

I lay back on the chair, take a swig, and offer her a lazy grin. "If you want me and Lennox to fuck you, just say it, little girl. But you'll never be in the Murder of Crows."

Color creeps into her cheeks. "What does that have to do with it? You get to fuck all your crew?"

I shrug. "Sure."

"So I guess Scarlet's a Crow?"

I give her a little grin. "You jealous, *o qué?*"

"Why would I be jealous?"

Her eyes flash with that spark of defiance that kindles something inside me, some urge to either own her or crush her. I'm not sure which one I want yet. Up close, I can see the gold flecks in the green of her eyes, ringed with a fringe of dark lashes. I imagine them peeking up at me while those pouty lips stretch around my cock…

I shove the thought away and sit up straighter, though if she wanted to look at my dick, she would have done it when I was shoving it down Scarlet's throat.

"She's not my type," I say, the words surprising me as they leave my mouth. "Just a hole."

Rae looks at me skeptically while I take another drink. "A hot blonde cheerleader is not your type?"

"Nah," I say. "She's a whore who knows how to ride a dick, but she's only trying to rebel against her daddy by slumming it with the crew. One taste of Skull dick and she'll be chasing us like a bitch in heat for the rest of high school. She doesn't want our respect, and she'll never get it."

"Wow," Rae says. "Do you have everyone figured out, or just her?"

"People are easy to figure out if you stop thinking about yourself long enough to look."

"Okay, I'll bite," she says, crossing her arms and lying back against my brother. "Tell me all about myself then."

I take a drink and let my gaze linger as it takes her in from head to toe. When I get back to her face, it's a little flushed, and Lennox is glaring at me like I'm eye-fucking his bitch.

"Maybe next time," I say, turning up the bottle again, even though I've already got a good buzz going. "I'm still looking."

two for joy

eleven

#1 on the Billboard Chart:
"Goodbye England's Rose"—Elton John

Rae West

After the second party, things are both better and worse. That morning, Lennox, Maddox, Billy, Lola, and Lexi stay until the last shard of glass is swept up and the last can thrown away. My neighbors take the trash to their house, so Lee won't see it by our trashcan again. No one mentions why they're doing it, but they seem to have a little more respect for me now. Or maybe they just take care of the people they consider to belong, and by mingling and drinking with them instead of fighting the idea of a party, I've proven that I can hang.

So, I don't get in trouble with Lee, since Mom would never intentionally bring down his wrath on me. She keeps her mouth shut, and so do I. No reason to give him extra ammunition. He'll think of a reason to knock us around when he wants one.

At school, no one seems to hate me anymore, and no one calls me a pig or a rat. They all know about the "Rae Ban," as Billy calls it. Besides, I let everyone come party at my house, even people I don't like who showed up without an invitation. Not that I handed out invitations, but I don't think the North brothers invited them, either.

I barely see Maddox, since I'm in advanced placement classes and he isn't. But I see Lennox, who's in several of my classes and makes sure to sit by me in each one. Everyone seems to know I'm under their protection, and they don't mess with me. At least, not directly.

But a few weeks after the party, I start getting rude comments from guys when Lennox isn't around. Not the ones I used to get about being a rat, but more sexual ones. No one pushes me, knocks my books out of my hands, or puts gum in the combination of my locker. But over the next month, I hear the comments behind my back, whispers, speculation that I came to this school because I got kicked out of my last one. The variety of fabricated reasons range from, I was blowing the principal, to I got pregnant and my parents didn't want anyone to remember.

Midway through the year, my name appears on desks and bathroom walls along with Lexi's and the other girls' who sit with us at lunch.

For a good time, call Lexi Gunn/Marilyn Boehner/ any of their friends… Followed by a phone number. Now, *Rae West* is added in with a plus sign. I try not to care. Fuck those people. Lexi's nice, and I'm not going to stop sitting with her at lunch just because everyone calls her a slut. She and her friends are tight, an impenetrable, unbreakable bond of girlhood that makes me miss my old friends, who I spent the first three years of high school with, even though we were never that close. They stopped calling pretty soon after I moved, since none of us had cars or ways to visit each other.

Also, we were the nerds, while Lexi and her friends are the self-proclaimed Slut Club. If it bothers them that others call them names, they don't talk to me about it, and after the rumors about me go around, I know better than to believe the gossip at this school has any basis in reality.

Just before Christmas break, I finally get an answer when Scarlet and her demon cheerleader squad clear it up for me.

"So, what's it like?" Scarlet asks behind me as I grab my gross uniform from my locker to dress out for PE.

"What?" I ask.

"Being the Murder of Crows' whore," she asks, then blows a big pink bubble with her gum. Her friends all snicker, and Diana flicks her shoulder-length brown hair back and smirks at me with pale, glossy lips.

"Why don't you tell me?" I ask. "You're the one who stuck Maddox's dick in your mouth in the middle of my party."

Her friends all widen their eyes at each other, and Scarlet's face goes red.

"I was drunk," she huffs. "And we haven't even hooked up. I don't sleep with guys I'm not dating, and I definitely don't let a whole crew pass me around."

"I don't either," I point out, but I remember what Maddox said, that they sleep with all the Crow girls. "I'm not even in the crew."

"Is that why you don't sit with them at lunch?" Diana asks, peeling off her baby tee and tugging a new uniform shirt over her head. I had to get one of the loaner ones from the school, since I don't have money like these girls.

Now that she mentions the lunch situation, I think of the little group of gangsters from my neighborhood who sit together every day, about a dozen guys and three or four girls, including Mariana. But they didn't invite me to share their table, and Lexi doesn't sit with them, so I don't either. I guess she isn't a Crow, though Billy is. She's like me and everyone in the neighborhood who they protect even though we aren't crew—peripheral to the gang, but not members.

"That's even worse," Scarlet says, giving me a disgusted look as she parades around in her bra and panties, looking like a porn star. "So you just spread your legs for all of them, and you're not even a member?"

"I don't spread my legs for anyone," I snap, tossing my jeans into my locker and pulling on the dingy grey PE shorts. "Not that it's any of your business."

"Does that mean they just pass you around instead of running a train on you?" Keisha asks, pulling her ponytail out the back of her t-shirt. "I mean, everyone knows that's how you get in the Skull and Crossbones crews."

I gulp, trying not to let her words get to me. Trying not to remember that Maddox said basically the same thing when he was trying to intimidate me. "That's not true," I say, squaring my shoulders.

The girls snicker and give me pitying looks that make me feel even more lame in my second-hand gym uniform.

"Okay," Scarlet says, barely holding back laughter. "I'm sure you know better than I do."

She tosses her pretty blonde hair back and struts away to get her clean new uniform. The school gets slightly new designs each year, which means that everyone knows if you're too poor for a new one and have to wear one of the old ones the school saves for poor kids. I turn to my locker and quickly duck into my used Wampus Cats shirt, my thoughts racing.

Do Maddox and Lennox really do that to girls to get them in the crew? Not that I think they're above that—at least Maddox. I've literally seen him with his dick in three different girls' mouths at this point. And Lennox never seems to lack female attention, either, though I've never seen him indulge girls to the extent that Maddox does.

I knew they were a lot rougher than me, but I'm finally having to face that this is who they are. I'm way out of my element in our new neighborhood, but here am I, making the best of a bad situation. Sure, my friends are gangsters and a group of girls who proudly wear the label of *slut*, but at least I'm not alone with my crow anymore.

My mother must be proud.

In PE, the coaches set up a volleyball net, crank up some music on a boombox, and sit around talking and ignoring us. They clearly don't give two shits about teaching us. They're just there to break up fights and make sure the school doesn't get sued. I don't know how to play, but thankfully I'm not totally hopeless at sports. At least a third of the class has decided not to play, so they sit in the bleachers talking, doing their makeup, looking at magazines, playing cards, and passing notes. If it weren't for the participation grade, I'd sit up there and read *IT*.

But like any good nerd, I'm determined to have a straight-A transcript when I graduate, and that means not tarnishing my report card with a B in an easy class. Not even when half the boys PE class, which is supposed to be playing basketball on the far end of the gym, comes over and joins us instead. They spike the ball at the pretty girls, making them duck and cover their heads, hump the air and sing "Pony" when I bend over to pick up the ball, and generally harass us. Maddox is in the class, but he stays on the other end, playing basketball and drawing the attention of the girls on the bleachers.

I have PE the last hour of the day, so at least I don't have to choose between showering in the nasty locker room or going through the day all sweaty. I'm happy to retreat to the locker room after class—a lot less happy when I open my locker and don't see my regular clothes inside.

"Looking for something?" asks a sweet voice behind me. I turn to see Scarlet smirking at me, her arms crossed and one toe tapping.

"Where are my clothes?" I demand.

"Maybe they're where they belong," she says, blowing a big pink bubble with her gum. "Have you checked the trash?"

Gritting my teeth and digging my nails into my palms, I stomp over to the trash can. I'm not going to let this bitch get under my skin, no matter how vile she is. If she wants to stand there laughing at me while I pull my clothes from the trash and put them back on, there's not much I can do about it. What I can control is my reaction. I'll never cower in front of anyone like my mom does, never give her the reaction she wants. I'll walk out of here with my head held high just to piss her off.

I pull the lid off the big plastic can, but all I see are paper towels and a used maxi pad wrapped up in its yellow plastic. The girls behind me are all snickering and giving me looks that have me as mortified as I am angry. I refuse to actually dig in the trash and have them laugh more.

"Where are they?" I snap, turning back to Scarlet and her little group of minions.

She taps her chin with one finger, her eyes rolling up toward the ceiling as if she's thinking, her pretty pink lips pursed to one side. "Oh, that's right," she says. "The ones you're wearing now are the trash. That's why the last girl threw them away."

I clench my teeth and glare. This bitch doesn't know how far she's pushing it.

Keisha snaps her fingers impatiently. "Throw them away, and we'll give your clothes back."

"Fat chance," I snap. "Now give them back, or you'll be sorry."

"Girls," she says, giving me a derisive look and crooking a finger to beckon them forward. "I think this bitch needs a lesson."

They step toward me, and suddenly, fear spikes through me. I refuse to run, though. I'll fight back as long as I can, and when they overwhelm me—there are five of them against one of me, and I'm not stupid enough to think I'll actually win this fight—I'll take it the same way I take Lee's beatings. Silently, without giving them the satisfaction of breaking my will, even if they break my bones. I'll walk out with my dignity intact, if nothing else.

Scarlet grabs me, and I take great satisfaction in the look on her face when I punch her in her smug, glossy mouth. But the girls all pile on, grabbing me and pinning me down. I tense, ready to receive the blows and hating that my face is exposed. When Lee kicks the shit out of me, I can at least cover my head and fend off most of the hits to the face.

Instead of punching me, though, the girls yank my shorts down.

A different kind of fear shoots along my limbs now. I twist and thrash, adrenaline charging through me.

"Please," I manage through gasping breaths. "Don't!"

"Oh my god, she thinks we're going to rape her," Scarlet squeals, snorting with laughter and wiping the blood off her lip. "As if."

"I'm sure there's a broom around here somewhere," Keisha says.

Scarlet's eyes widen for a second, but then she sneers at me. "You really think we'd touch your diseased little hole? It's probably crawling with crabs and crusted over with herpes."

I keep fighting to free myself as they peel off my shorts. Scarlet stands up and smooths down her hair, tosses the shorts in the trash, and spits a spray of blood onto them. Then she adjusts her butterfly clips before motioning for the girls to continue. They wrestle my shirt over my head, handing it up to her. I struggle harder as they peel off my underwear, but I can't do more than land a few punches before they pin my arms again.

"Oh my god," Diana howls, making a face and jumping back from me. "Haven't you ever heard of a razor?"

The girls all start howling with laughter.

"She's got a full bush," Scarlet screams. "Like a twelve-year-old!"

"I'm surprised all those guys have found their way through that," Diana adds, wiping away her tears of laughter. They finally let me up, and I stand, shaking with rage and humiliation.

So much for walking out with dignity. I can take a beating, but this… This is more than a beating. They didn't leave a single bruise, and yet, this will stay with me far longer, the shame burned into my psyche.

"Give me my clothes," I say, my voice unsteady. I'm going to be sobbing into my pillow about this for months, but I'll take that secret to the grave with me. I'd fucking die before I cry in front of the demon cheerleaders from hell.

"Fine," Scarlet says, rolling her eyes. She steps back, giving the other cheerleaders a minute to straighten themselves out. They all step aside, making sure I'm fully exposed to the entire locker room. Half the class has already cleared out, since people are eager to head home at the end of the day, but the ones who remain are snickering and giving me looks that range from pity to scorn to amusement. No one gets fully nude in the locker room, which means they're all staring. I want to crawl into a bathroom stall and hide until the rest of them are gone.

Scarlet, who's already back in her snug Calvin Klein jeans and a striped baby tee, leads me to one of the stalls and shoves the door open. "There's your clothes," she says, barely containing her laughter. "I think we improved them."

I stare in disbelief at the jeans and t-shirt that are stuffed down into one of the toilets. Gagging at the smell, I try to step back, but Keisha shoves me forward into the stall, and Diana pulls the door closed, holding the top.

"Are you fucking serious?" I ask, glad they've shocked the tears away. "You *shit* on my clothes?"

"Hey, I said your gym clothes were trash," Scarlet says, giggling. "Your regular clothes are shit, so that seemed fitting."

I stare at the clothes, trying not to puke at the sight of the pile of human excrement on my "If My Mouth Doesn't Say It, My Face Definitely Will" shirt. It would be bad enough if they just soaked my clothes with toilet water. I could at least bring them home and wash them. Now, there's no way I'm fishing the clothes out. I want to slam the lid of the toilet, but of course it's in the gym of a public school, which means we're lucky it has a seat. To get lids, I'd probably have to move across town to Willow Heights, the fancy private school.

I turn around and yank on the door, trying to open it while the girls outside hold it closed.

"What's going on in here?" demands a male voice, one of the coaches who likes to stick his head in the locker room while the girls are changing.

"We're just holding the door for Rae while she changes," Keisha calls back sweetly. "The lock's broken."

"Well, hurry up," the coach shouts. "Clear out and go home!"

I hear the door to the locker room settle closed. "Let's go," Keisha says. "She's had enough, and I don't want to miss the bus."

"Because Tommy's on your bus?" teases Diana.

Suddenly they shove the door toward me, the one I've been pulling, and I stumble backwards, my legs hitting the edge of the toilet. The seat rattles, and Scarlet shrieks. "She fell in the toilet!"

This time, they don't snicker and hold back. They're all out guffawing.

I stumbled out of the stall, my hair a mess from the fight, my rage burning up through me like magma in a volcano. I see the flicker of fear in Scarlet's eyes as she takes a step back, her tongue darting out to taste the split I left in her lip. Backing up another step, she swallows, her eyes rolling back and forth like an animal looking for an escape.

"I said you'll be sorry," I growl, my breath unsteady. I don't know what's going to come out if the volcano erupts. Tears or murder are equally viable options at this point.

Keisha snorts. "What are *you* going to do? You don't even have clothes."

Scarlet bumps into the big plastic trash can where she threw my gym uniform. Her gaze drops, and the next second, she snatches the clothes out of the trash and runs for the door. She's got a head start, and I have to shove past her friends, but she's in a pair of platform boots, and I'm barefoot. I race after her, arriving at the door just when she does. We wrestle for the clothes, the door handle, the upper hand. Then Diana grabs me from behind, fisting a handful of my hair and yanking my head back.

I cry out, and Scarlet yanks open the door. I hear her footsteps clomping across the hardwood, moving as fast as she can go in her thick boots. I also hear the squeak of basketball shoes, the *choing!* sound of balls hitting the floor, the clank of the rim when they bounce off.

Shit. The team has practice after school.

I'm just going to have to hide until the place clears out, and then I'll find… Something… To wear home.

As if she's reading my mind, Keisha swings open the door. "Put her out," she says, like I'm a bag of trash.

"No," I scream, the word tearing from me unbidden. Adrenaline spikes through me, and I kick the door, trying to force it closed. I grab Keisha's hair, yanking it askew. My nails rake down Diana's arm, scratching like a cat being thrust into a sink full of water. She shrieks and releases me, but someone else shoves me from behind. I go stumbling out the door, instinct taking over as I try to keep my feet. When I straighten, I'm standing at the edge of the basketball court, fully naked in front of the whole team.

twelve

Rae West

My blood is ice. I can't even move for a second. Half the team is gaping. Someone whistles. Another guy nudges someone who hasn't turned to see me yet.

That jerks me out of my coma, and I throw myself back against the door. The girls are holding it from the other side, and it only rattles, bringing more attention my way. I try to cover myself with my hands, slamming my shoulder into the door again as a few of the guys start to murmur and chuckle.

Balls bounce across the floor and roll away, forgotten. The last squeak of a shoe echoes through the space as Maddox turns from rebounding, the ball held between both hands. His gaze falls on me, and his eyes widen so far you'd think he'd never seen a naked chick before. Surprising he even noticed one more, with all the others who are always naked around him.

He throws the ball at Reggie. It bounces off his chest, as his hands are hanging at his sides and he's too busy looking at me to notice the flying object coming his way. Then his view is blocked by the towering wall of muscle barreling toward me, his eyes like the darkest pits of hell. As he approaches, he lifts one arm, gripping the bottom of his t-shirt with the other hand.

I let myself be completely absorbed by watching him, so I don't have to feel all the eyes watching *me*.

He drags the hem of his shirt up, and my breath catches as I watch the muscles ripple along his arm, up his side. He's even got muscles on his ribs. His long, silky basketball shorts sit low on his hips, and when he lifts his arms to peel the t-shirt over his head, the V of muscle inside his hipbones makes my head swim. His shoulder muscles bunch and flex as he wrenches the shirt over his head, down his other bulging, tattooed arm.

Usually I think Lennox is the fine one. Maddox is too big, too rough, too angry. Lennox would be a fun boyfriend. Maddox would be… Brutal.

But today, it doesn't matter. Today, I watch him like my life depends on it, until he's standing right in front of me, his inside-out shirt dangling from one hand, his bare chest heaving with each breath, the tattoos flexing. He shoves the shirt at me. "Put this on," he snaps, his voice low and trembling with rage.

I stare at the sweaty wad of fabric, not wanting to take my arms away from my body and show him everything. "Can you get my clothes back?"

"Put it on," he roars, his voice so loud it makes me jump back against the door, cowering away from him. He jerks the shirt the right way out, then wrestles it down over my head before I can question him again. I try not to notice that his body heat is in the shirt, that the smell of a summer storm engulfs me. He manhandles the garment over my shoulders, roughly jostling me against the door until he can let the long shirt fall down over my body. Then he steps back, his breathing harsh and his dark eyes deadly. He doesn't look at me like the other guys, like he's appreciating seeing me like this. He looks like he wants to kill me.

"Who did this?" he asks, his fists clenching, his inked arms flexing, his abs tight.

I swallow, trembling with fear at the power in his sculpted body, each muscle chiseled to perfection, as if an artist carved him from marble for the sole purpose of inflicting pain.

"No one," I say quickly, the answer coming automatically. "I—I fell against the door, w-while I was changing, and it came open and…"

My answer doesn't even make sense, since the door opens inward, but eighteen years of training to keep my mouth shut has programmed the excuses into me.

"Who?" Maddox demands, his jaw clenching, the veins along his thick arms standing out like a map. I try to focus on those and not the fact that he's looking at me like he might grab my head, twist it around, and snap my neck with his bare hands if I don't tell the truth.

I know better.

Keep your mouth shut.

"No one," I whisper. Somewhere along the way, protect the family turned into protecting all enemies. Otherwise, they just make it worse. Everyone knows that. I've already felt what it's like to be called a rat at this school, and that was without actually ratting anyone out. It will be a hundred times worse if I actually snitch.

"I'm going to ask you one more time," Maddox says slowly, each word low and laced with menace. "Who did this to you?"

"It's nothing," I insist. "I'm fine. Not a scratch on me."

His jaw clenches, and he brings up a hand and swings. I almost scream, but instead, the muscle memory of how to protect myself in an attack takes over, ingrained in me since I was five years old. In an instant, my eyes snap closed, my head ducks down, and my hands fly up, covering my face.

I hear the blow, a crack that echoes through the gym, and feel the door give behind me. I stumble backward, pinwheeling my arms and trying not to fall on the other side of this door for the second time in five minutes. Once I get my balance, it takes a second for my brain to catch up, to realize Maddox didn't hit me—he hit the door beside me. Now he's towering over me in the doorway to the locker room, still breathing hard, his murderous gaze bouncing from one girl to another. He grabs the back of my neck like he did the other time, like I'm a doll he's going to dangle from his grip and shake at them.

"Who's responsible for this?" he demands, his deep voice echoing off the tiles.

A girl I must have hit while I was thrashing to free myself is sitting on a bench, covering her face and crying. Keisha and Diana are huddling around her, Diana with a wad of wet paper towels on her bleeding arm where I scratched her.

"She attacked us," Keisha says flatly. "That bitch gave me a bald spot and took off half the skin on Dee's arm. Not to mention she gave Cassie a black eye and Scar a fat lip right before the game. How's my squad going to cheer for y'all looking all busted up?"

"You took her clothes?" he demands.

"No," says a voice behind him. "I did."

We all turn to see Scarlet standing in the doorway, looking kinda badass taking responsibility instead of sniveling like usual. She crosses her arms and smirks up at Maddox, and I see the other girls exchange glances, looking impressed as hell that she's standing up to the most feared guy in school, a dangerous gangster with neck tats that make him look like he could run a gang in prison.

"You did?" he asks, no inflection in his voice, almost like he's just stating facts.

"What about it?" Scarlet asks. "I don't see the big deal. We do shit to lots of girls who are losers. It's not like she's a Crow."

"She's mine," Maddox growls, drawing me closer to his body as if by instinct. He's still looking at her, and again I get that feeling like he's holding onto me for his sake as much as mine. Like maybe I'm holding him up too, in some way I don't understand.

"I don't see what's so special about her," Scarlet says, her fat lip curling in disgust as she looks at me standing there in a t-shirt that swallows my body, the body she laughed at for being unshaven and childish. How was I supposed to know what girls are doing with their pubes nowadays? No one's ever seen mine, so it didn't really seem important to find out. And who am I going to ask, anyway? My mother? The bird on my roof?

Maddox takes a slow step toward her, dragging me along. His voice is low and deadly, iced with loathing. He speaks each word carefully, delivering them slowly, as if he knows the devastation they'll cause her self-esteem. "What's so special about *you?*"

Scarlet swallows, her eyes widening with real hurt. "I…"

"If you were anyone else, I'd grab you by the throat and pin you against the wall and let you hang there, struggling to breathe until you passed out," he says. "But you'd like that shit too much, wouldn't you, you fucking whore? You don't deserve to feel that good. And the janitor doesn't deserve the mess he'd have to clean up when you'd cum all over the floor like a fucking dog."

Scarlet's face goes as red as her name, and she looks at the floor and blinks hard, not saying a word.

"Because that's what you really want," Maddox says, prowling forward. "For someone to treat you like what you are. You know that's all you deserve. To be treated like a pathetic little mutt, just begging for a scrap of attention, so desperate you'd do anything to get it. Isn't it?"

His words hang in the silence, not one person moving or daring to breathe. Scarlet swallows so hard I can hear it echo in the silent locker room. Then, slowly, she nods.

Maddox chuckles. "What was that?"

"Yes," she whispers, a tear spilling from her lashes and trickling slowly down her cheek.

"That's what I thought," Maddox says. "Now apologize."

"I'm sorry," Scarlet says, her voice shaking.

Finally Maddox turns to me, acknowledging my existence instead of using me like a crutch. He moves his hand under my hair, from gripping the back of my neck like he was about to shake me around like a ragdoll again to gently cradling the back of my head like a basketball in his huge palm. He uses his other hand to stroke my disheveled hair back from my face, letting his knuckles linger on my skin. His lips quirk into the softest smile, one I've never even imagined could grace his hardened features. His eyes are sharp and burning, though, and when our gazes lock, I understand.

I understand that it's a lie, just like Lennox's flirtations and dimpled smiles that feel like they're just for me, like we share a secret. But Lennox doesn't share the secret. The lies are at my expense.

This lie isn't meant to deceive me. Maddox is letting me in on the lie. It's one we'll share, only the two of us knowing, like we're on the same side against these bitches. These outsiders.

For once, he's letting me in. I'm not the outsider. Because I may not be a Crow, but I'm from Mill, like him.

"You good?" he asks quietly, moving a step closer, so we're almost touching. His hand behind my head guides me, turning my face up to his. His gaze smolders into mine, and suddenly, it doesn't feel like a lie. I swallow hard, my pulse thrumming in my throat. The corner of his mouth quirks again, and I wonder if he can feel it, how hard my heart is hammering. His thumb gently strokes my cheek, and I'm not sure how long my knees will hold me.

I nod faintly, and he chuckles and brings me in, his arm circling me and holding me tight against him. I'm relieved for the moment to hide my face in his chest and get my wits about me, even though it's not easy with his warm, bare skin all pressed up against me. I can smell the sweat on his damp skin from the workout, and it's all I can do not to run my fingers down his torso, exploring every ridge of muscle, tracing every line of ink. I want to know what they mean, each tattoo, each secret.

"You got off easy this time," he growls over my head at Scarlet. "But if I ever hear about you fucking with this girl again, there will be consequences. And crew consequences aren't the kind of thing a girl like you wants to get mixed up in. Go back to your daddy and your rich little frat boys while you still can. You don't want to fuck around in our world and find out the hard way. And next time, you will."

"Her gym unform is in the trash can on the far side of the gym," Scarlet says, still staring at the floor.

"Where are her regular clothes?" he asks, looking around at the others.

No one moves.

"Who the fuck has her clothes?" Maddox demands.

"They're ruined," I say. "I can wear my gym clothes."

"Fuck that," he snaps. "You're not wearing clothes from the trash."

"It's fine," I assure him, pulling away to pick up my shoes from where the girls dropped them when they were stripping me. I grab my backpack before returning to him, laying a hand on his chest and trying not to feel how hot his bare skin is, how smooth and masculine. "Really. Come on. You've done enough. You need to get back to practice."

He frowns down at me a moment, then nods and takes my hand, leading me out of the locker room. His grip completely swallows my small fingers. When the door falls shut behind us, the noise of the gym quickly replaces the stifling silence. A couple guys whistle, clap, or laugh, when they see me still in Maddox's shirt, but it's the sort of good-natured ribbing that makes me blush because I know they're admiring the view, not disgusted by me. Maddox silences them with one glower before turning back to me.

"I could have had Scarlet give you her clothes."

I shrug. "They wouldn't fit. She's curvier than me."

His gaze flickers to my chest, and I'm suddenly aware that it's cold enough that my nipples are peaked against the fabric of his thin shirt. That explains the guys cheering when they saw me.

"Go sit in the bleachers," he says gruffly, releasing my hand and giving me a little push in that direction. "You missed your bus. I'll take you home after practice."

I don't argue. Mom doesn't drive and Lee's at work, and he'd be pissed as hell if he had to swing by and pick me up in his squad car.

I head to the bleachers and pull out my homework. Whatever moment passed between me and Maddox, it did exactly that—passed. Still, I try to figure him out as I sit there in his oversized shirt. Ninety percent of the time, he seems to hate me. But whenever I'm in trouble, he doesn't hesitate to step in and protect me, even to dole out justice. I decide it's just neighborhood loyalty. Like Lennox told me that first day at the pool, their Murder of Crows is like a Neighborhood Watch. Maddox would look out for anyone from Mill. He feels some crew obligation to stand up for me, even if he doesn't like me.

An hour later, Lexi comes in and sees me and climbs up the bleachers to sit beside me. I quickly close my composition notebook, where I'm planning out my next short story, and tuck it into my backpack.

Lexi drops her heavy backpack onto the bench seat below us and blows a strand of hair out of her eyes. It settles right back in the same place. "Hey, ho," she says. "What are you doing here?"

"Waiting for a ride."

"Same, same," she says, bracing her Chucks on either side of her backpack. "Billy's my ride. You going home with Maddox?"

"He's giving me a ride," I say, not liking the connotation in her words.

She grins. "You hit that yet?"

"What?"

She rolls her eyes. "Maddox. He's fine as hell, in case you hadn't noticed."

I smooth the notebook on my knees and mumble, "He's okay, I guess. If you're into jacked up assholes."

Lexi laughs. "Lennox then?"

"What about him?"

She rolls her eyes again. "If you're not fucking Maddox, that means you're not fucking both of them, which means you're fucking Lennox. Which, if you're not into jacked up assholes, makes sense. I mean, the boy might not be popular, but he's drop dead gorgeous. Mariana said he's into some freaky stuff, though. Is he?" She wiggles her brows at me and grins.

"I don't know," I mumble, trying not to think about him and Mariana.

"Well, she'd know," she says. "The crew guys pass around the crew girls. And don't look at me like that. The girls know that's the deal before they join."

"I'm not a crew girl."

"Right, but they still usually share with the crew," she says. "Especially Maddox. He doesn't respect any girl enough to keep her for himself. Lennox though…" She trails off, studying me.

"I'm not fucking either of them," I assure her. "They're all yours."

A little flare of jealousy rises in me at the thought of her swimming naked in my pool that night, of them watching. She's my friend now, and I should be happy if she gets what she wants. But the thought of her with either of them makes my fingers twitch, wanting to curl into a fist.

She laughs and unzips her bag. "No way. Been there, done that, have way too much self-respect now."

I cough to clear my throat. "You fucked both of them?"

"Just Maddox," she says, digging through her books, her hair falling like a long, tawny curtain between us. "I think Lennox only fucks crew girls. But back in my sluttier days, when I didn't know my worth, I let his brother string me along for a while. Not that you have to stop being a slut once you know your worth. You can do both. That's just not how it worked for me."

"You don't care that people still call you that?"

"What, a slut?" she asks, grinning. "Nope. We made the Slut Club to take back that word from the assholes who used it against us. That's where I was just now. At a meeting. If you're interested, I can feel them out, see if they'd take a new member."

I hold up a hand. "Thanks, but not interested. Still a virgin here."

"Really?" she asks, looking impressed. "With the North brothers next door, just waiting to sneak in your window every night?"

I shrug, embarrassed. "I don't see them as the sneaking-through-a-bedroom-window type."

She cocks her head. "Are you a lesbian?"

"No," I say, frowning. "I barely know those guys. I'm not just going to sleep with them because they're hot."

She gives me a funny look. "Why not? You've lived next door to them for six months."

"And?" I say, tugging at the hem of Maddox's shirt, suddenly becoming aware of the smell of him on it again, how it envelopes me in the masculine scent, how it caresses my bare skin.

"I'm just surprised, that's all," she says. "Though now that I know you've never done it, I'd advise against it for your first time. I mean, damn, does that boy know how to *fuck*. He'll eat that pussy from dust 'til dawn to make sure you cum, too. But he's big—way too big for a virgin. You'd be icing that shit for *days*."

I can barely swallow. It's bad enough seeing random girls sucking his dick. I don't need to think about him eating out my friends, how intimate that is. "He took your virginity?" I manage at last.

"No way," Lexi says, waving a dismissive hand. "I was a regular slut by then, but he still left me hobbling around like I had a dislocated hip. Which, now that I think of it, maybe I did. Do those pop back in on their own?"

"I don't know," I say, shifting on the seat and watching Maddox drive to the basket, swarmed by teammates. His bare skin is glistening with sweat, and my fingers tingle with the memory of how it felt against them. "Can we talk about something else?"

Lexi laughs and swings her hair back, gathering it into a high ponytail. "I knew that would make you jealous. You totally like him."

"I totally do not," I insist, leaning down to get my book out of my backpack, pretending the blood rushing to my face is from bending over too fast.

thirteen

Lennox North

"What the hell is she wearing?" I demand as Maddox holds the door open, letting Rae slip out under his arm. My gaze drops to her bare legs, lightly tanned and fully toned, the kind of legs you can picture pumping hard, giving you a good chase.

My cock twitches as I watch her stride out toward my car. Her ass is nice too, firm and high as it flexes against the inside of his shirt.

I know she runs. I bet she's fast.

Maddox gives me a cool look when I return my attention to him. He lets the door fall shut, and we both follow her into the parking lot, now deserted except for a few cars—the team, the coach, a few teachers staying late.

"Her clothes got ruined," he says. "She needed something to wear."

"You just can't help yourself, can you?" I demand, glaring at him.

"I can," he says. "But I don't see why I should."

"She's too fucking pure for you," I snap.

He shrugs, his eyes hooded as he tries to get a rise out of me the way he always does. "You gonna pretend you're any better?"

I scowl at him. "I'm not pretending anything. I won't hurt her."

He scoffs. "Like you don't hurt the crew girls?"

"I don't do anything to a girl that she doesn't agree to," I say, glaring as we approach my shitty little fifteen-year-old El Camino. Rae stands beside it with her thumbs hooked in the straps of her backpack, the t-shirt hugging her tight tits and highlighting her hard, pointed nipples.

"*Vení,* I don't either," he says with an arrogant smirk. "Trust me, she'll be agreeing so loud it shakes the house when I fuck her."

I fight the urge to punch his teeth in. Instead, I open the passenger door for Rae, letting her in through Maddox's side. She smiles and climbs in carefully, holding the shirt down to keep from giving us a peek at her pussy as she swings her legs in and scoots into the bitch seat. Blood pulses in my temple at the thought of what must have happened. She's naked under his shirt, which means he saw her already.

I glare over the top of the car at Maddox as I circle and climb into the driver's seat. He just grins and climbs into the passenger seat beside her.

The asshole knows I'm interested, and he said he wasn't. As usual, though, he can't stand for anyone else to get a girl he can't. Not that he tries. He refuses to put in any effort, and then gets pissed when one of them has the audacity to not fall all over herself at his hard-to-get act.

But he can't stand to leave one pussy unfucked, so now he'll put in the minimum amount of effort necessary to get her to open her legs, and then he'll leave her crying and expect me to clean up his mess. That's how it works every fucking time.

Normally, I don't care. I don't want those girls anyway.

But Rae? I want her.

And he knows it.

Instead of being a decent friend or a good brother and backing off, now that he sees I want something, he wants it too. And Maddox always gets what he wants, fuck everyone else. The rest of us are left with his sloppy seconds, even when we saw her first.

Aside from the crew girls, who are community property, I don't fuck girls he's already fucked. Which leaves me with next to nothing, since by now, he's gotten his dick in every willing pussy at Faulkner High. Any girl who will fuck guys like us is already ruined for me. I'm not going to let him ruin Rae, too. If he wants her, he can have what's left when I'm done.

I glance sideways at her as I shift into gear, letting the back of my hand drag along the outside of her knee longer than necessary. She doesn't move away. I've seen the way she looks at me. I could fuck her too. I'm sure of it.

But she's innocent, too sweet for what I like. Maybe I could feel her out, see if she'd be into it. I wonder how fast she runs. If she'd run for me, fight for me, cry real tears for me. If she'd make her cunt so tight around my cock I couldn't help but cum inside her.

Does she get off thinking about me next door when she's in her bedroom upstairs? Does she fantasize about me climbing through her window, holding a hand over her mouth so her policeman daddy can't hear her scream, and taking what I want?

Or would she run screaming if she knew that's what I fantasize about?

fourteen

Rae West

Lennox parks in front of his house, and we all get out. I'm flustered from sitting squeezed between the North brothers, and the palpable tension inside the car didn't help. It crackled like the energy in the air before a storm, the same atmosphere that's outside. Every time I'm near them, I want to simultaneously do a happy dance and faint dead away, and being squeezed in between their big, strong bodies while wearing nothing but a long t-shirt with nothing under it nearly did me in. I definitely don't need to get my head any more fucked than it already is.

I thank Lennox for the ride and start for my porch next door, but he calls for me to wait and comes around the car. "I'll walk you over," he says, giving me one of those grins that he hands out like candy.

"I think I can make it myself," I point out, unable to keep my mouth from smiling back at him. "It's like ten steps away."

"At least twenty," he says easily, falling in beside me. "Besides, I wanted to talk to you."

"That doesn't sound good."

"I just wanted to tell you, if anything like that ever happens again, you know you can come to me. I would have dealt with it." He looks so earnest I feel a little bad for joking around.

"I'm fine," I say. "Maddox dealt with it."

"Yeah," Lennox says, casting an angry glance back toward his house, where Maddox went. "But you had to sit there for two hours in his shirt. I could have gotten you some clothes. You should have come to find me. *He* should have sent you to me."

I shrug. "He took care of it. It's fine, really. He wasn't even a dick about it. In fact, if I didn't know better, I'd think maybe he doesn't hate me after all."

I smile at the thought, but Lennox scowls. "Listen…"

He takes my hands and looks into my eyes, and my tummy flips at the concern I see in those warm, golden depths. We're standing on my front porch now, in front of the door. I have this horrifying thought that this is where people kiss goodbye after a date. Not because I don't want to kiss him, but because Lee would murder me if he saw me kissing a boy on his porch.

"Just come to me next time," Lennox says, squeezing my hands.

"Okay," I say, swallowing hard. "I will."

He keeps gazing into my eyes until I swear I'm dizzy with him. "I don't want you to get hurt," he says. "And that includes by my brother. He's my brother, my blood, and I won't say anything against him, but keep your eyes open, Rae. Watch what he does, and decide if you want to be one of those girls. Make that decision with your head, not your heart."

He drops one of my hands and taps a finger gently against my temple, stepping even closer, until I'm forced to look up at him or take a step back. His gaze searches mine, then drops to my lips, and for one horrifying, heart stopping moment, I think he's going to kiss me, really kiss me, in broad daylight on my front porch.

But then he chuckles and steps back. "Don't be a stranger," he says, walking backwards down the steps with a grin on his face again. "You can come over to our house too, you know. We may not have a pool, but we have us."

"I know," I say, my heart still doing funny things and my stomach full of nervous butterflies. I turn to the door, letting a wide grin overtake my face as I step through. I feel high, like I could float away, or cheer, or dance around my room like a maniac. I can't wait to recount my week to Poe, like I do every weekend.

"Where the hell have you been?" demands a gruff voice from the other room.

The balloon of sparkling joy inside my chest deflates, and I'm back to being myself, back to my dark house and the danger lurking there.

"I missed the bus," I say, wondering if I can stay out of sight of him and sneak up the stairs.

"I know you missed the damn bus," he snaps, and I hear the pause while he sucks on his cigarette. "Get in here, girl."

I think about making a run for the stairs, but my programming is too strong. My feet carry me slowly into the living room, where he sits in front of the little boxy TV as usual. I can't feel my fingers, and my throat is so tight I can barely get air in. I'm starting to feel lightheaded, the world receding into grey as I slip further from my body.

"What's this I hear about you getting into a fight?" he asks, staring at the TV instead of me.

"What?"

"Didn't think I'd hear about it, huh?" he asks, his gaze swinging my way at last.

I flinch back.

"I got a call from the school," he goes on, swishing the end of his cigarette in the ash and butts left in the ashtray on the arm of his chair. "Three girls say you attacked them in the locker room after school."

"I…" I fight for breath, for words. "I was defending myself."

"What in god's name are you wearing?" he asks, narrowing his eyes at me and taking in the knee-length t-shirt and tennis shoes that make up my entire outfit. I'm suddenly very, very aware that I'm not wearing anything under it. Lee's not that kind of creep, but I still don't want to be around him when I'm wearing so little.

"It's from the fight," I say, relieved I have a reasonable explanation, even if I'd rather him not know about that. "My clothes got torn."

"And who gave you that?" he asks.

"Some guy had it in his locker," I say. "He offered it to me."

Lee stares at me through the haze of smoke. I have one second to take in the way his hands suddenly tighten on the arms of his chair, and then I'm spinning on my heel and running. I hear his footsteps behind me, but I don't look back. My heart races frantically in my chest, my Reeboks hitting the hardwood with each step, and then I'm at the stairs. Lee grabs my arm and spins me around, his hand cracking across my cheek.

My head whips back, and I stumble on the stairs and fall onto my ass. The edge of the next step bites painfully into my back, but I don't make a sound. Lee grabs my hair, thundering about me thinking I can run from him. His fist sinks into my gut, and the pain takes my breath as thoroughly as his fist. He holds me by the hair on the crown of my head.

"You want a fight?" he growls, slugging my stomach again, my arms, my knees. Finally he lets my hair go, and I curl up on my side while he batters my side and back. And then his palm cracks across my bare ass, my shirt having ridden up.

"Why the fuck aren't you wearing underwear?" he demands. "You expect me to believe those got ruined in a girl fight? You think I'm blind? You think I work my ass off to house a dirty slut who can't make it through the day with her clothes on?"

I reach down and tug the shirt over my ass, even though it leaves me open for the next blow, this one landing on the side of my breast. I think I'm going to pass out from pain. Finally, Lee steps back, breathing hard. "Get some damn clothes on," he snaps. "You're grounded from going out, and if I see a boy come around here looking for you, he's going to end up in the back of my cruiser. You're not even eighteen yet."

I don't say anything. My ears are ringing, and pain is crashing over my body in waves.

I wait for him to walk away, and then I pick up my backpack and drag myself upstairs, where I crumple into bed. Every good thing that happens to me turns on its head in moments. It's like I'm cursed. Lexi told me that crows are a bad omen, and that the Murder of Crows chose them because they're so common in our neighborhood and they mean death is near. I hope it's Lee's death, but so far, no such luck.

I lie in bed staring out the window as the sky turns grey and then darker with the approaching storm. Then I see her outside my window.

"Poe," I cry, dragging myself to sitting. She comes in the middle of the day every day, even though I'm in school. I know because she's always here on the weekends. She usually doesn't come in the evenings, but here she is. Maybe the storm scared her from her nest.

I hobble to the window and open the glass, letting in a gust of bitterly cold, damp air. A few fat drops of cold rain splatter down from the blackened sky.

"You hungry, girl?" I ask.

I prop the window open and hurry as fast as I can back to my bag, pulling out a package of square, orange, peanut butter sandwich crackers. I dump out the last two and return to the window, where Poe is cawing angrily.

"You and me both," I mutter, breaking off a piece of the cracker. I drop it out onto the roof, and she hops over and picks it up, gulping it down and ruffling her wings as she stares at me expectantly. I break off another piece and set it out, leaving my fingertips against the edge of it. She watches me and caws as if to tell me to back off. I don't. I wait, and eventually she hops over, looks at me, and then snatches up the bit of cracker.

My heart starts beating harder again, this time with excitement. I break off a piece of cracker and lay it in my palm, extending my hand out the window. I murmur a few soothing words to the bird as she hops closer and then back, flaps her wings, and caws in agitation. Finally, she stalks forward on her little crow legs and pecks the cracker with her black beak. She's so close I can see her nostrils, can see each soft feather on her small head.

Suddenly, my bedroom door flies open, and Lee stands silhouetted there like a madman from a horror movie. I jerk back from the window. In a flurry of feathers and squawks, Poe takes off and disappears into the coming darkness.

My heart beats erratically as I stare back at Lee, wondering if he turned into that kind of creep from seeing my bare ass.

"What the hell are you doing?" he demands.

"Nothing," I say, brushing off my hands and gripping the window. It hurts to tense enough to hold it up, but it's too cold to leave it open. I pull the stack of books in with one sweep and lower the glass.

"I don't buy the food around here so you can feed it to pests," he snaps. "You got some mice in here you're feeding too? You fancy yourself Cinderella? Is that why we got rats in the wall?"

"It's just a bird," I say, feeling the need to defend Poe.

"It's a crow," he says flatly. "They're a nuisance in this neighborhood, always squawking and bickering so there's no peace and quiet to be had."

"Sorry," I lie. "Won't happen again."

I don't bother pointing out that I only fed her half a cracker, and the whole package costs exactly a quarter at the gas station. Lee thinks his money is god. When he thinks it's being wasted, there's no point in arguing.

"The pool cover's falling in," he says. "You did a piss poor job of it last fall. Go out and fix it before the storm blows leaves in."

"Now?" I ask incredulously. I can't even move without panting from pain.

"Yes, now, goddamn it," he roars.

"Okay," I say quickly. "Just let me get dressed."

He gives me a long, baleful look, and then closes my door. I wait until I hear his heavy footfalls stomping back along the hall before I let out a breath. My hands shake as I quickly peel off Maddox's shirt and rush into a pair of underwear and a sports bra, terrified the door will fly open at any moment and Lee will be back. I flinch as I pull on a pair of jeans, the bruises on my thighs throbbing with pain as the denim scrapes over them, my back and arms throbbing when I have to bend and pull them on. I shrug into a long sleeve tee, then layer it with a regular t-shirt, and then grab a beanie on my way out.

Downstairs, mom is scurrying around the kitchen, her eyes downcast. From the looks of it, she's been in there a while. She must have heard Lee whaling on me, but of course she wouldn't try to help. If she did, he'd turn his wrath on her.

I step out the back door, and the loose screen door whips back at me in the wind, nearly smacking me in the face. As if I'm not bruised up enough already. If I'm not cursed, this day definitely is.

Lightning sizzles across the sky, and thunder builds, the kind that starts far away and rolls across the earth, shaking the ground as it grows louder and louder with its approach. Instantly, I'm shaking all over, and I can hardly swallow. But I know I can't go back in without obeying Lee's command. I take a deep breath, duck my head, and dive into what feels like a march down death row.

Icy rain pings off the tin roof of the dilapidated shed as I hurry to the pool to where the cover is sagging down into the empty pit. I grip the edge and heave to pull the heavy tarp up. Pain lances through my ribs and grips my entire torso in a spasm so intense that I cry out and fall on my knees, cradling my body and taking a ragged breath. When the worst of it subsides, I carefully lean forward and reach down, tugging the edge of the tarp up slowly this time, gritting my teeth when the rib starts to ache again.

"Hey there, Sunshine," Lennox's voice calls from the broken spot in the fence. "Need some help?"

"Fuck," I mutter under my breath, ducking my head and trying to collect myself. Then I lift my face and wave, clenching my teeth past the pain and hoping he sees it as a smile. "I got it, thanks!"

He steps through the gap, Maddox close on his heel. They hurry over, and within minutes, the pool cover is secure again and rain is falling in a steady, grey drizzle. I'm still on my knees, having reached down to help so they didn't notice anything was off. But now they're both standing there looking at me, and I know I have to stand, and I know I can't do it without wincing.

"Thanks for your help," I say, smiling brightly.

Lennox holds out a hand to me, smiling back. "What did I *just* tell you about coming to me when you need help?" he asks. "We take care of what's ours, Sunshine."

"Am I yours?" I ask, cocking my head and squinting up at him through the streaks of dismal, icy rain. "Because I seem to remember you telling me I couldn't join your Murder of Crows."

Maddox frowns down at me. Somehow, he looks right at home in the December rain, like the king of this dark, depressing season. "You're in our territory, aren't you?"

"Yeah, but so are lots of people."

"If you're on our turf, you're either our responsibility or our problem to take care of."

I gulp at the thought of him 'taking care of' someone. He's not talking about the way he takes care of me. He's talking about literal murder, taking someone's life. The very first time they came to the pool, his friends told me he had bodies buried in his backyard.

I push the thought away and focus on my current predicament. I've reached the point where it's going to be completely obvious that something's wrong if I keep stalling. I take Lennox's hand because I know that'll get me on my feet faster and save me from rising myself and looking like an eighty-year-old grandma with bad joints.

Lennox's warm fingers close tightly around mine, and he heaves me to my feet in one go. The pain is blinding, so white hot my vision goes out for a second, and I sway on my feet.

When my eyes clear, Maddox is frowning at me, icy rain tracking down his sculpted face. He jerks his chin at me. "You good?"

"Yeah," I say, forcing a laugh that comes out breathy from pain. "Head rush."

The guys exchange a look, like they're deciding whether to believe me. Then Maddox steps in and yanks up my shirt.

"Hey!" I yell, trying to jerk my hand from Lennox's and slam my elbow down so Maddox won't see the bruises blooming like poppies across my ribs and torso.

Lennox's hand tightens, and I suck in a gasp when another spasm of pain slams into me as I tense, trying to wrest control of my arm from him.

"What…the…fuck," Maddox says slowly, his sexy voice going low with a growl that's pure animal, something made to go with the soundtrack of thunder overhead and the pelting of freezing rain on the world around us. The way he's looking at me sends a shiver of instinctual terror through me, freezing the blood that throbs in my hot bruises. His gaze rises to mine, and in that moment, I see exactly how far apart we are. I may belong to his neighborhood, but he's a man in every way, and like he says, in comparison I'm just a little girl.

I already knew we were different. He fucks girls like it's no different from playing a video game or swimming in my pool. I've barely ever even kissed a boy.

But I've never let myself think about what they do in their gang.

Looking into his burning eyes, though, I realize how deep his affiliation goes, how serious it is. He's capable of murder, and right now, he looks it. This isn't about him fucking lots of girls. Our differences go so much deeper than sex.

I'm just a girl who likes to read and run and talk to a crow.

He *is* a Crow. He's an animal, one with another beast inside him, something primal and simple. Something godlike.

He lowers my shirt without a word, his dark gaze holding mine through the curtain of icy rain. "Who did this to you?" he asks quietly.

"No one," I say, forcing a laugh. "It was an accident."

"Fell down the stairs again, did you?" he asks, his tone laced with cruelty.

I gulp, hot tears stinging my eyes.

"Come on," Lennox says. "You can stay with us."

"I can't," I say, my throat thick.

"You can," he says, pulling me to his side and sliding an arm around my shoulders. "Our mom's cooking. She made friends with a couple Mexican ladies at church, and now she thinks she can cook tamales. Granted, you'll be eating a melted pile of cornmeal mush, but once she goes to sleep, we can order Little Caesar's."

I shake my head, glancing back at the house. "I can't. I'm grounded."

"Bullshit." Maddox is the one who speaks this time, his intense gaze still boring into me, his dark green eyes like onyx in the dark.

"*Vení,*" Lennox says, giving me his pleading puppy dog eyes and the smile that shows his dimple, with his lips closed. "I said we should hang out during the break. Let's start tonight. I'll be good—I promise. Maddox?"

"I'm not going to fucking make a move on a girl who just got used as a punching bag," Maddox snaps. "What the fuck, *parce?*"

Lennox snaps back at him in Spanish, and they argue heatedly. I'm totally lost, but I know it doesn't matter what they decide. They don't understand. I'm not going home to protect Lee. I'm going to protect them *from* Lee.

"I can't go to your house," I interrupt, shrugging out from under Lennox's arm. "Thanks for the offer. But my stepdad's a cop. He'll arrest you. Just go home, okay? Can we just pretend you didn't see anything? It's not even that bad. I'm fine. It's just a couple bruises, and most of them are from the stairs anyway."

"Take her home." Maddox isn't speaking to me, he's speaking to his brother, but the command in his voice leaves no room for argument.

Still, I try as Lennox takes my arm and pulls me across the lawn, through the gap in the fence where so long ago, I stepped through and went for a run. Someone pulled all the broken boards from the hole, so it's easier to climb through now. I got so used to the guys using it that it just seems like a gate now, the normal passage from one yard to the next.

"What's he going to do?" I ask, twisting to look behind us. Maddox stands unmoving by the pool, the rain falling around him, each drop turned silver by the back porch light. For one moment, he's standing in a spotlight, his huge imposing figure like a king waiting to be worshipped, every drop of rain racing to bow at his feet.

Then Lennox pulls me away, wrapping an arm around my shoulders and guiding me into his house. "He's going to talk to your dad, that's all," Lennox says. "He'll take care of him, and I'll take care of you. *Sí?*"

I don't know what to say. I'm struggling not to cry too hard to speak anyway. These boys owe me nothing, have no obligation to help me or even be kind to me. And yet, here they are, taking care of me in the way Lennox does, and my stepdad in the way Maddox does.

I swallow hard at the thought, fear gripping my chest and making it hard to breathe. Lee has guns—lots of guns. Maddox isn't the only one who knows how to kill.

fifteen

Rae West

I balk just inside the door, trying to turn back. "He shouldn't go over there alone," I blurt out, the fear overwhelming me. "Lee will kill him!"

"He's fine," Lennox assures me, his arm tightening around my shoulders. "You'll sleep here tonight, and you'll hear him come back, and he'll be fine. He knows what he's doing. I promise."

I'm breathing hard, fighting the urge to freak out. But I'm trained in the art of keeping quiet and not disturbing things, so I swallow the terror and press my nails in until the pain settles my spinning thoughts. I let Lennox pull me into their small, cozy house without further protest. It's as old and drab as mine, but the kitchen is painted yellow, and the curtains are white with little yellow flowers on them. There's a little altar set up in one corner of the living room with candles and a crucifix, dried flowers and faded pictures with the corners curling inwards propped up between other things.

"You boys ready for tamales?" sings a cheerful voice, and Valeria comes dancing into the hall from the kitchen before pulling up short when she sees us.

A short, rapid-fire exchange in Spanish ensues, during which I stand there awkwardly wondering if he's telling her what happened and where Maddox is. Surely she'll send me home and demand that I send her son back in exchange. But after a minute, she goes back to the kitchen, and Lennox leads me down the hall and into the room with the two twin beds and the painting on the wall.

He closes the door behind us and smiles down at me, and my heart flips as I realize we're alone this time. In his bedroom.

"Look at you, you're soaking wet," he says, that soft smile still on his lips. He reaches up and pulls off my beanie, dropping it to the floor. He cups my face, skimming his thumb lightly over the red mark on my face from Lee's palm. That one won't leave a bruise, though it's swollen and hot tonight.

Lennox slides his hand back, threading his fingers through my hair and wrapping his hand around the back of my head. Then he pulls me in, angling his face down to meet mine. My heart stops. His kiss is slow and sensual this time, nothing like the one in the hall at school. This is a real kiss, one that sends waves of pleasure rocking through my body. His lips move against mine, increasing and decreasing the pressure in a rhythm that makes my toes curl and my hands rise to touch him of their own accord. I run my palm up his back, feeling the heat and lean muscle beneath his wet t-shirt.

He gives a soft moan, and a rush of heat floods my center. I fist my hand in the back of his hair, and he growls and grips my hip, pulling me flush against his body. I gasp in pain, and he must take it as pleasure, because he pushes his tongue inside. He rocks his hips against mine and angles his mouth to go deeper. He tastes me, slow and sensuous.

I think my knees will give way, but he tightens his hold on my hip. I wince, brought back to the battered state of my body by the pain. I forgot it for a moment, forgot everything but Lennox's lips, his tongue expertly guiding me, his hand cradling my head and holding me tight to him so his tongue can slide deep inside my mouth, fucking it slowly and thoroughly.

"Lennox," I gasp, tearing my mouth away, suddenly scared. He's too good at this.

"Rae," he says, lifting his other hand to the other side of my head, holding my face while he drops his forehead to mine. "Let me make you feel good."

"I don't know," I whisper, scared to say yes, scared to say no.

He runs his finger down the side of my nose and over my lips, rolling my bottom lip down. Groaning, he leans in and nips it, drawing my lower lip between his teeth and biting down gently. Warm tingles of pleasure race through my body, and between my legs throbs with pleasure the way my bruises throb with pain. He drags his tongue along my lip, holding my face more roughly and tugging my lip between his, sucking at it for a second. Then he pulls away, his tawny eyes hazy with heat.

"Fuck, this mouth," he groans, thumbing my wet lip with paint-stained skin.

When I don't answer, he chuckles and drops his hands, stepping back from me. I curse myself for being such a naïve little virgin that I froze with nervousness.

"Let's get you out of those wet clothes," he says, reaching for my shirt. When I tense, he pauses, gripping the bottom hem. "*Vení,* Rae. I won't do anything you don't want. Just relax. I know you're not ready to be fucked. We're just going to get you in some dry pajamas. *Sí?*"

I nod, relaxing and reaching for my shirt. I pull it up, but he sees me wince at the movement and covers my hands with his, stopping me. "Let me."

"I'm fine," I say, still not quite able to let go and let someone take care of me.

"You're not fine," he says softly. "Stop trying to do it on your own. I'm here. I'm going to take care of you now. So let me."

I nod again, too nervous to speak as he slowly peels my wet shirt off and drops it on the floor. He stares at my body, not with horror at the marks but with hunger. Then he peels off my sports bra, which is tight and makes me suck in shuddering breaths through the pain at having to wriggle out of it.

When that's off, he swears under his breath and steps back again, holding my body between his hands and studying me from behind his glasses. My nipples pebble with cold, exposed to the air and damp from the rain. Lennox moves his hand in, skimming his thumb over the tight tip. I shiver, and his eyes blaze with heat again.

"Dios mío," he groans, dropping to his knees. He peels down my damp jeans, leaving my underwear in place, and then he kneels up, laying soft kisses over the bruise forming on my ribs, red and purple. He moves over, kissing down the ones Lee left on my side, my hips, my belly. He slows there, his thumbs caressing my sides as if to calm me. I'm shaking with nerves, with fear and excitement. I've only just had my first real kiss, and now

I'm almost naked in front of a boy. It's nothing like in the gym earlier.

"Lennox," I manage, my voice coming out with a slight croak.

"Trust me?" he asks, holding my hips and looking up at me. His warm breath comes quick, skimming over my skin and making more goosebumps rise. I can't see his eyes behind his glasses with the light reflecting off them, but after a second, I bite my lip and nod.

Lennox leans in, his mouth lingering as it gently worships each inch of bruised skin. At the same time, he moves one hand lower. I quake when his thumb skims over the front of my panties. Tingles race along my limbs and swirl between my thighs as the blood rushes there, pulsing with hunger. His mouth moves lower, and he tugs the side strap of my panties lower, kissing from my hipbone inwards.

I suddenly remember all those girls laughing, and I grab his head.

"I—I don't know about that," I say.

"Trust me, *mi cariña*," he says again. "You'll like it."

I gulp. "What if I don't?"

"Then I'll stop," he says. "Promise."

I try to relax and calm my racing thoughts and shaking limbs as he kisses down the side of my mound. It's ticklish, and my body jerks with a spasm. Lennox moans softly, moving inwards, kissing onto the front of my panties. All I can think about is that I'm not shaved like the other girls he must have been with. I feel stupid and naïve, and I know I should like this because girls always talk about how great it is, and how if a guy knows how to do this, you keep him.

Lennox kisses me there, harder, moving his mouth in slow, erotic circles. His warm breath passes through the fabric, warming me, and I shiver again. It feels good, but all I can do is stare at the wall and feel cold and exposed, self-conscious and unsure of what to actually do with myself. He hooks his finger through the edge of my panties and pulls them aside, and I quake with embarrassment that he's seeing what those girls saw when they laughed at me.

But he doesn't laugh. He makes a low noise in his throat and parts my hair with his fingers before he leans in, kissing me again, with nothing between us. A shock of pure pleasure rocks through me when his warm lips meet my bare skin.

The front door slams hard, shaking the whole house.

I jump a mile, and Lennox chuckles and sits back on his heels. He licks his lips and smiles up at me, not seeming at all concerned that his brother just walked into the house. I can hear Maddox's voice in the other room, talking to their mom.

"To be continued," Lennox says, standing and opening his dresser drawer. I see a gun on top, in plain sight, before he shifts his position so I can't see. He pulls out a pair of pajama pants with the St. Louis Blues logo printed on them and hands them to me, along with a FHS Wampus Cats t-shirt.

I hear footsteps in the hall and practically dive into the shirt, my heart hammering like I'm about to be caught alone with a boy by Lee instead of Maddox. "Hey," Lennox says, gently taking my arm to slow my panicked movements as I try to find the neck hole with my head. "Slow down. You'll hurt yourself more."

"But he—"

"Has seen more tits and asses than the owner of *Girls Girls Girls!*," he says with a chuckle as he eases the neck of the shirt over my head, smoothing my hair and giving me a soft, dimpled smile. I've heard a couple guys at school talk about sneaking into that strip club, so I know what it is, but somehow thinking about Maddox seeing a million other girls naked makes me feel worse, not better.

I reach for the pants, but Lennox's hand closes around mine, stilling me again.

He looks down at me, his gaze earnest as he cups my cheek in one palm. "You're okay now," he says. "Trust me, Rae. You're safe here. I promise."

That wasn't even what I was thinking. I knew Lee wasn't coming to get me. That's not his style. He prefers not to be inconvenienced. He'll sit in his chair smoking and watching TV, waiting for me to come to him, and then he'll strike. I can hear his voice in my head already.

"I work all day, I'm not going to work to discipline a kid who's not even mine."

He's the kind of bastard who made me go pick out my own switch before he whipped me when I was a kid. Somewhere along the way, that became too much work. He'll be the first to brag that bare hands work just as well, the first to tell the story of how he killed a bad guy with his bare hands in the line of duty.

I wonder if Mom and I fall into the category of bad guy when we disobey or displease him. I'm sure we do. That's why we deserve the punishment. Maybe one day, his hands will end up around our throats, and that's how he'll spin that story too.

I hear water running in a bathroom down the hall, and I relax the slightest bit.

"Step into these," Lennox says, lowering himself to his knees again after helping ease my arms into the shirt. He holds open the pajama pants, and I brace a hand on his shoulder and step into them. I'm relieved to be covered before Maddox comes in. Besides the guilt about what I was doing with his brother, I'm gripped with a terror that he'll see me before I'm dressed. Which is ridiculous, since he saw me stark naked at school just hours ago.

Two taps come at the door, and it opens before I can tell him we're busy. Maddox steps inside, his gaze falling on his brother, who's still at my feet. A scowl forms on his face, and he glares at me like I'm some temptress who's intentionally luring in his brother, instead of the opposite.

Lennox settles the pants around my hips and gives the drawstring a little tug, securing them and grinning up at me. Slowly, he stands and turns to face his brother. He tips his chin at him.

"*Quíubo, parcero?*" he asks.

"What the hell are you doing?" Maddox demands. "She's injured, for fuck's sake."

Lennox grins. "I know. I was just making her feel a little better. Isn't that right, Sunshine?" He winks at me before pulling out another pair of pajama pants. He strips out of his jeans, not even turning his back to me. I can see a long, thick ridge in his boxer briefs, and I swallow and look away, as uncomfortable seeing him undress as I am with the crackling tension between the two of them.

Maddox glowers at me like he wants to kill me while Lennox pulls on his pajamas, unclips his wallet chain, and tosses his wet clothes into a hamper in the corner.

"I can go home," I say, crossing my arms over my chest to warm myself and stop the jittery shakes in my body. "In fact, I probably should. I don't want to make things worse for any of us."

"Shut up," Maddox growls at me, his eyes still on his twin.

His pissy attitude arouses my own anger. "Look, I'm not here to cause problems between the two of you, but I'm also not here to be your whipping girl. If you have beef, that's something you'll have to sort out on your own without using me as an excuse."

"Oh, no, it couldn't be about you," Maddox says with a derisive sneer. "You're so sweet and innocent, you've never caused a problem in your whole fucking life."

"That's not what I'm saying," I growl back at him. "If it's about me, fine. I'm flattered, actually. But even if you're pissed at each other about me, don't make it my problem when it's clearly your problem. Just let me go home so the two of you can work it out on your own."

I take one step before Lennox grabs my arm again. "Stay."

His one simple word makes the bravado drain from me, and suddenly, the whole horrible day feels like too much. I just want to be home, to crawl in my bed and curl up and cry. I bite my lip to keep it from trembling and stare at Maddox's feet like my life depends on it.

"Mom said you could stay as long as you want," Lennox says. "If your dad's hurting you, you'll be safer here. One of us will even give you our bed, and we'll sleep on the couch until we clear out the little office space across the hall for you."

I shake my head, my eyes welling with his kindness. "I'd never make you do any of that."

"That's the thing," he says, stepping in front of me and ducking down to look into my eyes, lifting my chin gently with two fingers. "You're not making us do anything. We want you here. *I* want you here. Stay for me?"

He gives me the sweetest smile, and I can't help but return it through my tears. I nod, wiping them away. "I'll stay tonight," I say. "But I'm sleeping on the couch. I'll be gone in the morning."

"The perfect woman," Maddox says, his voice cutting. He turns away and unloads his pockets, pulling up the back of his shirt and removing a gun from his waistband. I swallow hard and turn my gaze back to Lennox.

"I can't live with another guy who hates me," I whisper. "Lee is the devil I know."

I didn't mean for Maddox to hear me, but he snorts at my words, turns, and walks out of the bedroom, slamming the door behind him. I feel even more guilty now, and awkward that I've caused tension. I open my mouth to say I can leave again, but Lennox takes my hand and leads me out of the room and back to the kitchen.

We all sit around the little round Formica table with gold flecks in the white surface, filling the four chairs. I wonder if their dad used to sit here. All Maddox told me was that he's still in Faulkner. He didn't say when he left, just that he and Lennox had to take care of things afterwards.

Valeria scoops cornhusk wrapped packages from a pan on the stove, laying them onto plates and bringing them over. I can already see what looks like cornbread batter leaking out the edge of mine, but I smile at her with gratitude. She's letting me stay. I don't expect her to cook for me.

Lennox slowly opens his wrapper and grins at me, nudging it up so I can see the combination of paste and little chunks of meat floating inside.

"These are great, Mom," Maddox says, wolfing down the mush like he doesn't notice.

"*Gracias, gracias,*" Valeria says. "I think I'm getting better at them, don't you?"

"Definitely," Maddox says, opening his second tamale.

I take a bite. It doesn't taste bad, if you can get past the looks and consistency. It's sort of like grits. When I look up, Valeria is watching me. "What do you think?" she asks.

"Not bad," I say, nodding and forcing myself to take another bite. I catch Maddox frowning at me and hurry to correct myself. "Good, actually. Really good."

Valeria smiles, her mouth open as if to speak, but she falls silent at the sound of sirens in the distance. Her gaze falls on Maddox, who's eating like he can't hear them growing closer. The rest of us sit in silence, no one eating, no one moving.

I remember the gun he pulled out of the back of his jeans, the matte black of it making it look almost like a toy. I remember the look in his eyes when he saw the bruises on me. I remember him standing there in the rain outside my house as Lennox pulled me away, into the safety of their house. Maybe Lee's not the person he was worried about leaving me with.

When the sirens are so loud it sounds like they're right outside the house, Valeria reaches over and covers Maddox's hand with hers, giving him a sad smile.

"What did you do?" I whisper, trying to pretend the flashing lights outside are just lightning, even though I know better.

Maddox shrugs and pushes his plate away. "I took care of him. He won't hurt you again."

"He's a cop," I say, my voice breathy with fear.

"Fuck the police," he says, echoing the songs on the radio. "I'm done eating. I'm going to go put on a movie." He stands, then leans down and kisses the top of Valeria's head, finding her hand and giving it a quick squeeze. "That was fucking great, Mom. Your best yet."

He walks out without a glance toward me and Lennox, who sit frozen at the table.

"Are they coming here?" I ask, peeking at the window.

"I'm going to clean up," Valeria says, pushing back from the table. "You kids done?"

"Yeah, Mom," Lennox says, though he's barely touched his food. "I'll help you clean up."

"No, no, I need something to do," she says. "Go watch a movie with your brother."

Lennox stands and holds out a hand to me. "*Venga*, Sunshine. Let's take your mind off things, *sí?*"

I nod and let him help me out of my chair and lead me to the living room. Maddox is in the midst of laying down a layer of blankets, pillows, and sleeping bags on the floor.

"What are you doing?" I ask.

"Making you a bed," he says. "You think I'd sleep on the floor for you? If Lennox wants to give up his bed, though, I'd be happy to share my room."

"Nobody has to give up their bed," I insist, hating that I'm imposing so much.

Lennox frowns, but Maddox just smirks and scoots under the blankets on one side of the double bed he's assembled on the floor. He shoots us a challenging look. "We watching this, *o qué?*" he asks. "Or are you scared to lay next to a man who hates you, little girl?"

sixteen

Rae West

Lennox picks up two Blockbuster cases from next to the TV and holds them up. "*Scream* or *Trainspotting*?"

"Seems more like a *Scream* night," I say, startled to hear shouting outside.

My eyes widen, and I check Maddox's reaction, but he doesn't look at all concerned. Meanwhile, I'm scared out of my mind. Lee has friends in high places, not just the police force but prosecutors and even judges. Maddox didn't kill him, but he did something my stepdad doesn't like. Whatever he did, he's going to pay for it.

And he did it for me.

I quickly cross the room and slide into the makeshift bed next to him. "Thank you," I say, before I lose my nerve. "For… Whatever you did."

"Don't go getting stupid about me over it, little girl," he says, picking up the remote and fast-forwarding through the previews. "That's what the crew's here for. It's my job."

"Okay," I say, nodding. "I get it."

I slide down between the sheets, trying to get comfortable on the shifting, uneven bed that's made up of cushions from the couch, pillows, and several sleeping bags. The sheet slides on them as I adjust my position so I'm not touching Maddox but also leaving enough room for Lennox to scoot in on my other side.

Even when Lennox slides in and wraps his arms around me, pulling me close, I'm acutely aware of the animal warmth and nearness of Maddox on my other side, of how nervous he makes me. He's harsh and violent, a dangerous gangster, and if he can do that kind of thing to other people, he could do it to me.

At the same time, he's protected me instead of hurting me at every opportunity. Every word out of his mouth reminds me what a dick he is, and yet, he's fiercely protective of me even when I did nothing to earn his loyalty or protection.

When the movie starts, I snuggle down into Lennox's arms, grateful for the warmth of his body and the blankets, since I've been freezing since I came inside. I can hear pellets of ice hitting the windows along with the rain, and I fix my gaze on the TV screen, studiously ignoring the flashing lights still outside the window. I'm tense, waiting for the knock at the door, for the police to come and drag Maddox away.

I wish I could wrap my arms around him, hold onto him and keep him here with me, but I know he'd just push me away and make some cutting remark about my maturity level if I tried. So I content myself with reveling in the warmth of his brother, who doesn't confuse the hell out of me, even if I'm a little scared of him too. They both make their feelings for me clear, but Maddox's words contradict his actions. Lennox has been steadfast since the day Maddox declared me as their property.

I barely breathe, even as the lights outside cease and I hear the tires on pavement as the vehicle pulls away.

Lennox cuddles me into his lap, kissing the back of my neck, and I'm impressed to feel that he's not hard, not rubbing his dick on me. He's just being here for me. I pull his arms tight around me and cuddle into him, grateful for the comfort. Halfway through the movie, I adjust my position and roll onto my back, my head pillowed on Lennox's arm. He's still facing me, but his eyes are closed, his breathing deep.

A minute later, a warm hand slides onto my other thigh. I lay frozen, not sure what to do. I can feel the scalding heat of him through my pajama pants, and every fiber of my being tingles at the contact. Slowly, his hand moves up, until it reaches the apex of my thighs.

I give a little gasp and start to turn to check Lennox, but Maddox's hand shoots up, coming out from under the blanket to grip my chin. He turns my face towards him instead. For a long moment, we study each other in the blue light flickering from the TV. Then he raises up on his elbow, leaning down over me until he's only a few inches from my face. My heart is hammering like a drum, and I can't even breathe.

"Eyes on me, little girl," Maddox murmurs.

Then he kisses me. His kiss is firm and dominating, leaving no room for argument. His mouth takes mine quickly, without gentleness, without hesitation, like he knows I'm his to take. His tongue sweeps between my lips, tasting mine, taking mine. His hand moves from my chin to my throat, his long fingers wrapping around it and making me suck in a breath. Though he doesn't squeeze, his position is one of dominance, reminding me he's in control here. He's a dangerous animal who could kill with his bare hands as easily as my stepfather, and I'm at his mercy.

The thought should scare me, but as he feasts on my mouth while I lay on his brother's arm, the only thing I feel is arousal, potent and incinerating. Somehow, the thought of Lennox beside us doesn't deter me. It makes me feel guilty, like I'm cheating, but also sexy, like I'm doing something naughty.

I squirm on the sheets, making them shift on the sleeping bag underneath. Maddox's fingers pulse tighter for a second, wordlessly conveying that he's not done, that I'm to wait for him to make the next move. I'm not the one calling the shots. He's the one who says when it's over, who decides what he's going to do to me. I'm the one having my mouth used, devoured, eaten like he's eating me out.

He licks and bites and sucks and moans until I'm dizzy, my whole body shimmering with heat. Between my legs throbs with wetness as his tongue strokes mine in a relentless, hungry rhythm. At the same time, he starts to stroke the side of my throat with his thumb, feeling my pulse point. I know he must feel the racing of my heart, how scared and aroused I am as I squirm on the pillows, sure I'll cum from his kiss alone if he keeps it up.

At last, he pulls back, his blazing gaze falling to my swollen lips. "*Dios mío*, your mouth is so fucking sexy," he rasps, his voice thick with lust. "If it were any other night, I'd have you show me what you can do with it."

I swallow, and he groans low in his throat, his fingers pulsing tighter for a second. I stare up at him, my heart thundering in my ears.

"Do that again," he commands.

"What?"

"Swallow," he orders. "When you swallow with my hand around your throat, it's the hottest fucking thing I've ever felt in my life."

I obey, and he closes his eyes and takes a deep, shuddering breath. At last, he moves his hand from my throat, slowly down over one of my breasts. He thumbs my nipple through the fabric of Lennox's shirt.

"You ever sucked a guy's cock?" he asks, his fingers closing around my nipple.

I shake my head, gasping when he tugs gently.

He smirks down at me. "Didn't think so."

"Is that what you want?" I whisper, my throat thick with trepidation.

"I want everything," he says. "But not tonight. Tonight's for you."

"It is?"

He leans down, flicking the tip of his tongue over my lower lip. "Still think I hate you?"

"I don't know," I whisper honestly. I don't go around kissing randos on the regular, but even I know that kissing someone doesn't mean you like them. At least not for guys like him.

For me? Yeah, maybe.

He angles his face to one side, burying it in my hair, his hot breath on my neck making waves of shivery longing spread through me.

"Roll over, and I'll show you," he murmurs into my neck. Wrapping an arm around me, and he scoots me into the curve of his body, rolling me onto my side again. I wince at the pain from my bruises, but I quickly forget them when he turns me so I'm facing Lennox.

His eyes are open, and he's watching us, not moving.

Shame floods through me. How long has he been awake?

Maddox pushes his hips against me, and I can feel the steel ridge of his erection pressed firmly to my ass. He nudges my head, and I lift it. Lennox moves his arm from under it, and Maddox slips his massive bicep under my head like a pillow. Instead of cradling it there, he bends his arm and grips the hair on top of my head, fisting it until my scalp burns. He pushes his hips against mine again, and I gulp, my pulse fluttering at the sensation of being maneuvered this way.

He's taken complete control by holding my head gripped in his massive arm like he's going to try to crush my skull with his powerful muscles. I feel like a puppet, like my body is no longer under my jurisdiction. It's an object for giving and receiving pleasure, whatever he wants to do to it while he has it in his power.

He nips the skin on my jaw, my ear, my throat, his huge body rhythmically rocking against mine, his cock throbbing against me with each push.

I meet Lennox's eyes, wondering if he can see the terror in mine, if he's going to stop his brother. I don't think I can stop him. If he wants me, he'll take me. My head is clamped in his grip, and there's no way I could free myself if I tried. And I'm not sure he'd stop if I told him to.

Lennox folds his arm under his head and rolls toward me, so he's only a few inches away, watching me try not to freak out. I can see his other hand moving under the blanket, but I can't see what he's doing. If he touches me, I might lose control entirely, scream for help. But he only watches, his breath coming almost as quick as mine.

Maddox's hand moves down the front of my body, dipping between my legs, and I'm sure he can feel how wet I am. Humiliation floods through me.

"Maddox," I gasp, squirming against his hand as it massages me through my pants.

"Does that feel good?" he purrs in my ear, cupping me from the front while he grinds his cock into my ass from behind. "Say it, little girl. Tell me how good it feels."

"Yes," I whisper, closing my eyes and drawing a breath through shaking lips.

He eases off, his arms relaxing to cradle me more gently than the forceful way he was, his grip loosening in my hair, his hips moving back from mine. "We're not going to fuck you with our cocks tonight," he says, laying a soft kiss just below my ear. "Relax, little girl. We just want to make you feel good. I'll fuck you like this another night, when you're ready. *Si?*"

I nod, my pulse still fluttering frantically. My eyes meet Lennox's, searching for the same promise from him. He nods and brings his hand from under the blanket to stroke a strand of hair off my damp cheek where Maddox was kissing. "Trust us?"

I swallow and then slowly nod. Lennox smiles and scoots in, and I can feel the heat of his rigid cock through the thin material of my pants. His lips meet mine, his kiss gentle and coaxing, bringing me back to them after Maddox's overly domineering treatment spooked me. Lennox's hand cups my breast, massaging until my nipples harden and I squirm for more, for him to squeeze my nipple the way his brother did.

Maddox lifts my knee, opening my thighs, and rolls his hips against mine, pushing me forward onto Lennox's cock. Lennox moans and grinds against the damp softness between my thighs. Without breaking the kiss, he moves his fingers inwards, finding my nipple and tugging, stretching it. My clit throbs so hard I gasp, and he slides his tongue into my mouth, fucking me with his tongue the way he did in the bedroom, grinding slowly against me in the same rhythm.

I'm so hot I think I'll explode when Maddox's hand dips under my shirt, his fingers sliding along the soft skin of my belly before dipping into my pants. I squirm against their bodies that hold me pinned between them, so aroused I barely feel the deep ache of my bruises. I think I'll burst into flame at any moment. Maddox slides his hand lower, into the front of my panties. He spreads my lips open, his finger skimming over my clit. My whole body rocks and shudders in response. No one's ever touched me there before, and it's more than I could have dreamed.

Lennox pushes forward, then pauses when he feels his brother's hand between us.

"Are you fingering her?" he asks.

"Fuck yeah," Maddox says, his breath coming short, his grip on my head tightening again, holding me in place while he strokes through my slit and rubs the pad of his finger over my untouched opening. "She's so fucking wet."

"Let me see," Lennox says, throwing back the blankets to watch me be touched for the first time. In all my life, I never would have imagined the first time I did something intimate, it would be with another person there. My instinct is to pull the blanket back, to cover my bruised skin and hide myself like I always have. But when his eyes burn with lust at the sight of his twin's hand moving in my panties, heat pulses between my thighs, and new wetness slicks Maddox's fingers.

"You like that, little girl?" Maddox asks with a taunting edge to his voice as he explores me with sensuous, teasing strokes.

I catch a glimpse of Lennox's bare cock, standing straight and dark against his belly, and I know he must have taken it out and been stroking himself earlier. Then Maddox yanks my head back by the hair, making tears blur my eyes. Twisting my face towards his, he takes my mouth roughly, devouring my cry of protest. Lennox pulls my pants and underwear down over my hips, then sits up and pulls them off my feet, discarding them beside the bed while I'm silenced by Maddox's kiss.

When he lies back, Lennox grips the hem of my shirt and pulls it off over my head, leaving my bruised body bare between them. They're still clothed, and it makes me feel even more naked, exposed to their hands and hungry gazes. I'm self-conscious, but somehow the shame only makes me hotter as I realize how much I enjoy being at their mercy, being wanted so badly. I've always liked being in control, having my feet on the ground, but somehow the exhilaration of flying, falling, being helpless between them sends me spiraling not into terror but into eager anticipation.

Lennox lifts my knee, spreading my thighs to watch his brother's fingers open me and smear over the sensitive bud of my clit. Another moment of self-consciousness freezes my body as he watches someone do the most intimate thing that's ever been done to me, see the most intimate place on my body spread open for his examination. To my utter humiliation, it makes more blood rush to my center, my wetness increasing again.

I want to hide my face. What is wrong with me?

Maddox groans when he feels the increased arousal, stopping long enough to shove down the top of his jeans. His bare, hot cock presses to my cool skin, and I gasp in shock, my clit throbbing against his fingers.

"Ah, fuck," he breathes. "You're going to make me cum all over you, aren't you, little girl?"

"Not yet," Lennox says, and I can barely see from the edge of my vision as he grips his long, thick shaft and begins to stroke himself. "Spread her cunt so I can see how wet she is."

My head is spinning, my body throbbing with pleasure. The hunger in Lennox's gaze combined with the expert strokes of Maddox's fingers and their dirty words drives me mad.

"Maddox," I gasp, my hips trembling against his, straining for relief.

"Good fucking girl," he breathes, rhythmically pumping his cock against my ass and teasing my entrance with the tip of his finger. "I'm right here. You're doing so well. Now say my name again. Say it while I bury a finger in this sweet little cunt and make your cum rain down on us."

"Maddox," I say again, shuddering against him as he pushes the tip of his finger inside me. I'm so wet and ready it barely hurts, only a twinge of pain as he works it deeper, pushing in slow and letting me adjust.

"Fuck," he groans, his words strangled by desire. His breath is hot and heavy against my cheek as he grips my head in his arm, his muscles shaking. His cock throbs against my ass, the bare length of it biting into my crack. "Oh fuck, little girl. You feel so fucking good."

"Is she tight?" Lennox asks, jerking his cock faster and moving in closer. "Move your hand so I can feel her too."

"So fucking tight," Maddox breathes, laying his cheek on mine. *"Ella es caliente."* He spreads my legs wider, pushing my knee up and adjusting the angle of his hand without withdrawing his finger. I can feel it pushed up deep inside me, squeezed snugly inside my walls. Tension builds in my core, and I want to scream with how good I feel right now. And then Lennox pushes his hips against mine, grinding the base of his cock against my clit.

"Oh god," I moan. "Lennox…"

"Feel how wet she is," Maddox says through rapid breaths.

I whimper out loud, not sure how long I can last before I shatter. Lennox grips his cock, pulling the skin back and sliding the tip around my slippery clit and then through my folds, mingling our arousal. Maddox curls his finger inside me, slowly pulsing it until I see stars. I grip Lennox's shoulder, panting as my hips spasm and a throbbing ache builds inside my core, where Maddox is tormenting me with a skillful finger.

Maddox takes a few ragged breaths before turning to whisper in my ear. "Are you a virgin, little girl?"

I nod, my face burning with shame. "Yes."

Maddox curses in Spanish, his finger convulsing inside me, his hips jerking forward, the ridge of his cock throbbing against my ass. He yanks my head back, gripping my hair so tightly my mouth drops open in wordless agony. Warm, thick liquid spurts onto my back.

It's so shocking, so dirty, that it snaps the last thread of my control. I cry out, bucking between the twins, who both push inward at once, pinning my bruised body between their hips.

"Shhh," Lennox says, covering my mouth with his hand and forcing me to keep the cries of pleasure inside. It only intensifies the sensations rolling through me, as if making sound would let the pleasure out into the world. Lennox forces me to keep it all in, building inside my body as he grinds the base of his cock against my clit, sending another wave of orgasm through me.

"Feel her cum with me," Maddox says, sliding his finger out. I make a muffled cry of protest behind Lennox's hand, but the next second, two fingers strain at my entrance. They both push a finger in at once, stretching me so far I think I'll tear apart. The pleasure and pain overwhelm me. I can't think about anything, not even what they're doing to me. My toes curl, my core clenches, and my vision goes dim as I cum, and cum, and cum.

I'm overwhelmed by them, the amount of pleasure being forced into me, the fact that it's both of them, the pleasure, the pain, the shame and vulnerability of being naked while they're clothed, being watched as their fingers fuck me, the filthiness of feeling Maddox's hot cum running down my back, my helplessness as Maddox holds my head and they both use my body at once. I can't stop coming.

I'm still trembling and shaking, pulses fluttering through me, when Maddox turns and kisses my sweaty temple. "*Dios mio*, woman," he says through labored breaths. "I don't think I can call you little girl anymore. You cum like a fucking porn star."

Lennox pulls his finger out and slides a hand around the curve of my backside and down into my crack.

"Use my cum," Maddox says, scooting back.

The sticky wetness of his cum on my back is instantly cold when it hits the air, but my body's so feverish with heat and sweat that it feels good. Lennox smears his finger through it, then scoots in, tugging my knee over his hip to secure me against him. I gasp when he pushes his slick finger against the knot of my rear entrance. I tense, and he groans and pushes hard, breaching the opening and sinking his finger all the way in. It feels so weird, and I'm so shocked, I don't even move.

"You're taking us so well," Lennox says, pumping in and out, fucking my asshole with his finger while his brother's finger is still inside my cunt. "You feel so fucking good. Do we feel good to you, Sunshine?"

"Yes," I whisper, my face heating at the admission. But god, it does, once I adjust to the new sensation.

"Good," he says, thrusting harder, his jaw going tight. "Because in a minute I'm going to ram my cock in this dirty little hole and wreck your virgin ass while Maddox rips open your virgin cunt and fucks it raw at the same time. Our mother's just in the other room, so you better not fucking scream. You keep your pretty mouth shut, or we'll slit your throat before we fill every hole in your body with cum and then bury you in the backyard."

I start to struggle, but Maddox pulls his hand from between my legs and clamps it over my mouth. I can smell myself on his hand with each frantic breath I draw as he holds my head with both hands while Lennox keeps elbowing my knee aside when I try to close my legs. He pushes his hips in close, and I cry out behind his brother's hand when I feel the head of Lennox's hard cock nudging at my entrance.

I squeeze my eyes closed, tears spurting from my lids.

"Let me see those pretty hazel eyes, and I might go easy on you," Lennox croons, his finger pumping hard and fast into my ass.

I open my eyes, blinking away tears of terror, my mouth still silenced by his brother's bruising grip. I make a muffled sound of fear, my breaths heaving, my back crushed to the wall of Maddox's massive chest. Lennox groans and pushes forward, the head of his cock straining against my tightness before slipping in my wetness and grinding up through my slit.

"Oh fuck yeah," he manages before his hips jerk in a spasm. He grabs his cock, aiming it and letting warm, sticky liquid flow from the tip and over my clit, down through my slit, my folds, bathing my pussy in his cum.

Maddox releases my mouth and leans up on his elbow, pulling my knees open to watch. I burn with humiliation as he slides his hand down the inside of my thigh and spreads my pussy open, watching cum trickle through my folds. Lennox pushes the head of his cock firmly against my entrance again, squeezing a drop inside me when his cock throbs again. They both groan at the same time, and I feel Maddox's cock nudge against my back again, already hard a second time.

"Let me fuck it into her," Lennox says, straining against my entrance until I feel the slick head stretching me. "I want to fuck her to death."

Maddox shoves his shoulder, pushing him back. "Not tonight," he snaps. Then he slicks his finger through Lennox's cum and slides it deep inside me with one strong, powerful thrust. His thumb slicks rhythmically over my clit while the finger inside me crooks forward, stroking the spot inside me that makes stars appear in my vision. Lennox ads a second finger and grinds the other one deep in my ass at the same time. Soul crushing shame crashes over me as I lose control of my body and cum again, whimpering and sobbing with humiliation even as my limbs tremble and my core clenches and pulses around their fingers.

When I'm done, Lennox rolls away with a chuckle, letting his hand rest on his chest as it rises and falls with his rapid breathing. "That was fucking hot," he says to the ceiling. "The way you looked at me made me go *loco*, Rae."

The credits are rolling on the movie that we stopped watching a long time ago.

A shuddering sob escapes me, my body quaking, my cheeks aching from Maddox's grip.

"Fuck," Maddox says, relaxing his grip on my head and releasing my knee. "*Vení.* You good, *o qué?*"

He strokes back my hair and kisses just in front of my ear, trying to roll me so he can see my face. I cover it with both hands, curling into a ball. I can feel his cum on my back, but it doesn't feel hot and dirty anymore. I can feel Lennox's cum wetting my pubic hair and trickling down my hips crease in both directions. My ass is sore, and my core feels achy and raw from their fingers.

"*Vení*, Rae," Lennox says, rolling toward me and stroking my arm. "Don't be upset. I didn't mean any of that. It's just something that gets me off, *sí?* I thought you knew. I told you to trust me, that we weren't going to fuck you. I mean, I wanted to. God, I wanted to cum inside you just now, even if I just put the tip in…"

I don't say anything because for one, how would I know to trust that promise when afterwards he started saying other horrible things he was going to do to me. Secondly, I'm too humiliated by my response, crying like a stupid little virgin, to even show my face.

"Asshole," Maddox says, shoving Lennox before lying back, pulling me into his arms. I curl into him and breathe in the stormy summer smell of his skin, seeking some comfort, even if it's from the people who hurt me. "Listen, *mi cariña*, you're not a crew girl. I wouldn't let my brother hurt you any more than anyone else. You're safe here. We just wanted to make you feel good."

"I'm sorry," Lennox says. "I should have gone to sleep without getting off. I just felt you coming, and it felt so good, I wanted to do it too. But I'd never hurt you. I promise." He scoots in on the other side, and they cocoon me between them like something precious.

I begin to relax, but I can't turn my mind off. When they're both asleep, I wriggle out from between them and pull on the pants Lennox lent me. Then I creep to the door. I step outside and hesitate. The rain has stopped, and the grass sparkles with a thin layer of ice. If I pull the door closed behind me, it'll lock. I won't be able to go back if things are shitty at home.

But this isn't my house.

After a few hours of distance, I feel stupid and naïve for freaking out about their treatment. I came. Maddox came. Of course Lennox should be able to come too. It's not fair to be mad about it. They did all that for me. I know if I were anyone else, a crew girl or even Scarlet, they would have fucked me. But they didn't because I said I wasn't ready. They respected that. I'm grateful they distracted me from my fears, that they made me cum so hard I think my soul left my body for a minute.

I'm grateful they took me in when they saw what Lee had done, without me even having to say it. Maddox saw my bruise-free body at school earlier, so he knew the marks were new, and he put it together and spared me the humiliation of trying to explain it. Lennox gave me clothes and made me feel comfortable. And yeah, his dirty talk was rough, but what did I expect? They're in a gang, for fuck's sake. They gangbang girls to initiate them into their Murder of Crows.

I'm not one of those girls, though. I don't know what I was thinking, how I let myself get so carried away, so hypnotized by their touch. I know better now.

I run across the lawn, the ice-glazed grass crunching under my bare feet, and let myself in the back door. Then I sneak up to my room and change into my own pajamas, not sure if Lee is home. He'd murder me if he saw me in a boy's pajamas, if he knew what I let them do to me.

I shove Lennox's cum-stained pajamas into the bottom of my closet and crawl into bed. The sheets are cold, the bed empty and lonely after being held in two pairs of protective arms for a few hours. I hate that I miss them already, hate that I need them to hold me, want them to wrap me up and keep me safe and warm. But I'm not part of their world, part of their crew. I have to get by on my own. They have each other, a whole gang at their backs. I only have me.

They're a murder of crows.

I'm a murder of one.

seventeen

Maddox North

"We should initiate her," Lennox says, turning up the box of Waffle Crisp and filling his bowl.

Our eyes meet, and an understanding passes between us. She needs protection. We can't protect her from someone living under her own roof, though. Not while she's living there. It makes the most sense. I know it's the right thing to do.

But a dozen jerk-off fantasies flood my mind, and my cock stiffens again even though I just took care of it in the shower. Rae riding me, her achingly tight cunt milking every drop of cum from my cock. Rae sitting on my face, her thighs shaking as she cries my name while I taste her sweet cunt, fuck her with my tongue until her cum runs down my chin. Rae smiling up at me with that coy smile, that pouty little mouth just begging to be fucked hard and deep.

What the fuck is wrong with me?

"She's a fucking virgin," I snap, grabbing the cereal and dumping it into my bowl. Half of it misses, and the little yellow discs scatter across the surface of the table.

"So we break her in before the crew takes their turn," Lennox says, watching me sweep the mess back into my bowl.

I know he's right, it's the best way to protect her, but the thought of all those guys… I picture her perfect, untouched body laid out before them, her delicate, rosebud pink nipples and ivory skin looking so fucking innocent. I picture her wild, dark hair spread out around her head, that fuck-me look in her eyes and the saucy little smirk on her pink lips.

The crew would fucking go nuts for her. I picture fifteen men seeing every inch of her, spreading her legs and stabbing into her, feeling the tight squeeze of her slick cunt, hearing her soft moans and watching her tears fall as they use her one after another, coming in her hot core until cum runs out of wrecked, gaping cunt like blood from a wound.

"No," I say, shaking my head and frowning at my brother. I can't believe he'd even suggest it. "She's too good for that."

"Then she's too good for us," he says quietly.

"Yeah," I say, dumping milk into my bowl and ignoring the way he's watching me. "We both knew that already."

Lennox takes a bite and chews, not speaking for a long minute. I wait, knowing it's coming. "Since when do you give a fuck whether a girl's too good for you? It's never stopped you from fucking one before."

I shrug. "You expect me to convince every chick with issues that I'm really not what she needs? If she wants to get on her knees for me, who am I to deny her? Her self-esteem is her problem."

He shakes his head. "That's what I'm talking about."

"What?" I ask. "It's free hot pussy. Not everyone's going to say no to that, Saint Lennox."

"I'm no saint," he growls. "As you know all too fucking well."

I remember Rae's tears last night when he said the shit he likes to say to chicks when we bang them. Dude's got more issues than the girls who throw themselves on my dick. I must have just as many, because it was worth her tears to watch his cum bathe her sweet little virgin pussy, pour over her swollen pink clit, drip through her folds.

"That makes two of us," I say, reaching down to adjust myself since now I'm hard as a fucking rock. "What's your point?"

"My point is, *that's* how you treat girls," he says. "Why do you care if we initiate Rae? She didn't even care enough to stick around for breakfast. She ducked out while we were sleeping."

"I don't fucking care," I snap. "I just don't think she's a good fit. She's not tough enough to be a Crow."

Lennox looks less than convinced, which just pisses me off more. The truth is, Rae's tough as hell. When people fucked with her for the first few months of school, she walked around like it didn't bother her one bit. She's been taking a beating from her piece of shit stepfather for who the fuck knows how long, and she dealt with her shit on her own, not making it anyone else's problem. She would have kept dealing with it and never asked for a hand up, if we hadn't found out on our own.

But that doesn't mean I'm going to share her with the whole crew. Fuck that. I know she's tough enough, but fuck if I'm letting any of those bastards get their hands on her. Yeah, they're my boys, my *parceros.* But they'll treat her exactly the way they treat all the crew girls, the way we all threat them. The way I treat every girl.

I don't know why I fucking care, but I do. I want her for myself, and it fucking pisses me off.

I turn up my bowl, draining the sugary milk before wiping my mouth on the back of my hand. "I'm going to go set up the office for her, in case she needs a place to stay again. That way she'll be out of reach of that asshole *and* us. Both of us. She needs protection, not a spit roast. We've got crew girls for that."

"Whatever," Lennox grumbles, looking pissed that he won't get to hunt the sweet treat next door and devour his prey once he catches her. I'm just as pissed about not getting to fuck her, but I can control myself. I'm not an animal.

THE RAIN KING

eighteen

#1 on the Billboard Chart:
"Truly Madly Deeply"—Savage Garden

Rae West

"Do you think she'll end up here?" Marilyn asks, glancing over her shoulder. "I mean, I'd vote her into the Club for sure."

"Nah," Lexi says, biting into her tepid, paper-thin hamburger and watching three girls head for their table. "The Crows will take care of her."

The girls slide in next to the North twins, and I focus in on who they are. The girls in their Murder of Crows. A stab of jealousy goes through me. Not that I've tried to prove myself or done any extraordinary feats to get into their gang. I don't want to be a Crow.

I just hate feeling left out, like I'm an outsider they're keeping at arm's length. Since the night on their living room floor, I've felt too awkward to go over. They never came over to get me, either. Of course not. Lee would kill us all if they tried.

"Who?" I ask, prying open my burger so I won't look too interested. A film of the bun remains on the brown, bumpy meat substance. I drown it in ketchup and mustard, so I won't taste the nasty cafeteria fare.

"Mariana," Lexi says. "She's pregnant."

"I wonder who the father is," Lola muses. "Think she knows?"

"She's been with Reggie Thomas since before Christmas," Lexi says. "I bet it's his."

"Wait, the Crows date?" I ask.

"Obviously," Lola says with a grin.

"I thought they just passed the girls around."

"Yeah, but if they get interested in a girl, they'll call off the others," Lexi says. "Billy says they all respect that, if one of them gets attached and wants a girl for himself."

"Huh," I say, watching the Crows' table. "How'd Billy get in anyway? He doesn't live in our neighborhood."

"He did when he joined," Lexi says. "Before his mom and him moved in with us."

"Of course, we don't know how far along she is," Marilyn says, still focusing on Mariana. "She was all over Maddox last fall, and he always shares with Lennox. But if Reggie dumps her and she needs a place to hang, I say we take her in. You know people are going to talk."

My stomach turns, and I drop my burger and push my tray away. Is it one of my boys'?

And when did I start thinking of them as mine? I have no right to them. They've already done far more for me than I deserve. And I know they're experienced, that Maddox sleeps around and Lennox at least hooks up with crew girls. It's not like I expect them to become monks because a dumb little virgin moved in next door.

But the thought of either of them getting a girl pregnant… That's permanent.

Even if he doesn't marry her, he'd be off limits in some way. I'd lose him forever. I'm not sure which one would devastate me more, if I lost one of my Crows.

Which is stupid. They're not mine. I'm not even sure we're friends. I haven't talked to them since the night in their living room, a night that feels like it happened in a dream, under the cover of darkness. It's like it never happened, that impossibly filthy thing we did together. If none of us ever acknowledge it, and the only witnesses are Skeet Ulrich and Matthew Lillard, did it really happen at all?

The day after I spent the night at the Norths' house, Mom went to get Lee from the hospital in the middle of the day. She never told him I was gone all night. Maybe she didn't even notice, having bigger things to worry about. Lee came home with both arms in full, white casts bent at the elbows. The first sight of him made my stomach turn. Maddox did that.

But then I thought how he'd done it for me, and my belly filled with warmth, and I could hardly keep from smiling at the perfect, poetic justice he dealt out.

Unable to use his hands for much of anything, Lee's been a nightmare, but he can't even feed himself, let alone beat the shit out of us. I still have no idea how Maddox pulled it off without getting shot or arrested.

I waited for him to come check on me, for one of them to. Which is dumb, since I snuck out on them. I'm the one who should have gone back, thanked them for taking me in, for what they did for me. But I felt way too awkward about it, and I didn't want to look needy and have them make fun of me or treat me the way they treat Scarlet. I hoped that, since they're experienced and they knew I wasn't, that they'd check in. Even after the weird note the night ended on, I expected… Something.

But that's expecting them to be boyfriend material, and everyone knows they're not. They're not going to get attached after one kiss, one hookup where we didn't even go all the way. That's my problem to deal with.

So, I sat in my window seat during Christmas break, reading *The Green Mile,* which I'd been waiting to read since it came out, but it was always checked out from the library. I finally got it, which gave me an excuse to sit up there and feed Poe and spy on the neighbor's house like a complete stalker.

I know Maddox's schedule, when he runs, and I could have gone at the same time and pretended it was a coincidence. Instead, I hid in my room like a coward, too awkward to face him after what they'd done to me, how much they'd seen of me. And more than that, how they'd treated me, and how I'd reacted. I don't know how the crew girls can ever face them again, let alone sit with them every day like it's nothing to feel their hands on you, in you, all over you. To know they've seen you and touched you and whispered things in your ear that make you blush so hard you think your skin will peel like a sunburn.

That afternoon, I climb off the bus at the stop right in front of my house. I wave to Reggie, who's outside sweeping his driveway and looking sullen about the chore. I wonder if he's brooding about Mariana's baby. He tips his chin at me, and I resist the urge to check the Norths' house as I walk up the short, cracked sidewalk to my front steps. The white paint is mostly worn off our wide, wooden front steps, and one of them is rotting along the center of the board. I'm busy thinking about whether I should replace it before Lee asks when I reach the top step and pull up short, a scream lodging in my throat.

A black lump lies on the welcome mat, looking so small and insignificant you'd never know she was so bossy and demanding, so full of bravado and sass and life. But the moment I see her, I know.

"Poe," I cry, racing forward and falling to my knees. Tears clog my throat as I gently lift her body. It's still warm, but not enough. Not nearly enough.

"No," I whisper, my voice trembling, my hands shaking so hard that I can hardly hold her.

Her head hangs at an unnatural angle, flopping down instead of staying intact with her body, and the fine feathers around her neck are crushed and bent.

I hold her gently, as if I could spook her now, as if I could hurt her. Tears blur my eyes and trickle down my cheeks as I stroke her beautiful black feathers, so much softer than I imagined before I touched her the first time.

Over winter break, she reluctantly allowed me to pet her silky feathers once or twice before she'd hop away and watch me distrustfully. Now I can pet her, but it's only with a rising sense of horror. It's too late. There's no triumph in it, only the finality of it, the realization that she'll never look at me with consternation again.

She'd never let me hold her this way if she was alive.

I stroke her side, my shoulders shaking with sobs. Only her wing feathers are stiff. Feathers that should have helped her fly away from danger, not toward it. Did she fly into the door?

That's impossible, though. Our door is heavy wood, with no windows. She wouldn't fly into a solid door. She wouldn't even fly into my window. Would she?

On trembling legs, I stand. Cradling her gently in my arm, I open the door and enter the house. The smell of smoke hangs in the air, the haze coming from the living room where Lee now sits all day, barking orders at my mother and watching TV. He can't work, and the investigation into his attack hasn't led anywhere yet. Apparently Maddox jumped him from behind when he was going to his squad car for something. He knelt on his back and broke both his arms and then left Lee lying in the freezing rain.

Now Mom rushes from the living room toward the kitchen with an empty plate and a glass. She stops when she sees me. "Oh—honey," she says. "What's that?"

"Poe," I say, my voice cracking. "My… My bird."

I don't know how to tell my mother what she really is, that she's so much more than a bird. She was my only company for most of the summer, my comfort when I was filled with helpless fury or loneliness, when the North brothers wouldn't leave our pool or stop using it. She was there for me every time I exiled myself to my room to let the bruises fade. She listened to me rant about Lee and confess stupid, naïve fantasies about the North brothers. When I felt left out, she came to see me on the regular. With her, I wasn't a murder of one.

"Get that rodent out of here," Lee calls, though he can't even see us from his spot in front of the TV. "I told you, those birds are a nuisance."

Cold fury settles into my bones, and I step into the doorway to face him. "Did you do this?" I ask, my voice trembling with rage now.

"It probably flew into your window," he says, not bothering to look my way. "It's right above that porch. That's what happens when you teach a dumb animal to get food from your hand."

I swallow hard, staring down at her lifeless form, so small and vulnerable. Did I do this? Is it my fault for teaching her to come to my window?

"But then how'd she get onto the porch?" I ask, my voice small. "She would have been on the roof outside my window, not under the awning on our doorstep."

"She probably flopped her way up there," Lee says. "Birds do that after you wring their necks. That's how you know they got no brains. They'll keep running around even without a head on their necks."

"She was smart," I whisper.

"Sure she was," he says. "That's what we'd say about the chickens, but they'd still walk right up to us and let us grab their heads. You pick 'em up like that, whip 'em straight down, and the neck snaps like kindling."

He turns his cold eyes to me, staring at me from beneath the ridge of his jutting brow, as if challenging me to contradict him. To accuse him. I let my finger run over the bent feathers on her neck, and my gorge rises. Lee's hands aren't in the cast. He can still grab things.

On stiff legs, I turn and walk up the stairs to my room. I don't know what I'd do if I stayed there, where I can see that terrible man.

I sit on the bed, staring at the window where so many days I put out bread for Poe. I never should have fed her. I should have chased her away and shut the window in her face, locked her out and never let her get close. She was a wild animal, and I tamed her so I'd have company, never knowing that it came with dangers, just like letting a human close comes with dangers.

This wasn't an accident. It was an execution. A warning.

If it weren't for me, she'd be flying free, soaring through the ice blue January sky.

Now she's dead. Not because I taught her to fly into the window and break her neck, but because I taught her to trust humans, to fly to my hand to get food. That's how I killed her.

I should have known Lee would never let me have anything that brought me so much comfort, so much joy. Something he couldn't take away from me.

Carefully, I lay her on the cushion in my reading nook. I open my drawers and pull out my three full composition notebooks, a handful of my favorite T-shirts, a few pairs of jeans, and enough socks and underwear to get me through a week. After reconstructing a box that's been flattened in my closet since the move, I shove my things inside, line the edge of the box with a few fat paperbacks, and look around. Then I grab my pillow and lay it on top, carefully transferring Poe's body onto it before donning my heaviest jacket and my school backpack. I cast one longing glance at my lovely window nook before turning my back on my room for the last time.

"Where are you going?" Mom asks when I reach the bottom of the stairs.

"Away," I say flatly. "I can't live in the house with that monster anymore."

"She's running away from home because her bird died," Lee mocks with a harsh chuckle. "Let her go, Maren. She'll be back in an hour."

"Fuck you," I say, glaring at him. I'm not afraid of him anymore. He can't hurt me with his arms in mummy casts. Not the way he used to, anyway.

His eyes narrow, and his jaw clenches. "What did you say, girl?"

"I said, fuck you," I repeat. My heart is skittering crazily inside my chest, but I have to do this. If I don't do it now, I might get cold and come back like he said. If I tell him what I think of him now, there's no going back. He'll wait, biding his time, until the casts are off, and then he'll break my neck the way he did that person he arrested. The way he did Poe.

"You ungrateful little slut," he growls, struggling to rise by leaning the forearm of his cast on the arm of his chair.

"What do I have to be grateful for?" I ask. "You murdering my pet? Beating the shit out of me and Mom? You're lucky she cooks the meals around here. I'd have put poison in your soup a long time ago."

Lee's face turns red, his bushy brows drawing together into a unibrow. "Get out of my house," he bellows. "And if you ever set foot in here again, I swear to god…"

"You'll snap my neck like those chickens you killed on your farm as a kid?" I ask. "Are you going to eat my corpse so there's no evidence? Or just pretend it was an accident? We all know your friends down at the precinct will take your side. That's how it works, right? Don't cross the blue line or some shit?"

"Out," he thunders.

"Gladly," I say, starting for the back door. "Don't fall down the stairs while you're all clumsy with those casts on. I'd hate to see you die a quick death without much suffering."

I wish I had a free hand just so I could flip him off on my way out the door, like I always imagined. I figured I'd wait it out until I graduated, but plans change.

I stride out the back door and slam it shut behind me. I'm too proud to beg someone for shelter, even the Norths, so I head for the shed. Inside, I make a little pallet of my clothes and shiver through the night in my jacket.

nineteen

Rae West

I make it an entire week before I run out of clothes and my hair is greasy enough that I'm afraid Mrs. Peterson is going to call me into her office and offer me deodorant. Finally, I gather all my dirty clothes, shove them in my backpack, and head next door after school. Maddox has basketball practice, and Lennox's car isn't out front, so they won't know. I stand under the tiny awning over the front door, trying to stay out of the drizzling rain, until Valeria pulls up in her gold Ford Taurus.

She steps out of the car and picks her way up the cracked walkway to the front door, jumping over a puddle that's formed near the front step. She's wearing a Hastings shirt, her black hair pulled back in a low ponytail. "Rae," she says, smiling at me as she unlocks the front door. "The boys aren't here. Is everything okay?"

"Yeah, fine," I say, following her in. "It's just, our washing machine broke, and I was wondering if I could wash a few clothes? I'm so sorry to bother you, but we only have the one car, and Lee can't drive with his casts on, so we can't go to a laundromat…"

"Of course, of course," she says. "You don't even have to ask, *chica*. You come over any time you need. *Venga*, I'll show you where it is."

After the clothes are loaded, I stare down at my muddy shoes, curling my toes inside. "Thank you so much," I say. "I don't want to ask for more, but, like… Would it be weird if I took a shower here? Just while my clothes are washing, so I don't have to sit here and do nothing until they're done. I mean, it's not a big deal, I can wait until I get home…"

"Rae," she says, taking my hand. When I meet her gaze, I see such sympathy that tears spring to my eyes. "Go right ahead. Any time you need. And you know we're right here if you need anything else. Our house may not be big and fancy like yours, but we have everything you need inside."

She squeezes my hand before letting go. I turn and flee, ashamed of my tears, my neediness. I curse myself for asking. Of course that's weird. Of course she knows something's going on. But even though it's cold so I'm not a gross, sweaty mess, a week without a shower is way too long. I don't even know what I'm going to do when I get my period. I'm going to have to shower in the locker room, and that will be a whole other nightmare. I was too embarrassed to do it this week, but this may be even worse.

Still, I don't have to worry about people staring and giggling and whispering while I shower here. The water is warm and heavenly. I've never been so relieved in my life. I scrub every inch of myself clean, borrow one of the twins' razors, and shave my legs and armpits. After a moment's hesitation, I turn my back to the warm spray and slather some shaving cream along the creases of my legs and onto my thighs, shaving the edges of my pubes until I'm neatly trimmed.

I know I shouldn't be using the guys' razor for this, but this will save me at least a bit of humiliation when I have to shower in the locker room at school. As I shave inwards a bit, I can't help the thoughts that creep into my mind. One of the guys has had this razor on his face. One of them will shave his face with this again, after it's shaved me down there.

A naughty little thrill runs through me, and tingles of excitement bloom between my legs.

I shave a neat landing strip, then rinse out the razor. I don't want to get out yet, don't want the precious shower to be over. I make sure there's no hair left in the tub, then run my fingers along the newly bare skin. My clit throbs, and I sink back against the wall of the shower, closing my eyes and letting my head fall back, the warm water sluicing down my body, over my breasts. My nipples harden at the attention, and I slip my finger inwards, between my lips and into my slit.

Valeria said they have everything I need in their house. God, she's so right.

Biting my lip so I don't moan, I let the warm water run down my hand and over the exposed flesh. I picture Maddox walking in, seeing me like this. I picture him stepping into the shower, fully clothed, grabbing my head and kissing me the way he did, like he was fucking the mouth of a blowup doll. My own wetness coats my fingers, and I slowly push a finger inside. I've rubbed my clit and gotten off before, but I've never done this, never felt what Maddox felt that night. I remember his sounds of pleasure at how tight I was, how he whispered in my ear, asking if I was a virgin. How he came on my back when I told him I was.

Suddenly, we're not alone in the shower. His brother is watching, like he did that night. I ride my hand, Maddox's hand, moaning for relief. I watch Lennox's warm, golden eyes heat to molten as Maddox bites my ear, the skin of my jaw.

"Fuck me," I whisper.

Lennox drops his clothes and steps into the shower with us. He slides in behind me, his warm, bare body against mine, his arm snaking down the front of my body. It's his hand that squeezes my breast, pinching and stretching my nipple until I whimper. Maddox leans down, and Lennox pushes it between his hungry lips. Maddox sucks a mouthful of my flesh into his mouth with my nipple, and I moan, rocking my hips faster, fucking my fingers as I imagine it's them.

It's Maddox's finger curling inside me, finding the spot he found on the floor that night. It's Lennox's finger, not my second one, that stretches me open to join his brother's. It's his thumb on my clit, rubbing as he pushes his cock to my ass the way Maddox did last time.

I remember his horrible words, but they only make me hot when it's not real. In my imagination, when I'm safe and alone, it's the sexiest thing I've ever heard as he whispers in my ear. He fists his cock, slicking it with soap, and then pushes it down, entering me from behind. He grips my hair, pulling my head back and thrusting roughly into my ass while his other hand reaches around me, spreading me open.

"Take her virginity," he tells his brother. Maddox leans down over my upturned face, taking my mouth again while he wraps my legs around his hips and forces his cock past my entrance. I buck against them as they fill me at once, each of them driving into me and driving me deeper onto the other's cock, impaling me until I'm panting and crying out, lost in bliss as they push me over the edge.

I come back to myself slowly, gasping for breath. The echo of my cry bounces around the empty bathroom. Shit. Did I do that out loud? And did I really just make myself cum in their shower? What is wrong with me?

I quickly wash and climb out, shame burning through me as I towel off. Realizing I have no clean clothes in here, I wrap the towel securely around myself, wind my dirty clothes into a ball, and step out of the bathroom, steam billowing with me. Humiliation slams into me so hard I stumble backwards, catching myself on the bathroom door when I see I'm not alone.

Maddox stands in the doorway of their room, his muscular arms folded over his even more muscular chest, a smirk firmly in place as he watches me. "Hey, little girl," he drawls. "Enjoying that showerhead, were you?"

"You—you scared me," I manage.

"Nah," he says. "I know what you look like when you're scared, and this isn't it. This is post-orgasm afterglow."

"I—I wasn't," I blurt. "I was just showering off while I waited for my clothes."

"Sure you were," he says, pushing off the doorframe and prowling closer. "Or maybe you were fingering that tight little cunt, imagining what I would do to it if you weren't such a good little girl."

"I'm not a little girl," I say, swallowing hard but refusing to back up a step when he closes in on me until he's only a step away. "I'm eighteen."

He snorts. "Next month."

I narrow my eyes at him. "How do you know that?"

"You live in *la olla*," he says, reaching out to finger the edge of my towel, his knuckles barely brushing the skin on my thigh. Even the barest touch makes my head swim. A smile plays on his lips, and his eyes shutter to half closed as he smirks down at me. "I know everything about you, little girl."

"Everything?" I whisper, my skin heating as I remember his eyes on me as he pushed up to watch his brother's cum melt over my spread pussy.

He tugs gently at the edge of the towel and leans down, the movement as smooth and hypnotizing as a snake. His hand rises to grip my jaw, and he moves my head to one side, angling his face in so his lips brush my ear.

"Everything except how you taste," he whispers, his voice a deep masculine growl that sends blood coursing to my core and goosebumps cascading over every inch of my skin. His tongue slides out, dipping into my ear and flicking against my ear hole.

Chills explode through me, and I cringe down, giggling at the strange, ticklish sensation. "How my ear tastes?" I tease, rubbing it with my shoulder.

Maddox chuckles and releases my jaw, straightening to stare down at me again. "How your cunt tastes."

The laughter dies on my lips, and I gulp down my nerves, searching his gaze. We stand there a moment, tension crackling in the air between us, every blood cell in my body blooming like a firework in the night sky on the Fourth of July.

"Maddox?" I whisper, my voice suddenly deserting me.

"Are you scared?"

I nod slowly, grateful I don't have to answer aloud.

He chuckles and leans in, pressing his lips to my forehead. "Some other time, then," he says. "Though if you keep coming over to finger yourself in my shower, I can't promise I won't come in next time and give you something to really moan about."

Before I can answer, the washing machine beeps, and I escape down the hall. The washer and dryer are stacked in an alcove off the kitchen, and I can feel Maddox's eyes on me, still watching as I switch the load over into the dryer and make small talk with Valeria. When I finish, Maddox gestures for me to follow and steps into their bedroom. I retrace my steps down the hall, wary of what I'll find. But when I reach his room, he's coming back with a pair of Adidas pants and an oversized Wampus Cat shirt with his number on the back.

"You sure you don't mind lending me this?" I ask, picking up the shirt. "It looks like something important."

He jerks his chin toward their room. "Put it on."

I start to turn toward the bathroom, but he stops me. "Where you going, little girl?"

"To change?"

"Here," he orders, hooking his thumb toward the bedroom.

"I'm not going to change in front of you," I say, my skin prickling with heat.

He smirks. "Seen it all before, little girl. Many, many, *many* times."

"Ugh, you're such a manwhore," I say, stepping past him. He catches my arm, swings me around into their bedroom, and closes the door behind us.

Leaning against the door, he crosses his arms and looks down at me. "Strip for me, little girl. Or if you'd rather, I can strip you."

I glare at him, anger and defiance rising in me. If he wants to see me, fine. It's not like he hasn't seen something a lot more intimate than me changing clothes.

I open the towel and let it drop to my feet, standing in front of Maddox completely bare, refusing to cover myself with my arms like I did in the gym.

"Happy?" I taunt, spreading my arms wide.

He smirks. "Getting there. Now show me what you were doing in my shower, little girl."

"Stop calling me that, and I might," I say, not sure where the bravery is coming from. Maybe it's just that I know he's seeing me, all of me. There's nothing more I can take off.

Or maybe it's this new, exhilarating power that I feel rolling through me like thunder when I see the heat in his gaze, the desire. He might play all tough and indifferent, like he's done it a million times, but he *wants* me. There's something addicting in that knowledge, in the way his eyes linger on my breasts, the bulge I can see growing in his jeans.

"Show me," he says, his voice so commanding, so dominant, that a tremor goes through me. I watch him watch me as I run my fingertips up my bare thigh. His Adam's apple bobs as he swallows, but he doesn't move.

"Then call me by my name," I say, feeling brave and reckless and high with power.

"Keep going, little mama," he says, his breath coming a little faster as I trace my middle finger along the edged of my newly shaven skin.

"Like this?" I ask. With my other hand, I reach for my breast, cupping it gently, then squeezing a little. When he doesn't respond, I tug on my nipple with two fingers. "You like that?"

Maddox gulps again, not even blinking as he watches me run my hand over my hip, the curve of my waist, my ribs, to my other breast.

I'm skating on some edge I can't see, that I'm feeling out as I go, and I know one misstep will plunge me into humiliation or even danger. On the other side of that line is the thrilling sense of this careening power I've just discovered, though—one I want to explore. Terror and exhilaration churn like storm clouds inside me. I know that at any moment he could snap, could grab me and force me to do whatever he wants.

But maybe that's the thrill. That I'm playing with fire. The danger is what's making me so hot, so bold. I'm shaking with fear, and yet, I don't want to stop. I want to push. I want to see that animal inside him again. And I want to feel this new power, to revel in it, after so many years of being powerless.

I squeeze my breasts together and then move them apart, thumbing my stiff nipples. "Do you know my name, Maddox?" I tease.

"Yes, I know your fucking name," he grits out.

I lift my breasts, leaning down and keeping my eyes on his. Slowly, I flick out my tongue, tracing the end of it along the pink rosebud of my nipple.

"You fucking tease," he growls, prowling forward and grabbing me by both arms. We stare at each other, both of us breathing fast. Fear spikes inside me, but some part of me wants this, too. Some part of me knew what would happen, and I pushed because I wanted it. I wanted him to show me he wants me, but more than that, I wanted him to take what he wants. To give me what I want, what he gives to all those other girls. I wanted him to stop seeing me as a little girl and let me in, to treat me like the girls in his gang.

I don't want to be alone anymore.

I want to be in his Murder.

Just then, the door swings open. Lennox freezes, something unreadable flickering through his gaze before it rakes over me, taking in every inch of my naked body. Suddenly, I'm thrust back into my real body, and humiliation rushes over me, replacing the surge of power. I snatch up the clothes, trying to cover myself with my other hand as I do.

"What the fuck," Lennox snaps, striding in and slamming the door behind him. He shoves Maddox, who stumbles against the dresser.

The dresser where he keeps his gun. Adrenaline courses through me, and I yank the shirt over my head.

"Nothing happened," I rush to explain. "I was just changing and—"

"I'm not talking to you right now," Lennox snaps, shoving his brother again. "What the fuck do you think you're doing?"

"I can tell you what I was about to do," Maddox drawls, shoving Lennox off him, not rising to match his brother's anger. "I was about to teach this little girl not to fuck with a real man unless she wants to get fucked back. But your dumb ass had to walk in before I could start the lesson."

"You said you didn't want her," Lennox growls, glaring at his brother through his glasses. "You said she couldn't hang, that she wasn't strong or tough enough to join the crew."

"What?" I whisper, hurt biting into me as I stand, fully dressed in Maddox's clothes. He told me once that I'd never be a Crow, but that was before. Now that we're closer…

I can't believe I was stupid enough to think he wanted me, that he'd let me in their crew, that I had any kind of power over anyone, let alone Maddox North.

"Who said anything about joining the crew?" Maddox asks, back to his usual cool demeanor, though Lennox is still seething. "I just wanted to pop that cherry before you. Maybe hear her scream my name while she milks my cock like a porn star with that hot little vice grip of a cunt she's got between her legs."

Lennox takes a swing, but Maddox ducks aside and steps back, taunting his brother. "Don't pretend you're any better. I know you're plotting to get in her pants the second my back is turned, too. You just like to charm them first, make sure to make them cry so you can get off on it. Isn't that right, little brother?"

"You son of a bitch, *malparido*, motherfucker," Lennox splutters, rushing at Maddox again.

Maddox pushes him off and grins, then palms his erection through his pants and gyrates his hips, slowly pumping into his hand. "Don't worry, *parce*. I'll pass her on to you after I break her in, bust in all her holes a few times, wear them out. The ones who don't know what they're doing are no use after that."

"Good to know," I say, a storm of humiliation and rage boiling inside me, threatening to spill over into tears. I'm damn sure not crying in front of them again, though. "I'll just be going now."

"No offense, little girl," Maddox says, tipping his chin at me. "But the good gangster dick gets chicks like you all clingy and shit."

"Well, thanks for the clothes." I give him a two-finger salute. "Jerk face."

He smirks. "You look good in my shirt, little mama. Like you're playing dress-up in daddy's clothes."

"Is that what we're calling you now?" I ask, batting my eyes. "Daddy Maddox?"

Without waiting for a reply, I spin on my heel and march out, closing the door behind me. I'm too mad to stay, even when I hear them continue arguing. My clothes aren't dry yet, so I go to the kitchen and help Valeria chop vegetables. She keeps insisting I stay for dinner, but there's no way I'm sitting across from her sons tonight.

So I insist I can't stay, that my parents want me home for dinner. I leave with my dry clothes, duck through the hole in the fence, and sneak into the shed.

I'm so busy trying to keep from tearing the shed down board by board to get out my rage that I almost don't see the disturbance in my tiny home. When my eyes adjust to the dim interior of the windowless room, I skid to a stop. Beside the bench where I've been sleeping sits a two-liter bottle of Diet Coke, a bag of Doritos, a bowl of congealed, cold Hamburger Helper with a plastic spoon in it, and a familiar, faded sleeping bag.

"Mom," I whisper, feeling unaccountably touched. Of course she'd try to take care of me when Lee's not looking. Now that he can't work, he's running her ragged, making her wait on him hand and foot. But she still took a moment to sneak me something to help, even knowing what it will cost her if he finds out.

I hug the sleeping bag to my chest, pressing my nose into it and inhaling the smell of home. Tears blur my eyes, but I blink them away. I pull on my coat because the damp chill never quite goes away, and then I start my homework. Gotta get it done in the few minutes remaining before dark, since there's no electricity out here. The steady rain continues falling, though there's no thunder or lightning, no ominous clouds. It's just drab and wet and cold, the whole world the colorless, grey nothingness of winter in Arkansas.

When the light fades from the dull evening, I slide into the sleeping bag, almost tearing up at my mother's small, kind gesture. It's so much better than trying to hug my knees up inside my jacket all night.

"Goodnight, Poe," I whisper, reaching out to run a finger over the cold feathers on the stiff bird. I know I should bury her, that once spring comes I won't have a choice. But for now, I can't bear to let go of the one companion I have in the world, the one Crow who will never hurt or betray me.

twenty

#1 on the Billboard Chart:
"Together Again"—Janet

Rae West

After the incident at the North's, I decide that taking showers in the locker room after school isn't so bad after all. Since it's my last class of the day, I just have to dawdle until everyone else has gone home. Hoping the creepy coach doesn't stick his head in and see me, I frantically shower and dive back into my clothes before the girls basketball team arrives for practice, then run for the bus.

I miss it a few times over the next few weeks, but Faulkner's small enough that most everything is within walking distance if you've got an hour or two to kill. My house isn't even an hour's walk from school, so I just shoulder my bag and head for home.

One afternoon I'm walking home under a slurry grey sky, hurrying to make it before the rain, when a two-tone brown Ford Lariat pulls up beside me. After a glance, I ignore it, since when people pull over to talk to me, it's usually older men who want 'directions to the highway' and offer to take me back to school afterwards if I'll just get in and show them how to get there.

A few fat droplets of rain splatter down, and I increase my pace.

I hear the window cranking down and then a familiar voice. "Hey," Lexi calls. "Hop in, slut! We'll take you home."

I glance up and see her hanging out the window, and beyond her, Billy in the driver's seat. "Oh, hey," I say. "That's okay. It's not far. I can walk."

"It's a good ways yet," Billy says, leaning forward to see me past his cousin. "You still live next door to the Norths, right? Get your ass up in here and out of the rain, girlie."

He's smiling, and Lexi's already thrown open the door, and big fat drops are quickly eating up the dry spots remaining on the sidewalk. Lexi scoots over, shoving the backpacks under her feet aside to make room for me.

"Okay," I say, forcing a laugh as I grab the oh-shit handle and haul myself up in. "I thought you were one of those people trying to lure girls into their vehicles by asking for directions."

"You get those too?" Lexi asks. "I swear, every time I walk alone, one of them comes cruising by. Why are men such soulless pigs?"

I lean over and slam the door, and she turns to Billy.

"What, you think I know?" he asks. "Why don't you ask that pig whose dick you've been riding?"

"Oh my god, shut up," she says, smacking his arm just as he pulls back into the lane. "Or I'll grab the wheel and run us off the road. Besides, he's not like that, and you are, so I'm asking you."

"Like what?" Billy asks, scowling at her. "A child molester who picks up girls off the side of the road?"

"Well, no," she says. "But an odious pig? Hell yeah. Half the girls in the Slut Club would go Lorena Bobbitt on you if they got the chance."

"Hey, that's not fair," he protests. "Don't hate the player, hate the game, baby."

She rolls her eyes and shakes her head at me, like we're sharing some inside knowledge with just our eyes. I want to be in that club—not the Slut Club, but the not-a-total-virgin club. I want to be able to know what she means by that look, and not in some vague, abstract way. I'm tired of being left out when they talk at lunch about what guys are good in bed, and who has a crooked dick, and whose spunk tastes weird.

Not that I want to know about the guys they're talking about, but I want to be able to relate. I've already gathered that Billy's a total manwhore who doesn't do girlfriends any more than the other Crows. After the way the North brothers treated me, though, there's no way I'm asking them for such an intimate favor. But maybe Billy would rid me of my V-card—just get it over with, no muss, no fuss. He's hot, he's my friend, and he definitely knows what he's doing.

"Anyway, back to your problem, Rae Rae," Billy says, hopping a curb as he takes a turn too fast. He flips the wipers to high as the rain starts pelting down on the truck.

"What?" I ask, feeling heat creep up my neck. He can't possibly know what I was thinking, but I did tell Lexi I was a virgin. Is that the problem he's talking about?

"The dudes harassing you when you're walking," he says. "Just tell them you belong to the Murder of Crows, and they'll burn rubber."

"Oh," I say with a nervous laugh. Of course he's not going to offer up his dick for me to sit on and break myself in with. That would be too easy. Besides, there's the whole Rae Ban to contend with. Just because I belong to the Crows, according to Maddox, that doesn't mean they can touch me. Apparently I'm off limits to everyone.

"And as for your comment, Lex, you know I like a real woman who knows her way around the D."

So much for that fantasy.

"Ah, right, the perks of being a pool boy," she says, cracking a smile.

"Fuck you," he says. "I'll dump your ass on the side of the road right now."

"Kidding, kidding," she says, holding up her hands. "I know you only bang the hot moms."

"Which is more than you can say," he mutters. "Picking up daddies at the playground and shit."

"If you call me a homewrecker, I will punch you in both testicles."

As I watch their easy camaraderie, a twist of wistfulness winds through me, making goosebumps stand up on my arms. They bicker nonstop, but they're family. They have each other, just like Maddox and Lennox, even when they fight. On top of that, Billy has the Murder of Crows, and Lexi has the Slut Club. I wouldn't even care if people called me a slut if I had friends like that.

Instead, I have a dead bird for company.

Billy turns onto Sullivan, and I wish he'd drive slower, make the ride last a little longer. Even if they're only talking to each other, using the secret language of their history that leaves me as lost in translation as when the Norths speak Spanish, at least I'm not alone.

"Hey, you want to come over?" Lexi asks, turning to me. "You can stay the night. I have my own room. And my mom doesn't care if I have people over on a school night, as long as I do my homework."

I want to cry at the prospect of sleeping in a real bed again, but then I think of Poe, alone in my shed. Lexi even gave me the perfect excuse, if I want to use it. I can just tell her my parents don't allow me to spend the night on school days.

Billy pulls up along the curb in front of my house, leaving the engine running. "Go get your stuff," he says, picking up a canvas CD case and unzipping it. "I'll rock out while I wait."

"Okay," I say, climbing out of the car.

"Hey, can I come in with you?" Lexi asks, hopping out before I can answer. "I've always wanted to see inside this house. You know, Marilyn's grandma or… great aunt or something… Owned this house? I'm pretty sure she died in there, too. People said it was haunted before y'all moved in. How many rooms does this have, anyway? It's so big."

"Uh… Yeah," I say, not moving. "So, my stepdad's actually hurt, and he doesn't really like people coming inside…"

"Oh, right," she says, nodding. "I heard about that. Is he okay?"

"Yeah," I say. "Yeah, he's fine. He just… He doesn't like people seeing him that way."

"Bummer," she says, reaching back to open the truck door. "Maybe next time?"

"Yeah," I say. "For sure. Sorry."

She climbs back into the truck, and I wait for them to speed away and leave me standing on the sidewalk alone. But she waves a hand impatiently. "Go get your clothes, homegirl. There's only so many Monster Ballads

I can listen to before I punch this idiot to remind him it's not the 80s anymore, and he dumps me on your doorstep, and then I'll have to stay the night with you instead."

That gets me going in a hurry, and I rush up the front steps, since I can't exactly skirt around with them watching. But I stop at the door, realizing I can't go in anyway. I cast a nervous glance over my shoulder and then hurry around the side of the house. Hopefully they'll just think the door was locked and my key is in my backpack.

When I've circled the house on the wraparound porch, I jog down the back steps and hurry across the soggy backyard to the shed. It's been raining for weeks, like it does this time of year, and a thin layer of water sits in the yard under the dead grass. The floor of the shed is dirt, which has turned to mud from me going in and out. All my clothes are damp, and the sleeping bag has gotten a little muddy too. I know I need to find somewhere else to live, that once Lee gets better and starts coming out to see his precious pool, he'll notice the footprints and find me.

I'm so busy fretting I don't even notice that the shed door is cracked open until I get there. It has a hook for a padlock, but it's never been locked. I always make sure to push it closed so rain doesn't come in, though.

I'm shaking even before I see the black feathers at my feet.

Then my blood turns to ice.

I don't know how long I stand there, the cold rain beating down on me, soaking my hair and clothes. I can't move. I can only stare at the feathers, anguish twisting inside me.

She must have only been stunned. That's it. She woke up and flew out…

I know it's impossible, but I can't consider another possibility.

I hear Lexi calling my name, and it snaps me out of my trance. Gulping down my nerves, I slowly ease open the door. My heart stops.

I rush in and fall to my knees in the bed of black feathers. Her body is mangled, nothing left but a few bones and so many feathers…

"Poe!" I scream, frantically gathering them up, as if I can put her back together, make her whole again.

A sob catches in my throat, and even though I know it's stupid, all I can think is that it's my fault because I was going to abandon her, go spend the night with a friend and leave her here alone.

"Poe," I sob, grasping at her downy feathers.

"Oh! My god…" I hear Lexi's voice behind me, and I know I should be embarrassed about… Something… But I can't remember what it is.

All I can think about is Poe. I've lost her. She's really gone. I can't pretend anymore.

"Shit," Billy says, his voice practically in my ear. "Don't touch that."

"Yeah," Lexi says. "I mean, I support anyone's right to go all Ozzy and bite off bat heads and shit, but for real, those things carry diseases."

"She doesn't have a disease!" I yell, gripping her tighter, like they might pry her bones from my fingers. "Go away!"

"I'll get help," Billy says.

He backs away, and I fold over her, crying at the hollow that's been carved out inside my chest, trying not to scream from the pain and the fury that the one thing I had in my life, the one thing that's mine, is gone. I want to tear the shed to pieces, throw the rain back up into the sky, rip the covering from the pool, fill it with water, and slam my hand into it so hard it makes a tidal wave that washes away the house, the whole fucking town.

"Okay," Lexi says behind me, her gentle hand settling onto my shoulder. "Hey, it's okay, *chica*."

"It's not okay," I whisper, raising my tear-streaked face at last. She's looking at me like… Like I'm everything I never wanted to be.

Weak. Broken. Pitiful.

This is why I don't have friends, why I don't let myself need people. This is why it's best to keep them out, like my parents taught me. When they get too close, they see all the ugly things, all the real things, and that's too dangerous.

"Jesus fucking Christ," says a deep, accented voice, the last voice in the world I want to hear right now. I close my eyes and will him away.

Maddox grabs me under the arms and hauls me up, dragging me backwards out of the shed. I don't care enough to scramble up when he drops me, and I land on my ass in the mud.

"*Vení*, it's okay," Lennox says, kneeling in front of me in the mud. He takes my face in both hands and pulls it up, letting the rain fall down my cheeks with the tears.

"It's not okay," Maddox snaps. "It's a dead crow. You know what that means."

"Shut up about the omen already," Lennox snaps back. "Can't you see there's more than that going on here?"

I don't want him to see. I don't want to watch as his eyes take in what Lennox must have already deduced from the contents of my little nest in the shed. I don't want to see the way his gaze shifts from the muddy sleeping bag to the bottle with an inch of flat soda in the bottom to the pile of damp clothes and finally, to me.

"It's a bad fucking omen, alright," Maddox says quietly, his mouth tight. "Someone's going to die."

"She already died," I say, holding out her remains in both hands, begging them to understand.

Lexi wrinkles her nose and takes my wrist in her hand, pushing it down. "Okay, maybe let's stop waving the roadkill around."

"How long have you been living out here?" Lennox asks, pulling my face toward his again. His glasses are streaked with rain, but I can see the kindness and pain in his eyes—pain that's for me, on my behalf. Suddenly all I want is to curl up in his arms and cry, forget all the things he's said and other people have told me to warn me about him that don't fit with this caring, kind, nurturing side of him.

I shake my head, fighting to get myself back under control, to make the tears stop falling and my lips stop trembling.

"You could have come to us," he says quietly. "I told you that. To come to us if you needed anything."

"I couldn't," I say, shaking my head.

"Bullshit," Maddox growls, slamming the shed door closed. It doesn't latch, and with the wood swollen from all the rain, it doesn't even close all the way unless you really push it. But there's no reason to make sure it's tightly closed now. There's nothing precious left inside.

Fresh, hot tears stream down my cheeks. "I couldn't," I say again. "Every time I came to you, something bad happened. *You're* the bad omen, not Poe."

The muscle in Maddox's jaw flexes as he clenches his teeth, but Billy clamps a hand on his shoulder and pulls him back before he can speak. "Let Lennox take this one," he says. "He and Lexi are better at this shit. Come on."

Maddox glares at me one long moment and then turns and stalks away with Billy. My shoulders shake, and Lennox sinks to sit in the mud with me, scooting in so his legs bracket mine as he faces me, taking my head between his hands again. "Listen, Rae," he says. "I'm sorry about how the last time went down, that you felt like you couldn't come to us with this. But you can. You can now. Whatever happened, it doesn't matter. You're with us now."

His words only make me cry harder. "I'm not," I manage. "You're with the Crows, and you said I couldn't join. That I would never be one of you."

"That doesn't mean we won't look out for you."

I shake my head, wiping my cheek with the back of my hand. "But you already have someone. You have each other."

"That doesn't mean you don't have us, too," he says, lifting my chin. "You have me."

He leans in and kisses me softly, right there with the dull grey sky above and the cold grey rain falling and the cold grey world around us. Right there in the mud, with a mangled crow carcass in my hands, he kisses me, like he doesn't care about any of it. He just wants me, and he wants me to be safe, and to take care of me. No one has ever wanted to do that before.

He pulls back slowly, stroking my wet, bedraggled hair behind my ear and giving me a little smile that only hints at the dip of his dimple. "Okay?" he says, searching my eyes. "You always have me."

I nod, feeling so stupid and gross right now that I don't want to look at his gorgeous, movie star face another second.

"Good," he says. "Now, here's what's going to happen. We're going to have a funeral for your friend here, and then you're going to go inside and take a shower, and this time, you're going to stay afterwards. Not just for a night. Forever."

I nod, another tear tracking down my cheek.

Lennox pulls me close and kisses my cheek, then the other, then my lips again, his mouth salty with my tears. "Okay," he says, standing and holding out a hand. "*Venga.*"

I don't want to put my gory hand in his, so I sit there, holding what's left of Poe cupped between my palms. After a second, he sees what's wrong and takes my elbow, pulling me up. Lexi steps in to help on my other side. "Always the man with a plan," she says. "Though can we do the shower first? Or at least wash her hands off? I mean, I'm not afraid to get my hands dirty, but cuddling corpses is going a little far."

I manage a smile through my embarrassment as we step through the gap in the fence and into the Norths' yard. "I'll wash my hands."

"Cool beans," she says. "So, what are we doing about a coffin? Anyone got a cool black shoebox? A decorative coffin from Hot Topic? I could call Marilyn. She's all gothy and shit. Did you know she didn't go goth until Billy dumped her? If he wasn't my cousin, I'd hate that boy. But my dude, I bet she's got something coffin-y. Coffin-esque?"

"No," I say quickly, not because I don't like her friend, but because it's humiliating enough with only four people to witness my complete mental breakdown.

She strides ahead to open the door, looking as much like a cute little fairy girl as always, even with her hair soaked and her oversized flannel and baggy jeans weighing down her tiny body. She gestures for us to enter, and Lennox leads me inside. I'm glad he's not making me leave Poe outside or acting like it's gross that I'm holding her.

Billy and Maddox are sitting at the table, a bottle of tequila on the gold-flecked surface between them. Maddox glowers at me resentfully, obviously of a different mind than his twin.

"We're going to bury her bird," Lexi announces. "Y'all coming to the funeral?"

"Poe," I say. "Her name is—was—Poe."

I swallow past the ache in my throat and avoid looking at Maddox, waiting for his cutting remark. "Yeah, we're coming," he grumbles, swiping the tequila bottle and standing.

"So… Shoebox?" Lexi asks, turning on her heel from one North brother to the other. Lennox pulls me in from behind, so my back is flush to his strong chest, and wraps his comforting arms around me.

Maddox frowns even deeper and takes a swig of tequila. Then he pushes past us and stalks down the hall.

A minute later, he appears with an absolutely gigantic orange box from a pair of basketball shoes.

"Yeah, we were hoping for something a little more black and gothy," Lexi says wiggling her fingers like she's a witch who expects a spell to come out and transform the box. She smiles up at Maddox hopefully. "Got anything like that?"

"No," he says flatly, opening the box and holding it out to me.

I don't want to let Poe go, especially when I wouldn't put it past Maddox to chuck the box in the trash and be done with it.

"Go on," Lennox prods, nudging me gently. "You can let her go now."

"Ooh, maybe a silk handkerchief would be good," Lexi says. "Anyone got one of those?"

"Yes, because we're all the fucking Queen of England," Billy says, standing from the table and adjusting his ball cap. "Come on, Lex. It's a bird."

"It's her pet," she says, glaring at him. Then she turns to me. "My bra's satiny, Rae. I know it's not a satin lining, but maybe…?"

"You don't have to do that," I say, but she's already unhooking it and working it over her arm while the North brothers watch as if hypnotized.

Billy snags the tequila from Maddox and takes a drink, then punches his teammate in the arm, hard. "Dude."

"Sorry," Maddox mutters, staring down into the box while Lexi pulls the bra out her sleeve and nestles it into the cavernous box. How big are his feet, anyway? And if what they say is true, he's damn sure got it right about being too big for a virgin.

I shake the completely inappropriate thought away and carefully scoot Poe from my hands into the space Lexi arranged between the cups of her pink satin bra. Which is the last sort of undergarment I'd have expected from an irreverent grunge chick who lives in flannel, giant t-shirts, and shapeless jeans.

"Okay, great," she says, clapping her hands together. "Now, let the handwashing commence before we all die of bird flu."

I go to the sink and wash thoroughly, glancing over my shoulder at Maddox every few seconds to make sure he's not lighting the coffin on fire. He's good in the kind of crisis where someone needs their arms snapped in four places, but when it comes to being sensitive to someone's feelings, he's beyond clueless.

But he only closes the lid and waits, expressionless, while I finish up and join the procession. In the backyard, we stand near the fence where they dumped the pool sludge into a long, raised garden bed that runs the length of our privacy fence on their side. A stack of wire tomato cages sits at the end, and a dozen metal posts lean against the fence.

Lennox grabs a shovel out of their garden shed and comes back to dig a hole.

Maddox turns to me. "You want to lower it in?" he asks, holding out the box.

I take it, silently thanking him for not being a total dick for once in his life. When Lennox is done digging, I kneel and settle the box into the shallow grave.

"Want to say a few words?" Lennox asks me.

I shake my head, feeling silly enough already. Now that the shock has worn off, I can't help wonder what they're all thinking, if they'll tell everyone at school that I went psycho over a dead bird. Lexi will only tell her friends, who are my friends, but Maddox knows everyone. He might just tell the whole school, like they told everyone that I broke up their party and turned them against me from the start.

At least they don't know what happened before today, that I've been living in a shed for almost a month and talking to a dead animal.

"I'll say something," Billy volunteers before Lennox can throw the first shovel of heavy, wet dirt onto the garish orange box.

I look at him in surprise.

"I know I'm not real good with words like Lennox here," he says. "Me and Mad, we're better with actions.

You know, fists and dicks." He breaks off and grins at me.

Maddox's scowl deepens.

"Not the time," Lexi warns.

"Right," Billy says, clearing his throat and adjusting the bill of his cap before going on. "Now, I didn't know this crow, but if it was anything like the Crows I do know, then she was a damn fine bird. And I'm sure her murder will miss her like the devil."

"Thank you," I say, smiling weakly. "I will."

"I'll say something too," Lexi says, wiping rain off her face and turning to the grave. "I'm sorry I never met you, Poe the Crow, but you must have been a pretty kick-ass bird if Rae loved you so much. I can tell you were real special. Oh, and please don't curse us with your bad-omen dead crow juju."

I give her a grateful smile, tears blurring my eyes.

"Rest in Peace," Lennox says, taking my hand and squeezing as he addresses the box. "You're already missed. We'll honor your memory and your spirit, and please know that we'll take care of Rae. The promise of one Crow to another." He taps his chest, then kisses two fingers and holds them up, like he's watching her spirit go.

"Rae?" Lexi prompts.

And even though they've been so great, I can't say what I want to say with an audience. It's private, the things I would say to the second member of my murder. So I just recite the nursery rhyme.

"One for sorrow, two for joy

Three for girls and four for boys

Five for silver, six for gold

Seven for a secret, never to be told."

Poe was one, a sorrowful loner, until she found me. Then there were two of us, and she brought me the only joy I found in that dark, creaky old house.

When I'm done speaking, I kneel and pick up a handful of dirt with my clean hands, dropping it on top of the box. It makes a hollow sound, and I think of how small what's left of her is in that big box. I start crying again, and a second later, a pair of knees lands on the soggy ground beside mine. When I glance over, I'm surprised to see Maddox beside me. He picks up a handful of dirt and adds it to mine on top of the cheap orange casket. After it's covered, and she's buried completely, he stands and takes the bottle of tequila from Billy.

"For Poe," he says, tipping it and dumping some on the grave. It falls onto the dirt like the rain still slicing down, soaking us.

Then he tips up the bottle, taking a drink before passing it to me. I take a drink and pass it on, and we all stand there above the grave for a few minutes.

Finally Lexi hiccups and then lets out a soundless breath of a laugh. "Well, this is not what I had in mind when I asked you to hang out today, but if you still want to come over..."

"Rain check?" I ask.

"For sure, for sure."

"And I'm... Sorry."

It's so inadequate it's embarrassing, but I don't know what else to say or where to even start.

"We cool," she says, slinging an arm around my neck. "You're an honorary slut, and now an honorary Crow. No apologies, 'kay?"

I nod and give her a quick squeeze around her tiny waist, thankful she's letting me skip the awkward stuff. "Cool," I echo.

"Well, I don't know about y'all, but I'm freezing my balls off," she says. "Ready to roll, Billy?"

"Yeah, let's bounce," he says, holding out a hand to Maddox. They clasp, and then he does the same to Lennox, then to me. "Keep it real, crow girl."

After they're gone, an awkward silence falls over our group as we huddle in the icy drizzle.

"*Vení,* let's get you inside," Lennox says after a minute. "Mad, you gonna grab her clothes from the shed, *o qué?*"

Maddox gives us a resentful look before turning and walking away. I guess we're back to him hating me and not talking, like last summer, though I'm not sure what I did to piss him off so badly. I don't have it in me to think about it right now, so I let his brother take my hand in his warm, comforting grip and lead me into the house and away from Maddox's grudge.

twenty-one

Maddox North

When I get back with Rae's stuff, I can hear the shower running in the bathroom at the end of the hall. I'm tempted to go straight to our room, since the walls between that and the bathroom are paper thin, and I want to know if I'll get a repeat of the last time she showered here, when she surprised the hell out of me. I didn't think she was the kind of girl who would finger herself in someone else's shower. I assumed that because she's still a virgin as a senior, she must be some uptight little prude, but maybe I had her all wrong.

She came while we fingered her ass hole and her cunt at once, after all. Maybe it's time to see what else my dirty little girl likes.

"You got everything?" Lennox asks, dropping onto the couch and adjusting his glasses.

"Surprised you're not in there with her," I say, shoving the whole pile of clothes into the washer.

"She's messed up right now," he says. "It's not the time."

"Oh, right," I say, picking up the box and dumping powder on top of her clothes. "Because you'd have to traumatize her to get off."

"Fuck you," he snaps.

"I'd rather fuck her," I say. "Maybe I should go in there now, make her forget her problems for a while, like we did the last time she stayed over."

"Don't touch her," Lennox growls.

I raise a brow and close the door of the washing machine. "Oh, so now she's yours? I thought you wanted to share her with the entire crew."

"I changed my mind," he says. "And so what if she is mine? You got a problem with that?"

I start the machine and turn to him, crossing my arms over my chest in the way that always intimidates people. "Maybe I do."

We stare at each other for a minute. "Since when is she anything more than a piece of ass to you?" he asks at last.

I shrug. "Who said she's more than that?"

"She's more than that," he says, glaring at me.

"You wanting to prove that you're a good guy by not touching her doesn't make you any better than me wanting to fuck her," I say. "We're both using her."

"You said she was too good for us," he points out. "That we shouldn't mess with her because she's too innocent."

I remember the feel of her struggling in my arms, bucking against me; of her bare ass nestled into my groin, my dick between her cheeks and my finger in the hot, wet squeeze of her cunt. My cock stirs at the image of my brother slicking his finger with my cum and sticking it up her ass, and how her pussy looked when I spread it open and let him shoot his load over her glistening pink flesh.

I push off the washer, grinning down at him. “You don’t think we’ve corrupted her enough, little brother? Because I’m down for round two if you think she’s still not ready.”

“You’ll ruin her,” he says quietly.

I stare back at him. “So will you.”

We stay like that, in a standoff, for at least five minutes. The time ticks by, neither of us willing to back down, to give her up to the other. Finally, Lennox caves by speaking first.

“Then it’s agreed,” he says. “Neither of us touches her.” He turns and walks past me into the kitchen, picking up the cordless phone and plucking a page of coupons down from where Mom stuck it on the fridge. “I’m ordering pizza.”

When Rae emerges from the shower a good half hour later, she’s wearing a pair of Lennox’s boxers and one of his shirts, which immediately sets off some primal part of my brain. I want to rip them off her and replace them with mine—after I devour her one lick at a time, like a fucking ice cream cone.

"We ordered pizza," Lennox calls, glancing back over his shoulder. We're on the couch playing video games. As much as we give each other shit and argue, we're brothers, and that never ends. But the air between us is unsettled, filled with the strain of our unsolved argument still lingering like cobwebs.

"Is your mom not home yet?" Rae asks, standing awkwardly at the end of the hall, like she's afraid to step into the lion's den where we had her between us the last time.

"She's on late shift tonight."

"I could have made something," she says. "I don't know anything fancy, but I can make an omelet or Hamburger Helper or…"

She trails off, biting at her lip.

"You don't have to cook for us," I say, my voice coming out gruffer than I meant.

"I don't want to be a burden," she says. "If she really doesn't mind me staying for a few days, just until…"

"Until what?" I ask. "Your fairy godmother shows up and turns your shitty little shed into a castle with a flick of her magic wand?"

"No." She scowls at me and crosses her arms, which just makes her perky little tits poke out even more, highlighting her pointy nipples inside Lennox's YMCA shirt. Of course she chose my fucking brother. He's actually halfway decent to her, and she doesn't know him well enough to know it's all an act. He'll try, but in the end, he can't keep it up. He'll show his true colors. No one can live their whole life pretending to be someone else.

It's better to just be up front about who you are and what you want. And we're both pieces of shit.

"Then what?" I ask, tossing down the controller and turning on the couch, laying my arm along the top and facing Rae. "You think your real daddy's going to show up and tell you that he's a billionaire and you're an heiress? Or he's a king and you're a princess? Tell me the fairytale that you're living in your head, little girl."

"If I could live in a fairytale, you wouldn't exist," she says, leveling me with those luminous hazel eyes ringed with dark lashes, the ones that blink up at me with helpless submission as she deep throats my cock every night in my dreams. "So obviously I'm not the one living in some fantasy inside my head."

Our eyes meet, and for a second, I'm sure she's remembering what happened on the floor in this very room. That she somehow knows that's the fantasy in my head, the one I jerk off to every fucking day. And now that I think about it, when did she take the starring role in every jerk-off fantasy I have? How the fuck did she get in my head anyway?

Is it just because I can't have her? Because Lennox told me to leave her alone? Because *he* wants her?

"Vení," Lennox says, scooting over and patting the couch between us.

Rae gives me a triumphant look that makes me want to wrap my hand around her neck like I did that night, but this time, I'd squeeze until she was gasping for breath while I pounded into her sweet little body and showed it who it belongs to.

No. What the fuck?

She doesn't belong to me. I don't play that game. I'm a free agent. I don't own girls any more than they own me. I've never wanted to, never wanted that responsibility. Owning someone means you're attached to them, and fuck if I'm ever attaching myself to one girl when I can fuck anyone I want, any time I want.

She circles the end of the couch to sit in the spot Lennox made for her, curling her legs up with her knees angled toward him, her back angled toward me. His gaze flicks to me, and I see the same glimmer of triumph in his eyes. I want to punch his fucking face in. He's winning her over, and he knows it's fucking killing me. It's killing me that I'm losing. I never lose.

He knows it, too. He knows it's killing me that she isn't all over my dick without me having to lift a finger, that she won't let me have her without working for her.

Fuck that. I don't chase girls, don't work for them, any more than I get attached. If she wants him, she can have him. She'll learn her mistake soon enough, and when she comes crying to me, I'll show her what she could have had if she hadn't been so fucking determined to prove her point. I'll make her pay for that, and then I'll leave her with nothing, like I've left every other bitch who chased my dick, *begged* for it, even knowing how it would end.

They all think they'll be different, that they'll be the one to tie me down. They don't see the irony—that thinking they're different is what makes them all the same.

I pick up the controller and start playing by myself while they sit next to me, talking like I'm not fucking here.

"What does your mom do?" she asks Lennox, leaning her elbow on the top of the back of the couch.

"She's a manager at Hastings," he says. "She mostly works days, but sometimes she closes."

"I was thinking," she says. "If I'm going to stay here more than a few days…"

She glances back at me, and the movement makes her back arch just a fraction, her tight little ass pushing out. I see it from the corner of my eye, but I pretend I'm not looking, that I don't want to touch it, to squeeze it, to feel it fill my hands while I devour her delicious little cunt. I hate Lennox for being the one to finger that ass last time. It was for her that time. It felt natural to share her. We've shared lots of girls. But now…

I don't know what changed. Maybe the fact that he wants her for himself, that he's *not* willing to share, even when I was. The selfish bastard.

When I refuse to look at her, she turns back to my brother. "I'm sure I can figure something else out," she says. "But if your mom wouldn't mind me staying for a month, I can get a job and save up enough to get my own place by the time I turn eighteen."

"You don't have to leave," he says, tucking her hair behind her ear. "You can stay as long as you want. Stay until graduation."

I lose my last life in the game and have to start over, since I can't pay any fucking attention with them practically fucking right up against me.

"I'd still want to get a job and help out," she says. "It wouldn't be fair to make your mom support me. I'm not here to mooch off y'all."

"I can think of a way you can pay for your room," I say, smirking at the screen as I start over in the game.

I don't look at her bare legs, muscled from running, long enough to throw over my shoulders while I pound her into the bed, strong enough to ride me while she grinds her clit on my pelvic bone until she cums so hard she can't stop saying my name…

"Ignore him," Lennox says, taking her hand. "He's a sore loser."

Fuck this.

I throw down the controller and stalk to the door, yanking it open and stepping out into the cloying, cold night. The rain has stopped, but the air is heavy with moisture, and the clouds are churning overhead, promising a second, more violent storm is brewing.

Reggie's sitting on the trunk of his dad's brown Oldsmobile across the street, smoking a cigarette. I cross and jerk my chin at the pack beside him. "Give me one of those, would you?"

He hands me the pack and leans back to fish out his lighter, his eyes staying on me. "Bitch problems?" he asks.

"*Qué mas?*"

"I saw y'all go in with Rae earlier," he says, watching me light up. "Not giving you shit, man. I got plenty of bitch problems of my own right now."

"Yeah," I say, hoisting myself onto the trunk beside him. "Mariana your bitch now, *o qué?*"

He shrugs. "*Sí.* Until her dad finds out and curb stomps me like a Skull Serpent."

"Not gonna happen," I assure him. "The Murder's got your back."

"I don't know how I'm going to pay for all this shit," he says. "She's going to have to move in here, and then the baby…" He glances at me as he drags on his cigarette. "Lennox said he was going to figure out our cash problem."

"I'm sure he's cooking up something," I say. Lennox is the brains and the moral compass of our crew, but the cash problem is one he can't seem to solve. He wants to make the Murder of Crows a legit organization, to help our members and their families, to provide safe spaces for the kids to have fun and be normal, like Rae's pool, and honest work for the parents. But to do that you need funding, and if there's a legal way to make fast, good cash, he hasn't found it yet.

"Maybe it's time to think about moving a little product," Reggie says.

"He'd never go for that," I say. We've already had this conversation, so I know his answers, and they make sense, even if I don't fully agree. But when it comes to the crew, we're equals, and we need majority rule to move on something like that.

"Maybe he doesn't need to know," Reggie says, tossing his cigarette butt in the gutter. "For those of us who need the cash, we could run the whole operation without him being involved. Just for a little while, to get on our feet."

"I know," I say, holding up a hand. "I don't disagree. But you know how he is. It's the principle of it."

"Fuck his principles," he says. "We're talking about a baby's life here, man."

A car turns onto the street, its lights sweeping over us, and I reach for my gun on instinct. But when it pulls up on the other side of the street, I see the pizzas stacked in the passenger seat.

"I'll talk to him about it," I promise Reggie, sliding off the hood of the car. "You've still got… What? Six months to go before it becomes a problem?"

He gets up too, and we clasp hands before I head across the street and pay for the pizza. The little dweeb looks like he's about to shit himself when he sees all six-foot-four inches of my tattooed Colombian ass, and he splits with a quickness. I go inside, halfway expecting to see Lennox balls deep in Rae despite his good guy act earlier.

Instead, he's sitting behind her on the couch, showing her how to play Grand Theft Auto. Somehow, that's even worse. His thighs block her in on either side as she sits between them, and his arms bracket hers as he shows her how to hold the controller. She clutches it with both hands, a little stitch pulling between her brows. Her tongue pokes out the corner of her mouth in concentration, and it's the cutest fucking thing I've ever seen.

But that just reminds me that neither of us has any business destroying that.

twenty-two

#1 on the Billboard Chart:
"Nice & Slow"—Usher

Rae West

It takes me a few nights to get used to sleeping in my new room, knowing the twins are just across the hall. They set up a squeaky old cot in the room, which is a little office space without a proper door. Lennox hangs a sheet over the doorway to give me privacy. Neither of them offer me their bed—not that I'd let them give up that much for me anyway. I'm pretty sure Maddox is intentionally being a dick to prove he doesn't care about me, despite what he said before. Lennox is too nice to make me share a room with his brother—and too jealous.

By the time I've shared a roof with them for a few weeks, I can tell how deeply he feels the sting of rejection when Maddox gets chosen first. He knows that in every way that matters to people in high school, he's inferior to his twin. I can't imagine how much that blows, so I try to show him that I favor him over Maddox's moody brooding. It would help if Maddox wasn't so damn fine on top of being huge and good at sports and, for reasons I can't figure out, far more popular with girls.

Valeria says I don't have to pay her back and that I'm welcome to stay as long as I want, but I insist on getting a job anyway. She promises she'll hire me as soon as a job opens at Hastings, but in the meantime, I get a job collecting the coins from the newspaper machines around town. The first few days, Lennox drives me around in the El Camino, but once I have enough to buy a used bike at a pawn shop, I assure him that I'm fine and go it alone.

It's nice to be able to pay Valeria back a little, so I don't feel like such a charity case. And it's nice to ride my bike around, to get out and even to be alone. As much as I enjoy the twins' company, even Maddox's when he's not going out of his way to be an ass, they're a lot. Their masculine, dominant energy is overwhelming at times, and they're always either at each other's throats or subtly goading each other. So, even though I'm doing the world's lamest job, working is its own reward in a way…

Except when it rains.

And February in Central Arkansas sees plenty of rain.

A few weeks after I move in, I huddle down into my narrow cot as rain slashes the windows and thunder rumbles far away. At last, I fall asleep, only to be visited in my dream by a murder of crows. I'm running, and they chase after me, shrieking and diving at me as I try to escape. They're angry because I killed Poe. Because I brought her into my human world that's no place for a crow. The faster I run, the closer they get, until they're scratching and clawing at me, tearing my hair and diving at me with screaming, open beaks.

I jolt awake when a boom of thunder shakes the house. I'm covered in sweat and trembling all over, aware of my own voice echoing in the room. I sit up and squint at the clock radio. The red, digital numbers blink back at me. Shit. The power went out for a second, and it reset to midnight. I have no idea if it's close to time to get up, or if I should wait it out while the angry gods overhead battle to the death.

I hear footsteps padding in the hall and pray I didn't wake up anyone when I cried out in my sleep. The next second, the curtain in my doorway moves aside and a huge figure looms in the doorframe. I bite down on my fist, trying to rid myself of the residual terror from my dream before he comes in and torments me about it.

"You good?" Maddox asks, stepping inside. Lighting flashes, lighting his way as he crosses the room. He's shirtless, his muscles straining under his skin the way they always do, making him look huge and even more imposing in the darkness. As if sensing my discomfort, he crouches beside the bed, bringing himself down to my level.

"Fine," I manage, unable to meet his eyes. I curl my hand into a fist under the blankets to steady myself, pressing my nails in and focusing on the pain instead of my embarrassment.

"I heard you crying. Did the thunder scare you?"

"Are you here to make fun of me and call me a little girl?" I ask, squeezing until my nails bite into my palm. "Because I'm fine. Go back to bed."

"*Veni.*" He strokes back my hair, and I start to turn away, but another crack of thunder sounds, and I jump a mile. My fingers latch onto his wrist involuntarily. I squeeze my eyes closed and wait for him to make me feel small and stupid, how he always does.

But he doesn't say anything, just twists his wrist to loosen my grasp and slides his hand down to match my palm with his before I can pull away. He links his fingers through mine and squeezes. "You know, you don't have to be such a fucking pain in the ass all the time," he says. "You don't have to be tougher than everyone else. You can be scared. You can ask for help. You're not alone anymore, and you fucking know it."

"The storm woke me up," I admit, swallowing hard.

"See how easy that was?"

"Shit. Did I wake you?"

"I'm glad you woke me, little girl."

He rises and scoots onto the edge of the cot, which groans like it's dying. Ignoring it, he leans down over me.

"I'm sorry," I whisper, embarrassed but also keenly aware of his nearness, how electric I feel when he's just a breath away, teasing me with the painful anticipation of his touch.

"I'm not sorry," he says, sliding down on top of the blankets so we're lying face to face on the tiny bed. He circles an arm around my back, pulling me tight to his bare chest. "You're scared, and I'm here."

"You're not going to make fun of me?" I ask, so distracted by all that hot, bare skin that I almost forget the storm outside and the dream haunting me.

"Not even a little," he says, his voice low, his face so close that my lips tingle with the memory of his kiss. "I'll stay right here until you fall asleep again."

A moment of crackling tension stretches between us, and my body starts to warm in a way I can't control when he's so close, his big body only separated from mine by a sheet and a single blanket. I try to shift away, but the bed creaks in protest, barely holding our combined weight.

Then another flash of lightning bathes the room in stark, white light, and I cringe, my body tensing for the thunder.

"Promise?" I whisper, curling my fingers around the edge of the sheet.

Maddox tips my chin up with a finger and presses his soft lips to mine, then draws back and cups my cheek in his palm. "Promise."

Lightning flickers again, and he tightens his arms around me.

"I'm glad too," I confess, the words tumbling out despite my better judgment. "Glad you're here. I was having a bad dream. I must have cried out in my sleep."

"Want to tell me?"

"No," I say. A beat of silence follows, and I go on, even though I didn't intend to. "It was about Poe. It's stupid."

"Why's it stupid?"

"I don't know," I say, tugging at the edge of the sheet, wanting to hide under it, but Maddox's weight pins it in place. I stare at my hand, not daring to look at him.

He doesn't speak, waiting for me to be ready. Finally I am. My voice trembles when I speak. "I just… It's my fault. I was feeding her, and my stepdad saw. He knew she was tame, and he… He…"

My voice catches, and I have to stop, my breath hitching.

"Is that why you're scared of thunder?" he asks. "Your stepdad?"

"I don't know," I admit. "Maybe. Maybe it's like his footsteps thundering around when he's pissed. I used to hide in the closet when he was coming, and he'd go apeshit trying to find me."

Maddox pulls me in closer, ignoring the straining bed, and presses his lips to my forehead.

I take a breath to calm myself, my usual defenses falling back into place automatically. "I'm not that scared. It was mostly the dream. I mean, I've gotten through all the other storms myself. I'm fine. Really. You don't have to stay."

"And I'm fine staying," he says. "Really."

I nod, swallowing hard, my eyes on the dark ink on his neck, illuminated by the next stroke of lightning. I raise a finger and run it slowly down the front of his neck, over his Adam's apple and the crow's body. "What about you?" I whisper. "What are you afraid of?"

He takes my hand, gently moving it from his throat and bringing it around the back of his neck before letting his hand fall to my hip. I swallow hard and look up at him, sure he's going to kiss me instead of answering. My heart hammers in my chest, and I can hardly breathe with the anticipation.

"You," he murmurs, his dark eyes burning into mine as his thumb strokes my cheek. "What you're doing to me. To us."

"What am I doing?" I whisper, my throat tight.

He chuckles. "You tell me, little girl."

"I—I don't know."

"Sure you don't," he says, smirking. "Want to take this to my bed? I'm not sure this cot is going to hold us much longer. You can stay until the storm is gone. I'll even be a good boy like Lennox."

I gulp down my nerves, ones that have nothing to do with the storm still raging outside. In his arms, I feel safe and warm, like he'll hold out the rain and wind, drown out the thunder. I guess he already has, because I've stopped shaking and I'm not thinking about anything but him, how good he feels against me, how right we feel together. "I'm not afraid of you, Maddox," I say, looking up into his fathomless gaze. "Or what you're doing to me."

He sits up, swinging his legs off the bed. "You should be."

I sit up too, watching him stand, his powerful body displayed before me like a work of art, drawn in a thousand masculine lines, so beautiful that it makes an ache build behind my sternum. I want more than the seconds of flickering lighting to look at it, to memorize it.

"I'm not," I whisper. "I'm not scared to be alone with you. I know you could take what you wanted, and I couldn't stop you. But I know you wouldn't."

"Then you don't know me at all," he says, holding out a hand. "*Venga*, little mama."

I want to say more, to make him understand that even when he stepped through the curtain, I never had a moment of fear. Not even after the last two weeks, when he's been cold and bitter as day old coffee. I know that if he wanted me, I wouldn't try to stop him. I want him, want whatever comes next. I don't know what that is, but I'm ready for it, even if he breaks my heart afterwards. Whatever he's doing to me, whatever he's going to do, I'm all in.

So I follow him into their room with the two twin beds in the two halves, one so messy and the other so neat, one with regular teenage boy posters of movies and bands and scantily clad women on the wall and the other with beautiful art, each side reflecting the boy who sleeps there.

When Maddox picks up the blanket, I slide under, huddling down into the bed that's still warm from his body. He scoots in with me, under the blankets, curling his massive frame around mine like armor to keep out everything I fear. When he pulls me into the curve of his body, spooning me from behind, I can feel that he's hard.

I squirm against him, frustrated and wanting, and he lets out a low, sleepy moan. "You better stop that, little girl," he growls into my ear. "Unless you want me to rail that ass so hard you can't walk for a week."

"What if that is what I want?" I whisper.

"You don't," he says. "I told you, I'm too big for a virgin. And Lennox may be a heavy sleeper, but he won't sleep through your screams when I make you cum so hard the whole block thinks I'm killing you. And neither will our mother."

Shit. Their mom is sleeping just down the hall.

I'm suddenly awkward, unsure how she'd feel about finding me in her son's bed after she was kind enough to take me in. Would she kick me out? Think I'm a slut?

And why does the thought of her finding me in his bed, or Lennox waking up and hearing us, make me even hotter instead of dousing the fire raging inside me?

I try to stay still, but the sensation of Maddox's long, thick cock pressed against my ass, with just his thin, drawstring pajama pants covering it, makes it hard to breathe, let alone sleep. All I can think about is the night on the living room floor, how it felt against my bare skin, how dirty it felt when he came on my back—and how much I liked it. His cock throbs against me, and my pulse throbs in return.

"Maddox?" I whisper.

"Mmm," he murmurs, slowly rolling his hips forward, grinding his cock against me. He sounds like he's half asleep, but I'm so hungry for him I could scream. I wonder what he'd do if I pulled my pants down, freed his cock, and impaled myself on it. Would he stop saying he was too much for me? Would he see that I'm not some innocent little girl who needs to be shielded from him?

I'm ready. I want to see where it goes, even knowing it goes nowhere. Even knowing it won't last, that he doesn't last in anyone's life except the Crows. Lennox told me to watch, and I have. I know he disposes of girls when he's gotten what he wants out of them, used them up. I know, and I'm not afraid. I want to be one of them, want him to use me up, devour me and leave nothing but bones, less than what was left of Poe after the animal got to her body.

I reach for Maddox's hand, wrapped around me and holding me spooned against him. I slide it from under me and move it down my belly. "Touch me," I whisper, moving his hand down and tucking it between my legs. I open my knees, hooking my top leg over his so he has access.

He cups my mound through my pajamas, pulling me tighter against him and making the softest sound of pleasure in his throat.

I squirm against him. "Touch me," I whisper again.

"I am touching you," he whispers back.

"More," I say, rocking against his hand.

"More what?" he asks, and I wonder if he was teasing me all along, if he knew how hard this is for me, how wet I am, that I'm lying here writhing with need.

"Finger me," I whisper, surprising myself with how bold I am.

He sucks in a breath, and I feel his cock throb against me again. "Little girl," he says. "You're asking for it."

"I am," I whisper. "And I'm not a little girl."

"Then tell me what you want," he growls into my ear, adjusting his position to cradle my head on his thick bicep like he did last time. His fingers fist my hair while his other hand kneads into the flesh between my legs, making me grind into his palm and bite down on my lip so I don't whimper for relief.

"I want you fingers inside me," I whisper. "Make me cum like last time."

"Where?" he asks. "Tell me where you want my fingers, little girl. In your pussy or your ass?"

"Both," I breathe. "Please."

I'm tired of being afraid. I'm tired of hiding. I want him to have me, to take me, to break me and make me his in every way, even if only for a night.

"Fuck," he breathes, dipping his hand into the top of my pajamas. He works it down the front of my panties and takes a slow, shuddering breath as he teases open my lips and dips a finger into my slit. His cock pulses against my ass, and I whimper with arousal.

"God, you're so fucking wet," he growls. His arm flexes as he drives a finger deep inside me in one slow, firm motion. Squeezing his hand closed, he fists my pussy, holding my hips in place as firmly as my head and grinding his cock against me so hard it hurts.

When he pulses his finger inside me, I bite down on my lip to stifle a cry of pleasure. Maddox pushes up on his elbow, gripping my hair and turning my head to his. His mouth comes down on mine, stifling my sounds of pleasure. He devours them like a starving man who's finally found sustenance, entering me with a finger while his tongue enters my mouth. I give myself, letting him do what he wants to me, push a second finger into me and then use one on my ass and two in my pussy, stroking my clit with his thumb until I explode, my cries muffled and swallowed by his rough, demanding kisses.

At last, he lays back, his chest heaving against my back. I can feel sweat sticking my shirt to me, and I sit up enough to tug it off, lying back and letting my sweat mingle with the sweat on his chest. I halfway expect him to send me back to my bed, since this seems more intimate than what I expect from a man like Maddox, and the thunder is faraway now. Only the faintest flickers of lightning bounce off the wall every few minutes, but the rain continues to fall. When he doesn't protest the intimate contact like he did at the pool that day, I snuggle down into his arms, relishing the delicious soreness of his fingers still buried inside me and the thrill of our bare skin pressed together.

He doesn't say a word, just fits his body tightly around mine and begins to relax, even though he's still hard against my back. Every few minutes, his fingers twitch inside me as his muscles fire off a little spasm of energy until he goes completely still, his breathing deep and slow when he's asleep.

He did it. He distracted me from the storm and my dream, just like the last time, when they distracted me from my worries about Lee. I know I'm doing something reckless, that anyone would tell me I was insane to take this leap with no parachute. Hell, I'm telling myself I'm insane. I'm not the girl who lets herself fall. I'm the girl who likes solid ground underfoot.

But I'm not afraid. For once, I'm not afraid.

I know he'll break my heart, but I'm ready to break. Not just by him, but by both of them. I'm not just a virgin because I've never had sex. I've never experienced anything. I've been alone so long, even when I had friends. I've never been in love. I've never had my heart broken. And I'm ready to do those things, ready to stop protecting my heart and lend it to someone else. I want to feel that terrifying thrill when I trust them with it, just like the terrifying thrill of letting Maddox come into my room and trusting him with my body tonight. Maybe he didn't take my virginity tonight, but he could have. And I wouldn't have stopped him.

I've guarded myself like a secret for so long, built a shell around my heart like a mother bird protecting her chick, keeping everyone out. But now I want them to see what's inside my shell. I want to emerge, spread my wings, and show off the parts of myself I've kept hidden away for so long, hoarding them like treasure when they were never meant to be mine. A heart isn't to keep. It's to give away.

I want these Crow boys to have it, even knowing they'll handle my heart carelessly, make my deepest fears come true. I can already tell that loving them will change me, leave me forever scarred. They'll leave marks on my heart that will last as long as the ink on their skin.

That thought has terrified me for so long. I don't let people in because I know I'll be hurt. If my own mother won't protect me, why would anyone else? If the people who are supposed to love me hurt me the most, why wouldn't the people who owe me nothing?

But in some strange way, I'm ready to be hurt. I want to love just so I'll know I'm not alone. I want to hurt because it proves that I loved, maybe even that someone loved me. If that's the price of not being alone with my heart anymore, then I'm ready to pay that price.

I already know they won't treat me gently. Maddox won't treasure my heart. He doesn't treasure anyone. He'll hold it for a moment just to watch it beat for him and feel his power over me, and then he'll crush it in his fist and discard it like a bad story idea scribbled hastily on a sheet of paper, never looking back when he walks away.

But loving them will be worth it.

No matter the pain, they'll be worth it. To have loved them, to have been theirs. To have belonged to someone other than myself, to have entrusted them with the heart I kept locked up so long.

I'll love the pain as much as I love the loving part. It's all part of the same thing. The terror, the thrill, the exhilaration of the fall. The pleasure, the hurt, the hope and devastation. It's all tied together, the threads winding into one rope. And if I admit what that thing is, what those strands of exquisite torment and aching beauty form, I know it's love.

I love them.

Not just Maddox, but Lennox too. Guilt settles heavy in my belly as I watch the rise and fall of the blanket that covers him where he lies on his bed, under the beautiful mural just across the room, his back turned to us. He's been so kind these past few weeks, so patient and nurturing. But it was Maddox I let into my bed tonight, when he's done nothing to deserve it. Just like all the other girls, I chose his brother who didn't work for it over Lennox, who's done everything right to earn my trust and my heart.

What am I doing?

If he knew, he'd be devastated. But I can't seem to stop my heart from feeling as much for his brother as I do for him, no matter how impossible he makes it. It's too late to turn back now, though. I'm in it now. They've tied that rope into a noose, and I put it around my own neck, hanging myself in the name of love.

And the worst part is, I don't know which one that love is supposed to be for, and which one tied the noose because it wasn't him.

twenty-three

Lennox North

When I wake and roll over, my stomach lurches and my balls shrink into my groin like I just jumped into the river in January. I grope on the nightstand for my glasses, my heart hammering as I pray that my poor vision is to blame for what's right in front of my eyes.

But there she lays on Maddox's bed, sleeping soundly, probably worn out from being used like a fuck doll all night. Rage shimmers through me, and my hands curl into fists. I throw off the blanket and sit up. I can sleep through anything, and apparently I just slept through my brother fucking my girl halfway across the room.

But no.

She's not my girl, is she?

Because she chose him. After all I've done, being patient and respectful, she chose the asshole like every other girl.

No one wants the nice guy, not even the nice girls.

That's why I only fuck the crew girls. They don't want nice guys, and with them, I don't have to pretend to be one.

With Rae, though…

With Rae I *wanted* to be nice. She deserves more than the crew girls. She demands more by her very nature, by her innocence, her resilience, her determination to carry the weight of the world on her back alone, even if she has to beat her wings twice as hard as the rest of us, who fly together.

I stand and stride over to the other side of the room. Maddox didn't even wait for her to wake. He'd never let a bitch interfere with his routine. So he left her and went to work out, like he does every morning, and now she'll wake up alone, probably heartbroken and full of regret that she gave herself to an asshole who will never care about her the way I can.

I lift the blanket to just to make sure. Her tits are bare, small but firm, and fuck, I'm getting hard just looking at them. I lift the blanket a little more and see that she's still wearing pajama pants.

What the fuck went on in here while I was lost in the oblivion of sleep?

Her nipples pucker with cold, and she squirms and reaches for the blanket, her lids fluttering. Before I can think too much about it, I slide in with her. I wrap my arms around her, holding onto her, my chest aching with the heartbreak I know I'll see in her eyes when she wakes. At least this way, she won't wake up alone on her birthday.

That asshole probably doesn't even know it's a special day. He doesn't care enough to know.

"Mm," she murmurs, pulling my arms around her and nestling her ass back into my groin. "Maddox…"

A fucking knife in my back couldn't have hurt more. Or maybe it hurts so much because it is a knife in my back, put there by my own blood, my own twin.

He knows how I feel about her. He knows I want her, that I want more than to fuck her, like he does.

I could, though. I could be Maddox right now, the way she wants. I could stave off her disappointment a while longer, just slide down the top of her pants and take her the way he would, not caring what she'd have to say about it. Maddox never cares about the bitches he fucks, never cares about their feelings or desires. He's not picky. As long as the pussy's wet, he'll fuck it. He doesn't give a fuck who it belongs to, not even if it's the girl his brother wants.

"Rae," I say, leaning up on my elbow. I stroke her dark chocolate hair back, tucking it behind her ear. I could let her sleep, let her go on believing Maddox is holding her the morning after instead of dipping out while she was sleeping.

But I'm not quite that much of a nice guy.

"Mmm," she murmurs, the corner of her pouty lips pulling into a smile.

"Maddox left," I say, leaning down to kiss her cheek. "But I'm here, Sunshine." I grip her hip, pulling her flush against me, so she can feel how hard I am, that I still want her even if his cum is still leaking out of her. So she knows it's not over.

He hasn't won until I admit defeat.

And this time, I'm not going down without a fight. I'm done letting him win and holding in my anger, pretending I don't care that the girls like him better, that the coaches chose him for the teams and cut me, that he's even physically superior—bigger, stronger, taller. The *malparido* even has perfect 20/20 vision. He took all the nutrients in the womb, and he hasn't stopped winning since.

But I won't sit back and accept it this time. This time, the nice guy wins.

Rae snuggles against me and sighs contentedly even knowing who I am. Maybe she thinks we're happy to share her, like we do the crew girls. Like we did last time. She doesn't know what's gone down between us, that this shit's become a competition for her heart, her body, her innocence.

Unless he already took it…

I lean down and continue kissing her cheek and jawline. She moans and stretches her chin up, giving me access to the graceful curve of her throat. I lick and bite along the column of her neck, coming back to her ear and gently tugging her earlobe between my teeth. I suck at the skin, feeling the back of her earring against my tongue. Releasing it, I blow a stream of cold air against the wet skin, making her squirm with ticklishness.

I lean down, letting my warm breath fill her ear. "Are you still a virgin?"

"Yes," she says, stretching her body against mine. My cock throbs, and I fight the urge to drag her off the bed, throw her on the floor on her back, and fuck her hard and fast, taking what I want so he can never have it. I wonder what her tears taste like, how tight she'd clench up around me with her sobs, if the fear in her eyes would fade too fast once I'm inside her.

But no.

She's not that kind of girl.

"Maddox didn't fuck you last night?" I ask, palming her tits and feeling each nipple stiffen under my touch.

My cock throbs against her again, and she pushes back into it, urging me on.

"Just with his fingers," she says, her voice breathy. She rolls over to face me, biting her lip to hide a smile as she reaches for me. I groan as she slides her hand along the front of my thin pajama pants, palming my erection. "Want me to even things out?"

So she does still think this is okay with both of us, that if we don't share her at the same time, we'll be happy to take turns. Hell, she's even asked about joining the Murder of Crows. Maybe she'd be okay with us passing her around. A month ago, *I* would have been okay with it.

Now, it's turned personal.

I lean in and kiss her, matching her smile with my own. "How about this," I say. "You owe me a rain check on that one. I think today you get to be on the receiving end, birthday girl."

"Oh!" Her eyes widen, and her fingers flex around my cock. "I totally forgot."

"Happy birthday," I murmur, leaning down to capture her soft, pouty lower lip between my teeth. I give it a gentle suck, running my hand down her tight tummy and pushing down her pants. I stroke my fingers over her mound, her panties warm and already a little damp under my fingers. I try not to think about why, if she's wet for me or still wet from last night with Maddox.

Of course it's all I can think about now.

"We have a tradition in our family," I say, drawing back from the kiss while I continue to tease her gently with my fingers. "On our birthdays, we always eat cake for breakfast."

"Uh huh," she says, her long dark lashes framing her deep hazel eyes, fluttering up at me as I draw her panties aside and run a finger slowly, lightly up the seam of her pussy lips.

"But this morning, I get dessert first, and then I'll make you breakfast. How does that sound?"

I give her a wicked grin, but it takes a second for her to catch on. Her cheeks pinken in the cutest way, but her gaze falters. "Are you sure?" she whispers. "I mean…

I've never done that before. Should I shower first or… Should we go to my room?"

"I've never been more sure in my life," I promise, pushing her panties down and touching her bare. I want to be the first, to take something Maddox hasn't. "This may seem like my present more than yours, but once you've done it, you'll know it's your present. Happy Birthday, Sunshine."

I smile and kiss the tip of her nose, shifting my body on top of hers and resting on my elbows.

She swallows, her eyes searching mine, so I grind a little to show her what I can do for her. "You can return the favor on my birthday. Or maybe give me your virginity?"

"What about Maddox?" she asks as I roll my hips against her. I can feel how wet she is even through my pants.

"Maddox knows not to come in when the door's closed," I say, irritated that she's so worried about him seeing us. She sure didn't give a fuck last night. She let Maddox finger fuck her, knowing I was sleeping across the room and could wake up and see them at any moment.

She seems satisfied by my answer, though my words are not the whole truth. Our signal is a closed door and the radio on. But I know Maddox won't be gone much longer, and I want the asshole to see that I'm not backing down and letting him have this one. Walking in on me eating her out on his bed should send the message.

"Okay," Rae says, still sounding doubtful. I kiss her mouth, pushing my hand into her pants and fingering her at the same time, until her objections are forgotten. I move lower, kissing her neck, her collarbones, sucking her nipples into my mouth one at a time. She buries her hands in my hair as I move lower, kissing down her smooth belly and sucking at her belly button.

Moving lower, I shift my weight to shove her pants over her knees, leaving her bare for me to explore. Sitting back, I spread her open and look down at her beautiful virgin cunt. I want to memorize it, to paint it, to immortalize it before I wreck it. Maybe she'll let me, pose for me with her legs spread while I look, paint, and then fuck it.

"Lennox," she whispers, and I look up to see that trepidation in her eyes, the edge of fear shining in every gold fleck on the green of her irises. It makes me so hard I think I'm going to lose control, fuck her like a crew girl, rough and violent and meant to hurt.

"Rae," I say back, opening her with my fingers and sliding a finger from my other hand deep inside her. She shudders, her thighs quake, and her lids flutter closed as she moans. I slide down the bed before I can lose the last shred of control that holds me to being a good guy, a nice guy, a guy who gives a girl head for her birthday.

I lick her clit, stroking it with my tongue, listening for her cues to tell me if I'm doing it right. I don't do this a lot, but I know where the clit is, and I know that's the main attraction. Still, I can't get out of my head, can't help but wonder if she likes it, if she's faking the little moans and gasps and tremors in her legs. I can't help but wonder if she's thinking about how Maddox would eat pussy, if he'd be better.

The fucker probably would. I can count on one hand the number of times I've done this. I'm a nice guy outside the bedroom, but inside it, not so much. In the bedroom I'm a selfish dick, and I know it, and I don't care.

It never mattered before. I never wanted to give head, to give pleasure. Everyone at school knows I only fuck crew girls. Everyone in the crew knows I don't eat pussy. The crew girls know it, and they don't expect this treatment. The times I've done it, it's been after I roughed up a Crow girl a little too bad and I felt guilty about it. Because I do respect those girls. I like them. They're crew, and I want to protect them like any other member. They know it's not personal, how I fuck. But I still feel bad when I hurt them.

Rae's fingers grip my hair tighter, her nails scratching my scalp. I suck her clit, drawing it into my mouth, stretching it a little. She whimpers, and I release the suction and lift my face. "Does that feel good?"

"Yes," she breathes, pushing her hips up, spreading her knees, and offering up her cunt. Her clit is red and swollen, her folds slick with arousal. Reassured, I go back to work, running my tongue along the inside of each lip, the outside of her folds, through the center of her slit. When I return to her clit, her thighs clamp shut on my head, and I know she's getting closer. I slide a finger back into her, pumping into the tightness that makes my head spin. I circle her clit with my tongue, and she grinds up against me, crying out. One hand grips my hair, and I hear the other one hit the sheets, digging in.

"Oh god," she moans. "Lennox…"

She's close. My tongue's getting fucking sore, but I'm not stopping for anything. She'll never forget her eighteenth birthday, the first time she got eaten out. She bucks her hips, pulling my face in with the hand gripping my hair so fucking hard my scalp burns. I thrust my finger into her harder, rougher, and she moans and grinds harder, obviously liking the roughness. Maybe one day, I'll tell her what I like, how I like it, and she'll be that for me. Not like the crew girls, but better. She'll be only mine, and she won't know any different.

Rae's thighs are wrapped around my head so tight I don't hear the door open. I don't know he's in the room until I'm yanked roughly backwards, away from Rae's naked, trembling body.

"In my fucking bed?" Maddox bellows, and then his fist connects with my face, and for a minute, I don't know anything but pain.

twenty-four

Maddox North

Rae screams when my brother hits the floor, but I don't give her time to go cold. I drop to my knees, throw her legs over my shoulders, and bury my face in her.

"Maddox," she cries, but I shove her hands away when she tries to grab my ears.

"He's fine," I snap, and then I bury my tongue inside her cunt as deep as it will go.

She cries out, her hips jerking against my mouth. I don't stop, not even to breathe. I wanted a taste, and now that I've gotten one, I may never stop. I've never tasted something so sweet, so erotically, mouthwateringly delicious. I moan, eating her like a starving man—no, a man with no taste buds tasting food for the first time.

"Maddox," she says again, her voice nothing but a gasp of pleasure. She's not trying to push me away anymore. She's bucking under me while I torment her clit and her tight little virgin opening at once.

She's slick and hot and tight, and she tastes so good I have to hold back from biting her, from eating her cunt right out from between her thighs. I fuck her hard with my tongue, going fast and deep, shoving my thumb over her swollen red clit at the same rhythm. I want to push my tongue all the way in, as deep as my cock will go when I fuck her senseless. I want to lick her cervix, open her like an orange and split her in half so I can taste all the way to her core, suck the marrow from her bones and leave her as dry as a skeleton in the desert.

I shove her thighs open and spread her pussy so I can get deeper.

"Maddox," she cries, even louder this time. It's my name on her tongue, not my brother's.

Mine.

She's mine.

All mine.

I suck and moan and thrust my tongue into her deep, so deep my teeth sink into her soft, tender flesh. I stroke her slippery clit rhythmically again as I hear Lennox moan and start to sit up. Fuck him. He'll have to fucking kill me to make me stop.

I lift her hips with one hand, pushing my thumb into her ass hole to hold her in place as I feast.

"Oh god…" She bucks under me, and I curl my tongue inside her, stroking upwards. She cries my name even louder, almost a scream, and slams her thighs shut on my head, her hips rising as her whole body tightens and she grinds her cunt over my nose and mouth so hard I can't fucking breathe.

I keep her impaled on my tongue, nearly coming in my pants when I feel her walls clenching rhythmically around my tongue and her ass hole strangling my thumb.

"Maddox," she cries, spasms going through her thighs as she fists the sheets, her head falling back, her tits heaving and her hair spread around her on my pillow. Her cum spreads over my tongue like melted ice cream with each pulse of her tight cunt squeezing and sucking and milking me as I lap up her sweet cream.

When her cunt finally releases my tongue, I sit back on my heel. Lennox is sitting up, holding his head, where an ugly purple bruise the size of an egg is already forming. His glasses are twisted and hanging from one ear, and the rage in his eyes is one I haven't seen since his first kill.

I wipe my mouth on the back of my hand and grin at him. "And that's how it's done, *brother.*"

"Because I got her warmed up for you," Lennox snaps, jumping to his feet.

"And I owe you a thank you for that," I say, standing and clapping him on the back. "You wouldn't believe how good it felt when her cunt clenched up on my tongue. God, she even tastes tight."

I must be drunk on the taste of her, because Lennox's fist connects with my nose before I even see him swing. I stumble back a step, but I get my feet under me while my head's still spinning and clock him in the eye. He tackles me, and we fall to the floor with a thud that shakes the house. Rae screams, but we're too busy punching the fuck out of each other to stop for her.

A minute later, a sharp, stinging pain goes through me as my mother appears, whacking my back and shoulders with a wooden spoon like she used to when we fought as kids and she couldn't pull us apart without risking injury to herself. She's yelling at us, but I can't hear her over the cursing and shouting and grunting from my brother, whose rage is the only thing making him my equal right now.

At last, Mom gets our ears, and the pain of nearly having our ears ripped from our heads finally ends the fight. She drags us apart, holding us each at the end of one arm to separate us, also like she did when we were kids.

"What's gotten into you?" she snaps. "And over a girl!"

Rae sits frozen against the wall, my blanket clutched to her chest, her face drained of color.

"No offense," Mom says to her without even glancing her way.

"It's fine," Rae mumbles.

"Now, you're brothers, so act like it," Mom snaps at us. "Girls come and go, but you'll always have each other. So work this out so she doesn't come between you, or she'll have to find somewhere else to stay. I'm sorry, Rae, but I can't have my boys at each other this way."

"I'm sorry," Rae says, her voice small.

"Now you boys better work out an apology, and then work out how you're going to solve this," Mom says. "I won't lose one of my sons. I already have to worry about you every goddamn day since you joined that gang, and now this? I won't lose you to them, and I won't lose one of you to the other. Never that."

"I'm not going to kill him," I grumble, wincing at the pain she's still inflicting. "Though you might lose me to blood loss if you rip my ear off my head."

She gives us a shake. "Are you finished?"

"Yes," I concede.

Lennox waits another second, but he finally breaks and agrees.

"Good," Mom says, releasing our ears and shoving us apart.

"Now Rae, why don't you get dressed and come help me with breakfast. Leave these two hot heads to figure out how to get along."

"Yes, ma'am." Rae nods, still clutching the blanket to her chest.

Mom turns to us. "And I better not hear any more of this fighting," she says. "Enough people spill our blood, don't they? We don't need to make it easy for them and spill our own."

three for girls

twenty-five

#1 on the Billboard Chart:
"Gettin' Jiggy Wit It"—Will Smith

Rae West

Things are different after the fight. That morning, I got dressed in silence with both of them watching like they wanted to pounce. Then I went to the kitchen to make breakfast with Valeria while the boys decided not just how they were going to get along, as she said, but my fate.

If they can't get along, I have to go.

But there haven't been any more fights since that morning, and no one at school even blinks twice when they show up all bruised. They're gangsters, after all.

When I ask what they decided, they're both tightlipped, which is par for the course for Maddox but unusual for Lennox. Despite my best efforts, I can't get a word out of him. Pretty soon, though, it becomes clear. For the next month, they treat me with respect, keeping their distance. They don't treat me like a sister, but they act like I'll erupt if they so much as touch me. It doesn't take a genius to figure out they came to the agreement that neither can have me.

That's the opposite of what I want.

If they'd asked me, let me in on the decision that affects where I'm living until graduation, I would have told them they could both have me. That's what I want, if I'm honest with myself. I can't choose between them.

How could I choose Maddox and be just another girl who liked him better and treated Lennox like he's second best?

But I can't choose Lennox, either.

It should be easy. Lennox holds me on his knee and kisses the back of my neck, wants to take care of not just me but the whole neighborhood, and smiles at me like we're in our own little world, where it's just the two of us. Despite being drop dead gorgeous, he's a bit of a nerd like me. We make more sense together. We're both artists of a sort, though I paint with words on paper while he uses brushes and canvas. He's incredible in nearly every way—brilliant and talented and sweet. He's no less special than Maddox.

It should be a given.

Most of the time, Maddox just glares at us like a broody, angry, unpredictable animal that might attack at any moment. Engaging with him is always a gamble. But like any good gambling addict, I can't quite quit him. It's the thrill, the hope, the chance that this time, you'll have the winning hand. The thing that keeps Lee overnight at his poker games, keeps him playing one more round. I have the same itch, the same need to try one more time because when I win with Maddox, the payout…

God, I can hardly sleep with them in the next room, knowing they're right across the hall, knowing what they can do to me, how good they can make me feel. I try to be good, to not tempt them, because I don't want them fighting any more than Valeria does. It's scary. But I have to slip a hand between my legs each night and try to quench the ache they put inside me. It only satisfies me for a moment, long enough to fall asleep, but it's better than nothing.

Sometimes, I think they're trying to drive me insane. They play video games, inviting me to join and putting me in the middle of the couch between them. Lennox will lean over and kiss my shoulder, or hug me and give me a quick, hard kiss on the mouth like he did in the hallway at school that first time. Then he'll see Maddox glowering and quickly let me go.

Maddox is only marginally better. He never kisses me, but he pulls my leg over his while we're playing or watching a movie. For some reason, the contact always short-circuits my brain, and I can't stop thinking of anything but how my legs are parted, and maybe he'll put his hand on my knee and work it up my thigh the way he did the first night on his living room floor. Of course that would be humiliating, since I'm always soaking wet by the time the movie ends and I escape to relieve the tension he winds so tight inside me I think the coil will snap.

I take on extra newspaper dispensers at work just to get out of the house. The guys start going out more too, and though I'm sure they're with the Murder of Crows, I'm also absolutely tormented by thoughts of them hooking up with the girls in the crew. Or hell, maybe they're going on real dates on those nights, taking girls to the movie theater, where Maddox really can run his hand up his date's thigh and under her skirt. He doesn't strike me as the dating type, but Lennox might be. The thought of him taking a girl out, holding her hand and buying her dinner and kissing her goodnight like a gentleman, is somehow even worse than the thought of him fucking a crew girl.

One night I hear one of them get home at two in the morning, and I'm so tired of obsessing about them that I'm tempted to just go back to the shed. I don't, but the next day, I cash in my rain check and stay the night with Lexi. The next week, I stay again, even though her house is full with her and her mom, Billy's mom, and Billy, who already sleeps on the couch because they don't have enough room. The moms both chain smoke, and the smell when I walk into the trailer the first time nearly knocks me out, but I get used to it after that.

One of Lexi's friends has a convertible, and we go cruising on the regular, whistling at guys out the window or just driving out of town on the winding, two-lane blacktop road to the north, listening to Nirvana and Meredith Brooks, Cowboy Junkies and Sublime, at deafening volumes. She puts the top down, and we let the wind whip our hair around until we look like wild women.

I get back from one of our drives one night to find Lennox on the couch, playing Grand Theft Auto by himself.

"Hey," I say, feeling the usual shyness I do around them now. I know I'm to blame for the tension, and I feel guilty, but I'm not sure what to do about it except to keep saving money so I can get my own place.

"Rae," Lennox says, glancing up at me. His hands pause on the controller, and he drops it and sits back on the couch, grinning. "Where you been?"

"I went out with the girls," I say with a shrug. "Lexi and them."

He nods. "Have fun?"

"Yeah."

"Where'd you go?"

"Just driving around."

"You ever been to the rock quarry?"

"Sure," I say. "We used to go to the swimming hole all the time when I lived in Ridgedale. Though, to be honest, I don't love to swim."

"The girl with the pool doesn't like to swim."

"Hey, I like the sun," I protest, then flash him a smile. "Laying out by the pool, sipping a drink like a rich bitch. That's the life."

Lennox grins, and my stomach drops at how devastatingly fine he is. "You could do that in your backyard without a pool."

"I didn't put in the pool," I say with a shrug. "It was there when we moved in. And it's not like I *can't* swim. I did it for exercise last summer, and I like playing in the shallow end. I just… I prefer my feet on the ground, thank you very much."

"You ever been to the quarry… When it's not summer?" he asks, a little smirk tugging at the corner of his lips.

I swallow, remembering the stories about parties up there, someone getting wasted and falling into the pit, someone drowning… And lots and lots of people hooking up while drunk, losing their virginity, or sleeping with someone else's boyfriend. "No," I admit.

"Want to go?" Lennox asks.

"Is that allowed?" I ask carefully.

He laughs. "Anything you agree to is allowed."

Before I can ask what that means, he stands and snags his keys. We slide into the El Camino, and a charged silence fills the car. The night is dark and oppressive, with no moon or stars visible behind the dense layer of low hanging clouds overhead. It's only March, but the humidity makes the air heavy and thick, an edge of irritability in the air, like you want to just throw it off already.

"Where's Maddox?" I ask after a minute.

"Out doing crew shit," Lennox says. "He's more into the shooting part than I am."

The shooting part.

Sometimes I forget they aren't just two fine guys who live across the hall, ones I can't have. They're gangsters. Now that I live with them, I hear a lot about the Murder of Crows. They don't treat it like a big secret, like something that has to be talked about in whispers or behind closed doors so I don't hear. It's such a big part of their life that it's ordinary to them, and they talk openly about it. I overhear plenty.

Still, it's hard to swallow the fact that Maddox actually enjoys killing people.

We turn onto the highway a few minutes later and head out of Faulkner, past rice paddies with swampy woods beyond, and toward the exit to Ridgedale. I think about my old friends, fellow nerds who were as sheltered from gangs as I was. At first, we didn't have a phone in our new place. Once we hooked it up, I called them on occasion, but the calls got fewer and further between as the weeks went by. Now, I can't remember the last time we spoke. We all knew that I wasn't coming back, and they moved on with new friends, crushes, boyfriends…

I turn to Lennox. "How'd you get into the Crows, anyway?"

He glances sideways at me and shifts into a higher gear. "We already told you, that's not for you," he says. "Those girls… They're not like you."

"Because they're tough?" I press.

"Because they're desperate," he says flatly. "They get fucked in by the whole crew. The guys get beaten in."

"You got beat up by the whole crew to get in?"

"Sí," he says, whipping off the interstate and onto the exit ramp. The speed makes my stomach drop, and a little knot of exhilaration and fear tangles up in my belly as we skid to a stop at the stop sign where the ramp ends.

"But why?" I ask after he's turned onto the winding two-lane road toward Ridgedale.

"Why can't you join?" he asks, shifting smoothly and sweeping around a long curve in the road. "Because I'm not going to let anyone touch you, which kind of makes being fucked *or* beaten in out of the question."

"No, I mean… Why'd you join?"

He shrugs. "Shit went down, and it became necessary."

I sigh in frustration. "Why won't you tell me?"

"It's not my story to tell," he says, turning onto the dirt road to the rock quarry.

"Whose story is it?"

He hesitates a moment before speaking. "It's Mom's."

"Oh," I say, nodding. "Maddox said it had to do with your dad leaving."

Lennox doesn't answer, just pulls up into the empty area beside the quarry. One other vehicle is parked at the end of the space, a truck sitting under the sprawling branches of an old oak.

"Did you both join at once?"

"Sí."

"I would have figured Maddox joined first," I muse. "And then gave you shit until you joined."

Lennox's jaw tenses, and he grips the top of the wheel with one hand, staring straight ahead. "Why? You think I'm a pussy?"

"No," I protest. "I just… Like you said, he seems more like the type who'd be into shooting people. You're… Caring. Sometimes it's hard to imagine you doing that stuff."

"It was my idea," he says quietly, still staring out over the abyss of the quarry ahead. "To become affiliated with the Skull and Crossbones. And to form crews by neighborhood, to take care of shit at home."

"How old were you?"

"We've been in four years. The Murder of Crows only formed two years ago, though. We've done a lot of good in that time."

"Lexi said you named it that because of all the crows on our street?"

"Sí," he says. "And because we're a flock, a family. We fight together. Fucking Serpents… What are they? They don't have a pack."

"What are you going to do when you graduate?" I ask. "It seems like most of the Crows are seniors."

"There are younger ones," he says. "But we'll still be here. I'm going to Dixon, so I'll be around, Rae. I'm not going anywhere."

He finally turns, smiling at me.

"I didn't know that," I say, surprised he hasn't mentioned that he's going to college in the fall. Dixon College is a small, fancy liberal arts school, and I already know the Norths don't have a lot of money.

"I'm an artist," he says, reaching for me. He slides his hands around my waist and pulls me across the bench seat, nuzzling into my neck.

"I know, but…"

"They have scholarships," he says, kissing along my skin. "What about you, my little ray of sunshine? Where are you headed in the fall?"

"I don't know," I admit. "I guess I'll take classes at a community college until I figure it out."

"You could come with me," he says, pulling me tight against him and kissing up the column of my throat. My head falls back on the seat, and I wrap my arms around him. After a month without this, I'm fiending like an addict, and it feels so good.

"Is this allowed?" I ask.

"Anything you want is allowed," he says. "Just tell me you want me."

"I do," I whisper. "But I thought you couldn't touch me."

"It's up to you," he says, kissing and sucking at my ear, sending shivers coiling around my whole body. "It was always up to you, Rae. We were just waiting for you to decide."

"Decide what?"

"Who you wanted," he says. "It's your choice. Now we just have to tell Maddox."

His mouth comes down on mine before I can answer, before I can protest that I need more time, that I didn't choose him yet. I need to think about it, now that I know this is what they were waiting for. And what does that even mean, that I get to choose? What am I choosing? If it's just which one gets to fuck me, my answer might be different than if it's more than that.

Finally he stops kissing me long enough for me to breathe. Diving into my neck, he kisses and nips my skin, moaning and dragging me into his lap. My head is spinning with it, with him, with trying to keep up. I can't think when his hot mouth is on my skin, sucking and biting, devouring me.

"Lennox, wait," I gasp, grasping his head in both hands and trying to pull him away.

"I'm done waiting," he says. "I can't wait anymore. I'm crazy about you, Rae. I want to be with you. Don't you want to be with me?"

He pulls back, his breathing ragged, his lips red from the kisses. He's so gorgeous I want to faint dead away.

"I…" I gasp, trying to catch my breath. "What do you mean, be with me? Like sleep with me?"

"I want to do everything with you," he says. "Yeah, I want to fuck you, I won't lie. But I don't want you to think that's what this is about. I want to do everything else, too. I want to play video games with you and make breakfast with you, go to sleep with you and wake up with you. I want you to be mine, Rae."

"But… What about the crew girls?" I ask.

"Fuck the crew girls," he says. "They don't mean anything. We have to participate in the initiations, but the rest of them don't matter. That's why I've been waiting for you, Sunshine. I respect you. I don't want to share you like the crew girls. I don't care about them. I care about you."

He kisses me again, but I push him away. "Stop," I say. "I need time to think."

"What is there to think about?" he asks, pulling me in again. I struggle against him, but the harder I struggle, the more insistent he gets. His hand and mouth are everywhere, and I can't breathe. Finally I tear myself free and shove myself backwards across the seat, onto the passenger side. Lennox dives on top of me, and my head hits the door.

"I'm going to fuck you so hard I break both your legs," he growls, thrusting his hips between mine. "I want to see the look in your eyes and hear your bones snap while I cum inside your bloody virgin cunt."

"Get off me," I yell, shoving him as hard as I can. His body lurches sideways from the force, his temple slamming into the dash.

He curses savagely, and I reach up and yank the door handle. The door flies open, and I tumble out, my back hitting the gravel. I barely feel the rocks cutting into my skin. All I feel is terror. I scuttle backwards on my hands like a crab, but Lennox dives out of the car the next moment, his hands grabbing for me. I roll, scramble to my feet, and run.

I hear his footsteps on the gravel behind me, and the next second, his body slams into mine from behind. I hit the gravel on my hands and knees, and his fingers wind into my hair. His breath is hot and fast on my ear. "You like to run, little mouse?" he growls in my ear, and I hear his belt clink as he unbuckles. "You want to know how perfect we are together? I like to chase. It makes me so fucking hard to hunt and catch my prey before I fuck her.

I bet your cunt's dripping wet, too. You couldn't be more perfect for me, could you, my sunshine?"

"I'm not your prey," I yell, twisting around as he tries to yank my jeans down. My back digs into the gravel again, and my scalp feels like it's being torn from my skull with the tightness of his fingers, but I don't care. All I want to do is get away. I kick his thigh as hard as I can, my heel connecting with solid force. "I'm not your anything. I didn't choose you. Now let me go, you psycho!"

Lennox releases my hair, and I scramble backwards on my bleeding hands. "What?" he asks, staring at me and breathing hard.

I hear a car door slam, footsteps on gravel, and a masculine voice calling out. A second later, a blond stranger appears behind Lennox. His blue eyes fix on me, though.

"You okay?" he asks, his voice a refined southern drawl that I've never heard outside old movies. "I saw this guy attack you…"

I look at Lennox, who's sitting back on his heels, staring at me. "I—I'm sorry," he says. "I thought you were playing."

"Playing?" I ask incredulously. "What the fuck kind of game is that?"

"I thought… You said you chose me," he says. "I thought you wanted me to catch you."

"You need help," I say, climbing to my feet and brushing off my palms. Blood and dirt grind through the cuts and scrapes.

"I'm sorry," Lennox says again, still on his knees. He looks up at me, his gaze so bewildered and miserable I start to soften despite myself.

"You need a ride?" asks the stranger, hooking his thumb back toward the truck. "I know you don't know me, but I'm Justin, and my girlfriend's in the truck. We got plenty of room for you. We can take you home. It's not a problem."

Lennox stands and wheels on him. "Fuck off, you pretty little Swan boy. This is none of your fucking concern."

The guy looks at me doubtfully.

I turn to Lennox. "Am I safe with you?"

"Rae," he says, his eyes full of emotion. He presses a hand to his chest. "Of course you're fucking safe with me. I'd never hurt you. I'm sorry. I fucked up, okay? I thought you were saying you were into that…"

"Who the fuck would be into that?" I ask.

"I'm sorry," he repeats quietly, looking away at the dark pit beside us where they mined for rocks and left the chasm like a gaping wound in the earth. "I know it's fucked up. You're right. I do need help. I don't want to be like this. To want that. I can't help it. But I'll never do that to you again. I swear, Rae. You can trust me. I'm not going to hurt you."

I swallow, searching his eyes for any sign of manipulation, but all I see is sorrow and regret. "Okay," I say, turning to the other guy. "I'm fine. It was just a misunderstanding. Thanks for checking though."

"You sure?" he asks, his brow furrowing with concern as he looks between us.

"Yeah, I'm sure," I say, heading back for the open door of the El Camino. "You can go."

I climb in and close the door, taking stock of the rips in the knees of my jeans from when I hit the ground. I pick little pieces of gravel and sand out of my palms while I wait. A minute later, Lennox climbs into the driver's side and slams the door. Neither of us speaks as he starts the car and turns it around, heading back down the dirt road the way we came.

"Rae…" he says after a bit.

"There's nothing you can say," I tell him.

"Let me try," he says, slowing as we reach the ramp to the highway. "Please? I'm so fucking sorry, Rae. I'd never want to hurt you. I… I care about you so much. I just… I got carried away. I was so excited when you said you chose me…"

"Except I didn't say that. And even if I had, and we were together, what happens the next time you get *excited*?"

"It'll never happen again," he says. "I swear to you, *mi cariña*. I just thought… I don't know why I thought you were giving me the signal that you were into that, and it made me lose my mind. You're so fucking perfect. But now I know you're not, so I'll never do anything like that again. I promise, Rae. I can control myself. I'm not an animal."

I turn my face and stare out the window at the rice fields, remembering how Maddox acted about my bruises, how he acted when he went down on me. He's the wild one. Lennox is so calm, so controlled and… And kind. When he makes a promise, he keeps it, even if it scares me when I think he won't. Like the first night on their living room floor, when he promised he wouldn't fuck me, and he didn't.

"Okay," I say finally.

"I'll make it up to you," he says, reaching over and laying a hand on my thigh. He gives a reassuring squeeze, and when I meet his eye, he flashes his dimples in a pleading, tentative smile. "I promise, Rae. That's not who I am. You know that, right?"

I do know that. Don't I?

I've been living with the guys for a while, and I think I know them pretty well. But they're both complicated. Maddox is hard to know, since he's so moody. Lennox seems easier to know, but then he goes and does something like this. He's all sweet and cute to me at home, but he's still a gangster.

I turn to him. "Can I ask you something?"

"*Si,*" he says, pulling off the interstate when we reach Faulkner.

"Have you ever killed someone?"

He takes his hand off my knee to hit the blinker while he comes to a stop at the bottom of the ramp. "You mean a girl?"

"Anyone."

He turns onto the empty road. It's late, and the streets are quiet, the lights magnified under the dark, restless sky.

"I've shot someone," he says. "We don't usually stick around to see how it turns out."

I swallow, a funny tremor going through me. I figured they both had, but hearing him say it…

"But I'd never hurt you," he says, reaching for my knee again. "I'm going to prove it to you, Rae. I meant what I said back there. I'm crazy about you. I went crazy with how much I want you, but I'll never hurt you again. I'm going to wait as long as you need, until you trust me again. I promise. I'll be the best boyfriend you've ever had."

"Boyfriend?" I ask, not mentioning that I haven't had a boyfriend since middle school. It makes a warm little swell of joy rise inside me, that this tattooed gangster artist wants to actually date me. "Are you asking me to be your girlfriend right now?"

"Yes," he says, smiling at me from the corner of his mouth. "Can you give me just one more chance? I fucked up, Rae. But doesn't everyone deserve the grace to make a mistake once, as long as they don't do it again?"

"Yeah," I say, my mouth answering his smile before my head is completely on board. "Yeah, I think I can forgive you this once."

He wants to be my *boyfriend.* I want to squeal with happiness. It's only a bit more than a month until graduation, and I was beginning to think I'd be the freak who didn't go out with a single guy in all of high school. Maddox publicly proclaimed me as property of the Murder of Crows, which means no one messes with me—and no guy would dare ask me out. It's a Crow or nothing, and despite my jealous imaginings, I didn't think they actually dated.

We pull up in front of the small brick house next to the dilapidated white one where I used to live. It seems like years ago that I first opened the window and fed my own crow on the roof. Everything has changed since then. Now the Crows feed me. Poe's gone, and I'm gone from that place.

Lennox turns off the engine and takes my hand gently. "Can you do something for me?"

"Okay…"

"Don't tell Maddox about this," he says. "You know how pissed he'll be that you chose me. He's never lost before, and he won't take it well."

"Lennox…" I say, my chest tightening. I don't want to hurt him, but I also don't want this decision made for me. I didn't even know it was my decision to make until tonight. I want to think through it, to really consider before I do something I can't take back. He's offering to be my boyfriend, and I know Maddox will never offer that. But is that what I really and truly want? Or is it just what everyone else does, and I don't want to be left out?

"He'll be looking for any excuse for violence," Lennox says. "If he thinks I hurt you, that'll be reason enough for him. He won't wait to see that it's not true. That I didn't hurt you."

I swallow, not sure what's wrong but feeling uneasy about the way he paints everything with words as easily as he does with his brush. But he's right—he didn't hurt me. I only have a few scrapes, and that's from where I fell. I was more scared than hurt, and now I'm all turned around and confused by what happened, and if it was really as big a deal as I'm making it.

Finally, I can't stand to sit there another minute with Lennox just staring at me with such a pleading look in his eyes. I don't want them to fight again, and not just for the selfish reason that Valeria will kick me out. I don't want them hurt—either of them. And I know Lennox is right. Maddox will hurt him. I don't want to be the reason for it, don't want to be a snitch and get his ass kicked.

"Okay," I say at last, tugging my hand from his. "Just let me think about things, okay?"

"Take all the time you need," he says, brushing my hair off my cheek and winding it gently behind my ear. "I told you, I can wait. I'm a patient man. When you're ready, we'll tell him."

"No," I say, drawing away from him. "When I'm ready for this, I'll tell *you*."

twenty-six

#1 on the Billboard Chart:
"All My Life"—K-Ci & JoJo

Rae West

Over the next few weeks, things are strained, but Lennox keeps his promise. He treats me with nothing but respect, never pushing my limits or even reminding me that he's waiting for my answer. Do I want to be his girlfriend?

The night we came back from the quarry, Maddox had waited up, watching some old western on TV. When we walked in, he took one look at us and stalked off to his room. But Lennox must have told him enough to satisfy him because they didn't fight about it like they did on my birthday morning. Maddox watches us closely, though, even pulling me to the Crows' table at lunch.

Lennox gives nothing away.

When Maddox goes to work out, though, Lennox steals a few sweet kisses or holds my hand while we watch TV. One evening I leave my room on my way to run, and smack into Maddox, who's stepping out of his room, also dressed in running shorts and a loose tank.

"Where are your jean shorts, little girl?" he asks with a smirk.

"Very funny, Jerk Face," I shoot back.

The corner of his lip twitches, and he reaches out and adjusts the ballcap I'm wearing with my ponytail out the back to keep it off my neck.

We step out the front door and pause.

"I go that way," he says, nodding toward Sullivan Street. "Think you can keep up?"

"Not a chance," I say honestly. He's an entire foot taller than me, and there's no way my legs can keep up with his long stride.

"Come on," he says. "Let's see what you got."

We take off, not saying anything else. But then, we don't need to. Our shoes hitting the pavement sets a comfortable rhythm, and there's no need for words. I know he could run faster, but he doesn't leave me in the dust or complain that my pace is holding him back. That makes me feel bad, and I push myself harder than I would if he'd given me shit about being slow.

After that, I run with Maddox nearly every evening, since we both run already, and it would be awkward to avoid each other and go in opposite directions. He never goes ahead, even when I tell him to. I arrive home completely wrung out after our runs, while he's barely winded, since I'm pushing myself hard while he holds back. Lennox doesn't seem too happy about our time together, but he doesn't say much, just retreats to his room and works out his feelings in his sketchbook.

One evening we arrive back after one of our runs and find the driveway empty. When Maddox turns the knob of the front door, we find it locked.

"Did he seriously lock us out?" I ask, distracted by the harsh sound of crows in the oak in our backyard next door.

Maddox shrugs, but a frown darkens his brow as he surveys the empty driveway. "He must have gone somewhere on crew business."

"Doesn't that usually happen somewhere closer to midnight?" I ask, since I hear them come and go on the regular, mostly after their mom is asleep. Clearly Faulkner's city curfew hasn't stopped the gangs from running around all hours of the night.

"There's no schedule for when people need help," Maddox says, looking annoyed at me, which he does pretty much always. I try not to take it personally, since that's his normal expression around everyone else too. And I did just make light of his gang, which they take very seriously.

"Are all the windows locked?" I ask. "We could pop out a screen."

"They're all locked," he says, glowering at me like I'm the reason we're locked out.

"We could break a window," I offer. "There's the little bathroom window on the back of the house that wouldn't cost as much to replace. I could crawl through and unlock the door for you."

"We're not breaking a window," he snaps.

"Okay," I say, holding up both hands. "We'll just have to hang out until he gets back. Good thing we're both so good at this conversation thing."

Maddox stares at me a second and then rattles the doorknob desperately, like it'll suddenly pop open with the force of his need to get away from me. I laugh, and he turns to glower at me again. "You think this is funny?"

I shrug. "Maybe a little."

"It's not funny."

"If you're worried about your brother, we should just break a window and you can check your voicemail or recent calls to see where he might have gone. They can't cost that much to replace. I'll pay for it with my newspaper money."

"I'm not breaking a fucking window." He lets his forehead thump to the door and mutters, "Mom would kill me."

I smack my hand over my mouth to stop the laugh that bubbles out of me.

He lifts his head and glares at me, his thunderous expression making me take a step back as I try to collect myself. "What?" he demands.

"I don't know," I say, my lips still twitching with amusement. "It's just funny, you know? You're this big scary gangster, but you're afraid of your tiny little mother."

"I'm not scared of her," he growls.

"Okay," I say. "I believe you."

"She brought us into this world," he says. "She can take us out. And she never misses an opportunity to remind us."

I've heard that saying before, but it's a little hard to take it seriously when it comes to Valeria. She loves her sons way too much for me to think she'd ever inflict serious harm on them. Just the thought has me holding back laughter again.

Maddox's thick, dark brows draw together in fury. "That's funny to you?"

"I mean, not that she'd 'take you out,'" I say, stifling laughter again. "That's dead serious."

"I'm going to fucking kill Lennox," Maddox fumes, turning back to the door and banging his fist on it like there's someone inside to answer.

"Come on, I'm not laughing at you," I say, stepping in and touching his elbow. "It's not a bad thing. It's funny in a cute way."

"Funny in a cute way?" he asks incredulously.

"Yeah," I say. "It shows how much you love and respect your mom. It's sweet."

"Of course I fucking love my mother," he snaps. "What do you think I am, some kind of heartless animal?"

I draw back. "Of course not. I don't think that at all."

He stares at me a second and then turns away from the door. "Well, maybe you should."

Before I can answer, he starts down the driveway. I hesitate a moment, then jog after him. He crosses the street and bangs on Reggie's door, ignoring the bell. A little girl opens the door and stares out at us. She's in a dress and pigtails with giant clear beads in the elastics. She chomps on her gum and stares up at Maddox. "Can I help you?" she asks, her voice full of sass.

"Get out of the door, loser," snaps another voice, and a girl who looks about twelve appears behind her. When she sees Maddox, she instantly transforms from annoyed big sister to sex kitten, batting her lashes and smirking up at him, leaning against the door frame in a provocative pose.

"Oh, hey, neighbor," she says, toying with her choker and pushing her chest out to make her boobs strain against her tight baby tee. "You come to borrow some sugar?"

Maddox chuckles at her antics. "I got plenty of sugar at home, Selma," he says. "Is Reggie in?"

"He might be," the girl says. "But what are you going to do for me?"

"Keep telling the Crows you're too young to join," Maddox says. "Trust me, you'll thank me someday."

She pouts up at him, but Reggie appears behind her before she can argue. "Hey, what's up?" Reggie asks, swinging the door wider.

They do their handshake, and Maddox asks if he's heard about any business that needs attending to. Reggie shrugs. "Haven't heard anything. Dad's at work, and I have to go in later, but y'all can hang out here until he gets home."

Maddox and I sit on the top step, and Reggie takes the porch swing, along with Selma, who brings out four beers and slips onto the seat beside her brother. He swipes the beer from her hand when she tries to open it, setting it down out of her reach on his end of the swing. "Don't be in such a hurry to grow up," he says. "You've seen what shit it got me in."

He and Maddox share a cigarette and talk about crew business while I watch the street, waiting for the El Camino to pull up. When we finish our beers, Selma crosses her arms and refuses to get more, since they're not letting her have any.

"Go get us some *polas*, would you?" Maddox asks me, stretching his leg across the concrete step to nudge my leg with the toe of his running shoe.

I think about being annoyed that he's ordering me around like usual, but I need to use the bathroom after the beer, and I've had enough of peeing in yards for this year. "Sure," I say, standing and brushing off the seat of my running shorts. "Bathroom?"

"End of the hall," Reggie says, picking up his cigarettes again. "Beer's in the fridge, bottom drawer."

The house is dark inside except for the TV, where the little girl who opened the door is watching *The Simpsons* with a big, bony dog. I go do my business and grab three beers, then pause when Selma's voice drifts in through the screen door.

"But is she your bitch or not?"

"Not," Maddox says flatly. "She lives with us. She's basically my sister."

Ouch.

I don't know what I expected. The truth is, I must have started to expect something, even without meaning to. Because these past few weeks, I haven't just been waiting for Lennox to prove himself. I've been waiting to see if I even needed to choose.

Guess not.

"Then you don't mind if I make her my bitch?" Reggie asks.

"The fuck I don't," Maddox growls.

"You said she's like your sister," Selma points out.

"Exactly," Maddox says, and I can practically hear the smug smile on his face. I can barely make out his form slumping back against the railing, his foot still extended to my spot, like he's saving me a seat. He drags on his cigarette and blows a slow stream of smoke toward Reggie. "Make her your bitch, and I'll make your sister mine."

Selma must be fainting with joy at the prospect. I decide to stop lurking, so I stride down the hall, purposefully making my footsteps heavy so they hear me coming. I elbow open the screen door and pass the beers around, then take my spot on the top step again. Maddox leaves his foot where it was on the second step, so it's under the crook of my knees.

Before any of us can start up a new conversation, we're interrupted by the sound of a trash can scraping along the sidewalk. My mother is out, dragging the can toward the curb. She looks up, her eyes sweeping over the four of us and moving away. My heart twists in my chest. Not that she was ever going to win Mom of the Year, but to not recognize her own daughter…

Just when I'm about to think the worst, her gaze snaps back, finding mine.

A small rush of relief goes through me. She's just out of it, like usual, and didn't expect to see me on Reggie's porch.

Maddox's foot nudges the back of my thigh. "You good?"

I swallow and nod, setting down my beer and wiping my hands on my shorts. "I'm going to say hi."

Without giving him a chance to argue, I stand and make my way across the street. Mom stands rooted to the spot, like a second trash can next to the first on the curb.

"Hey, Mom," I say.

"You're here," she says faintly. "I was so worried. When you disappeared from the shed…"

I shrug. "I'm sure they would have notified you if they found my body."

"Oh, I know," she says, giving me a pained smile. "They didn't even show up to see why you weren't at school, so I figured you were still going, that you'd found a place to stay with a friend."

"I did." I smile at her, but it must be as pained as hers, because all I feel is sadness. I can get out. Lee never wanted me around anyway. She's stuck there forever.

"And you're… You're doing okay?" Her expression is so painfully hopeful. She always did want the best for me, even when she couldn't give it. "You look good. Healthy. You're staying somewhere safe?"

"Yeah," I say, crossing my arms and squeezing my hands into fists, feeling my nails bite into my palms. "I'm okay, Mom."

"Good," she says, her eyes shiny with unshed tears. She reaches out and tucks my hair behind my ear. She gives me one last smile, then drops her hand. "I'm glad you're happy."

I don't say anything. What is there to say? I could be spiteful and point out that she never protected me, that all she can offer now is a lame sentiment about being happy for me because I got out when she didn't. We both know she'll never get out. She can't, and it makes me sad, but I won't stay for her.

I was strong enough to leave, and I'm safer living with gangsters than I was living under the same roof as my own mother. I could offer to help her, to get her out, but we both know she wouldn't survive it. Lee thinks she owes him for all the years he's supported her, and he wouldn't let her go that easily.

Plus, she's too broken to have a normal life, too damaged by all the blows to the head. One day, he'll hit her just a little too hard, and that'll be the last time. He'll say she fell down the stairs, and it'll be ruled an accident. There won't even be an investigation. His word will be enough. All three of us know it, but we never say it, just like we never said what happened behind closed doors.

But I escaped through those doors, and I'm never walking back into that hell.

"I better get back inside, or he'll wonder where I got off to."

"Yeah," I say, tears thickening my throat. "Yeah, Mom. I…I love you."

I reach out and give her a quick hug. "I love you too," she murmurs into my shoulder.

I let her go, and she turns and walks away. She doesn't offer me a place to stay, doesn't invite me to come home. We both know she can't, that it's not her home. It's Lee's home, and I'm not welcome there. I'm eighteen now, so I'm on my own.

And I don't ask her about Lee, don't ask how he's doing—not because I want to know, but because how he's doing tells me how she's doing. Maybe it's time for both of us to stop worrying about the other, to accept that we never helped each other before, and we're not going to help now. I take a few deep breaths and turn back toward Reggie's house. I don't want to hang out with friends anymore, but fucking Lennox locked us out, so I don't have the option of curling up in my bed and disappearing into a book so nothing else exists.

Maddox stands and comes down the walkway, stopping when he reaches the street. We just stare at each other across the gap, and then a car turns onto the street, the headlights all we can see in the dark. I don't look, anyway. I keep my eyes focused on Maddox. He tenses, his hand going behind him, but he doesn't drop my gaze. The car speeds by, and his shoulders relax.

"Quíubo, little mama?"

I shake my head.

"Reggie's going to work," he says. "But there's a good spot we can hang out. Come on."

He jerks his chin toward the side of the house and turns to walk away. I don't want to follow, but I don't have anywhere else to go. I drag my heavy feet across the street, along the side of Reggie's house, and through a gate in the chain link fence with a sign that says, "Beware of Dog." We cross the squelchy yard, and Maddox starts up a creaky wooden ladder. I stand back, eyeing it warily, since it shakes and groans like it might collapse under his impressive weight at any moment. He makes it to the top and turns to me.

"What you waiting for?" he asks. "Scared, little girl?"

"Shut up," I mutter, taking a breath and gripping the ladder. The wood is swollen and extra flexible from all the recent rain, which makes it even more shaky. But I make it to the top without falling and breaking my neck. Maddox crouches and holds out a hand, and I let him pull me onto the slightly slanted, asphalt shingled roof. We both stand, and he tips his chin toward the street.

"We can see when the asshole gets home," he says. "Or Mom. But we're in shadow if we sit down. No one will see us up here."

"Well, aren't you quite the peeping Tom?" I tease. "You ever look through my window from here?"

"If I want to see tits, I hit one of the numbers on our speed dial," he says, sitting down on the roof and pulling a beer from the pocket of his baggy shorts. He pulls another one from the other pocket and sets it next to his, between us. I hesitate only a second before taking a seat on the other side of the beers. I have nothing else to do, nowhere else to be. I can't even do homework, read, or write.

"Doesn't that ever get old?" I ask, propping my elbows on my knees and staring up at the silvery white disc of the moon overhead.

He snorts. "You think pussy gets old? Damn, you really are a virgin."

I shrug. "Yeah, I am. But it seems like after a while, you'd get tired of sleeping with every girl in school."

He laughs. "You have no idea what you're talking about, little girl. No dude gets tired of fucking hot, willing chicks. There's no such thing as too much pussy."

"I'm not saying you'd get tired of sex," I say. "Just with different girls. Don't you ever want it to mean something?"

"Yeah," he says, popping the top on his beer and lifting it like a toast. "It means I get to bust a nut in a tight little hole. If you knew how good it felt, you'd understand."

"I know," I mutter. Maybe not sex, but I'll remember the orgasms they gave me for the rest of my life.

Maddox chuckles. "Is that what you're really after? You're asking me to eat you out up here?"

"No," I protest, my face going hot. I reach for the beer so I'll have something to do with my hands. "I just think that maybe some day you'll meet one girl who's worth giving up all the others for."

Maddox throws back his head and laughs. It's a sound I've never heard before, a real, big, whole body laugh. It makes me feel small and large at the same time, like I'm important enough for him to share a secret with, the secret of what a real Maddox North laugh sounds like. At the same time, I feel like his kid sister suddenly. "You're funny as shit, you know that?" he asks, taking a swig of his beer and shaking his head when he's done laughing at me.

"You will," I say with a shrug, sounding like I know what I'm talking about.

"Let me guess," he says. "You think you're going to be the girl who ties me down? That's what you all think, isn't it?"

"I don't think any girl's going to tie you down in the way you think," I say. "Like you're some wild thing she's going to trap or tame by convincing you to stop playing the field. But I bet one day you'll meet someone who you like enough that you'll want to hang up your uniform and stop playing the game."

Maddox shakes his head and takes another drink. "Don't count on it, babe."

"I'm not," I say. "You're obviously not ready now. But I'd bet money that it'll happen. Everyone grows up eventually. One day, you'll *want* to be tied down. She won't tie you down. You'll tie yourself down for her, tie yourself to her."

"There's not a pussy in the world that's better than all the others combined," he says.

"You're probably right," I say. "I'm sure all the happily married men in the world are wrong."

"Show me one, and I'll hear him out," he says, leaning back on one hand and giving me that infuriating smirk. I want to slap it off his face. A more smug man cannot exist.

I run through the people I know in my head, determined to prove him wrong. My mom and stepdad. His single mom. Reggie's single dad. Lexi, Billy, Marilyn, Lola… Not a single set of married, biological parents between us.

"Well, we live in a fucked up part of the world," I say at last.

Maddox laughs, quietly this time. "Drink up, little girl," he says, bumping his can against mine. "And don't ever lose that."

"What?"

"Your ability to believe in that fairytale shit," he says. "Hold onto it as long as you can. That's rarer than a happily married man."

"Shut up."

"Plus, it's cute," he says, cracking a smile at me.

Tension tightens the air between us, and my breath catches. Then a car turns onto Mill—the El Camino at last. It pulls into the drive opposite us and idles for a minute before Lennox shuts off the engine and climbs out. I wonder where he's been. If he's been with a girl.

And suddenly, I don't want to go home, don't want to hear his excuses or know if he got done waiting for me to be ready.

I swallow hard and meet Maddox's piercing gaze. "Should we go?" I ask, bracing my hand on the roof to push myself up.

Maddox's huge hand covers mine, pinning it in place on the rough asphalt. His eyes search mine. "Not yet," he says. "Let the asshole sweat a while, wondering where we are."

I can't help the smile tugging at the corner of my lips. "Cool beans."

Maddox lies back on the roof, his hand moving from the top of mine to my wrist. Suddenly, I can't move. I can barely breathe. His thumb strokes the soft underside of my wrist, skimming over the sensitive skin and making my pulse race. I drop my head back and close my eyes, drawing a slow, deep breath through my trembling lips. Can he feel it, what he's doing to me?

"Maddox?" I whisper, my heart skittering crazily in my chest. I'm ready to tell him, to let him know that I choose him, even if it means nothing to him. It will mean something to me, and isn't that good enough? To have lost my virginity to a boy who makes my head spin and my temper flare and my heart die a little inside my chest every time I look at him?

If that's not love, then what is?

Does it really matter if he feels the same?

What if I never find someone where the love is equal? Would I rather give it to a boy who loves me, who feels the way about me that I feel about Maddox, like he can't breathe when our eyes meet, if I only like him and am flattered by his attention the way Maddox is by mine?

How can I ever really know, anyway? If a boy said he loved me, I'd have to believe him, but I'd never really know if he was just saying it to get in my pants. Does

Lennox really care about me as much as he says? He's been proving it to me, but what if I always have doubts?

Maddox is honest. He could have told me he cared about me, that I was the only one, worth giving up all the other girls. I gave him the perfect opening. And if he said it, I'd believe him because I want to, because I'm desperate to. He could say those things, make me trust him and believe he loved me, and then use me until there was nothing left he wanted, like he does all the other girls.

I hear about it at school, how he broke some Crow girl's heart so badly she left the crew and dropped out of school; how some rich girl took a month off to go to Hawaii and recover from the devastation of Maddox North.

"You ever get high?" he asks, pulling his hand from mine and digging in his pocket.

The tension that weighed heavy in the thick air for a moment is gone, and I lay back on my elbows and stare up at the sharp points of starlight twinkling in the velvet blue-black night sky, relief and regret warring inside me. What the fuck was I thinking?

"No," I admit. "Where do you even get that?"

"I have connections," he says, sitting up. He pulls out a small rectangle and pulls a delicate, folded paper from the pack. Then he opens a baggie, and the skunky smell invades the damp cool around us. I watch him break apart the fuzzy green buds and arrange them in the crease of the paper, watch his thumbs knead and tuck. My pulse flutters when the tip of his tongue drags along the edge of the paper, and I have to squeeze my knees together.

God, the things that tongue can do…

When he finishes rolling the joint, he doesn't offer it to me first, like a gentleman. Of course not. Maddox never pretends to be what he's not.

He lights the joint and takes a deep drag, then picks a fleck off his tongue before exhaling a white cloud of smoke. He flicks the lighter, taking another drag to make sure it's burning good before handing it to me.

"How do I do this?" I ask nervously.

"Just give it a little suck," he says, smirking at me. "Don't worry, you'll still be a virgin."

"Shut up," I protest, elbowing him. "I'm not as good as you seem to think."

"Yeah, look at you, breaking city curfew and smoking weed on the same night. Pretty soon you'll be doing time in lock-up."

He grins and watches me, a challenge in his eyes, like he doesn't think I'll do it. When I slip the end between my lips and feel the wetness of the tip, a little thrill goes through me, and I have to press my knees together again. I take a drag, feeling cool and grown up and badass like him.

Then I exhale and cough for a whole minute straight while Maddox laughs his ass off.

My head is spinning and foggy at once, and I lay down on the roof, this time flat on my back. The warmth of the tiles seeps into my back, and I'm grateful they absorbed so much from the sun today. It's still early enough in the year that the nights are a bit chilly to be out in shorts and a tank, especially when the dew settles.

It must be around midnight by now, but Maddox doesn't protest when I make myself comfortable.

I reach out and run my finger over a tattoo of a vaguely familiar man's face on the back of his forearm. "Who's this?"

He twists his arm around and looks at it, swiping his palm over it and smiling. "That's my boy Che," he says, leaning back on his hand again.

"A guy in your crew who died?" I ask, swallowing hard.

"Che Guevara, dumbass," he says, knocking his foot against mine to show he's just playing and doesn't mean the insult. Still, embarrassment washes over me. I should have recognized him. I make a mental note to study up on him on the Encarta at school, since Valeria doesn't have a computer. If he's important enough to Maddox that he wants him inked on his skin forever, he must be a pretty big influence on him.

"What about you, little mama?" he asks, nudging my foot again. "Got any ink I don't know about?"

I feel my face warming, and I'm glad it's too dark for him to see it up here. He's seen every inch of me—on several occasions.

"Not yet," I say lightly, leaning up on one elbow to snag my beer. "But I've always wanted one. They look really cool on y'all. I wouldn't mind having a few."

"Know what you'd get?" he asks, turning his head and looking down at me, like he's actually interested in the answer.

"No," I admit. "Maybe a quote from my favorite book."

He tips his chin, prompting me to go on. "What's your favorite book?"

"Yeah, see, that's the problem," I admit, smiling up at him. "It changes all the time. Right now it's *IT*. Last year, it was *Frankenstein*. Next year, it could be something else, so if I got a quote from that book, maybe I'd regret it."

"Maybe," he says, taking a swig from his beer.

I take one from mine. "Have you ever regretted any of yours?"

"No," he says. "They're part of me."

"What made you decide to put the crow on your neck?" I ask. "No one else has it there."

He shrugs one shoulder. "It's right up front, where you can't miss it," he says. "People know who I am and what I'm about from the first time they see me. I like that."

It strikes me how well I know him. I was just thinking the same thing earlier, that with him, there's no guessing. He is who he is, and he makes no apologies for it. I try not to let other people's opinions of me matter, but I'm nowhere near as confident as he is. "You're not worried about… I don't know… People not wanting to hire you because of it?"

He laughs quietly. "You sound like Mom."

"I mean, it's a legitimate concern."

"Nah, I'm not worried about it," he says, setting down his beer and leaning back on both hands. "I figure the only jobs I'll ever have will be for the Crosses, anyway. If I live that long."

"Wow," I say, sipping my beer. "That's morbid."

"I thought you were into that shit," he teases. "All those scary books and movies…"

He shoots me a grin, and my tummy flips. He's not as gorgeous as Lennox, not as perfectly symmetrical and flawless, not as well dressed. But when he smiles, the rough, carelessness of his appearance disappears, and there's only that smile, the one that tugs at the corners of his lips and crinkles the corners of his eyes, the one that makes me feel like I'm soaring high in the night sky, a crow who lost her bearings and is guided only by the silvery moonlight on her inky feathers.

I clear my throat, trying not to lose myself in his magnetism. "I like to read," I say, hearing how lame it sounds the moment the words leave my lips. "Not just scary stuff. I like everything. I figure one day I'll probably teach lit, or maybe… Write."

I've never said that out loud to anyone, and it makes me feel stupider than just saying I like to read.

"You write?" he asks, looking way too intrigued by that. "What kind of stuff?"

"Nothing," I mumble into my beer. "It's dumb."

"You have a diary, don't you?" he asks, smirking at me. "I bet it's pink and has a little lock on it. Do you use your glitter pens to draw my name in hearts on every page?"

"Shut up," I protest, shoving his arm. "I don't have a diary."

A diary was dangerous in my house growing up. I never knew when Lee would go through my stuff, and I wasn't about to leave any evidence of my hatred of him. He would have kicked me out of the house a long time ago if he knew how I felt about him.

Besides, I didn't need a diary once I moved here. Poe was my confidant, the one I poured out my anger and anguish to, the one I told about my dreams and silly crushes. She never judged, not even when I told her I liked both North brothers.

"Unless you tell me what you write, I'll never believe you," Maddox says.

"Fine," I say. "I write scary stories. Short ones, like Shirley Jackson. If I ever got famous, I'd want to be the girl version of Stephen King."

"Cool," he says. "Maybe I could read one sometime."

"Maybe," I say, my voice giving away my doubt.

"What?" he asks. "You think I'm a gangster, so I can't read?"

"I was going to say dumb jock, but y'know. Whatever works for you."

"You're a bitch, you know that?" he says, but he's smiling.

I smile back, feeling giddy and high. "Sometimes."

"For real," he says. "Why can't I read them?"

"Do you even like scary stories?"

"I don't know," he says. "If they're good."

"Well, you might be waiting a while for that," I say, leaning back on my elbows beside him. "I said they were short like Shirley Jackson, not that they were as good as hers. But hey, if I go to college, maybe I'll study abroad one year and really learn to write. Maybe get a room in a hotel in Paris where Hemingway wrote, and I'll write a great American short story that's good enough for someone besides me to read without me dying of shame."

"Damn," he says. "You'd do all that for me?"

I roll my eyes and hide my smile behind my beer can. "Of course, Maddox. The world revolves around you, after all."

"I know."

I shake my head and lay back, setting my beer down so I can rest my head on my arm and stare up at the starry sky. "No, I'd like to do that anyway," I say. "Travel. Eat croissants and drink coffee in a sidewalk café in Paris, just watching people until I was so inspired I couldn't help but write something brilliant."

"That's a long way to go for inspiration."

"Yeah, I told you it was stupid."

"It's not stupid," he says, lying down beside me. "I could see you living in Paris. You'll go over for school, meet some French dude named Pierre with one of those skinny mustaches. He'll propose in front of the Eiffel Tower. You'll get a French poodle and call it your baby and take it everywhere with you, even on your little Vespa."

"I wouldn't."

"Oh, and you'll go to wine tastings and lift your pinky when you take a sip."

"Shut up," I say, laughing when he reaches over and wiggles my pinky finger between his thumb and finger.

"Oh, it'll happen," he says, then makes a terrible French accent. "Pierre, you simply must taste this one, *mon chérie*. The bouquet is simply divine. Notes of rusty barrels, lime, and Chi-Chi's poo."

"I hate you," I say, covering my face with both hands. "I'm never telling you anything again."

He laughs quietly, and then we fall silent, watching the clouds move. It's well into morning now, but I'm too amped up to be sleepy. I can't think of anything but the boy beside me, aching with anticipation of what comes next. I'm attuned to his every breath, painfully charged with expectation, with the wonder of the endless possibilities.

"What'd your mom say?" he asks after a long time.

"Nothing." I watch a small cloud race across the moon and continue on, followed by another big, puffy bank.

"You're not going back there, are you?" Maddox asks.

I glance at him from the corner of my eye and lean up to take a sip of my beer, which is now tepid and almost flat. "Not unless you want me to."

He scowls at the moon. "Do you want me to kill a cop?"

"No," I say, lying back next to him. "I don't want you to kill anyone."

A silence falls between us, heavy with the question I can't bring myself to ask. I know he must have killed people. I don't really want to know, though.

"And I don't want you to leave," he says at last.

Those words hang even heavier, and I wait for him to amend it, to justify it.

"I don't want you to leave…

If that's the only place you have to go.

Until graduation.

If you want to stay.

Unless you make trouble between me and my brother."

But he doesn't say anything. For a long while, we just lie there, watching the clouds cover and uncover the moon. I can feel the heat of his bare arm crackling along mine even across the space between us. My fingers twitch, my palms tingling with the memory of his smooth skin under them. I ache for his touch, hope so hard my chest hurts that he'll reach over and lace his fingers through mine.

After what must be an hour or more, he sits up and smokes again, then leans back on his elbows, watching the sky full of the moon and clouds and stars passing us by, like time moving over us as we lie still, suspended in this moment, on this roof, on this night.

"See that cloud covering the moon now?" I ask. "That looks like a big fluffy bunny, right?"

Maddox squints and tilts his head. "Where's the ears?"

"Oh, and that one?" I say, pointing to a cumulous heap higher in the sky. "That's my big fluffy castle. Hey, I think there's even a princess in it."

"Either you're high as hell, or you're fucking with me," Maddox says.

"No, I'm serious," I insist. "See, she's leaning out the window, waving to her pet unicorn. Which is… Right there." I point to a little shapeless blob of clouds, edged by silvery moonlight.

"Shut the fuck up," Maddox says.

I bat my eyes and give him my most innocent look. "Just trying to live in the magical fairytale land inside my head."

Maddox growls and pounces on me, his strong fingers digging into my ribs painfully hard. I yelp and struggle as he pins me, laughing and tickling me so hard I know I'll have bruises. But I can't help but laugh too, thrashing around as he keeps going, tickling me until I'm laughing so hard I can't breathe.

"Stop, stop," I beg, gasping for breath. I shove at his hands, flopping back and forth to free myself. Suddenly, his hot palms are on my bare skin, my loose tank having ridden up while we wrestled. He stops moving, his big hands circling my waist, his face hovering over mine. Our eyes meet, and the laughter dies on my lips. His own smile slips away, and there's nothing between us. There's just him and me, my heart beating so hard I can hear it, my breath coming quick, my chest rising and falling between us.

He leans a fraction closer, his gaze dropping to my lips. My lids flutter closed, my heart stopping with anticipation.

I feel him move away. My eyes fly open in time to see him stand and brush off his shorts. I sit up quickly, confused and hurt and disappointed all at once.

"It's getting light," he says, holding out a hand. "Mom's home too, so the door's open. *Venga.*"

What the hell?

My head is spinning at how quickly he turned it off, how abruptly it all ended. He's right though. We stayed up all night, longer than I thought. I must have lost track of time when we were high, or talking, or tickling, or…

Just being together. It was so comfortable, surprisingly easy to be with him when he's not being a total dickhead. Is it because he thinks of me differently now, like a sister, as he told Reggie?

Is that why he freaked out when his hands touched my stomach?

I'm too confused to get my thoughts together, especially when I'm still a little stoned. So I just put my hand in his, and he yanks me to my feet in one pull. I stumble, and he steadies me, then releases my hand and snags the beer cans, dumping the backwash over the side of the roof and crushing the two cans in his hands while I climb down the ladder. He follows, then strides off across the street without waiting for me.

twenty-seven

Maddox North

I can't have her.

I keep reminding myself that, cursing that I let it get as far as it did. She shouldn't matter. She's just another hole. There are a hundred girls waiting by the phone, praying it will ring so they can race over and jump on my dick. She's no different.

Except she *is* different.

She's different because if I stick my dick in this one, it will ruin my family. And fuck if I'm going to let that happen, to let any chick come between me and my brother, to cause our mother any more grief than she's already gone through.

Sure, it would fuck me up to see my brother lose it again, like he did that one time. Despite our differences, it's my job to look out for him, as the "big brother," just like it's both of our jobs to look after Mom. If something tore us apart, a girl or some disagreement about how to run the crew, I could live with it. It would kill part of me, but I'd live.

What I can't live with is knowing what it would do to Mom. She couldn't live with it, with having her sons torn apart and her family broken. And I couldn't do that to her, couldn't be the cause of it. She's suffered enough already—more than enough.

Nothing will tear us apart though. That didn't, and this won't. No girl is going to be the cause of that kind of grief in our family, no matter how soft her skin is, no matter how willing her body feels when it trembles against mine, no matter how ready she looks with her pouty, pink lips and her dewy, do-me eyes blinking up at me with their gold flecks and fluttery lashes. I'll just jerk off in the shower like I have every fucking night since she moved in. I'll picture it's her hand around my cock, stroking my shaft, fisting the head as I cum. I'll picture her touching me, but I won't touch her.

"I… Guess I'll take a shower," she says uncertainly as we step through the back door, which Mom always leaves open for us when one of us is out, even though I've told her a million times it's not safe.

"Fine," I say, striding off down the hall. I throw myself on the couch and grab the remote, too pent up with sexual frustration to go to bed. I'm not going to jerk off with Lennox across the room anyway. Not when I'm thinking about the girl he wants as much as I do. I'm not that much of an animal. I'll wait until she's done, and I'll fuck my hand in the shower like a civilized person.

I won't listen for her breathy little cries, the ones I heard that first day she used the shower here, when she didn't know I was home to hear her. I won't think about her in there, thinking about me. I won't think about her peeling her clothes off the way she did at the pool that day last summer, except this time, she won't stop with a bathing suit on like a tease. This time, she'll shed all her clothes, leaving her smooth, creamy skin bare. But I won't think about that. I won't think about the hot water sliding over her skin when it should be my hands. I won't think about it making her pink silk nipples pucker when it should be my mouth. I won't think about her fingers between her legs when it should be my cock.

Fuck.

I throw the remote down and grab my head in my hands and squeeze, like that will make it go away. Make her go away. End the fucking torture I'm in every fucking night that she sleeps across the hall and *I. Can't. Fucking. Have. Her.*

I hear the soft pad of her footsteps in the hallway and pray she has the sense not to poke the tiger right now. She's so fucking good at that, at provoking me until I think she's doing it on purpose, that she wants me to bend her over and fuck the spark right out of her.

"Maddox?" she asks, her voice barely above a whisper. Her fingers touch my shoulder tentatively. "You good?"

That's my question, and hearing her ask it does something fucked up to my head. She noticed. She remembers.

I wrench my hands through my hair and straighten. "Yeah," I bite out. "I'm good."

Instead of leaving the way she's supposed to, she circles the arm of the couch and sits down next to me, pulling one leg up and folding it under her while the other dangles off the edge of the couch, not even reaching the floor. Her hair's a wet tangle, and she's wearing a tiny pair of pink pajama shorts with yellow flowers on them and a white cotton tank with pink spaghetti straps and one flower on the front. It's not lacy like she's trying to look sexy. It's something a kid would wear.

I tell myself that, so I won't look at the water trickling from her mess of towel-dried hair and slowly wetting the edge of the tank. It's so girlie and unlike her usual, casual t-shirt and jeans style that I can't help but stare, that's all. How long until the water gets to her nipple, and I can see it through the wet fabric?

Fuck.

No. No. No.

I'm not doing this to my family. No girl is worth losing my brother, my blood.

"Need something?" I ask, swiping the remote and switching off the TV. The blinds are down, and living room is dark, but I can see her in the pale light filtering in the kitchen window behind her.

"Maddox," she says, reaching over and taking the remote from me. She sets it on the coffee table and straightens, squaring her shoulders. "Can we just talk for a minute?"

"We talked all fucking night," I say, gesturing toward the kitchen. A rectangle of pink light falls on the linoleum floor from the east-facing window, where the sunrise is coloring the sky.

"Well, I just wanted to tell you one more thing," she says, balling her hands into fists on her bare thighs. I know she's digging her nails in. I've seen the marks on her palms. But I don't stop her. "I—I've never done that before. Talked to someone until the sun came up. That means something."

I let out a snort of breath. "It doesn't mean shit, little girl. Trust me on that."

"It means something to me," she says.

"Fine, got it," I say. "You said your one more thing. You done now?"

"No," she says, scowling at me. "Stop being a dick and let me say it."

I sigh. "Then spit it out, little girl. I'm late for an appointment with my fist."

She swallows and then slowly lifts her eyes to meet mine. "I… I wanted you to know… That I choose you."

"You… Choose me?" I ask, trying not to laugh.

"Yeah," she says, squeezing her fists tighter.

I wince, feeling the nails biting in like she's digging them into my skin. "Would you stop that?" I snap, grabbing her wrists and squeezing until she has to open her hands. "And what the fuck are you even talking about?"

She raises her gaze to mine again, and suddenly I'm aware of how fast her pulse is racing in her wrists, that I can feel her heartbeat in the delicate skin, can smell the shampoo she used—my shampoo—in her wet hair. My cock twitches in my shorts, and I know I'm going to get hard all over again if I don't get away from her. There's no way she'll miss it with what I'm wearing.

She swallows so hard I can hear it, then lifts up and slides onto my knee. I try not to fucking groan out loud like a virgin at the sensation of her soft skin against mine. She tugs her hand from mine and threads her fingers through my hair, and I can't help but think she's probably getting blood in the strands. Fucked up as I am, the thought only makes me harder.

"Maddox," she whispers. "I choose you. I want you."

As if it's that simple. As if that will make Lennox magically stop wanting her, and it will all be okay. Nothing is okay. We both promised not to touch her, that neither could have her. It doesn't matter what she wants.

Before I can stop this shit from going further, she presses her lips to mine. Fuck, they're so fucking soft I lose my mind. My hands are on her hips before I know how they got there, my mouth taking hers automatically, guided by the instinct to take what I want, to claim her like the spoils of victory.

Victory over my brother.

I tear my mouth from hers, ending the kiss. We're both breathing hard, and I can see the color in her cheeks, her lips, pinker already from our brief contact. My cock throbs at the sight of her arousal.

"What are you doing?" I ask, my fingers digging into her narrow hips.

"I want you," she whispers.

I shake my head. "No, you don't. I don't do forever. I do right now."

"I know."

Her gaze holds mine, bolder than usual. It makes me want to throw her on her back and plow into her, give her what she's asking for with no questions asked. Fuck. This is a nightmare.

"What do you mean, you know?" I demand.

"You told me," she says. "On the roof, and other times too, though maybe not in such clear terms. I know what I'm getting into Maddox. I'm not a little girl. Maybe in some ways I was when I met you, but I'm not anymore. I'm ready for this."

"I heard you on the roof, too," I say, moving her off me. "It's not what you want."

"It is," she insists. "It's what I want right now. Not everything has to last forever. That doesn't mean it's not worth it."

"Trust me, little girl," I say. "It's not."

"Maddox North," she says, a little smile tugging the corners of her pouty lips. "Are you saying you're not worthy?"

I scowl at her. "No," I snap. "I'm saying you won't think it's worth it when you're crying your eyes out because you got used like every other bitch who climbed on my dick."

"Who says I'll cry over you?" She reaches for the thin strap of her tank, slowly tugging it over one shoulder. Every fucking thought, every shred of decency and morality leaves my mind as I watch the pink strap slide down her pale shoulder. I can't stop staring, can't even take a breath as I wait, the anticipation making my cock strain painfully hard against my shorts as she edges it down her arm until the top slips down over her breast. My mouth instantly fills with saliva at the memory of the taste of her skin, imagining how soft her nipple would feel against my tongue.

"Little girl," I growl. "Cut it out."

"I'm ready for you Maddox," she says, her voice that soft, breathy murmur that makes my brain shut off and turns me into the animal that only she can bring out in me. She slips the other shoulder down, baring both breasts to me like an offering. "I'm giving myself to you. Take me. Use me. I'm yours. Do what you want with me."

"Fuck," I grit out, the only word I can manage as the primal instinct inside me takes over. I drag her into my lap, holding her back in both hands while my mouth clamps down on her nipple. She shudders against me, and I suck hard, not caring when she whimpers and grabs my head in both hands, trying to pull me away.

I move to the other side, sucking half her breast into my mouth this time.

"Oh god," she moans, her head falling back.

"There's no god here, little girl," I growl, moving up to devour her throat, sucking and biting at her skin. "If there were, He'd never let me do what I'm about to do to you."

She moves her knee around to straddle me while I take her mouth again, thrusting my tongue against hers, claiming it the way I claimed her cunt on my bed that morning.

The morning I swore I wouldn't do this.

It takes everything in me to pull away this time. "Fuck," I mutter. "We can't."

There's no conviction in my voice though. Not when she starts rocking her hips slowly, grinding along my shaft. I'm already a breath away from erupting. It takes everything in me not to plunge my cock to the hilt inside her and cum into her clenching core while she screams for me.

I grab her hips to still her. Because that's not how it would go. She'd scream alright, but it wouldn't be for more.

She's a fucking virgin.

"You're too small," I growl, trying to lift her off me.

She grips on tighter, wrapping her arms around my neck and speaking against my lips. "Then make me bigger," she says, kissing me with smiling, teasing lips.

I'm so hard my head is spinning, and I can't even think about what she's saying, asking me to stretch her out, wreck her, make her loose for me. I've never fucked a virgin before, and there's a reason for that. But fuck, the thought of it makes me nearly choke on my own tongue. God, what would it feel like to be inside a cunt as tight as hers?

Or maybe I'm just a defiant bastard, and the moment I can't have something, that makes me want it that much more. Just like her.

"I'll still be too big for you, little girl," I growl into her mouth, gripping her hips and moving them along the length of my erection so she can feel what she's dealing with.

"Make it fit," she whispers against my lips. "Or I will."

There's something about her bossy as fuck demand, bold as a crow going after what she wants, that makes me lose my head. I'm used to her sweet little lamb demeanor, not this…

She's not a crow. She's a tigress, taking control and taking what she wants like she deserves it. Whatever threads of self-control I'm holding onto snap. I lift her and slide sideways on the couch until I'm on my back, then jerk her down on my cock, thrusting up against her at the same moment. Her eyes widen, and I feel a tremor go through her belly. Without hesitation, she reaches down and tugs down the top of my basketball shorts, freeing my cock. Her small, soft hand wraps around my thick shaft, tugging the skin completely away from the tip. She strokes her hand up and down my length while I hold her hips and grind her clit against the base of my cock.

"Are you wet?" I ask.

"Yes," she pants, rocking harder.

"Good," I growl. "I want your cunt dripping for me before I fuck you so hard you black out. I'll use your body like a blow-up doll until you wake up and cum for me like a porn star, the way you do."

"Oh god," she gasps, her hips jerking against mine. "Maddox…"

"Yeah, baby girl," I say, rubbing my thumb over the soft, damp flesh of her mound.

"Do it," she says, cupping her hand around the head of my cock and squeezing a little pulse with her fingers. "Do everything you just said. I'm ready. I'm dripping. Feel me."

I reach down and pull aside the center of her shorts, hooking a thumb in her wet panties and pulling them aside too. She doesn't wait for me to finger her. She sinks her weight down until her slick cunt meets my shaft. I groan at the heat of her center, how wet she is, how ready to be fucked. My hips lift to grind into her, and my cock throbs out a drop of precum into her palm. With a moan, she slicks it over the head of my cock with her thumb. At the same time, she rocks her hips on mine, coating my shaft with her arousal from base to tip.

"Fuck," I grit out. "You're soaking me."

Releasing her grip on my cock, she grabs onto the back of the couch for leverage and starts riding me hard, pumping her hips along my length. I push up on one elbow to watch and nearly choke at the sight of my tip cresting between her lips. Another drop of precum squeezes from my tip at the sight. I palm her ass with my free hand, and she reaches down to hold her panties aside the way I was doing.

I watch her gliding along my length, my cock spreading her lips as she rides me. She rolls her hips forward, stroking me through her wet slit all the way to my tip. She grinds around it for a second and then slides back, the engorged head of my cock grinding her clit before she sinks along my shaft to the base again. Her tits sway above the top of her shirt, her pink nipples stiff and flushed.

"Fuck," I growl. "Are you sure you're a virgin?"

"You know I am."

"Say it."

"I'm a virgin," she whispers. "Take my virginity, Maddox."

I'm not sure I'm going to last that long if I have to keep watching her. I reach up, squeezing her tit so hard she bucks against me, the muscles in her taut tummy flexing as her hips gyrate on mine.

"Oh god," she gasps, grinding hard and fast, the slick sounds of her cunt filling the room with her breathy cries. "Maddox, I'm going to—"

"Oh fuck," I choke out. "Fuck, slow down, little girl. I—"

I'm about to fucking cum all over us both, but my animal need to rut her like a fucking bitch in heat is interrupted by the quiet rattle of a door closing down the hall. A bucket of ice water replaces the sweat coating my skin, and my hands freeze on Rae's hips. She's still moving, obviously not having heard my brother moving in the house. But I heard.

Oblivious to the sound, lost in her own gasping, panting, moaning little cries as she climaxes, she keeps grinding her clit against my frenulum as she cums.

"Maddox," she gasps, pumping her cunt against me, using my cock to get off like a greedy little slut. Her tits bounce, my handprint still marking one of them where I fisted her flesh. She throws her head back, her damp hair tumbling down her back, swaying with her rolling hips. "Oh god, Maddox, I love you."

If hearing my brother's door close didn't kill the fucking bird brain that runs on instinct, her words sure as fuck do. I didn't even fuck her, and she's already using a word that no girl in the world has any business even thinking when it comes to me.

I shove her off me, sitting up and swinging my legs off the couch. "Grow the fuck up," I snap. "What are you, twelve?"

"I—I'm sorry," she blurts, looking so stunned I think she's about to fucking cry. Her panties are still askew, and I can see her glistening wet cunt, swollen and flushed red after her release, begging to be pounded hard and deep by a cock she'll never forget. "I didn't mean it. It just came out."

"And this is why I didn't want to fuck you." I stand and yank my pants up over my dick. "You can't handle adult shit. You're a fucking child, Rae."

"You're mad at me?" she asks incredulously, sitting up and adjusting her shorts to cover that cunt that makes me lose my head. "Because I said something stupid when I came?"

"Because you climbed on me like my dick is community property," I say. "You want to use someone's dick so bad, go buy a fucking dildo."

She swallows, and her voice is small when it comes out. "I thought you wanted to."

"Why?" I demand. "Because I fuck a lot of girls, so I must want to fuck them all? I must want to fuck *you?*" I bite out a bitter laugh, leveling her with my coldest glare.

"I'm sorry," she whispers, pulling her shirt up over her tits that are so fucking gorgeous I want to bite them and fuck them and fuck her into the ground until she disappears into it like a corpse. Maybe then I could believe she was a fucking ghost who was never here at all. Then I could go back to being the asshole I always was instead of the one who just stabbed his twin brother through the throat like an animal that doesn't even know the meaning of the word *loyalty*. Rae brings out that side of me, the side that's ruled by wild, animal passion. I've never been this man before, and I don't want to be him now.

"You can't just take whatever you want when you want it and think there are no consequences," I grit out, glaring down at her. "That's not how life works, little girl."

"I'm the same age as you," she snaps, her eyes shining with anger and humiliation.

"You're a virgin," I say flatly. "You might as well be a child."

"And how am I supposed to change that without actually, you know, having sex?" She sounds mad, but when she stops speaking, she bites down on her trembling lip. I know I'm killing the sexy as fuck tigress who climbed on me with such bold assurance, but I don't have a choice. I need her to know with certainty that this isn't an option. She can't do this shit again. If she does, I don't think I'll be able to stop her.

As much as it kills me that this will never happen, it would kill Lennox if it *did* happen. Accepting the truth of it, that it's just not in the cards for us, is best for all of us.

"Go fuck someone else," I say, gesturing to the door. "There's a whole fucking school full of guys who would fight to the death to bust a nut in a sexy little virgin like you."

"Guys who *you* told to stay away from me," she bites out.

"I take it back," I say. "If you're so fucking horny, go jump on their dicks like the slut you are. What do I care? I wouldn't fuck a desperate virgin like you if you paid me. You don't even know where a dick goes. You probably think what we just did is fucking."

I stalk off when I see the first fat tear roll down her cheek. Fuck if she's going to draw me in again, get me with her tears and her quivering lip and her big, hurt, hazel eyes. Fuck if I'm going to be the one who falls for it, the one who tears apart our family. I may not have a single moral in my stupid animal brain when it comes to her, but she'll never break the bond I have with my own blood.

twenty-eight

Lennox North

I seethe as I fumble in the top drawer in the dark. I don't think. I only feel. Red hot rage pulses in my temples. I fit a bullet into the chamber, then hesitate before I dip my hand back in, fingering the smooth, rounded tips. After a moment, I fit a second one into the gun.

They were fucking.

He wasn't fucking her, bending her over the side of the couch and stabbing into her like a demon possessed by passion, like I'd expected.

I knew he couldn't last. He's weak.

I'm not weak.

I'll do what I should have done before. I will take care of the problem.

I didn't expect to see what I saw, though. I should have, but I didn't. I thought she was different, that she was smarter than the dirty cum sluts who grovel at the feet of my brother and then cry about it, like they didn't know they'd get fucked in more ways than one.

I thought Rae was better. She was pure, innocent. A virgin.

She's not anymore, though.

She's just another whore who ignored all the hard work I put in and went straight for the asshole who doesn't give a fuck about her. Once again, the nice guy finished last.

I step toward the door, holding the gun pointed at the floor.

Never again.

The nice guy finished last for the last time.

I stop when I hear footsteps thudding past my room. The bathroom door closes, and the shower goes on. The fucking bastard thinks I slept through this one like I did last time, that he'll get away with this. That he'll wash her blood off his dick and crash onto the bed across the room, and I'll never know that he broke our pact. That once again, he couldn't keep his dick out of every girl he lays eyes on. Even knowing it's the one I want didn't stop him. Nothing stops Maddox from getting what he wants. He doesn't give a fuck about loyalty, about brotherhood. Maddox cares about two things, and two things only—himself and his dick.

I step out into the hall and swing my body in the direction of the living room. I hear her soft sobs as I creep down the hall. What did she expect? The whore jumped on his dick after he told her he didn't care. I know he did. Maddox doesn't lie. It's not because he's above deception. He just doesn't care enough to pretend to give a fuck.

And yet, there she was, riding his dick and crying his name. I thought they'd crashed at Billy's when I got home to find them still gone, but they came home in time to fuck on the couch, probably hoping I'd hear. Or maybe they've been doing it all along, and they got sloppy because they know I'm a heavy sleeper. They didn't know

I'd get up to take a piss and see her bouncing on his dick. It didn't look like the first time.

Have they been sneaking around behind my back from the start? Maddox knows I honor my word, but it means nothing to him. His word has no meaning to him, so why would mine? He has no honor, so his word is cheap.

I'm only surprised he hasn't rubbed it in my face instead of keeping it a secret. It must have been her idea to hide it. My brother may not be deceptive, but this bitch is. She let me think she'd chosen me, let me work for her love and do nice things for her. She acted like she was respectable, a good girl. All the while she was spreading her legs like the cheapest whore, probably letting Maddox fuck every hole raw, fill them with his cum without even making him shower after he railed some cheer slut in the locker room after school.

I step up behind the couch, where I saw her head bobbing as she rode him like a porn star. Part of me hopes in that fraction of a second that it'll be some other slut he brought home to fuck, Scarlet or Lexi or Mariana.

If he'll fuck his own brother's girl, he's sure as hell not above fucking another Crow's bitch.

Rae's curled up on the couch, her small body shaking with sobs.

Of course she is. Maddox wouldn't be gentle.

It gives me a small amount of comfort that this was probably the first time.

Not that the tears prove that. Maddox is a savage to all his lays, from the easiest to the most resistant, forcing them to take every inch and then calling them loose when he's done wrecking their cunts. He's shared enough of his fuck toys for me to know how he operates.

Still holding the pistol aimed at the floor, I cock it, and she finally hears me. She looks up, her eyes puffy and swimming with tears, her nose swollen and red in the early morning light filtering in from the kitchen. She looks like shit. That makes me feel better somehow. I'm glad she's in pain, both physical and emotional. She deserves it for choosing him.

"Lennox?" she whispers, her voice tremulous.

"I told you to watch out for him."

Tears burst from her eyes, and she chokes on another sob. "You're right," she blubbers into her hands. "I'm sorry, Lennox. I'm so sorry. I should have listened."

Vindication swells inside me. She's not rubbing it in my face. She regrets it.

Of course she does. She's just like every other dumb bitch in the long line of hearts Maddox has trampled without even noticing.

Usually, I don't pick up the pieces because I don't care any more than he does. My brother's sociopathic nature is an annoyance, not much more. If he shares them, I take it like the fucking charity case I am. If he doesn't, she's just another girl to mark off the list of potential lays for me.

But this time, I do care. And if I care, maybe he could too.

I've never bothered with a girl he's used and discarded. But what if I did? Would he get pissed over it, or laugh at me for taking his sloppy seconds?

Maddox isn't possessive. Of course he'll give me shit for following in his footsteps.

But if I don't let it bother me… That's what would kill him. If I showed I don't care, and I won in the end anyway, it would drive him crazy in a way that no amount of breaking in a fresh pussy could do. At first, he'll gloat and mock me for picking up his discarded fuck doll. But once he sees I'm not letting her go, that I value her… Once I walk around with her on my arm, making her happier than he ever could… It will drive him out of his mind to know that I tricked him, let him think she was only worth a night, and then took her for keeps.

I put the safety on and slide the gun into the waistband of my boxers, then circle the couch and scoop her into my arms.

Maddox thinks he won, but this isn't over. He used her, and he thinks that's all I care about. By the time he realizes it was only halftime, he'll have long ago tossed her ass like every other girl. And I'm here to catch her when she falls.

That's why I'm the one who will be ahead at the final buzzer. He doesn't know it yet, doesn't know any better than she does, but I'm just getting started. I'm not going to walk away from her just because he ruined her. I'm going to put her back together and keep her forever. By the time he realizes that I won in the ultimate game, that I won in the end, she'll be mine.

Just as I'm carrying her down the hall, the bathroom door opens and Maddox steps out in a cloud of steam.

We stare at each other for a minute.

I expect some smirking and gloating, but he just frowns, and his jaw clenches. Then he walks into our room and closes the door. Not that I expected him to fight for her. He got what he wanted, after all. He plays the short game. He's a dumb *gilipollas*, and he thinks that her virginity is the prize. But I'm playing the long game. I'm playing for keeps.

And if I play my cards right, by the time he realizes that she's the prize, she'll be so in love with me she won't even remember tonight.

I step into her little room and lay her down on the cot. "I know you're hurting," I tell her. "But I meant what I said. I made a promise, and you know what that means. I'm not going to fuck you—especially now. Not until you're ready. Let me prove I'm not like him. I'm going to be here for you, Rae."

She nods, curling in on herself with another hiccupping sob. I go to Mom's desk and set my gun down, then return to the bed. It's narrow, and when I slide onto it, the metal railing on the side of the cot digs into my back. But it's worth it. I know that now. I know I won, and that's worth a little discomfort. It's worth the seething white rage in my chest that Maddox fucked her first. It's worth knowing that the real reason I'm not fucking her tonight is because his cum is still inside her, probably leaking out of her cunt as the tears leak out of her eyes while I hold her.

And she fucking lets me. She lets me dry her tears, the ones she cries for him. She lets me hold her while his cum drips out of her wrecked hole, no longer untouched and waiting for me. I waited for her, and she didn't wait for me.

But I have plenty of time to punish her for that.

I pry her hair off her tear-stained cheek, my touch gentle, and kiss the damp, salty skin. "I'm here," I whisper, pulling her into my chest and letting her cling to me until her sobs subside. "I'm not going anywhere, despite what you did. I'm going to wait for you, and I'm going to be with you in the end. I promise you, Rae. And I never break a promise."

twenty-nine

#1 on the Billboard Chart:
"Too Close"—Next

Rae West

Maddox doesn't come home for a full week after our night on the roof. I try not to think about where he is, if he's crashing at some girl's house. I'm sure he is. He's Maddox. He goes through girls faster than most people go through a bag of Doritos.

And it's none of my business.

He made it clear he didn't want me after all. Worse, he accused me of using him.

Was I? I didn't think I was. I didn't know I was.

But the way he made it sound when he pushed me off, it was like he didn't want it at all. Like I threw myself at him, or worse, forced myself on him.

I'm too confused and hurt to seek him out at school, either. I go to my classes, and at night, I crawl into bed and nurse my wounded heart until Lennox comes in and carries me to his room. He holds me and kisses me, but he never even tries to slide a hand up my shirt. He's patient and kind and all the things Maddox isn't.

After a few days of waking up and seeing the empty bed across the room, I work up the nerve to ask where his brother might have gone.

Lennox leans in and kisses my forehead. "He does this sometimes. Takes off like this. Don't worry about it."

"Do you know where he is?" I ask, watching Lennox's face carefully for signs that I've pissed him off. He's been nothing short of amazing since that night at the quarry, so patient I can almost convince myself I imagined it, that it wasn't that bad.

But I know it was real. That boy is still in there, under the sensitive artist soul.

He shrugs his top shoulder as we lie face to face on his narrow bed. "No," he says. "That would require him to actually care about people besides himself. If he didn't leave us worrying, how would he know we were thinking about him all week?"

"You really don't like your brother, do you?" I ask.

"I love him," Lennox says. "Like? I don't know. It's hard to like someone who goes out of his way to show he doesn't give a shit about anyone else."

"You don't think he cares about you?" I ask, drawing back.

"He cares about girls, and money, and power," Lennox says. "He wants to be the center of attention, the star of the show, and he'll do anything to make it happen. I guarantee he's only gone because he wants to make sure you're thinking about him and not me."

"I don't think so," I say, frowning at the button on the front of his pajamas. "He doesn't even like me. He told me he didn't want me, didn't want to be with me—ever."

"And then he saw me taking you to bed," Lennox says.

"Why would he care, if he doesn't want me?"

"He still wants you to want him," Lennox says. "That's what I'm telling you. As long as you're worshipping him, he's going to be happy with you. But when you stop…"

"What?"

"He's dangerous."

"You think he'd hurt me?"

"I think he'd hurt us both if he knew about us," Lennox says, pulling my leg over his hip.

I want to argue, to defend him, which is ridiculous. I don't owe Maddox any loyalty. He made it clear we're nothing, less than nothing. That he sees me as a joke, a child. Lennox is right. Maddox didn't give a single fuck about hurting me that morning. I think he actually enjoyed it, just like Lennox said he likes shooting people.

"I'm sure you know him better than anyone, but…" I search for words, but Lennox cuts me off.

"Don't worry about him," he says, stroking my hair behind my ear and tipping my chin up. "He's fine. I promise."

His lips meet mine, and I try to let my worries melt away. I need to let go and move on. It's not my business where Maddox is or who he's with.

I can't help thinking about him, though, and worrying just as Lennox said I would. Just as Maddox intends. His brother knows him best, and I'm not about to keep asking and look like the desperate little girl he says I am.

After a week, I finally spot him going into a coach's office off the gym when I come out of the locker room one stormy afternoon. I'm about to call out to him when Scarlet pushes past me. Glancing back over her shoulder, she gives me a once-over, her lips curled in a derisive sneer.

"Get lost, loser," she says. "He's with me now, and following him around just reeks of desperation."

"Oh, is that what I smell?" I ask, trailing her to the closed door of the office. "I thought you must have picked up some new perfume at the gas station, but now that you mention it, it's what you always smell like."

She huffs and stops at the coach's door, crossing her arms and glaring at me. "At least I can afford deodorant."

"Yeah, too bad dignity doesn't come with it, huh?"

Despite my quick comeback, her words sting. I don't want to think about him telling her that. Has he been staying with her all week? I figured he was crashing on another Crow's couch. I can't imagine some rich bitch's parents allowing a gangster to use their guest room with their daughter across the hall.

Her mouth drops open at the insult, then snaps shut. She grits her teeth and glares at me. "Why are you even here? He doesn't want to see you. Aren't you a nerd? I thought y'all were supposed to be smart."

"I'm smart enough to know you're full of shit," I say. "Maddox has better taste than you."

She raises her brows and lets her gaze rake over me with obvious distaste. "Like *you?*"

I cross my arms and mirror her pose, lifting my chin and refusing to be intimidated, even when a crack of thunder outside makes me jump. "Maybe."

"You have Lennox," she says, shaking her head. "Why do you even care? Are you such a slut that you actually miss them taking turns with you? I mean, I know you're in the Slut Club and everything, but that's nasty even for one of y'all."

"Like you wouldn't jump at the chance to get Lennox if he'd take you."

"Whatever," she says, rolling her eyes. "Projecting much?"

The coach's door opens, and Maddox looks back and forth between us. The coach steps out from behind him and pulls up short. "Y'all need something?" he asks.

"Just waiting on Maddox," Scarlet says, batting her eyes and taking Maddox's arm in both hands as if to make sure he can't escape her clutches.

"Of course you are," the coach mutters, pulling the door closed behind him. He steps around us and strolls off across the gym, probably happy to be done with his day early now that all the sports seasons are over.

"So, Maddy, what are we doing after school today?" Scarlet asks, leaning into Maddox's side. "Maybe we could hang out at your house?"

I wait for him to tell her she's nothing, like he did when she stole my clothes, or at least to snap at her not to call him *Maddy*. But his cool green eyes meet mine, and his jaw tenses.

"Sure," he says to Scarlet, his gaze still on me like a chokehold.

"Is it still your house?" I ask lightly, though my hand squeezes into a fist, my nails digging into my skin. "I hadn't seen you in so long I thought maybe you moved."

"It's not *your* house," he drawls, sliding an arm around Scarlet's slender middle. "Just because our mom takes in strays on occasion doesn't make it your home."

"Noted," I say. "So, want to give me a ride back to *your* house?"

"Don't you have Lennox for that?" he asks, his words iced with bitterness.

"Nothing happened between us," I say quietly, darting a glance at Scarlet. I know she's drinking it all up, ready to spread gossip and try to ruin me further in our last few weeks of school. I wish she wasn't here, but not because I give a shit about my reputation. I just want to talk to Maddox without an audience.

He lets out a quiet snort of breath, the corner of his lips twitching. "I know."

The way he says it, like it's glaringly obvious, like his brother couldn't possibly want me, cuts through my defenses and feigned indifference and slices straight to my heart.

"You do?" I ask, searching his dark eyes for signs of the boy who lay on the roof with me until sunrise, who makes me feel so good I think I'll expire every time he touches me.

"Yeah," he says, swinging his gym back over his shoulder and heading for the door. Scarlet scampers after and dives under his arm, pulling it around her and casting me a triumphant smile over her shoulder. As much as I want to let them go, I can't stand the thought of him leaving with her. Of her winning by default. At the very least, I should try, tell him…

What?

I accidentally told him I loved him, and that's how this whole shit-show started.

Still, some fucked up part of me can't let him go without a fight.

I follow them, which earns me another of Scarlet's glares. But Maddox doesn't even acknowledge her, which gives me enough satisfaction to lure me to the parking lot with them. Besides, the bus is already gone, and it's pouring rain out. The trees at the edges of the lot toss and bend with the force of the wind, and we're all instantly drenched when a sheet of rain hits us.

Only a dozen or so cars remain in the student lot. Lennox's car is among them, but I know he stays late for art sometimes. If I'm not waiting at his car, he'll assume I took the bus.

"Lennox isn't going to fuck with you any more than I am, little girl," Maddox says, opening the door of a shiny new Cadillac. "He's a good guy, and he knows you're not experienced enough to handle him. Go find some nerd-boy virgin to knock the cobwebs off for you.

I told you. I don't care what you do with your cunt as long as it doesn't fuck up my family."

Scarlet tosses her head and gives me a look that's pure savagery as she climbs into the passenger seat after Maddox tosses his bag in the back seat. He closes the door behind her, cocooning her in the dry safety of the car. I wonder if he even remembers I'm edgy during storms. I'm tempted to crawl under the nearest car just to get out of it.

Maddox turns to me, his thick arms bare below the sleeves of a wet black tee that stretches over his massive pecs, tight abs, and broad shoulders. He has new ink on his bicep, and his neck tattoo is on full display, up front and center, the way he said he likes it.

"Consider that your last warning," he says coolly, looking down at me through hooded eyes, his arm muscles bulging against the sleeves of his tee, which is practically painted onto his sculpted body from the rain. I have to fight not to watch the water running down the bulging muscles in his arms.

Anyone in Faulkner would quake at the threat from this gangster who looks like a straight up hitman, but I don't back down. Not this time. I'm tired of him pushing me around.

"You're wrong," I say. "Lennox does want me. He basically asked me to be his girlfriend already. Guess that's what happens when he has a week to breathe without worrying about what you'll think of him for going after a girl you think is beneath y'all."

Maddox's nostrils flare, and his eyes narrow to slits. "You better be fucking kidding me."

"Where'd you get the car?" I ask, raising my chin and smirking up at him. "Is that how much Scarlet thinks your dick is worth?"

Maddox's hand reaches for me, and I flinch despite myself. His eyes catch on the movement. He doesn't miss anything. He told me as much one time—that you could learn a lot about people just by watching. His hand wraps around the back of my neck, his fingers digging in painfully as he drags me flush against him.

My toes barely skimming the slick pavement, I have to bite down on my lip to keep from crying out. Turns out poking the beast wasn't such a good idea after all.

"I told you, I'm not a nice guy," he growls. "You want to fucking try me, little girl? Find out the hard way? I may have gone easy on you because you were an innocent bystander, but you fuck with my family, and you'll meet the Maddox North everyone else knows."

He squeezes harder, and I cringe against his grip, trying to twist free. Tears of pain spring to my lashes, and I gasp as he lifts me off my feet, so my mouth is only inches from his. He grips my chin in his other hand, swiping tears and rain from my cheek and smearing them over my trembling lower lip. Then he leans in and crushes my lips with his. It's not a kiss. It's harsh and painful, his teeth smashing my lip before drawing it between his. He bites down hard, and blood gushes into my mouth. I cry out, the sound muffled inside his mouth, and shove against his chest.

He pulls away and slowly licks his lips, his hooded eyes filled with a fire I've never seen in them before, something venomous and predatory as a shark who just tasted blood in the water. Leaning in, his tongue flicks out and swipes over my lip, lapping up the blood that spilled.

"You really don't want me for an enemy, little mama," he says, his voice a taunting purr. "Trust me when I say, you don't want to know what I'm capable of."

"Let go," I choke out. "You're hurting me, Maddox."

"Then think about that before you hurt my family," he says, lowering me back to my feet but keeping his hand firmly around the back of my neck. "Because if you do, there will be no end to the pain we'll inflict on you. You won't just wish you'd never met us. You'll wish we'd let your dad kill you."

"I'm sorry," I whisper, not sure he can even hear me over the drumming rain on the roof of his new car. "I never meant to hurt you."

He stares at me a second, then barks out a cold, mirthless laugh. "Hurt me?"

I swallow hard, my whole body shaking with fear of him, the storm, the rain. Squeezing my hands into fists, I let my nails bite in, focusing on the pain there instead of the confusion and pain of his cruelty.

Reaching past me, Maddox yanks open the door. "Get out of the car," he orders, his gaze still locked on mine.

"What?" Scarlet demands.

"Get out of the fucking car," he snaps.

"It's raining," she points out.

He doesn't answer.

She hesitates, then slowly climbs out, shooting me a look that's half wounded, half resentful. I have no idea where he thinks he's taking me alone, but I'm not about to get in the car with him after he showed his true colors. All along, I thought he was the honest one, the one who didn't play games and pretend to be something he wasn't. But he's just better at hiding it than Lennox. He lured me into a sense of security, let me believe he wouldn't hurt me, by protecting me all those times.

"Bend over the hood of my car and pull up your skirt," Maddox says, his eyes still locked on mine. Somehow, though, I can tell his words aren't for me.

"Right now?" Scarlet asks doubtfully, glancing around and hunching her shoulders against the hammering rain.

"You want me to fuck you or not?" he snaps.

"Yeah, but…"

"Then fucking bend over."

She licks her lips, her gaze darting around the lot again as she measures how much she wants his dick against how much she wants to keep her dignity. Or maybe she's just realizing she doesn't have much choice in the matter. Slowly, she stalks to the front of the car and bends over the hood, lifting up the back of her skirt. Maddox turns away from me, walks to her, and unzips his pants.

I'm frozen in place by his icy glare as he yanks out his dick and jerks it roughly, his eyes never leaving mine through the curtain of rain streaking down between us.

He's not going to do it. There's no way. He's challenging me, daring me to break first.

But I won't.

In the end, no matter how much he's watched me over the past year, he doesn't know me. He's seen me break, that day they pulled me out of the shed, and he thinks I'm fragile, that he'll break me by hurting me, just like Lee always did. But they underestimate me. If he knew me as well as he thinks, he'd know I'm just like him. I never break for myself.

When I don't back down, he pulls out his wallet, flips it open, and pulls out a condom. I still don't move, don't look away. Not even when he tears the package with his teeth and rolls the condom on, stroking his shaft as he goes. I try not to stare, not to notice how fucking wide his cock is. God, it's big. I almost pity Scarlet for what he's about to do to her.

I'm still not sure he's going to go through with it. Not until he yanks down Scarlet's underwear and thrusts into her. She yelps in pain, grasping uselessly at the wet surface under her, and he pulls back and spits on his palm. He slides his hand between her thighs, up through her crease, wetting her while his gaze locks mine in place. He pushes into her again, this time slower. From the corner of my eye, I can see her hair blow over her face in a gust of wind, can see the tortured expression twisting her pretty features as she takes his impossible size.

Thunder rumbles through the sky overhead, and rain slices down, running down my fingers, the cold making my hands numb. My whole body is numb as I watch him fuck her, pounding her against the car, spearing his cock into her again and again while she just lies there, her fingers clutching for purchase on the smooth metal. I think she's crying, but it's hard to tell through the rain.

"You think you can hurt me?" Maddox snarls at me. "You think you have anything I want? Scarlet knows what she's doing, knows how to take it like a woman, not a little girl. She's not some pathetic virgin who thinks her cunt's so fucking special I'd lose sleep over it."

I stumble back a step, wanting to run to Lennox's car, to dive inside and make this all a nightmare, make it so Maddox never fucked Scarlet in front of me just to hurt me.

He smirks and drags his cock out before plunging it to the hilt inside her. "She's tight as a virgin too, which means you have literally nothing to offer that I can't find a hundred other places. You really think you were special to me? I took pity on you because you're a sad little girl desperate for attention because Daddy doesn't love you."

"You're right about one thing," I say, my voice shaking as tears streak down my cheeks with the rain. "Lennox is a good guy. A good man. A better man than you could ever hope to be. That's why I choose him."

I turn away, my throat burning, my world burning, my heart nothing but ashes in my chest.

Behind me, Maddox laughs. "If you can't handle watching, how are you going to handle taking a beating like this from my brother?"

His taunting words follow me across the parking lot, the wet pavement. When I get to Lennox's car, I have to circle to the other side to climb in.

I won't look at them. I won't. I won't.

Hot tears gush down my face as I climb into the passenger seat. Now that the rain won't mask my tears, though, I force them to stop. I won't let him see me sitting in here sobbing. I won't cry over him. Never again. And definitely not in his brother's car.

I don't want to see them, but my eyes betray me, attracted by the movement when Maddox pulls her up off the hood of his car like he's picking up a dead animal from the road. She stands unmoving while he pulls up her underwear and straightens her skirt.

Then he turns her to face him, and another wave of incinerating, blinding pain hits me as he pushes her hair back and cups her cheek in his palm, turning her face up toward his. I watch his lips move, and I can hear him speak as clearly as if he were in the car with me when he says, "You good?"

thirty

Lennox North

I hurry through the pounding rain and open my door, stopping for only a second when I see Rae in the passenger seat. She's soaked through, like she was standing outside for a while before trying the passenger door and realizing it doesn't lock.

"Hey, Sunshine," I say, leaning over to give her a quick kiss. She winces, and when I pull back, I notice her lip is swollen, and there are traces of blood in the corners of her mouth. I frown and tip her chin up, touching her broken lip gently, even though rage boils up in my gut. No one hurts my girl. "What happened?"

"Your brother," she says, nodding toward a car a few rows over and two spaces up in the lot. The black

Cadillac is running, the vertical taillights glowing red in the stormy grey afternoon.

I reach for the glove box, pop it open and pull out my gun.

"What are you doing?" Rae cries.

"You said he hurt you," I say, though inside I'm thanking him. The asshole did just what I predicted. All those years of watching him eviscerate hearts has finally paid off. I knew he couldn't help himself, that he'd hurt her like he does everyone. And every time he hurt her, I was there to pick up the pieces, to hold and comfort her. Each time drove her deeper into my arms, and now she's mine.

"That doesn't mean I want you to shoot him," she says, grabbing my wrist. I open the chamber and see the two bullets I loaded a week ago. Her gaze falls on it too, and for a second, neither of us move.

"Why's it loaded?" she asks at last.

"You think we just carry guns for show?" I ask, laughing.

"No, but… You had that the other night."

"I heard you crying," I say. "I thought you were being hurt."

"You can't just shoot someone any time they hurt me."

"Why not?" I ask, smiling as I lean over to kiss her. "They deserve it."

She kisses me back, but just a little. Then she pulls back, biting her lip and looking down at my gun again. "Why does it have two bullets?"

I shrug and close the chamber, putting the safety on again. "Must be what's left from the last time I used it," I lie.

What took me over that night, that was temporary insanity. Now I'm thinking clear though. No crimes of passion will land me in jail. I'll be patient, and when the time comes, I'll make her pay. It takes time to create a masterpiece. Right now, I'm only priming the canvas.

I take her hand and squeeze. "I'm sorry my brother's such a dick. Let's get out of here, and you can tell me what happened. I hear ice cream makes everything better."

"I'm too cold," she says, a shudder wracking her body. I turn on the car and crank up the heat, rubbing her hand to warm it.

"Then what do you want?" I ask. "Anything. My treat."

"I don't know," she says, then looks at me hopefully. "Maybe doughnuts? And a hot coffee."

I can't help but laugh. "If that's what you want, it's yours, Sunshine. Anything to see your smile."

She does smile, and a swell of triumph warms my insides. There's nothing that says I can't make her happy or that she won't make me happy. We'll come to an understanding about what she did, and after she pays for her crime, we'll have a life together. I cared about her before Maddox did, after all. I care about her more. It's almost as if this were meant to happen, like it proves how perfect she is for me.

She had to get Maddox out of her system, see him for who he truly is. And she had to betray me so that she can earn my forgiveness by satisfying the hunger inside me that she refuses to acknowledge otherwise. If it weren't for this, I might have thought I could never be with her fully because she can't fulfill that need. But her punishment, her payment, is to fulfill me in a way she never would otherwise. Knowing she doesn't get off on it like I do, but she'll do it for me, makes it that much sweeter.

We're made for each other, and soon enough, she'll see it too.

And the longer I'm with her, the more Maddox will realize what he lost. I'll know that I finally won one, using my wits and charm. That will never stop making me happy.

Ten minutes later, I'm climbing back into the car outside the doughnut shop.

"Oh my god," she says, laughing. "I said just one glazed doughnut. What did you do?"

I flip open the lid on the box of a dozen doughnuts and present them to her. "Anything for my sunshine."

"You're crazy," she says, shaking her head. But she's grinning as she selects one with yellow frosting and sprinkles.

"I knew you wanted something fancier than glazed," I say. "You don't have to settle for the minimum anymore, Rae. You're with me. I want to give you everything."

She nods, looking a little embarrassed, and bites into the doughnut.

I bite into mine and lace my fingers through hers on my free hand. "Good choice. There's no good ice cream places in town anyway. Now, tell me what happened."

"It's stupid," she says. "I don't know why I was even upset. It's nothing, really. Just Maddox being Maddox."

"Did he say where he's been?" I ask, though I'm pretty sure I know. There's more to life than a girl, after all. She's been distracting me, but Maddox never lets his passions carry him away.

She shakes her head. "No. But he was with Scarlet, and he has that car."

"Scarlet's following the money," I say, staring out the windshield as I chew.

"Isn't she rich?" Rae asks, licking her fingers with that pretty pink tongue.

"Nah," I say, shaking my head. "Compared to us, maybe. She's a subdivision bitch, not gated community rich. The kind of chick that got her parents' Honda when she turned sixteen, not a new Porsche."

"That's rich to me," Rae says.

"One day, we're going to be so rich that will look poor to us. I've got big plans for us, Sunshine."

"Is that right?" she asks lightly, the corner of her pouty lips tilting up.

I did that. Not Maddox. He made her bleed. I make her smile.

"That's right, Sunshine."

Maybe he drew first blood, fucked her first, took her virginity. But I'll fuck her last. She'll do more than bleed for me. She'll break for me. Watching her crumble will be like watching Michelangelo paint the Sistine Chapel. Agonizingly slow, but worth it a thousand times over in the end.

First, I have to remove her from his reach, so he can't take this from me the way he takes everything.

"So, he didn't get the car from her?" she asks. "She's been after him all year. I figured she finally lured him in by giving him a fancy car."

"She's a whore," I say, dropping my doughnut back into the box in disgust at the thought of girls like her. "She wants to be somebody, but she has nothing of her own to get there, so she attaches herself to people who do. Her dad was a coach, so she tried to make herself popular through that, but it wasn't quite enough, so she started spreading her legs for the football team. That's all she has to offer."

Rae winces. "Not your favorite person?"

"She's a slut and a leach," I say, my tone scathing.

There was a time when she pursed her pretty pink lips in my direction, batted her pretty blue eyes at me, giggled at my jokes. That month, I felt like a king.

Then I didn't make the football team, and she pretended she didn't know me. A poor art dork like me, what could I possibly offer a girl like her?

My brother, though, he had lots to offer. She didn't turn her nose up at him. She joined his fucking fan parade. I've never quite forgiven him for that.

But now that I have Rae, maybe I will.

"She follows money, status, power," I go on. "If Maddox didn't have a reputation or a football jersey, she wouldn't give him the time of day. Now that we're graduating, his football god status won't matter, so I guess he had to get a car to keep her attention."

"Yeah, but where?" she asks.

I pick up my doughnut and bite off a piece, though heaviness sinks into me when I face what I've suspected for a while. "Remember when I said Maddox doesn't care about anyone but himself?"

She swallows and pulls a half-full bottle of Diet Coke from her backpack, and I remember I was supposed to get coffee too. She's too sweet to complain, though. "Yeah…"

I turn in the seat to face her. "There's been conflict in the Skull and Crossbones organization for a while," I say. "Lately there's even talk about it breaking up. As part of that, we're affected."

"So… They gave Maddox a car to get him to stay?"

I shake my head. "It's not just a Crow problem. We started the crew to help the neighborhood, but some people... They'd rather help themselves. That's what the whole argument has come down to. Half of the members want to better the community, help people. The other wants to make money. And there's one quick and dirty way to do that."

"Drugs," she says, realization dawning. "That's how Maddox got the pot. He said he had *connections.*"

I nod, even though I know they're not moving drugs. If she thinks that's worse than the truth, I'll take whatever advantage I can. They're doing something illegal either way. What does it matter if it's drugs or hot cars?

"The Crows have always landed on the cleaner, more law-abiding side of the argument—now that side is pulling away, calling themselves the Crossbones. The Skull side says money is the way to take care of people, so it starts with the money. But we all know once you introduce drugs into it, the neighborhood's not just going to get the money. They're going to get the drugs. I joined to take care of people, to help neighborhood kids, not get them hooked on crack. Getting into that business won't save us. It'll destroy us. And they know that. They're just using that argument as an excuse to line their own pockets and buy themselves fancy cars."

Rae sets down her half-eaten doughnut, looking sick. "Maddox got that car from selling drugs?"

I nod. "*Lo siento, mi querida.* I know that's not what you want to hear, but I think so. That's what he's been doing the past week, where he's been staying. With some supplier on the Skull side. I don't know if the Murder of Crows is going to survive this, but if it does… Say you'll be with me."

Her hazel eyes search mine, flecks of emerald and gold shining in those complicated depths. She's too sensitive, too complex, for my brother. I deserve a girl like that. He can have Scarlet and all the other sluts he fucks. Rae has been waiting for someone worthy, for her match.

And now she's found me.

Waiting for her, proving myself worthy, will only make it that much sweeter when I break her. I'll show her I'm more than a match for her. I'll make her sorry she chose my brother over me, like she's just some dumb bitch like Scarlet. I'll make her see she's better than that. And so am I.

I'll build her up until she feels like a queen, and then I'll tear her down piece by piece until she crawls like a dog and begs for mercy. Until she recognizes that I am superior to my brother. He may have more brute force, but that's a finite power, bound by the laws of physics. My power is infinite, limited only by my imagination. I create reality as easily as art. I can create and destroy her reality until she doesn't know what's real and what's illusion without asking me. She will be mine, bending to my will, dependent on me for her very sanity.

I take her hand in mine. "Are you with me, Rae?"

Finally, she nods. "I don't want to be part of something that sells drugs to kids," she says, dropping her gaze to the eight remaining doughnuts in the box between us. "But I don't think I can go back home with you, Lennox."

"Why not?" I demand.

She swallows and glances up at me. "He got pissed when I told him we might be together. Like, really pissed. I don't think I should live in his house anymore."

Fury builds inside me, but triumph winds through it. I knew he'd fucking implode when he found out. He thinks because we signed a contract and because I have morals, that I'll stick to it even when he doesn't. But he broke the contract, which means it no longer holds me, either. And he can't fucking stand that I want her even after he ruined her. Now that he sees she's desirable even after he took her virginity, he'll want her back.

"You're right," I say. "He's dangerous to us both now."

"I'm sure he was exaggerating," she says with a nervous laugh, like she can't quite believe her own judgment. She's already trying to convince herself she was wrong. He made it almost too easy for me, making her fall for him and then being a dick like he always does when he realizes feelings are involved.

He forgets other people have those.

That's his mistake. I learned from the best, but I don't make that mistake. I have feelings, so I never forget that part. That's where the real power lies. I can see when someone's vulnerable, when she's ready for me.

I watch too, after all.

But I'm done being a spectator. I'm ready to play.

"No, I think you're right," I say. "It's probably better if we find somewhere else to stay."

"I'd just rather be safe than sorry," she says. "I'm eighteen, and I've saved up some money. I can put down a deposit on a place. It's just a couple weeks until graduation, and then I can get a full-time job to pay rent every month."

"We'll both get jobs," I say, stroking the back of her ring finger with my thumb.

"Wait, you're moving out too?"

"Well, yeah," I say. "I mean, he's just as dangerous to me as he is to you. Maybe more. And you know I'm a heavy sleeper. I'm not trying to go to sleep one night and be easy prey when he comes home."

"Oh," she says faintly. "Are you sure?"

"Sure this is worth it?" I ask, stroking her chestnut hair back and tucking it behind her ear. "*Sí.* I'm more than sure. I know you are."

I kiss her until she responds, and I taste her blood, and it's so sweet I don't even care that Maddox drew it first. I sit back, and I pick up a glazed doughnut.

"I want to be with you, Rae. Just you and me. No matter what." Slowly, I push it onto her finger.

She stares down at it for a second, then raises her startled gaze to mine. Her voice comes out a choked whisper. "Lennox… What are you doing?"

"I'm asking you to choose me."

"What?" she breathes, looking like she might faint.

"I want you to be mine," I say, stroking back her damp hair and searching her gaze. "I've wanted it since the first moment we met, when you told me your name and I said we'd be the North-Wests. I know you had to figure yourself out this past year, figure out what you wanted and learn who my brother really was. But I haven't changed. You haven't changed. I still want you despite what you did. I want you just as much today as I did then. Even more. I've never met someone like you, Rae."

"What are you talking about?" she asks. "Someone like what?"

I slide my hand around the back of her head and make her look at me. "Someone who voluntarily chooses to sit with the Slut Club because you like them, and you don't care what people think. Someone who walked around school alone, when people called you a snitch, and didn't let a single one of them get to you, but who will completely lose her shit over a bird dying. And the way you make *me* lose my shit when I touch you… You're spectacular, Rae. I've never felt this way about anyone."

She swallows and drops her gaze, but I hold her head so she can't duck away. "How do I know you don't say that to every girl you want to sleep with?"

"You should know by now this isn't about sex," I say. "I'm not going to pressure you into anything. I'm not my brother. Hell, I'll wait until our wedding night to prove to you that this isn't about sex. It's about you, Rae. You and me. My world's already a better place because you're in it. Let me make yours better too. Don't you want to make the world a better place with me?"

She hesitates a long moment, then nods, staring down at her doughnut ring.

"Don't worry, I'll get you something better than that," I say, rubbing the back of her sticky finger. "So what do you say? Will you marry me?"

thirty-one

#1 on the Billboard Chart:
"The Boy is Mine"—Brandy & Monica

Rae West

"You're not mad?" I ask Valeria, dropping a handful of carrot shavings onto the bed of lettuce in the big serving bowl she handed me.

"Mad? No," she says, setting aside the plate of arepas. "Sad, yes. I knew this day was coming, seeing my sons move out. I just didn't think it would come so soon."

"He's going to college in the fall," I point out, reaching over to flip the chicken in the pan so it doesn't burn. "It'll be good to have a place right by campus. And we'll be right across town…"

"I know," she says, shooing me away from the chicken. "I know. I just thought they'd live at home through college at least, but more likely until they got married."

I laugh nervously and sprinkle cheese over the salad. I just broke the news that we found an apartment, only a month after graduation. Lennox will have to share the other announcement. Since the day Lennox proposed, when I finally broke down and told him about Maddox's threats in the parking lot, he's insisted I stay with Lexi. So this visit serves a few purposes. I'm here to gather the last of my meager stash of clothes and other belongings, thank Valeria for her generosity, and to break the news.

"When did you get married?" I ask, hoping to ease us into the conversation.

"Too young," she says. "I met their father at my first job when I moved here. We both worked in the kitchen at El Chico. And here this handsome American wanted to sweep me off my feet. I was flattered at first, but I kept telling him no. But he kept asking, and finally I went out with him. Then I fell in love and lost my head."

She laughs, and I glance at her before placing the final cherry tomato on the salad.

"He wanted to marry me even though I couldn't cook to save my life," she says, turning the chicken and ignoring the smoke going up from the oil in the pan. "And then the boys came along…"

"So it worked out in some ways," I say. "I mean, you got the boys out of it."

"Of course," she says. "I wouldn't change it for anything. Even if I do put a curse on Mr. North every time I see him around town with his new wife who probably never burns the chicken."

The smoke alarm starts going off, and she runs to stand on a chair and wave a lid to one of her Tupperware containers at it. I pull the chicken off and take the smoking legs out of the oil before they get more charred.

"They're fine," I assure her. "I'm sure it's just the skin."

She grins at me and climbs off the chair when the alarm stops beeping. "You're a keeper," she says. "I'm glad one of my sons snatched you up before you got away."

"Thanks," I say, watching her from the corner of my eye. "So… Has Maddox been home at all?"

"Not much," she says. "He moved out a week before you."

"He never came back?" I ask, surprised. Since Lennox has been staying with someone from the Murder of Crows, and I haven't been here, I assumed Maddox would have come back. A ridiculous little dart of jealousy pierces into me before I can scold myself out of it.

"He comes by to see me," Valeria says. "You'll make sure Lennox does the same, *sí*?"

"Of course," I say still distracted by what she said about Maddox.

Which is ten kinds of stupid. Why does it matter if he's living with Scarlet now? I already know they're together. I endured the slap in the face that was the last few weeks before graduation, when I had to see them around school together. Every single time, my mind flashed back to that day in the parking lot, when he bent her over and fucked her in front of me.

I'll never be able to unsee that. Even if he showed up and begged forgiveness on bended knee, I'd never be able to stop seeing that. He wanted to hurt me, and he succeeded. There's no going back from that.

"Hey, can I ask you something?" I say, carrying the salad to the table. Might as well get all the awkwardness out now, since I'm already awkward as hell today. Lennox wanted us to dress up for the big announcement to his mom, so he asked me to wear a dress instead of my usual jeans. Which means I spent yesterday raiding every secondhand store in town with Lexi, both of us moaning about the weird smells and lack of clothing options for poor girls under fifty.

"You want to know where Maddox is?" Valeria asks, watching me closely.

"No," I say, frowning and smoothing down my thrift store dress. "That's not my business. I'm with Lennox."

"Then what?"

"Lennox said they joined the Crows because of you," I say. "But it was your story."

"Oh." Her face goes still, and I can see her struggling with some emotion before she speaks. Then she turns and picks up a bottle. "Do you want wine?"

"Sure," I say, going to the cabinet and pulling out three glasses. "You don't want to tell me?"

She sighs and pours wine into a glass before handing me the bottle. "No, but I will," she says, tucking an arm hand around her middle and resting her elbow on the back of her hand. She takes a sip of wine and forces a smile. "You should know, if you're going to live with a gangster. But you should also know that my boys, they didn't used to be like that. That's not how they were raised. I didn't do that to them. That damn *organization* did."

"Did what?" I ask.

"You know what they're like," she says. "They're still my sweet little boys to me, but I know what they're like to other people. To women. To your father. To everyone else."

I think of Lee's arms encased in white casts from wrist to shoulder, leaving him as immobile as a Ken doll, and I think maybe their version of sweet is just a little different than when they were her little boys. No one has ever done something like that for me before. Not even my own mother protected me.

But Maddox did.

I'll never forget that. No matter what else he did, Maddox protected me. Lennox took care of me. They both made me forget for a while.

"They're not so bad," I say, pouring a glass of wine and hiding my smile.

"The gang started after them when they were only kids," she says. "Twelve or thirteen. I wouldn't let them join of course. I watch the news, see the statistics on crime. The Skull & Crossbones is no organization, no matter what they say. Make no mistake, Rae. It's a gang."

"I know."

She nods. "Well, they weren't members, but they had friends. They got a lot of pressure, living in this neighborhood, and it only got worse the older they got.

Then about five years ago, I was raped outside my work one night. That's when they joined."

"Oh my god," I breathe.

She takes a sip of wine. "I forbid them from joining, but they said it would protect me and everyone in the family. I didn't see how. It couldn't change what had happened. But I knew who the man was. I knew him, and he came into work sometimes. So I went to the hospital afterwards and filed a report and did everything you're supposed to do. They brought him in for questioning, and I thought he'd go to prison, but they let him go the next day. He only spent one night in jail. A single night."

She shakes her head, swirling her wine in her glass, her jaw set.

"I'm so sorry," I say, sinking down into a chair at the table.

"I found out a few days later he'd been murdered. I saw it on the news. That's when the boys told me they'd joined the Skull & Crossbones, and that they'd protect other people on this street, get vengeance for them when they needed it. I would never have asked them for that."

"Of course not," I mumble, wondering if they did it themselves or just joined and told the gang they needed revenge on someone. It doesn't really matter now. I'm sure they've killed since then, even if they didn't kill that man. At least Maddox has. It's hard to imagine a sensitive artist type like Lennox being capable of murder.

Valeria stares off over my head. "Sometimes I wonder… If that man was hired or maybe even a member, and that was supposed to drive them to join. That's what they do to boys, push them into joining by saying it offers protection, even though it puts them in more danger. And my boys are the kind of people they want—strong and smart, real leaders. They formed the street crews, the Murder of Crows on Mill, and the whole idea. The other neighborhoods made their own to take care of their own. That was Lennox's idea, though."

Despite her disapproval of the gang, I can tell she's proud of them, too. I can't really blame her. They protected her, and I know exactly how good that feels.

The conversation is interrupted by heavy footsteps in the hall. I tense, for some reason expecting Maddox for a split second. But Lennox steps in, dressed in black slacks and a rust-colored button-up shirt that makes his golden eyes practically glow behind his glasses. He looks so beautiful I want to cry, knowing where the broken places under that beauty come from. He once told me that it was his idea to join. He may not rave about her terrible cooking the way Maddox does, but he's the one who wanted to avenge his mother. They love her so much it hurts deep in my chest, as much as it hurts to know how deeply she loves them.

No one has ever loved me that way, and I'm taking him from her.

"How's my two favorite ladies?" Lennox asks, kissing her cheek before coming to the table. He pulls out her chair across from mine then takes the one on my right, leaning in to kiss my cheek. He lays his hand over mine, and I turn my palm to face his and lace our fingers. Meeting his eyes, I smile at my beautiful, broken, bitter artist boy. I feel closer to him than I ever have now that I understand him in ways I didn't before.

"I was just telling Rae about how the Crossbones has damaged you boys," Valeria says, delivering the plate of blackened chicken to the table. "I'm glad you have a normal girlfriend who can remind you how to treat a woman."

"Mom," Lennox groans. "Don't."

She rolls her eyes. "*O qué?* I'm your mother. I worry about the ideas that crew put in your head."

"Rae's not a Crow, so I don't treat her like one," Lennox says, squeezing my hand. "She's wife material."

A tense silence falls, and I glance at Lennox from the corner of my eye. His beautiful face is frozen, his expression so still it's like he's carved from marble, a statue of the most beautiful man on earth. He seems to be having trouble speaking, so I slide my hand across the small table to touch Valeria's hand. "Are you okay with this?"

"You're getting married?" she asks, her gaze flitting from her son to me and then back.

"Yes," Lennox says, clearing his throat and picking up his wine glass. He takes a gulp and blinks hard at the burn, then flashes me an apologetic smile, like he's not allowed to have doubts about this too. Then he takes my hand again, and I give him a reassuring squeeze.

"We're engaged."

A charged silence fills the room, interrupted only by the slamming of the front door. I jump a mile and start to pull my hand away by instinct, like we did so many times the last few weeks we lived here, when Lennox was proving he was sorry for his mistake but would still love on me when Maddox wasn't around. Now, he tightens his grip, reminding me that we aren't hiding our love anymore.

"Well, what do we have here?" Maddox asks, striding in and pulling out the last empty chair. He drops his huge body into it and scoots in, sniffing the smoky air. "Smells amazing, Mom. Why isn't anyone eating?"

He digs in without waiting, sliding a couple burnt chicken legs onto his plate like this is just a normal dinner when we all lived here, like he didn't threaten me in the parking lot, fuck my enemy in front of me and then parade her around school for the next few weeks like he'd won a prize for how badly he hurt me.

Because it's Maddox, and of course he didn't beg forgiveness after he hurt me. He didn't flaunt her and throw it in my face the way she did, but in a way, that would have been better. Then at least I'd know he still cared enough to want to see my reaction. Instead, he acted like I didn't exist, like I was a ghost. And I wasn't about to follow him around begging him to talk to me. Not after he made it clear he wanted nothing to do with me.

Even though he and Lennox both told me he didn't do girlfriends before that, Scarlet must have changed his mind with her apparently virginal tightness, because he moved from the Crows' table to the football table after that. Every day, Scarlet perched on his knee and crowed louder than Poe ever did. I swear the bitch wanted the whole cafeteria to turn her way, so they'd see that she tied down the powerful, elusive, unattainable Maddox North.

She can have him. I have his brother, the one everyone else overlooks. I don't overlook him—not anymore. I don't know how I ever did. He's hotter than Maddox anyway, so beautiful he's a piece of art in himself.

Without him, I don't know how I would have survived the devastation to my ego that Maddox inflicted. Instead of getting dumped and having to walk around alone, seeing Maddox with his new, upgrade of a girlfriend, I had a gorgeous boyfriend of my own. Not only that, but Lennox did things Maddox would never do, showing him up and proving every day that I made the right choice. In the end, he was even more of an upgrade than Scarlet was for Maddox. Instead of looking pathetic and used, I spent the last few weeks of senior year with a doting boyfriend who held my hand, brought me flowers for no reason, and took me to dinner after graduation when everyone else went out with their families.

"Apparently this is an engagement dinner," Valeria says, breaking the silence at last. "So I'm glad you showed up. Now, if you and your brother can get along for a few hours, let's try to make this a celebratory evening."

She gives him a tight smile, but he's not looking at her.

The news seems to have derailed his plan to pretend everything is all hunky-dory. He stares at Lennox in disbelief, a bite of chicken forgotten halfway to his mouth.

Lennox slides his arm around my shoulder and squeezes. "That's right," he says, grinning proudly at his brother. "She said yes. Show them the ring, Sunshine."

I don't want to. This all feels terribly wrong. My stomach is tight, and my whole body feels shaky and weak. I can't even meet Maddox's eyes. Dread weighs my hand down, but Lennox picks it up and holds it out to show them the small ring he got me until we can afford something nicer. I should be happy. I'm engaged. We're announcing it to his family. He's happy, all smiles now as he shows off his girl and the ring. So what is my problem?

Maddox stares at my hand for a second, and then he laughs and shoves the bite of chicken in his mouth, blackened skin included. "You get that at the pawn shop or K-Mart?"

Lennox glares. "At least I bought it with honest money."

"Money is money," Maddox says. "Nothing honest about it. But I like the ring. *That's* honest."

"What does that mean?" Lennox growls.

"Boys," Valeria warns.

"It says someone's settling," Maddox says, leveling his brother with a stare. "That's she's okay with second best."

I feel Lennox tense beside me, and I grab his hand before we can have a repeat of the fight in the bedroom. "Or maybe it says that love matters more than money," I say. "That a marriage matters more than a ring."

"You should trademark that," Maddox says. "The universal slogan for a consolation prize."

"Rae's not a consolation prize," Lennox snaps.

"Oh, I wasn't talking about her," Maddox says, smirking down at me. His hand lands on my knee, and my whole body goes rigid. I hate the way I feel when he touches me—I hate that I love it. Despite everything he's done, and no matter how much I tell myself I hate him, I can't stop the way my blood flows hotter at his touch. I still crave it despite the cruelty of the man attached to those hands, wielding that touch like a deadly, seductive poison.

"Lennox isn't a consolation prize, either," I say, forcing myself to focus and not be distracted by the warmth of his hand on my knee. "He's a man who knows that a girl's worth lasts more than one night."

"Someone's pissed she got played," Maddox taunts. "Aw, does your pussy still hurt?"

"Not from you," I shoot back.

"That's enough," Valeria says, smacking her hand down on the table. "I will not have this talk at my dinner table. Rae, you're part of the family now, so you're going to have to learn to get along. Lennox, have some compassion for your brother. Maddox, I know you're upset, but could you at least try to find some happiness in your heart for your brother?"

"Oh, I'm very happy for him," Maddox says, his fingers biting into my flesh. "He gets to enjoy all this every night. Who wouldn't want that for his brother, his twin, the person he loves and trusts most in all the world?"

He relaxes his fingers and moves his hand up my thigh in one motion, pushing my dress with it. I almost yelp at the contact of his warm, strong fingers stroking up the sensitive skin of my inner thigh. I want to slap it away, but I know Lennox will pounce the moment he sees Maddox's hands on me. Tonight's supposed to be the night we move into our new place, not a hospital. And the way these guys brawl, that could very well be the end result if we don't keep it under control.

"Good," Valeria says, turning to us.

"Yes, ma'am," I say, managing to keep my voice normal despite the racing of my pulse.

"She's right," Lennox grumbles, glaring at Maddox. "Just because you don't see any use for a girl after one night, doesn't mean she's useless. And just because I saw something of value that you missed, that doesn't mean you can come in and take it from me."

"I said, that's enough," Valeria snarls. "I will not have you fighting under my roof."

Lennox answers in Spanish, his tone heated, and they argue for a minute.

While they're distracted, I shoot Maddox a murderous glare. He gives me a cool smile in return and hooks his foot around the leg of my chair, scooting it up until I'm pressed against the table. His hand is now buried deep between my thighs, pushing against the heat at my center. I think I'm going to faint when he strokes his little finger slowly against my panties. An explosion of tingling heat rushes over my body, and it's all I can do not to close my eyes and moan. I fight to swallow, casting a desperate glance at Lennox. How can I alert him without sending him over the edge and getting him killed?

I glance at Maddox again. He's watching me, a smug smile pulling at the corners of his lips. He knows what he's doing. He knows that if I tell Lennox, Lennox will pounce, and Maddox will get what he wants—to beat the shit out of his brother. He's bigger and stronger, and this time, I have a feeling he won't hold back.

Lennox and Valeria fall silent, and tension crackles in the air over the table. Maddox's finger traces the seam of my lips through my underwear while he takes a sip of wine and sets his glass down. My clit throbs at his touch, and I feel blood rushing between my legs, swelling my flesh and wetting me in anticipation.

"*Has terminado?*" Maddox asks, quirking a brow at his brother.

"*Sí,*" Lennox grunts, then turns to me. "Sorry."

I nod and almost choke when I feel Maddox's little finger move to my other thigh as he adjusts his hand, so his middle and first finger slip under the damp fabric of my panties. There's no way he won't feel how wet I am now.

I want to die of humiliation.

"I would never want to take something from you that you value," Maddox says to his brother while he works a finger into his fiancé's slit. "I'm offended that you think so little of me."

I grip the edge of the table, my head spinning so hard I think I'll faint or sigh and spread my legs. Instead, I squeeze my thighs together, trying to get his hand out, but it only holds it more firmly in place. I bite down on my lip as he works his middle finger against my swollen flesh, already slick with my arousal.

Maddox picks up a piece of chicken and bites into it like nothing's happening, like he's not fingering his brother's fiancé while he sits across the table from him, a picture of innocence. I consider picking up a fork and stabbing his hand with it, but that would require his hand to be on the table, not wedged between my thighs.

"*Vení*," Valeria says, smiling so tightly her lips lose their color, like petals pressed between the pages of a book. "This is nice. Having all three of you under my roof again, if only for a meal. But maybe it was a bad idea to invite a pretty girl to live here. I should have seen this was inevitable."

"No," I say quickly. "Thank you for doing that. I can't thank you enough."

I want to say more, but Maddox pushes the heel of his hand against my clit, and words desert me. I grab for my wine so I won't pitch out of the chair.

"It's not her fault," Maddox says, massaging my clit slowly while he palms my pussy. "We've always had our differences. They were bound to come to a head eventually."

"He's right," Lennox says, laying a hand on mine and making guilt wash over me like a tidal wave. "It's not your fault, Rae. It's easy to point fingers, but this is just the culmination of a lot of years of pent up frustration."

"So much frustration," Maddox says, spreading my lips and teasing my entrance with the tip of his finger.

"Well, I hope you boys can put those quarrels behind you now," Valeria says. "Rae's going to be a permanent part of the family, so you'll have to find a way to welcome her into our home, Maddox."

"Welcome to the family, little girl," he says, slowly sinking a finger deep inside me.

I choke on my wine. Maddox sucks in a sharp, audible breath when my core clenches around his finger reflexively. I'm grateful to have a reason to pull my hand from Lennox's to grab my napkin and hold it over my mouth. I'm grateful my coughing fit stifles the sound Maddox made, the one no one remembers as they ask me if I'm okay. Lennox reaches over to pat my back.

When I finally recover myself, Maddox is way ahead of me. He's already pumping his finger into me in a slow, relentless rhythm, no sign that his earlier slip even happened.

"You good?" he asks, smirking at me.

I press the napkin to my lips to stifle my gasp as he curls his finger inside me, hitting the spot that makes me explode every time. I squeeze my eyes closed and nod, willing myself not to climax in the middle of family dinner.

"I'll get you some water," Lennox says, pushing back and standing. He walks right behind me, and I freeze, my heart racing as Maddox torments that spot inside me, coaxing me closer to the edge.

Lennox comes back and sets the glass down next to my plate, leaning between me and Maddox. He pauses, and I tense, waiting for him to say something, though I can't tell how much he can tell by our positions. Can he see that Maddox's hand is aimed in my direction under the table?

He kisses the top of my head and returns to his chair.

"I think a toast is in order," Valeria says, picking up her wine. "Congratulations, you two. I never imagined I'd have a daughter so soon, but I think we can all agree you're a wonderful girl, Rae. We're happy to have you in our family and our lives."

My hands are shaking as I reach for my glass. I grip the stem for dear life and lift it to tap it against hers, then Lennox's. He gives me that dimpled smile that makes my heart shatter as Maddox circles his finger against my walls, grinding his palm onto my clit. I almost yelp, but I swallow it with a gulp of wine. Maddox raises his brows and holds his glass toward mine, reminding me I forgot to clink my glass with his.

Our eyes meet, and he gives me the smuggest smile that's ever graced a pair of lips. "Everyone loves a happy ending," he murmurs, bumping my glass and pulsing his finger against the spot inside me again. He touches his lips to the edge of his glass, flicking his tongue against the rim.

I remember that tongue inside me, and I can't hold back any longer. The orgasm explodes inside me, hard and fast. My hips jerk forward, and my wine glass topples as I try to set it down. I cry out, grabbing for the glass and pretending that's the reason for my gasps. I can't even see where the glass is, though. Black spots swim in my vision, and my walls clench and pulse rhythmically around Maddox's finger as it holds steady pressure against all the right places inside me. I grab the edge of the table, and my toes curl, and all I want to do is throw my head back and lift my hips, spreading my knees and letting him fuck me with his fingers until I fucking die.

Because I want to die. I want to die of embarrassment as Valeria rushes to get a roll of paper towels to clean up the mess I made. I want to die as

Lennox watches, a frown on his brow and realization dawning as he sees my cheeks flush and my eyes clear. I want to die as Maddox lazily strokes my swollen, tender clit with his soaked finger a few times before pulling my dress down and patting my knee in the most patronizing way imaginable.

"Isn't that right, Rae?" Maddox asks as Valeria comes back and drops a handful of paper towels onto the puddle of red.

"What?" I manage, avoiding their gazes and helping dab up the mess.

"That everyone loves a happy ending," he says. "Though if you ask me, you don't have to get married to get one of those. They can happen any time. Hell, even an engagement dinner can have a happy ending. Isn't that right, little girl?"

"That would be nice," Valeria says, looking at him like she knows something's up but she's not quite sure what. "Since I made a lovely dessert. Can we get through that without you boys killing each other?"

Lennox just stares across the table at his brother with cold fury burning in his eyes.

"I'll give it a shot," Maddox says cheerfully.

Valeria stands and stalks to fridge, apparently giving up on figuring out the reason for the tension. Thank god for small miracles, because I might actually drop dead if she knew I just came at her dinner table while being finger-banged by her son—not the one whose engagement to me was just announced.

"Though I'm really more in the mood for something salty," Maddox says, leaning back in his chair and sprawling his legs out. He meets my eyes and lifts his hand to his mouth, slowly sliding his tongue along his middle finger.

I swear my heart stops beating when he wraps his tongue around it, making a completely obscene show of licking off his finger. After the longest moment of silence in history, he pushes his finger into his mouth and sucks greedily.

Suddenly, the scrape of chair legs shatters the brittle silence, and Lennox dives around me and grabs Maddox by the front of his shirt. "Outside," he barks in his brother's face. "Right fucking now. We're going to get this over with for good."

Maddox stands, looking completely unconcerned. He towers at least four inches over his brother, his frame bulky enough to dwarf Lennox's lean, muscular one. "*O qué?*" Maddox asks, then adds a word that sounds more like a taunt than a term of endearment. "*Brother.*"

"Or I'm going to paint Mom's kitchen with your blood," Lennox fumes.

"Outside," Valeria barks, pointing to the door. "And get it out of your system this time, because I'm tired of this shit happening in my house."

I gape at her as Maddox shrugs off his brother's grip and saunters out. Lennox casts a furious look at me, one that makes my stomach twist into a cold knot of dread, and then stomps after him.

"What are you doing?" I hiss at Valeria. "Maddox is going to kill him!"

"He would never kill his brother," she says. "Sometimes, you have to let them just punch it out of their system until they tire themselves out. They'll go back to being friends tomorrow."

"They're not five years old," I say, my voice rising with panic. She doesn't understand that this shit has gotten serious—deadly serious. They'll always be her little boys, like she said. But they're not so little anymore, and the conflict between them has reached a breaking point. I can feel it in the desperation in my bones, but I know she's as helpless to stop it as I am.

We need someone bigger, someone their physical equal.

Neither of us has answers, but I turn and run for the door when I hear the first shout. I can't understand what they're saying, as they're yelling at each other in Spanish now, but there's already blood on Lennox's shirt by the time I throw open the door and charge onto the porch. He screams obscenities at Maddox and charges him, slamming his shoulder into Maddox's middle. They tumble to the ground in a blur of violence and power.

"Stop," I scream, lurching down the stairs in my heels. They won't stop for me, though. They don't even hear me, too absorbed in a conflict that started long before I showed up. I consider running next door for about two seconds, but I don't know if Lee's healed, and if he is, he'll bring a gun. So I pull off my heels, toss them over my shoulder, and run across the street in bare feet. I pound on Reggie's door with both fists.

"Reggie," I yell. "I need your help. They're going to kill each other!"

I can hear the sound of their blows landing all the way across the street, their grunts and curses, shouts and wordless exclamations of pain, the heart wrenching agony of brother turned against brother, of fist and bone, blood and fury.

"Please," I yell, pounding harder.

"What is it?" demands a familiar voice, and the door is wrenched open. Selma looks at me, then across the street. Her eyes widen. "Oh, shit."

She turns and yells for her brother, and the dog comes padding in, looking unconcerned. I keep glancing over my shoulder, nearly screaming in frustration for them to hurry. At last, Reggie appears.

"Come on," I say, grabbing his arm. "Maddox is killing him!"

And then I hear another shout, different exclamations. I turn back, my heart gripped with cold dread, just in time to see Lee with his knee on Maddox's back, wrenching his hands behind him. He snaps a pair of cuffs on him, even though he's not in uniform and probably not on the clock. I race back across the street, onto the grass where Lennox is curled, spitting and coughing and cursing.

"Don't hurt him," I scream at Lee.

He looks up at me, his face set in hard, cruel lines I know all too well. Is that how he looks when he arrests people? The same way he does when he beats the fuck out of his wife?

Maddox is spewing a stream of obscenities in Spanish, struggling under Lee's knee. Ignoring him, Lee barks for backup into his radio, then shoves it onto the simple holster he wears with jeans and looks me over from my bare feet to my black dress. "So this is where you been," he says, his lip curling in disgust.

"Don't hurt him," I say again, my voice pleading now.

"I'm not hurting him," he says, climbing off Maddox and dragging the cuffs with him, forcing Maddox to lurch clumsily to his feet or have his arms dislocated. Blood runs from his nose and mouth, and one eye is already swelling closed. "They're hurting themselves."

"Get your dirty, wife-beating hands off me, pig," Maddox snarls, jerking his arm free of Lee's grip.

"Go stand next to my cruiser," Lee says, then turns to Lennox, who pushes to sitting. His glasses are gone, crushed somewhere in the brawl, and his face looks even worse than Maddox's. His nose is skewed to one side, obviously broken, and blood pours down his mouth, chin, neck, and the front of his shirt.

"It was him," he says, his voice muffled by the blood. He stares at Maddox, who hasn't moved despite Lee's order.

"I'm sure it was," Lee says, reaching for a second pair of cuffs. "Now get your hands behind your back. You can both tell your side down at the station."

"No," Lennox says, stumbling to his feet and glaring at Maddox over Lee's head. "He's the one who attacked you. He broke your arms last spring."

Maddox stares back at him, his eyes going hooded in that way they do, like he's more snake than human. His jaw clenches, and the gaze he levels on Lennox could turn bones to dust. *"Qué sapo puto."*

"Is that true?" Lee asks, narrowing his eyes at Maddox.

Maddox's jaw works, and then he leans forward and spits a stream of blood at Lee's feet. *"Sí,"* he says, straightening and staring Lee down with eyes as green as emeralds but hard as diamond. "It was me. And I ever see you put your hands on your daughter again, I'll fucking kill you next time."

"You son of a bitch," Lee rages, baring his teeth in fury.

A police car turns onto the street, lights flashing and sirens wailing. Lee glances that way, and Maddox uses the momentary distraction to step forward and slam his forehead into Lee's face. I hear the bones in his nose snap, and I almost vomit on the spot.

"Maddox, no," I scream, leaping for him. He ignores me as if I don't exist.

"The only fucking bitch I see here is you," he snarls at Lee, who stumbles backwards, screaming curses.

My stepdad grabs his nose with one hand and reaches for his gun with the other. I throw myself onto him, wrestling his arm to stop him from shooting. Blood streams down his arm, but by the time he throws me off and gets his gun out, the cruiser screeches to a stop at the curb. The doors fly open, and two uniformed officers sprint into the yard and slam into Maddox, who hits the ground so hard I can feel it tremble beneath my feet.

Lennox helps me up, wrapping his arms around me and holding me together even though I want to blow to a million pieces. "It's going to be okay," he murmurs into my hair.

I don't think it will, though. I don't think it will ever be okay again. My heart is a stone in my chest, frozen in shock and heavy as lead.

"What are you doing?" I cry, burying my face in his chest so I won't see them wrestling to get Maddox under control. "You just ratted out your own brother."

Even though Maddox is cuffed on the ground, he's stronger than the two officers put together as he kicks and writhes, spits and curses. Finally, they whale on him with their Billy clubs to subdue him and then drag him to his feet. His face is battered and bleeding everywhere, and my stomach lurches like I'll be sick again. Tears burst from my eyes and a sob tears loose from somewhere deep inside, one I can feel all the way to my bones, as if the roots of some invisible tree are being torn from the very core of my being.

"Maddox," I cry in desperation, but Lennox pulls me back into his arms and holds me tighter.

"I did it for you, Rae," he says, watching the cops shove his twin into the back to their cruiser. "Now we'll be safe."

four for boys

thirty-two

#1 on the Billboard Chart:
"If You Had My Love"—Jennifer Lopez

Rae West

"Am I making a terrible mistake?"

I whisper the question to the girl who stands in front of me, looking the furthest thing from a black crow imaginable. In her layers of white chiffon and lace, she's like something out of a fairytale, a fantasy I dreamed into existence by the force of wanting it so badly. Not the wedding or the dress, but everything that comes with it—somewhere to belong, someone to belong to. Someday, a family to surround me the way mine never did, to anchor my feet to the ground like a tree, not a bird flying free.

I thought I was a lone crow for so long, a murder of one. I thought it was what I wanted to be. But Maddox was right back then. I'm not a crow. I never was, and I never will be. I thought I was flying, but really I was a seed blowing on the wind, looking for a place to grow, to put down roots. Lennox has given me that. I'm ready to grow, to be a tree, as I was always meant to be.

Not a crow, but somewhere one can nest and make its home.

I think of Poe on my roof. She always knew. She came to me looking to make her nest, her home.

And I got her killed.

"I wish you were here," I whisper to the mirror, letting my fingertips touch the glass as if to show myself it's not real. It doesn't feel real. I wish anyone was here, that I had someone to confess my doubts and insecurities to. But I haven't seen my mother since we left Mill Street. My chest still aches with the memory of that night, so I try not to think about it. Especially the night before my wedding.

I turn on the CD player and hit play. I've been listening to a lot of Poe lately, trying to find some connection with my dead crow. Or maybe it's just better than listening to the silence of my lone reflection and missing the crow tapping outside my window. I still remember the time she tapped on the glass while I was so engrossed in *The Tommyknockers* that for a split second, I thought they'd come for me.

Maybe she was a bad omen after all.

But that's silly. I'm getting married tomorrow, to the most patient, kind, beautiful boy who ever lived. My life is a fairytale.

I could ask Valeria what to do about cold feet, but it's her son, and I don't want her to think I don't love him. I do.

"I do," I whisper to the mirror. I practice it, fitting my lips around the words. They feel foreign, more clumsy than when I try to speak Spanish to impress Lennox.

I can't talk to him about it, obviously. And maybe that's a problem. Shouldn't I be able to talk to my husband about anything? Shouldn't I trust him to be able to handle it?

I don't want to hurt his feelings, though. He's so sensitive, so moody. By now I know it's part of his artist nature, that it won't change. We've lived together for a year, and I know I can handle a lifetime with him if that's the worst I have to deal with.

But is it?

Valeria might know. She might be straight with me if I come right out and ask. He's her son, after all. She must know things about him that could put my mind at ease.

She's the only person I see besides Lennox and my coworkers. Maybe it would help repair things. Reaching out to her could be the first step toward rebuilding the bridge we burned that night on her lawn, one year ago this month.

Now that she's speaking to us again, I could ask, even though we're not close. Until recently, she refused to take our calls. Lennox tried reaching out a few times, but she never responded. For eight long months, there was nothing between us but the ring of silence.

Eight months that Maddox spent behind bars.

I shove the thought away and pick up my veil, nestling it into my chestnut hair. Even though brides don't usually cover their faces anymore, I pull it forward and hide mine. Maybe that will make it easier to hide my fear.

What if he comes to the wedding?

My heart does a funny little lurch at the thought. But that's stupid. He's not coming to see me marry his brother. He hates us both. He hasn't spoken to us once since he's been home. I only know he's out because Valeria told us, and once, I ran into Scarlet at Hastings. She made a big deal of gloating about how she stuck with him through the eight months where he was in jail, and now they're madly in love.

I imagined reaching for the nearest shelf, pulling open the *Pulp Fiction* case, snapping the disc in half, and slicing her jugular with it.

A car pulls up outside, and I hear the door slam. I don't move from in front of the mirror, where I stand shrouded like something that belongs in a funeral. No one comes to visit me, anyway. When we left Mill, we left in shame. We'd ratted out one of the Crows, after all.

Lennox said he'd been thinking about leaving that life altogether, going clean when he started school. He felt like he'd outgrown the gang. But after that, it was too dangerous. We needed protection in case anyone retaliated, and the Crossbones provided it. They were more than happy to absorb a smart guy with vision into their ranks when they split from the Skulls.

Unlike me, Lennox has lots of friends now. Members of the Crossbones come and go from the house all the time. He's only one year into college, but he's already an important member. They consult him about things all the time. He says it's just business, but he hangs out with them so much I know they're more than that. They're friends, sometimes lovers.

I run my hands down my sides, sucking in my flat stomach. I imagine his hands on me tomorrow night. A warm tremor of excitement and nerves goes through me. He barely touches me anymore. He said he didn't want to scare me like he did at the quarry that night, that he wants me to know he loves me for who I am and that he thinks of me differently than the girls who came before—and after—our engagement.

I told him months ago that he'd proved himself, that I'd rather have him in my bed than all the flowers and promises in the world. That's when he finally broke down and told me he couldn't touch me without thinking about his brother being there first. I swore we didn't have sex, but I could tell he didn't believe me. He said it wasn't me, that he'd never been able to look at Maddox's conquests as options, but this time, I didn't believe him. I know it's me.

I know, because I know what it's like to look at someone and see the worst thing they've ever done. To feel the hurt and betrayal fresh every time you think of them fucking someone else.

I swallow hard, blinking back the ache behind my eyes. I tried to prove myself in every way after that conversation, even asked if Lennox wanted to break off the engagement. He insisted he wanted to marry me more than anything, that he loves me, even if he doesn't lust after me. He says the wedding will be a fresh start, and everything will be different once we're married.

I believe him.

I have to.

Tomorrow, I'll have everything I ever dreamed of. My forever someone. He promised that after the wedding, there would be no more crew girls. He'll be all mine.

Goosebumps rise on my arms, and I tell myself it's just from the argument I can hear downstairs, something about a contract. I turn up the music to drown it out. The Crossbones might be friends, but they're also dangerous. I've spent countless nights lying awake, waiting for him to come home. Praying he's with a crew girl and not in a ditch somewhere.

Because without him, where would I be? What would I have left?

I would have exactly one thing—a job. We're saving up so I can go to school, but with Lennox in school full time, it's hard enough to keep up with the bills, let alone put money aside. So I don't have school. I don't have family. I don't have friends. All I have is him.

That's normal though, right? All Valeria has is a job and her kids. All my mother has is a husband. That's how life works when you grow up. You leave behind childhood things, childhood friends, just like I did when I moved to Faulkner and again when we moved to college. I haven't seen anyone from Mill Street since we left that night, but Lennox says the Murder of Crows members and everyone in that area who was affiliated were absorbed into the Skulls with the chaos that ensued after Maddox's arrest. That means Billy, and by association Lexi, took Maddox's side.

Which blows, if I'm honest. I know Lennox is enough, and I'd never want him to think otherwise. But he's gone a lot, and I could really use someone's advice, a night away, or just a drive through the winding roads on the north side of town with the windows down and the music blaring.

I hear a few thuds, and I freeze. They're fighting. In a panic, I can't decide if I should go down, or if that would just distract Lennox and put him in more danger. After a minute, it's over, and I sink in relief. Footsteps thud on the stairs of our townhouse, and I freeze, praying Lennox sent them home, and he's coming to reassure me he's fine. I only remember he's not supposed to see me in my wedding dress when the door opens.

"Wait," I cry, turning my back. "You can't see me in my dress before the wedding! It's bad luck."

Bad luck, like a solitary crow.

I want to laugh and cry at the same time when the words leave my mouth. Everything has felt cursed since the night we sent Maddox away. Tomorrow's supposed to be the happiest day of my life, but all I can think about is climbing out the window, sliding down the rain gutter, and disappearing into the dark.

His footsteps cross the floor, and he slides his hand under my hair, gathering it at the nape of my neck. Fisting my hair, he jerks my head back. I catch a glimpse of my ghostly figure in the mirror, my face still hidden by the veil, before I can't see anything but the ceiling. I smell his rain-hay-sun scent a fraction of a second too late.

My heartbeat explodes into a sprint that thunders in my ears so hard it almost drowns out his deep, masculine growl.

"And what if I fuck you in your dress before your wedding to my brother? Is that bad luck?"

thirty-three

Maddox North

"Maddox," she gasps, her whole body tensing as she realizes who she's let into her room, who her chicken shit fiancé let into her house. I lean down and press my nose into the crook of her shoulder, breathing her scent through the filmy veil like it's the first breath I've taken in a year. I close my eyes and let myself enjoy it like I'm not here to punish her. She still smells as sweet and fresh as dew on a summer morning, like that day we crossed the grass on the way back from our night on Reggie's roof.

But she's not that girl anymore. She's got to be into some sick shit to put up with Lennox this long. Maybe she never was the girl I wanted to believe she was, someone good and pure, without black wings on her soul. Maybe no one is.

I'm sure as fuck not the man I was then. I guess I have her to thank for that. I didn't even have to spend a year behind bars to become the kind of man the Skulls respect and seek out for their organization—ruthless, fearless, and remorseless.

"That's right, little girl," I say, slapping the paper in my free hand down on the surface of her dresser. "You didn't think I'd forget a debt, did you?"

"What are you talking about?" she asks. "What are you doing here?"

"I'm here to collect," I say, sliding my free hand under her veil and wrapping it around her throat. "To claim what's mine."

I use her hair to pull her head to one side, then latch onto her neck, sucking hard, tasting her skin as she gasps and squirms. I thrust my tongue against her skin, moaning and licking, tightening my fist in her hair and squeezing her throat until I feel it flex against my hand as she swallows. My cock throbs at the erotic sensation, and a growl builds inside me. I bite down on her skin to stifle it, but it rumbles out anyway, vibrating up my chest and into her.

"Maddox," she cries, her nails biting into my skin. "You're leaving bruises."

"Good," I growl against her neck. "I want to leave marks all over your body, so my brother has to see them when he puts a ring on your finger and when he takes the dress off your body tomorrow night. I want him to know that I've tasted and fucked and owned his wife every hour of the night before he marries her."

"Maddox, don't," she says, trying to twist away. "Let me go."

I don't know when she grabbed my arm, trying to pull me free. I barely feel her nails breaking the skin. It's a pathetic effort. She has no chance of escaping me. If I had my brother's proclivities, I'd let her try, let her run. The thought of the chase does stir something primal inside me, but I've already caught my prey, and I don't play with my food.

"You never let me go," I growl, yanking her veil off and tossing it to the floor. "*Tu me tragaste.* I was fucking fine before you."

"I don't know what you're saying," she protests, her breath hitching. "Why are you here?"

I can feel her pulse racing under my thumb, and fuck if it doesn't make me hard. Being near her makes me hard. I've waited for this so long. I'm not going to waste it. I'm going to use every hour I've been given, every hour that she's mine. I'm going to use her every hour of the night.

"I'm here for you," I say, turning her toward the mirror above her dresser, where she was admiring her reflection. I can see her face clearly for the first time, how small and scared she looks, how pale and thin. She doesn't look radiant, the way a bride should look. She looks pathetic. Her big, hazel eyes shine with tears, though she tries to hide them by blinking her thick lashes against them.

I release her hair and run the back of my fingers down her arm from her shoulder to her wrist. Fuck, her skin is soft.

"I'm doing you a favor if you think about it," I say, smirking when our eyes meet in our reflections. "You'll never have to worry about the debt again. You'll start your new lives free and clear, without the fear of when I'll come to collect. It's the best wedding gift of all."

"Where's Lennox?" she demands, a glimpse of the defiance I remember returning to her eyes as she stares back at my reflection. "What did you to do him?"

"I only reminded him of our contract," I assure her. "He knows how this works. An oath signed in blood is paid in blood."

"What does that mean?" she snaps. "What contract? Can you just say what you mean for once in your life?"

"This contract," I snarl, snatching up the paper on the dresser. "The one we both signed that said we wouldn't touch you. The one *he* broke."

"He didn't," she says, her voice barely above a whisper as the realization sinks in. She takes it from my hand with shaking fingers. "He wouldn't."

"But he did," I say flatly. "We both swore we wouldn't touch you, and if we did, the other got to fuck you *and* his next girlfriend when you broke up."

She swallows, and the sensation of her throat pulsing inside my grip makes me practically cum in my jeans like a virgin. I watch her in the mirror, her pouty lips moving slightly as she reads the handwritten contract to herself. We each wrote out a copy, signed in blood, an unbreakable seal for a Crow. And even though the Murder of Crows no longer exists, my brother knew what it meant the moment I showed up tonight.

"And if you didn't break up…" she whispers, her eyes going wide as she reads the lines.

The other one gets her the night before the wedding.

At the time, I thought Lennox was insane for putting that in there. Now I wonder if he knew even then, long before I did, that this would never be over. He always thought ahead, had the strategies all planned out. That's why the fucking Crossbones wanted him so bad.

"No," Rae whispers, raising her gaze to mine in the mirror. Her face has gone even paler. For some reason, I thought he'd have told her by now. My damn ego is a little bruised that she doesn't even know about this, as if they haven't thought of me once since they sent me away in that police car.

"Oh yes," I say, gathering a handful of her puffy white skirt in my hand and dragging it up. Maybe it's unfair that she wasn't in on it, that she didn't know. But it won't stop me from fucking her. I'm not taking what's hers. I'm taking what's his, and her ignorance in the matter won't change the outcome. She may not have known about the contract, but she sent me to fucking jail just like he did.

"We were fucking kids when we signed that," he snarled at me when I barged in downstairs and waved it in his face.

"The devil doesn't care how old you are when you sign your away soul to him," I said. "When he's ready, he still comes to collect."

"You broke the contract first," he shouted. "You fucked her, so I got her when you were done. That was the agreement. Why should I honor it when you didn't? If anything, I should be knocking on your door, demanding a night with Scarlet."

"Then have your night with Scarlet," I snapped. "And I'll have mine with Rae."

"Don't fucking touch her, Maddox."

"I never have."

"Bullshit. I saw you with my own eyes," he raged. "Now you're going to lie to me because I caught you? Because you're pissed that after you hurt her, she ran to me? I didn't break the fucking contract, Maddox. You did."

"I didn't," I shouted. "You're the fucking pussy who snuck around like a snake and stole her instead of fighting for her like a man."

"I fought like the man I am," he said. "A smart one who doesn't use fists to solve every problem. I cared enough to figure out a way to get her. I cared enough to make sure you were out of the way so nothing could distract her from falling in love with me. I cared enough to treat her so well that you can be damn sure she did.

Maybe if you'd given a fuck about someone other than yourself, she would have chosen you."

"You mean, if I'd wanted to win so badly that I'd destroy my own twin's life?" I asked. "Not to mention hers. Do you even love her, Lennox? Or are you just marrying her to prove you finally beat me at something?"

"Fuck you," he said. "I'm marrying her."

"I'd rather fuck her," I answered. "I'll bring her back five minutes before the ceremony, and you can marry her tomorrow with my cum running down her legs. You fucking deserve each other."

At least the asshole fought me for her. I thought he'd just admit defeat and accept the inevitable.

It takes a minute to get all the layers of lace and silky stuff pulled up above Rae's thighs. She's wearing white cotton panties, like she's still as fucking innocent as the day we shared her on the living room floor of my mother's house. I should have known then that she was never sweet and innocent, even when she was inexperienced.

I can see her pussy through the fabric of her panties, and rage slams into my chest. Lennox took this from me.

He's had her all this time. Time I spent in jail for the night I fought back, even though they could never prove I was the one who broke that asshole's arms.

I tighten my grip on her throat, jerking her body against mine. "Touch yourself," I command.

"What?" she asks, her eyes rounding.

"You have one minute to get it wet for me," I say. "I'm not going to take my time and make it good for you, little girl. I'm not going to be gentle."

"Maddox, I've never… Please don't do this. You're scaring me."

"Time's up, little girl." I smile, but when I catch my reflection, I see a man baring his teeth, more savage than reassuring.

"Okay," Rae says quickly. She takes a breath and slides her hand down her panties. I watch her fingers move, and my cock throbs so hard I can feel it deep down in my groin, an ache for release.

"You should be used to being scared by now," I tell her. "Isn't that my brother's game? Or is this part of it? Your part to play, pretending you're scared?"

"No," she protests. "He's not like that with me. And I'm not pretending, you asshole."

"Go on, pull your panties aside," I say. "I want to see that sweet little cunt I'm going to be fucking tonight."

She hesitates, her fingers still moving, massaging her flesh. "You can't just take someone against their will," she says, but I can see in her eyes that she knows I can.

"I'm taking what's owed me," I say. "I'm not fucking you because I want to make you feel good. It doesn't matter if you like it. I'm fucking you for me, because I'm a man of principal, and I follow through with the contracts I sign."

"I didn't sign that contract," she points out.

"But your fiancé did," I say. "Deep down, you know he did, and you want it. You always wanted me, little girl. You were all over my dick like a regular slut, but you weren't ready then. You've had plenty of practice now, haven't you?"

"No," she snaps. "I haven't had any practice. We were waiting until the wedding."

I throw my head back and laugh the way only she can make me. Then I jerk her head back against my chest and growl into her ear. "Stop fucking around and show me what's mine tonight."

Still glaring at me in the mirror, she slowly pulls aside the white cotton fabric, spreading herself with her fingers. The moment I get a peek of her pink cunt, I'm gone. I spin her around, pick her up by her little waist, and set her on the dresser. Then I'm between her knees, buried in the billows of her dress, and her head is between my hands. My mouth crashes onto hers, muffling her cry of protest. I take her with my tongue, fucking her mouth the way I fucked her cunt with it once. Tonight, there will be no pussy licking, no sweetness. Tonight, I'll punish her for her part, and I'll enjoy taking what she gave to someone else when it should have been mine. She should always have been mine.

I wrap my hand around her throat from the front this time, caressing her racing pulse point as I draw back, leaving her lips red and swollen. "I'm going to take it so hard you feel it in your soul," I murmur. "Now spread your legs for me, little girl."

"No," she gasps, shoving me back. The moment my hands slip free of her, she launches herself off the dresser. Her bare feet hit the floor, and she runs for the door. I leap after her, fury pounding into me. She catches the door on her way out, slamming it in my face. A little scrap of her dress is caught in it, and I hear it tear as she yanks free. Then I hear her footsteps pattering down the hall. Instinct takes over, the years of crew girls and my prey drive sending me after her. Maybe Lennox is onto something, because I've never been harder as I prowl down the hall after her.

I don't run. I don't chase. I hunt.

I hear her footsteps thudding down the stairs, her exclamation of surprise when she finds her fiancé tied to a chair in the living room. She's trying to get the tape off when I reach the room.

"You should have kept running, little girl," I say, starting across the room toward her. "Did you forget he's the one who gave you to me?"

The fact that she didn't, that she stopped to try to save him, is the final blow. She fucking loves him. She loves him more than herself, stopped to try to free him even knowing she was sacrificing herself. Hatred and rage spread their wings inside me, the phoenix of fury rising and taking over.

When I reach for her, she darts around his chair, putting him between us. "I'll scream," she says, panic in her voice. "The neighbors will call the cops."

"Then scream," I say. "You already proved you have no problem sending me to jail. It'll be worth it to wreck that sweet cunt in front of your husband."

Lennox squirms and jerks his shoulders, his face red with rage behind the duct tape over his mouth, but I ignore him. I swipe for Rae again. She darts away, falling on her knees beside the couch. I think she tripped on her frilly dress until she yanks open a drawer in the little table. The next second, she swings around, aiming a pistol at me.

I cross the space between us in a single stride. "You think you're going to shoot me?" I ask.

Lennox bellows behind his gag.

"I will," Rae insists, aiming at me and releasing the safety. "Stay back."

I grab the barrel to wrench it away.

She squeezes the trigger.

The window behind me shatters.

She fucking shot at me. If I hadn't pushed the muzzle away when I grabbed it, she would have *shot* me.

We stare at each other for a long second, and then the rage takes over. I grab her, shoving her against the wall. We wrestle for control of her writhing body inside the ridiculous layers of her dress that's like fighting through a cloud of spiderwebs. The butt of the gun crashes against my temple, and I rip it from her hand and click on the safety before tossing it on the floor. My hand closes around her throat, and I yank down the top of my pants, freeing my cock. She lets out a mewl of protest, and behind me, I hear the door open, but I don't turn.

Reggie came, the way he said he would. But I don't need his help, and his presence won't stop me any more than Lennox's will.

Let them all watch me claim my prize, take what's mine.

I reach the center of her dress, grab the damp fabric of her panties, and wrench them off, dropping the torn scrap of fabric on the floor. "Maddox," she cries, but she doesn't get out another word.

I knock her legs apart, line up my cock, and ram it into her as hard as I can.

She's so tight I see stars. I've never been inside something so tight, so fucking hot and perfect. I draw out and slam into her again, relishing the fact that she still feels like a virgin when I don't get her ready, relishing the knowledge that her tightness means she's in pain. I bend my knees and crouch until only my tip is gripped in the vice of her cunt, then use all the power in my thighs to drive upwards, burying myself to the hilt in her slick, stranglehold of a cunt.

She doesn't scream. She doesn't even breathe. Her mouth drops open in silent anguish, though, as if the pain has stolen her voice, her breath, her soul.

It's stolen mine, too. I drive into her like a man possessed, a vicious animal, using my cock like a weapon, stabbing into her sweet little cunt until her eyes roll back in her head and tears pour like rain down her cheeks. I can feel how wet she is, how slick, can feel her wetness slicking my cock for easy entrance and running down my balls as I bury myself in her again and again, as if I can extract payment for the devastation she caused.

My family, broken. My crew, disbanded. My heart, buried somewhere deep in the ground, wrapped in the roots of a tree that feeds off it like a parasite. My mind, consumed by thoughts of this revenge. My soul, left inside the walls of that prison. This is all that kept me sane those months. Knowing that this was waiting, that I would find her and make her pay. So I do.

She sent me away so I couldn't come to collect, so she could make her fairytale life with my brother at the expense of my life. She didn't visit me there. She wanted me gone, out of the way, because I scorned her when I fucked Scarlet. She turned me into this animal. The one I became when it was the only way to survive. Now, she faces the consequences of her betrayal.

Her cunt stays clenched, making me force my way in with each pass. I know it hurts and I love it even more. This is her punishment, and her silence says she knows she deserves every savage blow as my hips slam against hers, my cock punching into her slick flesh. She grips me in a chokehold, tight as a fist, the fist I've used to erase thoughts of her so many times. Since the day we met, I've cum a hundred times picturing doing just this, imagined wrecking her little pink cunt every time I shot my load after masturbating in the shower or into the eager body of some faceless woman whose name I never bothered to learn.

I drop my hand from around her throat and bury it in her dress, finding her hips. Lifting her, I palm her ass in both hands, slamming her down on me hard and fast, impaling her tiny cunt to the hilt with my cock over and over. I don't feel anything else, not the rigidity of her body or her nails biting into me or her trembling in her limbs. I don't hear the crew behind me or Lennox's muffled screams. All I hear is the slick, wet sounds of her cunt as she takes me to the depths of her tight, dripping cunt.

"Maddox," she chokes out at last.

"That's right, little girl," I growl. "Say my name when you cum like a fucking porn star, the way you do. I can feel how much you want this. You're so wet you're fucking dripping for me. Taking every inch of me like the slut you are. Lennox really has fucked you up, if you like it this rough."

"Stop," she whispers, her lips trembling, her eyes bright and panicked as her gaze flies around the room to the people behind me.

But I don't care about them.

"I have you all night," I remind her. "I'm not stopping for the next eight hours."

I turn and dump her over the arm of the couch so I can fuck her from behind. When I fight through the mountain of lace and fluff, pulling up her dress to reveal her bare ass, I stop.

There's blood.

A lot of blood.

It's smeared on me, leaking out of her, trickling down her thighs.

"What the fuck?" I demand.

"I told you," she whispers, her hands balling into fists beside her head on the couch cushion.

"You're a virgin?" I ask incredulously. "How?"

She doesn't answer, and it doesn't matter. The sight of her virgin cunt bleeding for me breaks me. I am an animal, and this is my kill. I smell blood, and I can't be stopped.

The last of whatever is tethering me to my humanity slips away as I slide my bloody cock back into her slick grip and watch her take every inch of me to the hilt.

I know I should be gentle, but I can't. I can't stop. I take her, and take her, and take her, using her while she lies facedown on the couch, her ass raised like an offering, little whimpers and sniffles coming from her every few minutes. I fuck her hard, my hips smacking her ass with each thrust as I ram into her, possessed by this animal instinct to fuck and take and break and devour and destroy. I own her with each stroke, slamming myself to the depths of her core until I look down and see the blood again.

I can't hold back when I think of what it means. I took her virginity.

I drive deep into her with a final, brutal thrust. She cries out, and a roar rips from my throat. Gripping the crease of her hip to hold her tight to me, I grind into her. My balls draw up, my cock throbs thicker inside her crushing tightness, and I feel the release all the way to my roots when I cum. I let loose inside her, grinding and throbbing and growling as I give her every drop.

The orgasm leaves my whole body shaking and weak. I'm dizzy with her intoxicating scent, drunk on the knowledge of what this means. I'm the only man who's ever been inside her, the only man who's ever felt the addictive stretch of her cunt from the inside. I came to take what was owed to me, but I didn't know I'd be claiming her as mine and mine alone. I want to keep it that way forever, to pull her into my arms and never let her go.

I collapse onto her back, pushing her hair aside to lick and bite and suck the skin on the back of her neck, down between her shoulder blades, then over them.

"Fuck," I whisper at last, sinking against her neck, relishing the sight of goosebumps rising on her skin. "I've never cum like that in my life."

For a minute, we just lie there.

"Not to interrupt, but do you need us?" Billy asks from near the open front door, where he and Reggie are sharing a cigarette. "Because if I'm reading this right, it ain't a gangbang situation, and nobody else is getting a turn."

"Get the fuck out and go home to your girls," I bark, raising my head just enough that I'm not deafening Rae. I'm still inside her, and I don't ever want to move. I'll just spend the rest of my fucking life on the arm of Lennox's couch.

"Sure thing, bro," he says, tipping his head. "Got everything you need?"

"Go," I order. "And take Lennox with you. I'll call you with instructions in the morning."

I expect Rae to argue, but she doesn't say a word. The guys grab Lennox's chair and hoist it between them, carrying him out like he's a fucking prince on his throne.

When the door closes behind Daniel, there's no one left but us. I relax and kiss Rae's cheek, her ear, her neck, her shoulder and back. I wipe her tears when they start again, and I don't stop until they're gone. At last, I raise my head and push up enough to clear the strands of hair sticking to her damp skin and tuck them behind her ear. I kiss her salty cheek one more time. "You good?"

She nods mutely, and I pull out of her at last. I tuck myself back into my pants, then slide onto the couch and lift her onto my lap, wrapping my arms around her in case she gets any ideas about going anywhere before I recover my senses.

I'm not sure that'll ever happen now.

thirty-four

Rae West

We sit on the couch so long I think Maddox might have fallen asleep. I don't dare move and set him off again. Besides, as fucked up as it is, I need the closeness too, the comfort of his arms around me, human contact after the trauma. I nestle into his chest, remembering the first time I tried to do that, at the first party at the pool on Mill Street. This time, he doesn't push me away. Every now and then, he squeezes me against him, and when I shift even the slightest bit, his arms tighten around me as if by instinct.

I wonder absently if I'm in shock. Nothing feels real. In my real life, I'm Lennox's fiancé. In my real life, I'm a virgin. In my real life, Maddox is a painful ache of memory, not this solid body against mine, warm and animal and wild, with a beating heart and brutal strength and unpredictable fury, who smells like summer rain and cum.

Somehow, at the same time, nothing in the past year feels real. Maybe this is my reality, and my life with Lennox was nothing but a dream, a year of suspended animation while I waited for his brother to come for me. Because some part of me always knew he would. Some part of me is shocked, but I'm not surprised by his reappearance into our lives. In some hidden place inside me, a seed nestled down in the depths of my soul through the cold winter of my engagement, waiting for the rain of Maddox's wrath to awaken it.

I don't know if that seed was doubt or hope or dread, or something else altogether. But somewhere buried in the dark recesses of my mind, I was waiting. I knew we weren't done. That it wasn't over.

Is it over now?

"Maddox?" I whisper, twisting around to see him. Pain lances through me when I move, and I wince, not only from that but also the sound of my wedding dress rustling around me.

A jolt goes through me like lightning when our gazes lock. He's not sleeping. He's… Crying.

His eyes are open, their dark green depths soft and full of so much turmoil and emotion it stuns me. Silent tears leak down his stony, chiseled face. He doesn't try to hide it, just stares back at me.

"Maddox!" I cry, grabbing his face between my hands. An instinct that's close to panic rises inside me, and I lean in, holding his face and kissing his cheeks frantically until the tracks down them are gone. He just watches me, and I wait for the shutters to fall back over his emotions, for him to close himself off the way he always does and become the asshole he always is. I want the asshole. I miss him. That's the devil I know. I don't know what to do with this side of him. I never saw him as breakable, as even capable of this kind of emotion.

"I'm okay," I promise him, giving him one last kiss, this one on the mouth. His hands tighten on my waist, and he pulls me against him. I burrow into his chest, wrapping my arms around him and squeezing him hard. His long arms wind around me, securing me against his broad, muscular chest. His shoulders are so much wider than what I'm used to, his body like a wall that protects me from every danger except this one.

In his arms I feel small, delicate, like his little girl. Against all rational thought, I feel safe. He warned me not to make an enemy of him, and for the last year, I held my breath to see what the consequences of that mistake would be. I waited, weighed down by guilt, for my punishment. Now it's over. I've paid. I'm not his enemy anymore. I can breathe again.

I'm the one who falls asleep. I wake up disoriented, not knowing how long I've been out or where I am until I sit up straight and a knife of pain slices through my center.

"Where are the keys?" Maddox asks, standing and hoisting me into his arms. My arms circle his neck automatically.

"What?" I ask, still groggy.

"The car keys," he says. "Where are they?"

"By the door," I says, nodding to the hooks. "Where are we going?"

"Somewhere you've always wanted to go," he says. By the time he's stuffed all my dress into the passenger seat with me and buckled me in, my brain has dusted off the cobwebs of sleep and kicked into high gear. In fact, reality seems to have returned.

It's three in the morning, and this is my wedding day. Maddox may have come barging in and made me forget that for a few hours, but nothing can save me from the truth. He's not some white knight who magically appeared to whisk me away from my doubts and fears about marriage. He's not my savior. He's my destruction, and he's only doing this to get back at us—Lennox *and* me. We hurt him, and he wants to hurt us back, and he knows that he can only get to his brother through me. He only took me instead of Lennox because it's convenient for him. He can hurt us both through me.

He slides into the driver's seat of the El Camino and fires it up, shifting into gear and spinning the tires before the car thrusts forward. He shoots me a grin and shifts again, burning up the tires and leaving a cloud of smoke behind.

"Ready to have some fun, little mama?" he asks, apparently back to his old self. I can't remember why I missed this side of him, why I wanted it back. He's terrifying. He's a member of the rival gang to the one my fiancé is in, and he's basically just kidnapped me. I reach for the door handle, contemplating leaping out of the moving car.

What the fuck came over me earlier? I was fucking cuddling him like he was Lennox. But he's not. He's the furthest thing from his brother, and more than that, after a year of not seeing him, he's a stranger. I don't know what he's capable of. Is it worse than what he just did to me?

This man doesn't want me. He wants revenge. He doesn't even really want to fuck me. He only wants my body to take out his wrath on, to punish me and gloat to Lennox that he fucked me first.

Despite our tender moment earlier—if that wasn't just a dream—this man is dangerous and unhinged. I can't forget that. And now I'm in a car with him, going fuck only knows where. Getting kidnapped is not in my pre-wedding plan.

"Take me home," I say sharply, turning to him.

"The night's still young," he says, the car screaming through the night so fast it makes my chest feel like I'm being sucked back into the seat. "I've got you for five more hours, little girl."

"I don't care," I say. "I didn't sign or agree to that contract. If you want to take someone, take Lennox. He's the one who made that deal with you."

"But you're so much more fun," he says, his hand moving from the gear shift to my knee. "Besides, he's my brother. I can't fuck him later."

"You can't fuck me later." My stomach drops out as we hit the smallest dip, and I fight back the urge to scream. Is he going to drive us off a bridge? If he can't have me, then no one can?

"Oh, but I've been in jail for the past year," he says, his voice taunting. "You know how many nights I've gone without while he had you?"

"We didn't even do anything!"

"If my brother didn't fuck you to within an inch of your life every day for the past year, he doesn't deserve you," he says, letting off the gas at last.

"You weren't in jail for a year," I say, too shaken by his driving to even dignify that comment with a response. "You've been out for months. I'm sure Scarlet's been all too happy to impress you with her superior skill and experience."

"Scarlet's…" He glances at me and then shakes his head, pulling to a stop at a red light beside a mailbox on the corner. The streets are deserted, the only glow coming from the security lights inside the barred windows of a pawn shop and a few streetlights.

"What?" I ask, turning to Maddox. "You sure were impressed with her last year. She knew how to work your dick like a pro while being magically tight, or whatever shit you said to me that day in the parking lot after school."

"She is tight," he admits with a grin. "One time she stripped the condom right off me with her cunt."

"Take. Me. Home." I grit out the words, glaring at him.

When I reach for the door, he shifts roughly and shoots through the light, even though it hasn't turned.

"Not a chance, little girl," he says, squeezing my knee. "I'm not done with you."

"You already took my virginity," I point out. "You took something Lennox can never have, something I can never get back. You won. So just bring me home, and go fuck your girlfriend and her magical pussy."

"Are you jealous right now?" he teases.

"No," I say slowly, glaring at him. "I'm pissed."

"You're jealous," he says. "I can tell by the cute way you jut your little chin."

"Fuck you, Maddox," I say. "Or better yet, go fuck your girlfriend."

"Look, Scarlet's fine," he says, raking a hand through his hair, cut shorter now than when I saw him last. "I thought she just wanted to bounce on a gangster dick to piss off her daddy, but she's actually more complicated than that. She stuck by me when I was away, you know? That's not nothing."

"So I heard."

"But there's one little problem with her."

"What? I mean, besides the obvious fact that she's a soulless demon and isn't house trained, so she might take a dump on your clothes when she's pissed at you."

"Ella no es tu."

I drop my head back on the seat, fighting the urge to scream. "If you're so pissed that I ended up with Lennox, maybe you should think about what *you* did to make that happen."

"So you're only marrying him to piss me off?" he asks, swerving into the small, empty parking lot in front of a tiny, darkened tattoo shop. He turns to me, his dark gaze boring into mine. "To get back at me for fucking Scarlet?"

I cross my arms and glare at him. "I told you how I felt. You didn't want me."

"I didn't want to fuck up my family," he corrects. He shuts off the engine and stares out the windshield. "Clearly a poor choice, considering where we are now."

"I guess that's the difference between you and Lennox," I say. "You chose your family. They came first for you. That's honorable, and I can respect that. But Lennox chose me. I came first for him. Maybe that's not worthy of respect in your eyes. But it's worthy of love in mine."

"You love him because he tore apart our family for you?"

"No," I say, drawing back. "Of course not. I never wanted him to do that. I adore your mom. She loves y'all so much, and worked so hard to support you, and took me in when I had no place to go. I would never want to hurt her, and neither would Lennox. But he risked everything for me when you wouldn't. He lost everything, and he could have blamed me, but he didn't. He still loves me. And if you hurt him for that…"

I break off. I can't think about what Maddox did to him, what the Skulls are doing to him right now. If I do, I might shatter into a million pieces. He's all I have. He's supposed to marry me tomorrow. After tonight, will he still want to? Or is that Maddox's real plan—to tear us apart the way we tore his family apart?

Maddox scoffs quietly. "I'm the dickhead who puts his family first, remember? I'm not the one who stabbed his own brother in the back like a little bitch. When I give my word, I fucking mean it."

"Look, I'm sorry," I say, reaching for his hand. When my fingers connect, I pull back though. "I'm sorry about how it all went down. I never meant for you to go to jail. I didn't call Lee that night. You know I didn't. I went to get Reggie."

"I know."

"And I…I meant what I said that morning on the couch, Maddox. I loved you. I loved you both, but I would have chosen you. But you freaked out and left, and then you fucked Scarlet to hurt me. It wasn't just that day, either. You dated her for the rest of senior year. I had to see you with her, rubbing it in my face that you didn't feel the same. What did you expect me to do, crawl in the dirt and beg for you to love me back? You chose her, Maddox. So I chose Lennox."

"You chose wrong."

He climbs out of the car and slams the door. I think he's just going to pace and cool down, but he comes around and opens the door.

"What are you doing?" I ask, shrinking away from him.

He grabs my arm and drags me out of the car, ignoring my gasp of pain when I have to stand for the first time. "I told you, we're going to have a little fun. Remember when you told me you wanted a tattoo? Let's get tattoos."

"You want me to get a matching tattoo with you?" I ask, gaping at him.

He really is trying to ruin me so Lennox won't want me anymore.

"Sort of," he says, his mouth twisting into a smile that sends a chill racing down my spine. He drags me through an iron gate on the side of the tattoo parlor, then up a set of iron stairs. Every step is agony, and I can feel warm liquid leaking out of me now that I'm on my feet.

Maddox bangs on the door, waits, and bangs again.

"They're probably sleeping," I point out.

"They'll come out," he says. "Don't worry."

"I'm not worried," I say, crossing my arms. "And I didn't choose wrong with Lennox. He would never hurt me the way you did with Scarlet. I could never look at you the same after that. You fucked another girl right in front of me, deliberately trying to hurt me. What if I'd done that to you, made you watch me spread my legs and take every inch of Lennox and moan his name?"

"Then he'd be dead, and we'd still be here."

"So… What? I was supposed to kill Scarlet to stake my claim?"

He cracks a grin. "That would've been hot."

He knocks again, pounding on the door.

"Well, I didn't," I say. "And even if I had, it wouldn't have undone what you did. You wanted to hurt me, and you succeeded. I can't forget that, Maddox."

He shrugs. "You're just going to have to."

Before I can tell him that he's the most infuriating man to ever live, the door opens a crack, and a guy peers out from above a lock chain.

"We're here for tattoos," Maddox says, that terrifying joker grin stretching across his lips.

The man clears his throat. "We're closed," he grumbles. "Come back in the morning."

"I see that," Maddox says. "But if you take a minute to look at my face, you'll recognize me as one of your most valued patrons." He takes out his wallet as he speaks, counting out ten hundred-dollar bills and passing them through the crack in the door. "And someone you'll want to remember."

The man hesitates a minute, then looks past Maddox at me. "For your wedding?" he asks. "Hell, why not? Hold on a minute, let me get a shirt on."

"Bring your son," Maddox says. "We both need them, and I don't want to be here all night."

Ten minutes later, we're sitting in the reclining chairs in the tattoo parlor while they get the guns ready.

"What are we getting?" asks the older guy, who apparently owns the place. "Rings?"

"Not quite," Maddox says, climbing out of his chair and coming to mine.

I wait for his answer too, part of me expecting him to tell me he wants me to have a crow like the crew, even though it dissolved last year. I'm not sure if I hope he will, or if I hate the thought.

Without answering, he starts to pull up my dress. I grab it to keep from flashing the two other men. The owner's son is around our age, maybe a few years older, and doesn't look too happy about being dragged out of bed for this.

"What are you doing?" I hiss, widening my eyes at Maddox. "I'm not wearing underwear."

"Shit," he says, glancing around. Then he peels off his t-shirt and hands it to me. "Cover yourself."

Without waiting for an answer, he pulls my skirt all the way up. I shove at his hands, wrestling to get the layers of fabric down again. "What the hell, Maddox?" I whisper, mortified that the others will see.

They studiously ignore us as they get their equipment ready.

"Either obey, or I'll tie you up and have it done anyway," he growls. "You're damn sure going to remember this night for the rest of your life. And so is Lennox. How long that life lasts is up to you."

He pulls out his gun, aiming it at the tattoo shop owner. "I want the blood tattooed on her. I'll have this gun on you the entire time, so don't fuck up unless you want to watch your son and then your wife die before you."

Both the tattoo artists freeze, the son lifting his hands slowly.

"What the fuck?" I ask, whipping back to face Maddox. "Have you lost your mind?"

"Shut up," he growls. "You fucking sent me to jail to get rid of me so you could never think of me again. You think I don't have marks from that on me, ones I'll carry the rest of my life? Did you really think it was going to be that easy to forget me, little girl?"

"I didn't forget you," I say, my throat tight.

"Good," he says flatly, yanking my skirt up so he can see what he did to me. "And I'm going to make damn sure you never do. So sit there and take it. I know you can handle more pain than a little tattoo."

"I'm not having blood tattooed down my legs! I'll—I'll never be able to wear shorts again!" I know it's a ridiculous thing to worry about, but I'm too stunned by his request to think of a reasonable argument. He's beyond reason, possessed by some inner demon that's made him into something I don't know, something that terrifies me to my very soul. Who asks for something like that?

"I'll send you some of my basketball shorts for a wedding gift," he says coolly. "Now cover your cunt and let the man work."

He drops into the other chair and waves his gun at the son, unbuckling his belt with his other hand. "You'll be doing me. Same thing. I want the blood on me to last forever."

Maddox shoves his pants down around his thighs, and I look away, not wanting to see the evidence of what he did to me. He's insane. He's completely lost his mind. I should have known when he took my virginity like that, like a man possessed by demons or overtaken by that animal that rages inside him. It owns him now. He's not the Maddox I knew, the boy who was cold and aloof but strangely protective.

I should have listened when he said I didn't want to make an enemy of him. I saw how he treated Scarlet when she took my clothes, how he threatened the football players for messing with me and what he did to Lee when he saw the bruises. I've always known he has that inside him, but I loved him anyway. He was always a violent gangster, but he was *my* violent gangster. Now I know what it's like on the other side of his wrath.

He's no longer protecting me. He's destroying me.

Destroying his brother, his family, my marriage that hasn't even had a chance. How will Lennox ever be able to have sex with me now? If he couldn't before, when he only *thought* I'd fucked Maddox despite my promises I hadn't, how is he going to now that he's seen it with his own eyes? He's seen Maddox take my virginity, force me to take every inch of him, cum inside me. And now, he'll have to see it again every time he looks down and sees the tattoos on my thighs. He'll never be able to make love to his wife without remembering what his brother did to me, what he forced Lennox to watch.

The shop owner approaches me stiffly while Maddox keeps the gun trained on him. With shaking hands, I shove Maddox's shirt between my thighs to cover myself. The guy gets between my legs, scooting his chair in, and I startle when the machine goes on, buzzing in his hand.

"You sure about this?" he asks, his face pale with concern.

I bite my lip and nod, avoiding his eyes. I think I might cry if I look at him. So I stare at Maddox instead, hoping he can see the rage and pain and hatred fueling my every breath.

But he doesn't seem concerned. He's showing the other guy his dick, showing him the bloody marks he wants to remember forever. Whatever glimpse of humanity I saw on the couch, it must not have been the guilt I took it for. I thought he was sorry for taking me so roughly when he realized I was a virgin, but obviously he doesn't give a fuck. Maybe I fell asleep before that and dreamed the whole thing. A man who regrets his actions doesn't tattoo them on himself so he'll be reminded of them every day of his life.

The guy working on me looks at me every few minutes, but I can't look. I can't explain to him why I'm letting this monster mark me for life, can't explain to him that it's to save my husband.

Isn't it?

Even I'm not sure anymore. This will kill Lennox as much as a bullet would.

After an hour or so, the son says he's done, and Maddox says he can go back to bed. While he's leaving and Maddox is at least a little distracted, the guy working on me nudges my hip with his elbow. "You need help?"

I widen my eyes at him, shooting a startled glance in Maddox's direction. The door settles closed behind the son, and I don't dare speak. The silence in the shop is deafening. Then the older guy turns on his gun again and starts working on my other leg. I adjust the shirt, trying to keep myself covered.

"You better not be fucking looking at her cunt," Maddox barks, jumping up from his chair.

"I'm not," the guy says, holding up his gloved hands, the gun still in his right.

"He's not," I say quickly. "Maddox, he's just doing what you told him to do."

"Don't fucking touch her cunt," Maddox growls, setting his pistol down to zip his pants and buckle his belt.

The guy casts a nervous glance my way, and I open my thighs so he can get better access and hopefully not look like he's doing anything wrong. When he glances at me, I give a single nod, my heart racing so fast I think Maddox will hear it. Even though I made sure he was looking at his belt when I nodded, I'm terrified that he somehow saw it anyway, that he'll sense it or know. But he finishes up and stalks around the shop, then comes to stand at my feet.

While the artist's back is turned to Maddox and only I can see his face, he gives a long, meaningful look into a back corner. I swallow and thank him silently, not daring to nod while Maddox is standing there. I want to look where the guy's eyes directed me, but I wait, praying for the right moment to arrive.

It never comes. Finally, the guy sits back, and Maddox leans in to look over his shoulder and nods his approval. There's no more time.

Heart thundering in my ears, I gather up my skirt and sit up.

It's now or never.

I hop off the chair, turn in the direction the guy looked, and run. There's a door at the back of the shop, and thank god it doesn't need to be unlocked. It has a bar on the inside, and I slam into it so hard I almost don't hear the men hit the floor behind me. My heart nearly stops when the door flies open, but I force myself to keep going.

That guy, that stranger, just put himself in Maddox's path for me. I know I can never repay him, that Maddox will probably kill him for what he did to help me. Tears blur my eyes, but I blink them away. The only thing I can do to make that man's sacrifice worth it is to get away.

My bare feet pound the pavement of the street outside as I run, holding my wedding dress up in the front so I don't trip on it. I run like I've never run before, not with anger or to escape my shitty life, but to keep it. I run like my life depends on it, because in this moment, I know that it does.

"*Vení!*"

I hear footsteps pounding behind me, and I want to fall to my knees and scream, because it's too soon, and he's so much taller, so much faster, and he's wearing shoes, and it's all so fucking unfair. I never even got a chance.

But I don't give up, even when I know there's no hope. I run, and when he's almost on me, I see a phone booth half a block ahead. I dash toward it and dive inside, slamming the door closed just as Maddox reaches it. He smashes into it, banging the plexiglass with both fists. I try to hold it shut, gripping it with both hands and leaning back, but he gets his fingers in and rips it open.

I stare up at him, at the wild man standing there breathing hard, his eyes lost in some place I can't see. All I see is the savage madness in them.

I scream, and he dives inside, yanking the door closed and slamming me against the wall when I turn, as if there's somewhere to run. I scream again, twisting to get away. He grabs my wrists, yanking them over my head and pinning them to the glass.

"Oh my god, Maddox, stop, you're going to kill me!"

But it's too late. He's on me, yanking up my dress, growling and snarling and cursing. He shoves my legs apart and I hear the tape ripping as behind me, he yanks off the bandages covering his tattoos. Then he's inside me.

"Go on, scream," he snarls, ripping at my dress. "Scream my name, little girl. Not Lennox, not God. There's no one here to help you, *mi cariña.* You're stuck in hell with me now."

I scream, my breath bursting into a cloud on the window for only a second in the heat.

"Don't fucking run from me," he growls, thrusting up into me again. "You're fucking mine, little girl, and you'll always be mine. You'll never get away. If you try, I'll find you, and I'll throw you down and fuck you wherever you are, whether you're in a phone booth or in your husband's bed or in the middle of the grocery store. This cunt is *mine.*"

He drives into me hard and deep, his cock slippery with blood, though I don't know if it's his or mine or both mingling together like a blood oath as he takes over my body and claims it for his own. My feet leave the ground, and I scream again. He growls and snarls as he pounds into me from behind, yanking my head back by the hair, his teeth sinking into my neck.

I scream.

He releases my hands and slides his hand around my throat, slowing the pace but increasing the force of each thrust until I think he'll tear my body in half with the power and rage and strength of his.

"Take it," he growls, gripping my neck harder. "Take what's yours. Every fucking inch."

"Maddox," I choke out, gripping his hand, trying to pry his fingers loose. "That's too hard. I can't breathe."

He leans in, pressing his lips to my ear. "Swallow."

I struggle to swallow, at last managing to gulp past my fear.

Maddox groans when my throat flexes, his cock pulsing hard inside me. A cry of terror and pain chokes out of me, and he growls, tightening his fingers.

"Tell me you love me."

"What?" I ask, a strangled, humorless laugh escaping me before I can stop it.

He responds with a thrust so crushing I can hardly draw breath. "You said it before," he growls, his fingers tightening on my throat. "I want to hear it again."

"I can't," I manage, choking on my words, struggling for breath.

"Say it," he roars, slamming his hand down on the glass beside me so hard I see cracks spiderweb from his palm. He bites down on my ear until it rings, and I can feel blood running down my neck. He slides his hand around my body, fingering my cunt while he fucks me. "I'm not stopping until you cum on my cock and tell me you love me like you did that morning. That's all I've thought about for a whole fucking year. All I've wanted. Now give it to me."

I claw at his fingers on my neck as they tighten further, struggling for air, for consciousness. Horror barrels through me when I feel how close I am to obeying. I don't know what's wrong with me, how I can like this, but his finger massaging my clit makes my body respond in a way I didn't give permission for any more than I gave Maddox permission to fuck me like this, up against the wall of a phone booth in my wedding dress with his hand so tight around my throat I can't get oxygen.

I manage only a whisper as his finger keeps circling my clit relentlessly while his cock owns me over and over, as if to remind me I have control over nothing, not even my own body. "You're going to kill me."

I feel blackness closing in, taking over the edges of my vision. He drives his cock deep inside me, his fingers clenching around my neck and tormenting my clit until I'm pushed to an edge that's terrifying and humiliating, that's freedom and death and relief all in one.

"Then tell the truth with your dying breath," he growls into my ear.

I mouth the words, feeling the sensation leaving my fingers, my body jerking against his in some spasm as it searches for air, for life. It's a hundred times worse, more humiliating, because it's true. My body is saying it already, my walls clenching and squeezing around him in helpless, sucking pulses as I cum for his skillful fingers, his thick cock, his rough treatment and denial of oxygen. "I love you."

His fingers loosen, and he gives a final, quick, brutal thrust into me, groaning and cursing savagely. My walls are still squeezing rhythmically when I feel him cum, grunting and grinding, holding me gripped against him so hard I don't know where he ends and I begin. I only know that I'm drawing every drop from him, helpless to stop my body from responding to his claim. It knows where it belongs, who owns it already, just as my heart does. It wants more of him, his cum, his cock, his claim. But I refuse to listen to the insanity inside me. My mind knows better.

"Fuck," Maddox whispers against my neck, falling back against the far side of the booth, taking me with him. "Fuck, Rae. You're the only thing good in my world. I can't let you go. I can't."

He strokes my slippery clit, so sensitive now that my thighs quake with every touch. Pinching it between his fingers, he gives a little tug, and I cry out and buck against him, tightening up around his painful girth. He groans again, his hips jerking against mine, and I can feel an answering throb in his cock that's still lodged deep inside me, squeezing the last drops of cum into my core.

"Stop," I gasp, trying to close my knees and push him away.

"I can't," he says. "You feel too fucking good, *mi tesoro.* I want to live inside you." He's breathing so hard he's can barely speak, his words twisted with anguish. "I want to fuck you forever." He strokes my hair back with his other hand, kissing my neck with hot, fevered kisses. He keeps touching me, spreading me open, squeezing me closed, rubbing my clit until I think I'll scream.

"Let me go," I whisper at last, my throat aching from strangulation. "It's my wedding day, Maddox."

Suddenly I'm crying, tears streaking down my cheeks like rain. He's the only one who can make me cry, and he does it so well. He's the king of pain, and my heart and body bear the proof.

At last, he pulls out, and our mingled cum and blood gushes down my thighs. Shame pierces my very soul.

Maddox turns me around, holding me in his bare arms like they're a shelter and not a prison, like I'm a baby bird and he's my shell.

"It's not your wedding day," he says frantically. "It can't be. I can't… I just can't." He lifts my face, kissing me desperately, like he's trying to convey something too big for words. I hold onto him, and I let the force of him wash over me, pull me under, consume me. Because somewhere deep down, I know that he's right. I can't let him go, either. I know that he's still my brutal gangster, my wild crow, my devastating love.

At last, he's let down his walls for me. Behind them is an ocean of hurt, of tears, of rain. The dam has broken, and the flood of his love has washed me away. I never dared to risk a love like his, one that might force its way inside me before I'm ready, before he lets *me* in. That's the most terrifying part, having my feet off the ground, giving myself over to someone else, knowing he could break me. Even worse is knowing he already has. He's hurt me in ways I can never forget, and I still love him.

That's the most terrifying of all. I can't control my own heart anymore. I don't own it. He captured that too, stole it, and it's no longer mine. It belongs to Maddox now, and if he wants to use it against me, I am helpless to stop him. All I can do is hold on and love him as hard as I can and hope it's enough to keep us both afloat until the tidal wave of his rage and pain and love dissipates. All I can do is hold on with my roots, and hope that by some miracle, the heart of this tree I've become can save us both from drowning.

thirty-five

Rae West

I sit on the sidewalk, my back to the brick wall of a building, while Maddox makes a phone call. I could run, but I don't. I know I won't make it even a block. So I wait, and after a while, he comes out of the phone booth. He's still shirtless after the tattoo parlor, his body a brutal reminder of his strength, all bulging muscle and size, tattooed with new ink he must have gotten in prison. He holds out a hand as if to help me up. "You good?"

I make no move to get up. "I'm the furthest you can possibly get from good."

He stands there looking at me in my torn wedding dress with dirt on the outer layers and blood on the inner ones like he's just now noticing that I'm a mess. Then he sits down beside me and thumps his head back against the bricks and closes his eyes.

"I'm probably supposed to ask what's wrong?"

"You," I burst out. "I'm supposed to be getting married today, Maddox. Don't you get that? It's my wedding day. It's supposed to be the happiest day of my life, and now it's the worst day of my life, the worst day I'll ever have."

He gropes on the concrete until he finds my hand, lacing his fingers through mine. "Don't say that."

A broken, incredulous laugh escapes me. "Look, I know I fucked up by letting you go to jail, and maybe I even fucked up by choosing Lennox, but that was my mistake to make. This… This is yours. You just showed up and destroyed my entire life in a matter of hours. I can't get married. My dress is ruined. My body is ruined. My engagement is ruined. So I guess you got what you wanted. You ruined every single thing I have, Maddox. I wish you'd kept going in there. I wish you'd held onto my neck just a little longer. Because I'd rather be dead than here."

A tear rolls down my cheek, and Maddox just stares at me like I'm a stranger, like I'm as different now as he is. Maybe I am.

"You'd rather be dead than with me?"

"What does it matter?" I ask, dropping my head back and closing my eyes like he did earlier. "Lennox will kill me anyway. He'll kill us both."

"He'll try to kill me," Maddox says. "Not you."

"You think he's going to marry me now?" I ask with a bitter laugh. "The best case scenario is that he'll kick me out and be so disgusted he won't want anything to do with me. I'll sleep in the break room at work a while, and if they don't catch me, I'll save up enough to get a shitty car to sleep in and maybe someday, have enough for an apartment. And that's the *best* that could happen."

"Did you not hear what I said to you in there?" he asks, nodding to the phone booth.

I just shake my head. "How can we go back from this, Maddox? There's no way back."

"There's a way forward."

He stands and takes my hand, pulling me up. He doesn't let go as we walk back to the tattoo parlor, where his car is parked.

"Stay here," he says. "I have a little business to take care of inside."

He walks away without a word, knowing I'm beaten, that I won't run. I stand next to the car a minute, and then I walk toward the shop as if in a trance. Thunder rumbles low overhead, rolling across the sky with my footsteps on the pavement. It seems fitting that it's going to rain on my wedding day. It can't ruin it more than Maddox already has. He didn't just come to collect. He brought something to give back—destruction and disaster, tears and pain. His love is a prison, a curse. Even if I manage to hold on until it's over, until he's done with me, I'll never truly recover.

I know I don't want to see what he's doing, but I can't stop myself. When I get to the glass door, Maddox is holding a gun to the back of the guy's head while he writes something on a piece of paper. Maddox says something, and the guy kneels, his hands behind his head. He's crying and shaking.

He's paying.

Paying for crossing a gangster. For trying to help me escape.

I reach for the door handle, a cry lodging in my throat.

I jump when the shot rings out, a loud pop inside the shop. The man falls forward.

I clamp a hand over my mouth, swallowing the scream, terror racing from my heart and along my limbs.

Maddox tucks his gun into the back of his pants, folds the paper, and slips it into his wallet. He tugs on the t-shirt he had me hold over myself, ignoring the bloody spots, and picks up the phone on the desk. After making a call, he talks for a few minutes and then hangs up. He steps over the body like it's nothing and walks out the door.

I'm frozen to the spot, a tree that may never be uprooted again.

"I told you to wait in the car," he says, his voice completely flat and devoid of emotion as he passes me. He climbs into the car and starts the engine. I stare at the body lying face down on the floor, blood spreading slowly around it. It's my fault. If I hadn't run, he'd have left him alive.

I don't move until Maddox drives up right beside me. He hops out of the car, picks me up, and tucks me into the passenger seat, buckling me in before returning to the driver's side.

We drive away without a word.

"Why'd you do that?" I ask at last, surprised that my voice comes out as empty as his.

"He saw your pussy," he says. "I don't want a man alive who's seen you like I have."

"They'll find him," I say. "You'll be arrested."

"No, I won't," he says. "I called a cleanup crew. He signed the shop over to me before he died. It's mine now, and no one will ever know what happened there. Just us."

"Us," I echo, watching clouds roil in the sky overhead. I wonder how many times he's done this. How he lives with himself. I guess I know the answer to that.

"You're pretty chill, considering," he says. "I went loco the first time I saw a man die."

"When was that?"

He pauses, glancing at me while he drapes his hand over the top of the steering wheel. "When Lennox killed the guy who raped our mom."

We drive in silence for a minute, through the blue morning. A few cars are out, their bright yellow lights cutting through the stillness.

"I always knew it was a possibility," I say. "You're in a gang. People get stolen by rival crews. I wanted Lennox to do it before someone got me, but he refused. He had this obsession with saving it until the wedding. He said he couldn't touch me without thinking about you doing it first. It made me feel like I was damaged, dirty, for what I'd done with you, even though we did it with him the first time. I swore on my life we never fucked, but he wouldn't believe me. But it was like he thought if he didn't fuck me until the wedding, I'd reset and be truly his. Like once we got married, what happened before didn't count."

"Sounds like Lennox."

"He said he had something special planned, and it wouldn't be as special if we did it first."

"That part doesn't sound like my brother."

I run my finger down the inside of the windowpane, tracing the first streak of rain.

"I didn't think we'd make it this long," I say faintly. "I knew he could snap, that he might lose control and hurt me. At first, I was sure he would. Later, I wanted him to. Sometimes, I tried to get him to lose control just so he'd fuck me before someone else did."

Maddox is quiet, and then he reaches over, taking my other hand. We turn into the parking lot at Thorncrown, the only Catholic church in town, which sits on the border of its private, namesake university.

I'm getting married here in three hours. Or I was. I don't know how Lennox can marry me now, after what Maddox did to me.

Though it's morning already, I'm not sleepy. I have this deep, peaceful stillness inside me, nothing like the last time we stayed up all night together. That time, I was torn and agitated, trying to figure out this infuriating, mysterious, dangerous boy.

Now I know. It's over. There's nothing left to be conflicted about. Once, I told him I wasn't afraid of him, because I knew he wouldn't hurt me. Now he has, but I'm still not afraid. He's taken everything, left me broken like I always knew he would. He's one of those snakes that sneaks into bird nests and sucks out the inside of the eggs. There's nothing left inside me for him to take. He used me up until I'm nothing but an empty shell.

"I was scared every time he had the crew over," I say, staring down at our linked hands. "Silly, right? I know they have the crew girls. What did they need me for? But I'd hear them downstairs, and I'd lie awake, just waiting. I thought if he didn't want me, maybe one day, he'd give me to one of them. Or maybe they'd get in a fight and one of them would punish him through me. But mostly, I was scared the Skulls would take me to get to him. And I guess that's what happened. I was always afraid someone would do this. I just didn't think it would be you."

I wait for him to make excuses for what he did, justify it, call it by another name, or say it's different with him, that's not what he was doing. I wait for him to say it wasn't just about his brother, that it wasn't to punish either of us, and that it meant something to him too. But he doesn't say anything.

The rain outside comes harder, sweeping over the car and sending a wave of goosebumps up my arms. I watch it sluice down the window, too many tear tracks to trace, as if the sky itself can feel my anguish, the pain and betrayal. I lost everything, not just my virginity. I lost the twins too. Not just Lennox, but Maddox—the image I had of him, the idea of him. He's not the boy who always protected me. He's a man who will force another man to do something at gunpoint and then shoot him anyway.

I wonder where Lennox is, if Maddox had him killed. If not, how will he get here? What will he do to me when he sees me? To Maddox? What will Maddox do to him?

He's right. I tore their family apart.

"Do you think he was punishing me too?" I ask after a while. "Is that why he wouldn't sleep with me? He knew how much I wanted to. He knew it hurt me that he wouldn't. I told him how it made me feel, that he didn't want to fuck me but he'd fuck the Crossbones girls. Maybe it's for what I did to you, to your mom, your family. Just like you did tonight. Am I done paying off the debt now? Or do I still owe him?"

Maddox shakes his head but doesn't speak.

"Maybe it was the contract," I say, running my finger along the bottom of the fogged window, where water is gathering on the outside seal. "Maybe he really was honoring it all this time. That explains it, right?"

Maddox drops his head forward, resting it on the top of the steering wheel. I wonder if he's feeling guilty about what he did now that he knows Lennox hadn't fucked me after all. There was nothing in the contract about accidentally breaking it because one of them thought the other one had. Will there be some punishment for him now? Or will that one fall on me, too?

Suddenly I remember the two bullets in the gun that Lennox had the night he finally got me. He said later they'd just been left in there, but I always wondered. If I'd rejected him, was one of those bullets for me?

"He was still fucking crew girls?" Maddox asks, finally speaking for the first time since we got to the church.

I press one fingertip to the glass, raising it and then circling down, then back up and connecting it, making a crooked heart shape in the steam. "He said he'd stop when we were married. But it's part of your job, right? I mean, you kind of have to do it, don't you?"

"I haven't fucked a crew girl in over a year."

"You haven't?" I ask, turning to stare at him. "Why?"

His face is still turned down, his forehead resting on the wheel. He doesn't answer, and when the reason comes to me, I feel like I'll be sick. My eyes sting, and I have to blink hard to keep tears from welling.

"Scarlet," I whisper, dropping my head back on the seat. We sit there in silence a while, listening to the rain drum on the roof and windshield. Goosebumps rise on my arms again, and I wrap my arms around myself, feeling as cold as if I were out there getting beaten by the pouring rain instead of inside the steamy cocoon of the car.

Maybe I'm a crow after all, not a tree. Maybe I've been inside an egg this whole time, one that Lennox never let crack. Now Maddox has come along and taken a sledgehammer to my shell, stripping it off and leaving me disoriented and reeling with shock. I don't know how to go on from here. I thought I was putting down roots with Lennox, but now I'm standing in the wreckage of my life, once again a murder of one.

"Do you love her?" I ask, slowly sliding my finger down the middle of the heart I drew on the windshield. It seems more fitting. Maddox doesn't break hearts. He slices them cleanly in half.

"No."

He doesn't offer any more explanation, just slides across the bench seat, pulling me into his arms. Holding my face between his hands, he kisses me so softly I wouldn't believe he was capable of the brutality I endured last night.

"Do you love him?" he asks, pulling back and searching my gaze, his shadowy, emerald eyes searching mine like he can find the answer he wants there, even if my mouth can't say it.

"I don't know," I admit. "I thought I did. He gave me what I wanted. Roots. A family. A picture of the future we'd have together."

"A lie," Maddox whispers, pressing his forehead to mine. "Is that what you want, *mi tesoro?* You want me to lie to you, to pretend I'm someone else?"

"No," I say, wrapping my hands around the enormous bulge of his triceps. "I wouldn't believe it. I know who you are, Maddox."

He kisses me, this time deeper, longer, until my lips are raw and swollen and my head is spinning and I can't think of anything but him. Finally, he pulls away, sliding his hand up my back, over the bare skin above my dress, the back of my neck, and into my hair. His palm cradles the back of my skull, his fingers curving over the crown of my head. "I have to be inside you again," he says, his voice soft but rough with desire. "I have to, Rae. I'll try not to hurt you."

I swallow hard and then nod, sliding my arms around his neck and pressing my forehead to his. He lays me down on the bench seat, kissing my swollen lips with his until I'm not shaking anymore. I'm wet and throbbing for him, but every heartbeat pounding between my thighs reminds me of the excruciating pain he left me with.

He lifts to pull my dress up, piling the mountains of fabric around my waist. His fingers skim over the bandages on my inner thighs, and a shudder goes through me as he gently skims them over my pussy. "I want you to cum for me, little girl," he says against my lips. "I'm going to eat you out. Think you can handle it?"

I swallow hard, searching his eyes. "I'm pretty messy down there."

He groans and kisses me, swiping his tongue across mine one more time. "I want your mess, Rae. The mess, the laughter, the tears. The life. I want all of it. All of you."

He tips back the seat, pulling my hips up and slipping his head between my thighs. "Fuck, you are a mess," he says, stroking his thumb sideways across my folds. "Bloody and swollen and leaking my cum. God, I've never seen something so fucking hot."

I brace my hands beside my hips to push myself back to sitting, but his forearm clamps around my hips, and he buries his face in me. The sensation of his rough tongue against the flesh he tore into so roughly makes me shudder and gasp, but he only moans and presses deeper, licking and sucking and stroking me until I'm shaking and crying. For more. For relief. For him.

Car doors slam outside, but I can only make out vague shapes outside the fogged windows—a person, a giant bundle of white balloons bobbing past, someone with their arms full of flowers. Then Maddox enters me with his tongue, and my lids flutter closed. My hips rise and my hands fist in my ruined dress as he takes me away, carrying me higher and higher until I'm soaring above the world with him, and no one exists but us.

When I cum, he slows, pulsing his tongue against my clit as if he can't bear to stop until he's sucked every drop from me, gathered every pulse on the tip of his tongue like honey. He moans, tugging my sensitive clit between his lips and making my thighs clench involuntarily.

"Stop," I gasp. "It's too much."

"It's not enough," he growls, giving a last suck before lowering me to the bench seat. He's so big he seems to take up the entire car as he hovers over me, trying to fit himself between my legs. He finally settles for kneeling over me, his mouth finding mine. I can taste myself on his tongue, and I start to pull away, but he grips my chin and slides his tongue deep into my mouth.

"Taste how sweet your cunt is," he murmurs, drawing back and running his tongue over my lower lip. "Can you blame me for losing my mind over it?"

"I don't know if I can go again," I admit. "Even that hurt."

"You're going to have to try," he says. "Can you do that for me, *mi reina?*"

I search his eyes, looking for the malice I saw earlier, the crazed animal side of him that tore me up so badly. But all I see is the Maddox I always knew, the boy I loved so hard it hurt.

Finally, I nod, my pulse racing.

"Take me one more time." He presses his lips to mine, then trails down my chin, along my jawline. Taking my wrists in one of his huge hands, he pulls them over my head and holds them pinned to the seat. "I'll try to go slow this time," he murmurs in my ear. "I don't want to hurt you. But fuck, you feel good."

Adjusting his position, he piles the layers of my dress onto my belly and pushes down the top of his jeans. His bare skin burns against mine, and I gasp when he presses the thick head of his cock to my raw opening.

"Maddox," I whimper. "Please. Don't hurt me."

"I'm trying," he says, reaching down and pulling his skin back before grinding his tip through my slit and back to my entrance before pausing to take a shuddering breath. "But fuck, I want to rip you to pieces and eat you alive."

"Don't," I manage. "Please don't. I don't think I can take it one more time."

He shifts around, then lifts up and spits on his palm. He rubs it over himself, though I'm already soaked from his mouth and my own release. The problem isn't that. The problem is his size, and how sore I already am.

"You can take it," he coaxes, gripping his cock and straining the thick head against my opening. "You did it before. Relax, little girl. Let me in this time. Show me how well you can take all of me. *Tragarme, mi amante deliciosa.*"

He rocks forward, the head of his cock breaching my entrance. I cry out as he stretches the torn flesh, sending a wave of hot, burning pain crashing over me.

Maddox growls, and I tense, my walls clamping down on him in terror, expecting him to lose control and ravage me again.

"Oh, fuck," he groans. "You're so goddamn tight." His body starts to shake, and he bites down on his forearm that rests on the seat above my head, still gripping my wrists. I can hear his breaths, slow and shuddering, echoing around the car. For a minute, he just breathes, in and out. Then he draws back and enters me again, holding his cock and filling only my entrance with the tip. He draws back and goes in again, over and over, slow and firm, until the sound of his breathing and my wetness, and the feel of him stretching me so wide, has me squirming for friction.

"Maddox," I whisper.

"Fuck, I know," he rasps. Reaching between us, he digs under my dress until he finds my skin, bare for his touch. He strokes over my clit, pushing in a bit deeper.

I gasp in pain, then suck in a shaky breath. "You're too big."

"I know," he says. "You'll just have to learn to take me."

He moves faster, sliding in and out until the pain wars with pleasure inside my body as it takes him the way it wants to, the way it was meant to. I lift my hips to meet his, pushing him in the last inch, and he has to stop and bite down on his arm again. I squirm under him, panting and gripping his hand, digging my nails in.

"I'm ready," I gasp when I can't take another minute. "Let go."

He doesn't wait for me to change my mind. He draws back and plows into me hard and deep. I cry out, my back bowing. He pushes up on his hands for leverage, his powerful arms flexing, his enormous body tensing with each stroke, the force of it enough to destroy me. One of his hands binds my wrists like handcuffs while the other slips under the back of my neck, cradling it and resting his weight on his knuckles. He rolls his hips rhythmically into mine, never breaking eye contact as he pumps his thick cock in and out of my ruined body.

"You good?" he asks between strokes, driving me up the seat with each thrust.

"It hurts," I admit, my lip trembling.

"You'll get used to it," he assures me. "Now reach down and finger your clit. I want to feel your cunt milking my cock when I cum."

I obey, my self-conscious gone. We're well beyond that, so I let go, too. I close my eyes and let my head fall back, his hand on the back of my neck firm and supportive. There's no insecurity with Maddox, no fear that I'm not good enough or that he doesn't want me. He wants me too much, more than I want him, more than it's natural to want anyone.

I don't know what I did to unleash this beast inside him, but I know his desire is an animal that won't be caged. It takes what it wants, and it wants me. There's something freeing in his ravenousness. I don't have to wonder what I did wrong, wonder if he'll want me later. I'm enough for him. I'm it for him.

I feel myself cresting, and I open my eyes. He's watching me touch myself, watching his cock slide to the hilt inside me with each drive of his magnificent, powerful body. When my lids flutter open, his gaze rises to meet mine. His deep green eyes burn into mine, heated with lust, with a depth of emotion that thrills and terrifies me, like everything about him.

I hold his gaze, and I let myself go. Yes, it's terrifying and thrilling, but it makes me cum harder than I've ever cum in my life. My walls flutter and then clench around him, and I'm falling into the endless green depths of his gaze, a crow wheeling through the raging storm, plunging through the writhing trees, not searching for a place to land but letting the tumbling wind batter me and lift me and carry me away, taking me where he wants to go.

"Maddox," I cry, my hands flexing and clamping around his, as if I can cling to him forever and anchor myself to him, not to a tree but to the wind and lightning, to the rain and thunder and churning water. My back arches, my heels digging into the seat as I lift my hips, grinding out my climax against him. "Maddox, I love you. Oh god. I love you."

"I love the way you cum," he says through panting breaths, grinding me down into the seat. "Your bare cunt taking every inch of me. Take my cum."

"Maddox," I whisper, barely able to speak. "I'm not on birth control."

"Good." His hips jerk forward, and I feel the swell of his cock expanding inside me. I wince at the stretch, biting down on my lip as he growls and grinds, his hips locking against mine. "*Te amo, mi reina.*"

Our gazes still binding us together, he lets go, releasing deep inside me. He groans as the heat of his cum floods into me. My walls flutter with pleasure at the pure, erotic sensation. He grunts and shudders above me, his cock throbbing as he keeps coming, filling my core with each pulse. His whole body quakes with each flutter of my walls, each answering twitch of his cock inside me.

Finally, he lowers himself onto me, bracketing my body with his arms and pressing his chest to mine, squeezing us together. I want to say something, but I don't know how to put into words how I feel, how I felt some connection forming between us, and now I know my heart is bound to his. I belong to him in some way that I'm not sure can be undone, and it's terrifying.

Because in an hour, I'm supposed to marry his brother. His brother who has given me everything, but who I've never felt this way for.

I wish it could be different. I wish he'd touched me, fucked me, given me this intimacy that I craved so much over the past year, that I needed like I need air. I needed it so much that when I got it from someone else, even someone who brutalized me, my heart went to him.

It belongs to him. When it threw itself on his mercy, he took it greedily, as if he'd been hunting for it all along. He didn't shut it up in a box and save it for later. He gave me what I've ached for all this time, and I'm terrified by how much it meant to me. He caught me in his trap, caught my heart, and I don't think he'll give it back. Not even to the man I'm marrying.

Why couldn't Lennox see what was happening to me all that time? That I didn't need a ring or a wedding or a honeymoon to thrive. I just wanted him. I wanted to know he was fully mine, not have to share him with his gang girls. I wanted to be able to give myself fully without fear, without holding back. But he wouldn't take my heart when I gave it, wouldn't give me the intimacy of his love, his touch. I needed it so much that I withered without it like a tree without rain. I became small and shriveled, a wilted thing dying of drought.

And Maddox… Maddox brought the rain.

thirty-six

Maddox North

I lift my head and kiss the end of Rae's nose. "I have some things to take care of."

Her eyes widen, and she stares at me like she's shocked I'm leaving, like she thought I'd stick around and watch her tie the knot with my twin. She's still ready to go through with it, even after last night. That shouldn't surprise me, but it does.

I wait for her to stop me, but she just nods. I pull out of her wrecked cunt, feeling my cum slide out of her with my penis. After putting myself away, I lift up off her dress and help her sit. I like knowing my cum will be running down her legs under her dress when she walks up the aisle. I wonder what Lennox would say if he saw what I'd done to her. Would he fuck her to punish her more, or be disgusted by the mess of her bloody, torn cunt streaming with my cum?

"Yeah," she says. "I guess you're not coming."

I let out a bitter laugh. "Who's going to be there?"

"Just a few people," she says. "Your mom, my parents, some of Lennox's friends…" She trails off, her eyes widening as she realizes what she's asking.

"Yeah," I say. "A cop who sent me to jail for assault and a bunch of members of a rival gang. The only reason I'm alive right now is because we're in Lennox's car."

She nods, swallowing and looking down at her hands. Slowly, she begins to twist her ring off. "I don't think this is going to happen."

I grab her hand, stopping her. "Go get married, Rae."

"What?" She lifts her gorgeous hazel eyes to mine, hurt and vulnerability written all over her face.

"Go," I say. "Valeria will help get you cleaned up. I'll go get Lennox."

"You want me to marry him?" she asks, her voice small.

"It's the last thing in the world I want," I tell her, leaning in to kiss her. "But it's what you want. That tree. Those roots."

"Right," she says faintly. "I guess you really are a crow."

"What do you mean?"

"A crow isn't meant to be tamed. Just look what happened to Poe. She died when I tamed her. I don't want to do that to you."

I start the car and pull through the lot, around the cars clustered together, and up to the front entrance. "You're getting married in an hour. Go get ready."

She sits another minute, then leans across the seat and kisses my cheek. "I love you, Maddox."

"Te amo, mi tesoro preciosa."

She climbs out of the car and walks inside. I sit there for a minute, too stunned to move. She left. She's going through with it.

Rage swells inside me, replacing the sadness, and I floor the gas, shooting past the curb and away from the church.

If she won't do it, I will.

I'll do it for both of us. Because she doesn't see that she doesn't need roots. She *is* the roots. She is the nest, the comfort, the refuge. My refuge in the storm that tosses me from one disaster to another, that tears at my feathers and threatens to cripple my wings. She is my solace.

I am her wings.

I'm not just doing this for me, because I need her. I'm doing it for her too, because she needs me. She needs my wings, my wild, my freedom. That's what she needs. Not more stability, more roots. She'll stagnate and die if she lets Lennox tie her down that way. Just like I'll careen out of control and fly into a storm I can't get out of one of these days if I don't have somewhere safe to land. She is my safe place to rest, my nest. I am her escape.

Her crow.

I fly through town, slamming on the brake when I see a phone booth outside the pharmacy. I check my pockets, cursing when I don't find the change I need. I run inside and peel off a five, exchanging it for quarters before returning to the phone booth. This one isn't really a booth, just a phone. I turn my back to the lot for whatever privacy I can find. Then I drop the quarters into the slot and listen for the dial tone.

The first person I call is Scarlet.

Then I call Billy and Reggie to find out where they took Lennox.

Ten minutes later, I'm back on the road. Forty minutes to wedding bells.

When I pull up, they're already chiming. Nine o'clock.

Showtime.

thirty-seven

Rae West

"He's not coming."

I turn to Valeria and my mother, looking back and forth between them in desperation. Mom looks like she's about to cry. She keeps picking at my ruined dress, like she'll somehow fix all the dirt and tears if she tugs on it enough. Thankfully, no blood soaked through to the outer layer, though there's a few questionable smudges.

"He's coming," Valeria says firmly, taking both my hands. "My son wouldn't marry you without being sure. I talked to Maddox half an hour ago, and he'd just picked up his brother. He has the number for the rectory."

"Okay," I say, nodding and taking a deep breath. I'm not sure if I'm more scared of him seeing me or not showing up at all. But there's a church full of his friends out there, and the music is playing already. The bridesmaids and groomsmen will be taking their places. I'm shaking all over. He was supposed to be at the altar first, and when I snuck out of the room to take a peek, he wasn't there yet. I pray he won't come, that he'll call and say it's off.

The wedding march begins, and I can't breathe.

"That's you," Valeria says. "Go on."

I take Mom's arm, not sure which of us is trembling harder. I wasn't even going to invite them, since I haven't spoken to them since the night Lee arrested Maddox. But Lennox said I'd regret it if I didn't invite them to this one thing. Otherwise, he's pretty adamant about keeping our lives separate from the one we led on Mill.

We step out of the little room off the atrium and make our way to the door of the sanctuary. Everyone turns to watch me in my bedraggled dress, and I'm thankful Mom ran by and got my veil on her way. They've done their best to patch up my neck and ear and shoulder where Maddox bit me, and the veil covers most of the Band-Aids, so I won't get questions.

I squeeze Mom's arm and hold my head high despite my appearance. I focus on the altar, stumbling a little when I don't see Lennox. A few people around us gasp. I manage to keep my feet and continue. My whole body is numb. I feel like I'm marching to my death.

My gaze sweeps over the motley assemblage where the groomsmen should be. Instead of Lennox's Crossbones friends, I see the old Murder of Crows crew has reunited, none of them in tuxes. Billy, Reggie, Michael, Jeff, and Daniel wait where Lennox should be.

I'm almost there before I notice that none of my bridesmaids are dressed up either, aside from my boss, who's there in her place, looking flustered. Beside her, in a floral dress and yellow rain boots, Lexi's standing with a bouquet of wildflowers, beaming at me. Her friends are standing beside her, all dressed up but none of them matching.

Dread knots in my belly. Did Maddox murder my entire wedding party and grab random people from the guest list to put up here?

But no.

I didn't invite any of these people.

Mom delivers me to the altar and scampers back to her seat. The priest looks me over and frowns. "It looks like we're missing a groom," he says. "How would you like to proceed?"

"I… I'm not sure," I say, silently cursing Valeria for making me go ahead with this.

"He'll be here," Billy says, checking his watch and giving me an easy smile.

We stand there awkwardly for a minute, no one speaking. The small crowd assembled in the pews shifts and murmurs, and then a door off the side where the choir comes in flies open, and Maddox hurries in. His hair is unkempt and wet from the rain, and he's out of breath as he strides over and takes my hands. He's still wearing his jeans and the black tee shirt with bloody spots on it, the shoulders wet from the storm outside. He turns to the priest and nods. "Go ahead. Just switch the first names."

"What are you doing?" I hiss.

"I'm marrying you, little girl."

thirty-eight

Maddox North

"Would you like to proceed?" the priest asks Rae, frowning down at her.

"I..." She looks at him, and then me, and then the expectant crowd. "Can we have a second?"

"I would advise against this," he says.

She swallows and turns to me, searching my gaze. "What are you doing?"

I raise a brow. "Did you really think I'd let you walk up the aisle and stand here alone?"

"He's not coming?"

"No."

"How do you know?"

"Because I sent him to Oahu a few hours early," I say. "Now, you don't want to waste this wedding I planned in an hour, do you?"

"You want to marry me?"

"Of course I want to fucking marry you," I growl. "Now hurry up and say I do so I can kiss you. Or do I need to carry you out to that car and remind you that you're already mine?"

"What about never wanting to be tied down?" she asks. "And the crew girls…"

"No crew girls, ever," I say, fury knotting inside me at what Lennox put her through the last year. "And you said it yourself, that one day I'd want to be tied down."

"If I remember correctly, you laughed at me when I said that."

"Turns out you were right," I say. "So here I am. Tying myself down for you. Tying myself *to* you. You're the tether that can keep me grounded. My refuge."

"Okay," she says, biting back a smile. "I'm ready."

"About fucking time," I say, then tip my chin at the priest. "Go on. Make this little girl my wife before I run out of patience and desecrate your altar with every sin of lust known to man."

He glowers at me and turns to Rae, but either she remembers what happened to the tattoo artist or she really does want to marry me, because she tells him to go ahead.

We repeat our vows, but when he asks for the rings, we just blink at each other.

"Guess we should have gotten those tattoos after all," I say.

Rae stares at me a second, and then she laughs. The sound echoes through the church, the second sweetest sound to ever come out of her mouth. I grab her and kiss her, hard, holding her head between my hands and crushing her lips with mine until I taste blood.

We're both breathless when we pull apart. Her cheeks are flushed, her lips shiny, and she's never looked more fucking perfect, and more perfectly fuckable.

"I do," she says, smiling up at me.

"Me too," I say. "Of course I fucking do."

Then she's laughing, and I'm laughing, and our friends crowd around us. I keep an eye on the Crossbones in the audience, but even they won't shoot a guy inside a church, and I brought backup. We leave out a side door, forgoing tradition. In the parking lot, I pick Rae up and throw her over my shoulder, running through the rain to the El Camino. I dump her into the seat and slide in, pushing her across it.

"Holy shit," she says, laughing and flustered, her hair all a mess. "Did we really just do that?"

"Yeah," I say. "We really fucking did."

"We just got married."

"We did, little girl," I say. "But I'm not going to the reception with all those Crosses, so pull up that dress and let me have dessert here."

"I guess, if we won't be having cake," she says, smiling with a tease in those hazel eyes that makes my cock stir in my jeans.

I slide over and pull her into my lap. "Are you really mine?" I ask, not quite believing it myself. I have to keep touching her to prove it's real, that she's mine to touch.

"Are you mine?" she asks, looping her arms around my neck. "I thought crows couldn't be tamed."

"Maybe not tamed," I say. "But they can build nests, if they find a tree that welcomes even the darkest omen in her branches."

"The darkest," she whispers before pressing her lips to mine. "But only if you come down to visit me on solid ground on occasion."

"As long as you fly with me on occasion," I answer, sliding a hand around the back of her neck to keep her close. "See, I think there's a crow girl in there somewhere. She's just hiding in her nest right now. But I'll get her to come out, and then we can take that flight together."

"Okay," she says, biting her lip. "Together won't be so scary."

"Together," I assure her. "Just the two of us."

"Two for joy," she says, scooting in until our bodies are pressed together.

"You're happy it's me?"

"So happy," she whispers, laying soft kisses against my lips between words. "Thank you for choosing me, Maddox."

I grip her hips, rocking her against me. "*De nada*, little mama."

"It's everything," she says. "*We're* everything. You and me. A murder of two."

epilogue

Lennox North

"I'm not getting on that plane," I rage, fighting against the grip of the Skull on either side of me.

"What are you going to do, squeal like a little pig?" Reggie asks. "Like you did on Maddox?"

"You're lucky all he took was your bitch," Billy says. "He could have taken your life."

"Let me go," I fume, yanking to free my arms. "You know she's not just my bitch. I'm marrying her today. She's my wife."

"So you say," Reggie says, unmoved. My former crew shows no sign of loyalty, no indication that they ever knew me at all, as they hustle me through the airport. We reach the gate, the one where I'm supposed to be boarding a plane to Hawaii with my wife in a few hours. They hustle me up to the podium where a boarding agent is announcing a last call.

"I'm going to need to see your boarding passes," she says, hanging up the intercom when she finishes.

"Yes, ma'am," Billy says, handing one across. "Just one for this guy. We're just escorting him to his seat. To make sure there's not any trouble."

He gives her his most winning smile, and she looks a little flustered.

"I'm sorry, I don't understand," she says. "You only have one boarding pass for all three of you?"

"We're not flying," Reggie says. "We're just here to make sure he gets on board and finds his seat."

"He's a little… Different," Billy says, leaning in to whisper conspiratorially to the woman, resting his hand on top of hers.

"I'm sorry, I'm afraid I can't let you board without a pass," she says. "But a flight attendant will make sure he makes it to his seat."

"See that?" Billy asks, clapping me on the back. "A sexy stewardess is going to take care of you."

"I don't want a sexy stewardess," I say between clenched teeth. "I want my fiancé."

I chose this destination for a specific purpose. I planned the trip, down to the last detail, making sure it was all perfect, from the enormous maze to the secluded beach huts. I've saved for this trip for an entire year, saved *her* for it.

And now it's all gone. Ruined.

Rage swells inside me like a tsunami, an endless well that will never be filled.

I will have my revenge.

"Is there a problem?" the boarding agent asks. "Because we really need to close the doors. Should I call security for you?"

"That won't be necessary," Reggie says, clapping a hand on my back. He draws a small X on my back with his finger, like he's drawing a target. "He's just going to get on board now. Isn't that right, Lennox?"

I know a warning when I see one. I don't want to be arrested, and in the eyes of the world, I'm no better than them. We're all gangsters. If I fight, there are two more

Skulls in the car. I haven't been able to contact any of the Crossbones, so I'm on my own. I know I'm lucky they didn't already shoot me in the back like the *malparidos* they are.

So I look at the agent and nod stiffly. The Skulls finally release me, and I walk down the gangplank, my legs wooden, my stomach hollow. It doesn't matter anyway. Maddox already ruined Rae. If he has her for a week or a night, it's all the same.

He fucked her.

He took her virginity within minutes after I waited an entire fucking year, preserving it even when she was weak and gave in, wanting me to take it. I didn't believe she was one. If I'd known, I would have fucked her, just once, to take that from Maddox. But I thought he'd already taken it. So what did it matter if I waited a year, made her feel insecure, inadequate, unsexy? She needed to feel bad for what she'd done, and that was her penance. I dreamed of this trip every night, though, dreamed of the moment when I'd make her pay.

But he made her pay instead. He took my plan. He ruined it, ruined her. Everything I wanted, that I worked for and waited for all this time, gone in an instant. He took it like he takes everything, like he's always taken what he wanted, without a second thought. He didn't work for it. He didn't earn it.

And yet, he's the one who planted his cum in her virgin cunt while she shook and sobbed.

That was supposed to be my reward.

Her fear. Her escape. The chase. The tears. The claiming. The pain.

Those were mine to take.

Not his.

I should have killed them both that night on the couch, when I thought she fucked him.

I wish she had. I wish I never had to know that all that time, I could have fucked her first, but I didn't because I was punishing her for something she hadn't even done.

I barely hold myself back from punching the stewardess when she asks if she can help me find my seat.

I don't need fucking help. I need to turn back time, to take it all first.

I stomp along the aisle, looking at the numbers along the overhead bins. They're already closed for the flight. I'm the last one to board.

Maybe it won't be so bad to have this week to myself. I'll spend every minute of every hour plotting my revenge. They won't just pay with their bodies. They'll pay with their lives.

I find my seat and stop short, staring in disbelief. My heart starts hammering irregularly, and I can't get a breath for a second. Then the girl in the window seat looks up, her long hair falling to her elbows, perfect hair for grabbing when it streams out behind during a chase.

"Lennox?" she asks, her eyes widening. "Why are *you* here?"

A flicker of fear crosses her gaze, and my cock twitches in my pants.

My lips twist into a cold smile even as a hot ember of excitement sparks to life inside me.

"What, did your boyfriend tell you *he'd* be joining you on this trip?" I ask. "Sorry, he's too busy fucking my fiancé to take you on *my* honeymoon."

"No," she says, shaking her head and reaching for her seatbelt.

"Oh, yes." I slide into the aisle seat in case she gets any ideas about arguing her way off the plane. "It looks like the bastard followed through on his word at last."

"What does that mean?" she asks.

"It means you're mine for the week, Scarlet."

"No," she says again, shaking her head, a look of panic crossing her pretty features.

My cock starts to stiffen, and I lean in, lowering my voice to a conspiratorial whisper. "I hope you brought your running shoes."

acknowledgements

This book would not exist without the amazing input and encouragement of so many!

First and foremost, the main character was named and inspired by Michelle, my amazing Patron who gave me a reason to start a series I've been putting off for nearly a decade. I can't thank you enough for being the brilliant, supportive, fascinating human you are!

Next, a huge thank you to Gisell Butler, whose request for recs in a reader group sparked the idea that later became the love triangle in this book. Thank you for your blessing & encouragement to make it happen!

Another big, huge thank you to Issa and Lani for reading for sensitive content. Y'all give me life!

A giant thank you to my patrons who help my books come to life with your generosity and kindness! Susan, Valarie, Adriana, Nineette, DesiRae, Amanda, Rowena, Terra, Kandace, Kellie, Emily, Christina, Mindy, Tina, Tran, Alex, Hilary, Jessica, Audriana, Alysia, LRaven, Nikki, Emma, Mrs. A, Amy, Rhiannon, Krista, Crystal P, J, Jennifer, Lena, Jasmine, Megan, Margaret, Jennifer S, Kim, Courtney, Nicole, Nikki T, April, Jennifer S, Tasha, Ashley, Nayomi, Crystal W, Doe, Makayla, Kelly, Rebecca, & Sabrina.

other books by selena

Willow Heights Prep Academy: The Elite

1. Bully Me
2. Betray Me
3. Bury Me

Willow Heights Prep Academy: The Exile

1. Bad Apple
2. Brutal Boy
3. Boys Club
4. Broken Doll
5. Blood Empire

Willow Heights Prep Academy: The Endgame

1. Dangerous Defiance
2. Darling Doll
3. Deviant Deception
4. Dirty Demise (2023)